RONIN MATTHEWS

THE
CONCRETE
JUNGLE

The Concrete Jungle
© Ronin Matthews 2024

ISBN: 978-1-923289-13-0 (Paperback)

A catalogue record for this book is available from the National Library of Australia

Cover Design: Ronin Matthews and Clark & Mackay
Format and Typeset: Ronin Matthews and Clark & Mackay Published by Ronin Matthews and Clark & Mackay

Proudly printed in Australia by Clark & Mackay

ACKNOWLEDGEMENTS

I want to thank my father Adam Matthews and my mother Lisa Matthews for encouraging me to follow my dreams. Also, I would like to thank Marc Clayton for his contribution in editing the novel and teaching me the skills to write this book. I would also like to thank Skillshare for giving me the video tutorial I needed to write this book.

In particular, I would like to thank Jim Bruce, Jenna Moreci, David Ault, Nitay L, Preeti Shenoy, Tasmin Hansman, Johnathan LaPoma, Matthew Dewey, Daniel Jose Older and Nia Hogan. Finally, I would like to thank all my friends – Alisha Moyle, Cory Cooper, Patrick Janeway, Aiden Thomas and Hayden Smith – along with my family, like my sister, Emily, and colleagues who encouraged me to write this book. Thank you.

Most importantly, I thank God.

CHAPTER 1

Pre-War Era 01-01-2025

Our planet was once liveable and sustainable, just as God intended. Every piece of his divine creation was interconnected to create one massive ecological system brimming with crystal-clear skies, pure blue oceans and rich-brown dirt. This system was a perfect balance of sky, sea and land. The wonders that this ecological system hosted, from the rapid rivers to the green forests and each mountain, were hand-crafted as sculptures. The environmental system formed the building blocks to host all forms of flora, big and small, with rich colours from the rainbow. But, of course, with the building blocks of life came the creation of fauna, from mammals to reptiles to insects as small as microbes. But there was one creature so intelligent that it would go on to build many wonders, from the tallest towers to the most modern and complex of systems. However, these creatures became flawed, full of hatred, capable of causing great misery and, eventually, their potential destruction: human beings.

The military-industrialised United States of America and the authoritarian Chinese Regime clashed in a major war of the world, or, as the history books call it, World War Three. The conflict started as a simple proxy war between Ukraine and Russia. But once a fire is lit, it cannot be extinguished. Fear and anger soon took over leaders' and populations' minds, with nation after nation quickly being consumed by pride. This promptly turned to entitlement and the never-ending chase for power by taking from those too weak to fight.

Eventually, the old peace system promptly turned into a system of taking from the weak and keeping for themselves. When China took Taiwan, it was on! After four years of brutal, large-scale fighting.

The war soon turned nuclear. China fired the first blow, and just like that, the domino fell, with America retaliating within an hour. Nuclear warheads were launched from each side of the globe, wiping out Asia, North America and Europe. What the warhead didn't kill, the radioactive fallout and famine did, finishing the job and killing millions across the globe.

CHAPTER 2

At first, the city started as sustainable due to its low population. Now, this city has a rough estimate of over 20 million people, all crammed in and confined together within its 783 sq km area, encompassed within a 100-storey concrete and lead-line border wall with a 20-storey enclosed dome covering the top of the city, or at least that's what Ella tells me. Everyone in this storey is forced to eat their way up for a piece in this city. Humans started creating technologies to work around the nuclear-ravaged environment, technologies that allowed us to breathe, farm and make. But over the years, humans became comfortable and wanted more speed and convenience. Therefore, instead of learning their lesson from the past by being content with what they had and helping one another, they persisted in building higher and higher, spreading wider and wider, taking more and more. Humans took more than they needed, sparing no material or resource they could get their hands on. They spread the dome out further to keep up with the city's demand, at least my city's. The sustenance in this city is packaged and stuffed down our throats, as food is rationed off, with the top eating first and the bottom getting whatever is left.

Yes, we live in concrete hell; the only things you can see are skyscrapers. Apartment buildings everywhere, across every block and corner. There are always shops and buildings, but there is not an ounce of greenery or shrubbery anywhere, as they died out years ago. Instead, everything is artificial and packaged; even the air we breathe is either pumped into this city from machines or sold as packaged goods. To survive in this city, you need money, brains and social skills; if you don't have these three things, you are pretty much out of luck. Unfortunately, life is cruel, because I was born at the bottom of the city, where the poor, the mentally ill and the criminals reign supreme. Of course, I was burdened with the worst thing in a cold, logical world – a sense of morals and a conscience – so I couldn't work and kill my way to the top. Instead, I am condemned to live off the crumbs with the other.

Oh, well, we all have our place in this city. My place was at the bottom. That is not to say that I can't climb to the top. But like I said, I am just too sick and uneducated to make my way to the top. So, at the bottom I stay. Welcome to my slice of paradise, which I like to call the level of rats. This place hides underneath the high rise of the rich and the working class. In this place, there is no guarantee you will see sunlight; the only light down here is the neon light from buildings full of successful people or the bonfire some drug addict lit to keep himself warm. Crime ravages these communities like a plague; it's pretty much the only thing high in this place, except for the junkies. Everything else in this place is low: employment, opportunities and economic growth. Blame the system for that. But hey, where the hell else am I supposed to go? When you have no money …

CHAPTER 3

It was early morning, and the hypersonic monorail rushed by, rattling the house and shaking my bed around the room. Guessing that was my alarm to get up, I woke up with a hangover glaze in my eyes and a pounding headache in my brain, and all I could hear was my mum yelling, "Jacob, get your arse out of bed. It is time for work!"

Yes, that is my name, Jacob Turner. Just your average 27-year-old washed-up war vet with severe PTSD, bipolar and schizophrenia, with no medication to treat it. As I can't afford healthcare, I just let the drugs and alcohol take care of it.

I slowly descended the broken, worn stairs to find my half-Latino mum cooking me breakfast. My mum, Anna, was a broke, single, lower-class woman, barely getting by on the minimum wage she got from her retail job. I had no father around, as he decided to OD on crack about 10 years ago.

"What's for breakfast, Ma?"

"Pancakes."

"Yum."

I walked over and kissed her on the cheek.

"Now, I will be working a 12-hour shift today. Shouldn't you be on your way to work?"

"Yer, bite me."

Anna then kissed me on the head, grabbed an apple and rushed out the door, as I sat there eating my chocolate pancakes.

After breakfast, I walked down the street in my dirty, baggy work clothes, blasting "Short Change Hero" by The Heavy, my favourite song, on my old, outdated holographic projector. I was passing the small shop owners who were trying to get by with the few customers and the constant robberies around them. I went to my workshop at the armament factory, a weapon manufacturing plant. It was my job to repair the robots that assemble the machines. The pay was as good as a dog's breakfast, but hey, it pays the bills (well, barely, considering rent costs $280 a week).

Just an average day, spannering the bolts on the robot and crossing the wires, when I hear a shriek from the guy next to me, "AHHHHHH!"

It turns out that the guy next to me was working on the assembly line robot when the robot hand accidentally pressed the trigger, and the AR-27 laser rifle went off by accident and blew his arm clean off. The guy was lying there on the factory floor bleeding to death, and only I batted an eye to see, as the other employees just ignored him. Injuries like that are very common in this place.

Just then, a bolding, middle-aged man in a suit stumbled down the stairs and asked, "WHAT THE HELL IS GOING ON HERE? WHY IS OUR DAILY QUOTA NOT BEING MET!"

"Sir, I need to go to the hospital. I am bleeding to death."

"Oh, yer," replied the greedy regional manager. He then proceeded to shoot the employee in the head with a golden Magnum handgun that he pulled out of his back pants. "Guess you're dead now."

He then pointed to me. "You! Throw this trash in the bin and get back to work."

"Yes, sir!"

Grabbing the poor guy's dead body that was covered in blood, and with no other option, I just threw it in the trash and decided to have a 5-minute smoke break. I sat in the cold darkness with a cigarette in my hand, the only break I ever got. Now, I know what you are thinking. What about workers' rights? Well, down here, they are non-existent. Everyone needs work and will take anything they can get, regardless of the conditions or pay. Hell, in this place, people dying on the job is a weekly occurrence. In fact, it is so common that hardly anyone cares about the dead anymore, as at the end of the day, we're all products of the economic machine.

As I looked at the dead body in the garbage bin, I felt much sorrow for him. Poor guy didn't deserve to go out that way. With nothing to do, I just looked at the dark, dirty street and started to do what I always do: contemplate my life and wonder what life is like in the Upper Levels, to not have any crime or poverty or sickness.

Since this is my personal story, here is a little about me. I never completed high school; no point in it. I was too poor to afford to go. Education was a luxury only the wealthy could afford. So I did the only logical thing that a 14-year-old with no education is qualified to do: I joined the military. Hell, it was mandatory anyway at 18. I enlisted to serve in the American Division Defence Force as a radiation diver marine; my job was to dive into the radiated waters of the Pacific Ocean and kill our opponents, who at the time were the Asian Division Defence Force. Just like all of our enemies from different cities, they threatened our global position as the top power in the world, so we had to take them out. I served in the military for 10 years, serving from 1 July 3009 to 3 September 3019 before gaining an honourable discharge, where I wound up, returning home with PTSD and a medal covered in bronze. Luckily for me, I didn't become addicted to drugs … well, the bad kind anyway, like meth or xylazine. So I was able to find a job in this place, which is a very rare commodity in this neighbourhood. Break's over. I put out my ciggy and went back to work.

After a 12-hour shift, I clocked out, took my $7 wage and began to walk home. Proceeding to head home, I could hear talking coming from the alley. I saw a male wearing a Halloween mask pulling a knife on a girl in her early 20s.

The girl was screaming at the boy, "Don't bloody touch me!"

But the robber was persistent. "Give me your money, or I will cut you!"

The guy then looked at me, as I watched in horror. "What are you looking at? Get lost!"

Now, I could have intervened, but I ain't no superhero, just an average man, so I just proceeded to walk home. All the while, the scream of that poor girl pierced the night sky.

After that ugly encounter, I just erased it from my mind and began walking home. You see, in this part of the city, police presence is virtually non-existent. Only the Upper and Middle Levels could afford that, so you could pretty much get away with anything down here as long as it didn't gain media attention.

After a long walk home, I walked up the front stairs and walked into the living room to find Mum setting up plates for dinner. On her way home, she'd picked up some Chinese.

"Hi Mum. Oooh, Chinese! Yum!" I kissed her on the cheek.

"Help yourself, love."

We then sat down at the dinner table as we explained the content of our day. I told her about the guy who died at work and the woman in the alley, and she told me how she was physically assaulted by a large man over a bag of chips; you know, just a standard day working in retail. We then began to eat our dinner while hearing the screaming of the next-door neighbour beating his wife (a lot of domestic violence in this place). After hearing the screams, we just ate dinner in silence.

After dinner, I proceeded to walk up to my room, pour myself a glass of whisky, smoke a blunt and begin drinking my pain and sorrows away. After getting drunk and high at the same time, I headed to bed, hoping to get some sleep. With my PTSD, it was a rarity.

I woke up the next day, barely getting 3 hours of sleep, but it didn't matter. I was used to that by now. So, with nothing better to do, I drowned my sleep deprivation with coffee and headed to the local pharmacy, the only one in the Lower Levels to catch up with my best friend, Edward Matthews.

Edward was a 27-year-old white male with blond hair and blue eyes. I met him in high school. I used to help him out with the bullies, and eventually over time, he became like a brother from another mother to me. Since high school, we had done everything together. We took all sorts of drugs, went to all sorts of parties and nightclubs together, and he even taught me Kav Bitz Kar Do when we were kids (a combination of Krav Maga, Brazilian Jujitsu, Karate, Judo and Boxing).

Edward hadn't always lived in the Lower Levels; he was originally from the Upper Levels, as his family came from wealth. His dad was a crypto investor. However, he had to move with his family down to the Lower Levels after the Economic Crash of 2998. His family lost everything: their firm, their mansion and their savings. Edward's family couldn't even afford to send Edward to private school anymore, so Edward had to slum it in the public school system like me.

We hung out together during school, but we both lost contact for a couple of years after we both joined the military. Luckily for Edward, he received a prestigious education before going to public school, and his family could afford to keep him going to school, which helped him avoid getting drafted into the regular military. So at the age of 18, he finished high school and got a scholarship to attend officer school. He stuck it out in officer school for two years but was medically discharged after having "back" problems.

After leaving officer school, he went to university to study pharmacy, but due to his background and the lack of money, he couldn't afford to live in the Middle or Upper Levels, so he had to start his own pharmacy down in the Lower Levels. We met again after I left the military, as he was my dealer.

Today, we both had a day off, the first in almost two weeks, so we went to the local pub and ordered ourselves a few drinks. Nothing better than having five beers at 9:00 in the morning.

After downing a few drinks, we were both in happy, talkative moods. Edward talked about all the girls he slept with, and I just talked about life in general. Edward was a trusted friend and a mentor for me. My family loved him, and his family loved me.

After the pub kicked us out for rowdy behaviour, we began to walk down the street. Then, Edward did the weirdest thing; he kissed me on the left cheek.

"Dude, what was that for?"

"No reason."

There was an awkward silence. Then we both laughed it off and continued to walk down the street. We talked a lot of rubbish and had a few laughs, but as we passed the local gun shop, I stopped to look through the window to get a look at my crush, Ella Janeway. Ella was this girl I held a flame for since high school. She was a beautiful white girl with brown hair, blue eyes and a skinny body. I was staring at her through the window like a creep while my friend blabbered on about some random nonsense; I didn't know what he was saying, as I wasn't paying attention.

But quickly, he realised I wasn't listening to him and turned around to me. "Why don't you stop being so chicken and ask her out?"

After that comment, I laughed, and in the nicest voice possible, I told him, "Oh, get off it."

Then Ella noticed I was looking at her, so I pulled away from the window and continued to walk down the street with Edward. Then *wack!* The butt of an AR-15 hit the back of Edward's head, which knocked him off his feet, and he began to bleed from the hit. I quickly picked him up and turned around as two medium-built guys stood in front of us with clown masks on and holding old AR-15 rifles in their hands.

In the most aggressive voice possible, they both yelled, "You better have the toll for entering our side of the levels, or else you are about to meet the full force of our ARs here!"

Now, a normal person would just give them the items; however, Edward and I had grown up on the streets and served in the military (some more than others) and were both masters in Kav Bitz Kar Do, so I nodded to Edward, and he used a side kick on the first attacker, forcing him on the ground. Then Edward hunched his back over to allow himself to be a launching pad for my attack. Without thinking, I jumped onto Edward's back and sent the second attacker down to the ground with a flying kick to the jaw. Edward began punching the first offender on the ground, as I began attacking the other one. Eventually, the robbers gave up, knowing that they were not going to get anything from us, and ran off, even leaving behind their guns, which we slugged over our shoulders as trophies. Guess we will have to add these to our weapons collection. Having a weapon down here is a must.

After that whole encounter, both Edward and I began to laugh as dopamine and adrenaline rushed straight to our brains. Normally, a situation like that would have been traumatic, but we were used to situations like that. Without thinking or caring, we proceeded to walk home in victory. Just another casual Saturday in the Lower Levels.

We both eventually proceeded back to my house, where we whipped out the ancient movie projector, plugged it into our ancient flat-screen TV and stemmed a copy of the hit movie *Over the Wall* while getting high on some weed. We just sat there talking, laughing and eating our problems away.

Down here, there was nothing to do, no sports clubs or gyms, so we just sat on the couch eating cookies and drinking some beers. Then, Anna walked in from an exhausting day at work and noticed our two dumbasses sitting on the couch high, which she was used to by now.

"Oh hey, Edward."

"Sup, Anna? What's cooking?"

Anna then turned to me. "Jacob, don't forget we are having Chicken Fatah's for dinner. Care to join us, Edward?"

"Sure!"

I nodded, and since Anna had worked all day, Edward and I proceeded to set up plates for dinner.

Then Anna, in a joking tone of voice, said, "What's that smell? Smells like smoke."

Both Edward and I gave each other a smirk and began to laugh, and even Anna joined in.

After dinner, we all had a glass of whisky each and told life stories and reminisced about the good old days of high school when suddenly, we all heard the noise of car tyres screeching down the road at what sounded like it was travelling at least 160 km/h. Curious, I got up and peered out through the window to see where the noise had come from. As I looked out the window, I saw the sudden turn of a worn-out Humvee hurtling towards our house.

I knew what it was. Quickly, I turned to Anna and Edward and yelled, "Drive-by! Get down!"

Anna, Edward and I ducked under the table. Suddenly, the whole living room lit up with bullets, and the car drove away.

"Anyone hurt?"

We both replied, "We are all good!" Luckily, we were all fine. No one was hurt, as we all got down in time.

We went to the window to investigate. Drive-bys were normal in these types of neighbourhoods.

Anna looked out the window, turned around to me and asked, "The Klan again?"

I looked out the window for a few minutes and said, "I think so. Or it may have been the Crypts, telling by the Humvee."

Anna replied with a simple, "Man, I hate this place," walking up the stairs to grab a broom and a dustpan.

You see, the Lower Levels were constantly plagued with gang wars. This week it was a gang war between the Klan, a far-right white supremacy group, and the Crypts, a multicultural group seeking to run these streets. Both were suppliers of drugs and other illegal substances, so naturally, they would try to kill each other, and unfortunately, innocent people would end up the casualties of these killings. But oh well, welcome to the Lower Levels.

After that incident, Edward proceeded to head home, with Anna and I cleaning up the mess caused by the guns. We then proceeded to our bedroom, where I did my usual routine of staring out the window, drinking whisky and looking into the streets, contemplating life. Then I saw a man running down the street and another man chasing him, letting out a howling scream like a werewolf and running towards the guy like a zombie. The guy chasing the other guy was clearly high on something. Just then, the guy being chased tripped, and the other guy pounced on him and began to eat him while the first guy screamed out in pain. The guy must have been high on the drug Crocodile. All I did was stare out the window, put out my cigarette and go to bed. Nothing I could have done, really. It was a messed-up situation.

I was lying in my bed, with the alcohol making me dizzy and my PTSD hitting me while I was barely conscious. I was remembering the time – I remembered it vividly, 15 July 3012 – when I was a sergeant off the coast of what was known as Old Australia; it is now known as the Oceania Outpost. It was our objective to dive through the radiated waters and pull a sneak attack on the Asian Division troops, which were in Old Indonesia planning to attack the outpost of Oceania that was currently occupied by America. It was our job to attack them first.

With a company of marines, we swam in lead-lined scuba gear, armed with M100 automatic. These weapons were produced by WeapCo. Their design resembled an M4, except they were modified for underwater combat rifles with water-piercing bullets. We were swimming through the green, murky waters and chatting on the radio line. We had just passed the USS *Gerald R Ford*, which was destroyed off the coast of Indonesia by Chinese anti-ship missiles in 2025. It was a relic of the past but still majestic in its beauty with its rust-covered hull. What made it even more majestic was the old United States of America flag that was replaced every year by local divers as a sign of respect. But it was amazing seeing it wave back and forth by the water currents.

We were about to prepare to ascend and attack when my men and I began hearing a clicking sound coming through the waters. My men and I were looking around for the source of that sound when we heard a fin-flapping noise passing us at a high speed in the murky waters. We heard it again but couldn't see it due to the murky water. One man, out of panic, swam backwards when he turned around and felt this small, mammal hand on the back of his shoulder. He turned around, and it was a kangashark (a mixture of a brown kangaroo and a great white shark). The kangashark let out a shriek and, with his row of jagged teeth, bit into the guy's neck, causing the guy to bleed out in the water. Out of fear, the others screamed in fear and prepared their guns to kill the creature, as the creature swam around and took out the marines with its claws and its jaw.

I was in the back watching this take place. I was about to fire my gun, but it jammed from the seawater and wouldn't fire. *Oh no!*

Out of Panic, I reached for my knife that was in my back pocket. By that time, the kangashark had already killed 10 of my men and was staring directly at me, ready to attack and kill me. I was so nervous, as I looked it in its dead black eyes.

The kangashark then screamed out another shriek and began swimming towards me with its claws out and its mouth wide open, as I saw its jagged rows of teeth. There had to be at least 60 teeth in its mouth. I was ready in combat mode, standing there with my knife in my right hand, as it was about to attack. But as the kangashark charged at me and I stood there panicked but ready to die, all I heard was the alarm on my bedside table, waking me for work.

Just another day. Obviously, I survived of course, but that was a memory for another night.

I started the day by hearing Anna's voice screaming out, "Jacob, you have to get ready for work!"

I let out a sigh and looked over at my holographic projector projecting the blue date: 03-02-3025. Immediately, I got dressed, ready for work. I ran down the stairs, kissed Mum on the cheek and then walked out the front door. Now normally, I wouldn't, because I didn't have the money, but today, I thought I would treat myself to a $2 coffee from the local coffee van. I was there waiting in line, as the barista was making the coffee when I looked out the window and saw a crowd of people standing around and staring up at this woman on top of the building. It looked like we have another jumper. The woman on the building was a woman in her late 40s who was holding a magazine and preaching about the word of some random deity who would come down and strike the wicked. This poor woman was clearly suffering from mental health issues. The problem was that there was no hope or help for her.

I just watched as she preached to a sick world about the demons coming to eat us, then the barista handed me my coffee, and I began to walk to work, ignoring the woman on the building crying out, as there was nothing I could do.

Just before reaching work, I stopped by the gun shop, just to get a look at Ella working. Damn, she was beautiful. I wish I could talk to her, but I just don't know where I would start. I mean, look at her, she was far too good for this place. But today was a different day, as today, I was going to grow a pair and ask her out. I decided to enter the shop and pretend to browse the gun shop.

I entered the shop, and the little bell above the door rang. It was a really old shop by the sound of that bell. I walked over to the nearest aisle and pretended to seem interested in the semi-automatic rifles that were lined up on the rack.

Ella then looked up from the counter directly at me and asked, "Looking for something?"

Let's just say my talking with women needed a bit of work. "Ah, a gun," I said sounding like a dumbass.

Ella just smiled. "Yer, well, you are in a gun shop, but what type of gun are you looking for?"

Ella was a no-nonsense girl in a nonsense world. Ella and her father had run this shop for years, which really built her attitude. They struggled to keep business afloat while they were battling gangs and having thugs constantly asking for protection money, but somehow, they managed, though it left a few scars, some you could not see.

Anyway, I just looked directly at her, trying my hardest not to make eye contact, and in a dumbass voice said, "Maybe an AR-15 rifle."

Ella nodded her head. "Quite a beauty, isn't she? Bit of an old soul. Hey, what are you planning to hunt?"

I wanted to say the gangs that shot up my house, but best not sound like a psychopath, especially considering the fact I was going to ask her out. "Just collecting."

Ella just nodded her head. "Fair enough."

She looked away for a split second, and trying to sound tough, I said stupidly, "And I may go hunt some deer later." I hit my head metaphorically as I realised deer went extinct years ago.

Then her face turned into a look of concern. "Deer in this city? Do I have to run a drug test on you?"

She thought I was the biggest idiot on the planet, but I laughed it off. "Hah, no, sorry, I am just buying to collect. Plus, it wouldn't hurt to have some protection around here."

She nodded. "I get that. You need all the protection you can get in this hellhole."

"True."

After an awkward silence, I walked over to the counter and gave her the rifle. She bagged it up, and I paid for it with my card. Then stupidly I said out of nowhere, "Hey … Um, gun."

She then shot me a dirty look, and I was thinking to myself, *Why did you say that? I just blew my moment to ask her out.*

Out of embarrassment, I grabbed the gun and walked away. Way to waste $150 on gun that's going to collect dust. Oh well, another one for the arsenal. I already had two of them, anyway. Kicking myself, I just proceeded to make my way to my minimum-wage job with my head held in defeat. I pulled into the warehouse, where my boss decided today was a good day to chew my ear off.

"Jacob! Where the hell have you been? You're ten minutes late for work. You pull that rubbish again, and you will be out of a job. Do you understand me? Now get your arse back to work!"

"Yes, sir!" I replied timidly and headed to my workstation.

Today was an average day, I just repaired robot, after robot, after robot. Then, after a few hours had passed, I threw out my colleague who was too stupid to know the difference between a glue gun and a coolant adjuster and froze his head off, poor kid. So, in the bin he goes, and a ciggy for me as I look up at the dirty, concrete city, thinking about life ... you know, the usual lunch break. While smoking my ciggy, I just sat there thinking about old childhood trauma; I was thinking about how when I was seven, I was in bed, hearing Mum and Dad screaming at each other.

"Damn it, Anna, why are you and your damn son spending so much?"

"Bill, go to bed. You're drunk."

"No, I am sick of having to be the sole provider of this family."

"Sole provider? I am the one pulling eighty hours at work. When was the last time you worked?"

"You bitch!"

And all I hear is crying and screaming, and then I hear banging at my front door and my father saying, "Jacob, you spoilt brat, open this door now!"

I hid underneath my sheets and began covering my ears as I hid in fear.

I then zoned back to the real world, as my boss opened the back door and yelled at me, "What are you off in La La Land? Move your arse, Jacob! We have five robots malfunctioning in here. Move!"

The boss then slammed the door behind him, leaving me again in darkness. I sighed, threw my cigarette in the bin and walked inside, preparing to fix the chaos that was unfolding inside.

After my shift, I clocked out and proceeded to walk home, when I suddenly heard a bang sound coming out of the gun shop. It sounded like gunfire. That's strange. The shop wasn't big enough to hold a target range, so why was there gunfire coming from the shop? I was concerned. I hoped Ella was all right. I had to make sure. I peered through the window, but I couldn't see anything through the window. The shop was dark, and there was barely any lighting. As I looked closer through the window, I heard another loud bang coming from the shop and saw what looked like the spark from a gun.

Quickly, I peered through the front door and saw five guys – two with shotguns, two with handguns and one with a semi-automatic rifle. Luckily, I was able to see Ella faintly behind the counter, struggling to load an old pump-action shotgun due to the constant gunfire in front of her, keeping to the bottom of the counter. I knew she wasn't going to last long, as she was out-gunned and outnumbered, and in 5 minutes, they were going to flank her and do who knows what with her.

After thinking they had the upper hand, the robbers ceased firing, and the four men signalled to the one on the left, who slowly began to make his or her way to the counter (hard to tell with the masks on), but as the robber slowly approached the counter, Ella quickly flung up and blasted the robber straight in the head with her shotgun, killing him instantly. But her gun was a pump action, so she needed to reload the shells one after the other, and the robbers knew that. The four remaining robbers rushed towards her, grabbing her, and the four piled onto her, with two of them holding her to the ground and one standing in front of her holding a pistol as the other stood beside him. Just as the robber was about to shoot her, I barged through the door, which caught them off guard. The distraction gave Ella enough time to sack wack one and knee the other in the stomach. After getting to her feet, she tackled the robber, causing him to drop his handgun. But the other robber kicked her in the face, which knocked her off his friend.

I rushed in and tackled the robber and began punching him, but the other robber on the floor quickly grabbed the gun and whacked Ella in the face with enough force to break her nose. While I was attacking his friend, the robber on the floor pointed the handgun at me. *Oh no,* I thought.

The robber was about to pull the trigger, but Ella quickly rolled him over to the floor, and he accidentally discharged a shot into the ceiling, with Ella knocking the gun out of his hand. Now was my chance. I rushed for the gun and managed to grab it and point it at the robber, who had a look of shock on his face. But behind me laid the other robber that Ella sack-wacked. Behind my back, he tried to reach for the shotgun, but my reflexes kicked in, and I shot at the floor, which scared the living hell out of them all.

At this point, I looked around the room at all four of the robbers, and in a sharp tone of voice, I yelled, "Everyone, get the hell out of here, now!"

The robbers all got up from the floor and fled the shop. The three robbers all rushed out the door, but one decided to push his luck. Instead of rushing out with all his friends, he rushed to the counter and quickly turned around. Instead of heading for the door, he made a mad dash to grab the shotgun on the floor, and *bang!* I discharged a shot that hit him straight in the shoulder.

"Agh!" the robber screamed out in pain, and holding his wounded shoulder, he rushed out to join his friends.

"And stay out!" I yelled, as they all rushed out the door and into the night sky.

I turned around to Ella to see if she was all right. She had a look of pure shock on her face, as she was surprised at how I handled myself. Ella had thought I was just some nerdy, socially awkward person. Little did she know that I had gotten into my fair share of gunfights.

"Are you all right?"

Ella grabbed her nose. "Yer, I am fine, thank you."

I offered her a hand up, and I picked her off the floor.

"I had that situation under control, but thanks for the assist."

I just laughed. "Yer, I bet you did."

Ella looked around the shop, and she noticed something in the corner of her eye: the door out back slowly opened. At first, she thought it was her dad, but ...

"Get down!" she yelled, as there was a sixth robber who had snuck through the backdoor and had a gun pointed at me. Not thinking or realising, I turned around quickly. *Bang!* The robber shot me straight in the abdomen, and immediately, I collapsed on the floor. Dazed and confused, probably from the blood loss, I looked down at my abdomen, as the blood began to pour onto the floor. Then out of shock, I began slowly collapsing into unconsciousness. The last thing I saw was Ella grabbing my gun and discharging a few shots, and then I saw her face and collapsed into darkness.

I woke up, and I was lying on an old, stained couch that obviously hadn't been washed in ages. I looked down to find my abdomen bandaged, with a few blood spots tarnishing the bandage. After having a bit of a blurry look around, it looked like I was in some damp, old basement. I looked to my side to find the bullet that was in my abdomen lying on the coffee table covered in blood and some surgical equipment right next to it, all spread out over the coffee table. Then I saw Ella standing over the couch and looking at me.

"Well, look who's up?"

I looked in shock and slowly began pulling myself up while groaning in pain. Ella then cautioned me. "Don't move too much. You could bleed out."

"I will take my chances," I said, trying to sound like a tough guy, even though I was in massive amounts of pain.

"You're lucky I have had some medical training, or else you would be dead right now."

I then got up and put on a clean white shirt that was lying on the couch. "Where am I?"

"In our basement. We couldn't have you lying on the floor. That would be bad for business, and it would stink up the place." Ella said that while having a bit of a grin on her face.

I just smiled a little at that comment. "Thanks for stitching up my wound."

"Well, it's the least I could do, considering you helped me out."

I just smiled when she said that. "I thought you had that situation under control?"

"Yer, well, thanks anyway."

"Thanks for the shirt. Well, I better get going."

"OK." She then smiled at me and said, "Take care."

I began slowly making my way up the stairs when she stopped me. "Wait Jacob, I mean it, thank you! You saved me back there."

"Well, I couldn't let them kill you." I paused for a moment. "How do you know my name?"

It brought me a bit of a smile that she knew my name.

"While you were unconscious, I checked your wallet, just to find some info on you in case I needed to contact your next of kin." Ella then chucked my old leather wallet that I kept in my back pocket. I caught it with two hands.

"Good catch."

"Goodbye, Ella."

She just nodded, and I slowly walked up the stairs and out the door. I may have been in excruciating amounts of pain, but it was worth it. Holding onto my abdomen and moaning with every step I took, I finally made it home.

I was in immense amounts of pain, but I was just going to have to live with it.

Later that night, I just parked my arse on the couch to try and ease my pain while I just sat there, holding an ice pack while watching some old World War Three documentary on the video projector. Anna walked over and handed me a box of expired painkillers she had found in the dumpster out back. With some strong whisky, it would make an effective painkiller.

Anna sat next to me on the couch with a beer in her hand. "You know, that was a stupid move you made. I mean, what if you had gotten yourself killed?" she said, with a sharp, condescending tone in her voice.

"Couldn't be worse than living in this dump."

"I am serious, Jacob. I did not raise you to just die on me. You deserve better than to be the guy who dies because of some guy in a Halloween mask."

I just smiled at that comment. "Look around, Mum. Look where I live. Look at the state of the world. A warrior's death would be a merciful death for me."

Mum just kissed me on the cheek and hugged me. "Don't say that, Jacob. You are my son, and you are all I have left in this world."

I just looked down at the floor sad. "Sorry, Mum."

She kissed me on the cheek. Then I turned to her. "Couldn't have gotten me a beer too?"

She gave me another kiss on the cheek, and she got up to get me another beer from the fridge. Mum and I just sat on the couch watching the old show and eating our leftover Chinese food while drinking some whisky straight from the bottle.

Then Anna turned around to me and said, "You know Jacob, you are still quite young. If you want to go attend school for a bit up there, I would be more than happy to visit you in the Middle Levels. I don't want you stuck here; you deserve better."

"I don't have the money to get out of this place, you know that."

"But would you consider at least going back to school to get your GED?"

"With what money?"

"There's more to life than money, Jacob. Why don't you take a risk?"

"Na, I have had enough risk for one lifetime. I just want to live a quiet life. Plus, I will be too far away from you."

After drinking that whisky, I began to feel tired, so I kissed Mum on the cheek, picked myself off the couch and began making my way up the stairs. "All right, I am feeling tired. I am going to head up to bed. Night."

She just gave me a wave and sat there watching the rest of the TV show, drinking a beer.

While I lay there in my bed nursing my wound, I couldn't stop thinking about what Mum was saying. *Maybe she is right. Maybe I should really apply myself, and I could finally get out of here. Ugh!* I sighed. What could my life have been if I had been born into money, or what could I have been like if I had never served in the military, or even if I had finished school, or if I even kept in contact with my sister who ran away from home?

I just brushed these questions off. This was the whisky talking. It was making me depressed. After the whisky made me drowsy and I began to dose off, my PTSD kicked in to wake me straight up. I just lay there, staring at the ceiling, while my mind was plagued with more intense flashbacks from my time in the war, this time I was in Asia City and the squad I was leading had successfully conducted an attack on the border wall. With cooperation from the ADDF Air Force and Navy, we penetrated the radiation-proof concrete walls of the mega city.

As we took the first half of the city, we began to make our way down the main street. The 20 of us looked around at the beautiful Chinese architecture that was like nothing we had ever seen before, when we were suddenly ambushed by a battalion of enemy troops who had surrounded us from all different sides from different skyscrapers and buildings. The troops opened fire on us. They mowed us down, and I had no other option but to quickly rush underneath a car to cover myself from the gunfire. My other men weren't so lucky, as they were cut down by enemy machine guns, while I hid there underneath the car and watched in horror. One after the other, the soldiers, my friends, were mowed down right in front of me, as I shook and froze at the horror that was unfolding in front of my eyes. All I could do really was cover my ears, as I couldn't stand to hear the painful screams and the bullets flying from the constant machine gun fire.

After a long and arduous 30 minutes, the smoke cleared, and the bullets ceased. All around me lay the bodies of my friends. I couldn't help but scream and break down. Suddenly, the alarm in my room blared, and my eyes shot open back to reality. Just like that, ding, ding, ding, my holographic projector went off.

I could hear Mum screaming, "Jacob, time for breakfast."

And just like that, I did the same old stuff that I normally did, every single day: get up, walk downstairs, kiss Mum on the cheek and walk out the door. Really, to make my pay, I had turned into the robots I repaired.

After entering my workshop, I began tinkering on some robot that broke down on the assembly line, but I looked over at the far end of the room and saw people in white suits walking in. Today was the day when members from corporate would come down from the Middle Levels and visit our little warehouse. Five guys in white suits with fancy shoes and aviator sunglasses rocked up in their private limousines. One of them looked at me and proceeded to walk up the stairs into the boss's office, and I turned back to continue my work.

I didn't really pay attention. I wasn't paid enough to care about the inner workings of the company. Just as I was about to throw out the body of my next co-worker, I heard a voice coming from my boss's office, as the door of the office was open slightly an inch, just enough to hear faint whispers. While it was none of my business, and I really shouldn't have gotten involved, I was however a little bit curious, so I slowly looked around to see if anyone was watching, and once the coast was clear, I began slowly walking up the staircase and peered my eyes through the black wooden door to spy on what they were doing.

I could barely see anything, as the office room was pitch black. The only light source in the room was coming from the projector that projected the statistics of gun sales and weapons distribution numbers. The guys in the white suits were all sitting around with the boss at the end of the table, but there appeared to be someone else talking through a cell phone. I couldn't see who the person was, but I did instantly recognise the voice. It was John Speer, the CEO and founder of the corporation I work for, WeapCo Limited. Our company was one of the biggest producers of weaponry and defence equipment in the whole world. We built all sorts of weapons, from small arms to the most advanced technological weaponry such as fighter jets to tanks. Hell, we produced so many weapons that most of the arms that defend this city came from this corporation alone. This company was so powerful that it had its own private army at its disposal that was more equipped than the entire ADDF.

Anyway, my boss was discussing with the board and the CEO the stats of this area's production and distribution records. He was discussing why records were up, but the CEO cut in and said, "Let me stop you right there. Why is your area not producing at the 5 per cent required?"

The boss replied, "Well sir, the Lower Levels don't have much money. They don't have the money to buy food, let alone guns. Also, by having so many cartels and private weapon companies cutting in the Lower Levels selling guns for three-quarters the price of our weapons, we have no way of maximising our profits."

"Don't worry. We have a plan to take care of that. Let us open the plans of 'Operation Revitalisation'."

All the businessmen, including my boss, opened the secret documented files.

Operation Revitalisation? I wonder what the hell that is all about.

Just then, the body I was carrying slipped out of my hand and fell down the stairs. I totally forgot I was carrying it to the dumpster, and it came down the stairs with a thump. The boss yelled from the room, "What was that?"

In a panic, I ran as fast as I could, but I had to remember I still had my wound. I rushed down the stairs, carried the body, quickly threw it into the bin and got back to my station. There was no time for a break today.

Just as my shift was about to finish, I saw the guys in white suits exiting the building with my boss shaking their hands and them entering their fancy flying cars, and off they went.

I didn't know what Operation Revitalisation was, but I didn't care, honestly. I was tired and ready for bed.

While I was walking home, I stopped at the liquor shop and decided to buy a bottle of red wine for Ella as a thank-you gift for her saving my life. After buying the flowers, I stopped to stare through the window of the gun shop to check if she was in the shop. After peering through the shop window, I saw Ella behind the counter cleaning. I was about to enter the shop, but as I peered through the window one more time, I saw a man approach her and begin to kiss her on the cheek. Turns out, Ella had a boyfriend. My heart was crushed.

I threw the flowers and bottle aside, as it was kind of rude to give wine to some other guy's girl, and kept on walking home. After my shaky legs finally got me home, I began making my way up the front porch when I noticed something out of the ordinary, even for this place. I witnessed five Humvees pulling up. The Humvees were lined up in a row with their high beams as bright as the street lights themselves. I looked at the cars, wondering what was going on.

Suddenly, 25 guys came out of the Humvee, armed with AK-50s, wearing white masks with hangman nooses around their necks. My mouth just dropped at the looks of these men, as I knew exactly who they were. *Oh no! It's the KLAN!*

But what were they doing in this part of town? Telling by the looks of the guns in their hands, they were on a warpath. Suddenly, one of the guys noticed me and started to point their guns at me. Quickly, just as he was about to open fire, I opened the door in time to get out of the way. Then, the 50 guys began to break into people's houses around the neighbourhood. I thought to myself, *What is going on here? How did they get through Crypt territory?* And then, I heard the bang, bang, bang from machine guns. I peered out the window and noticed gunfire coming from every house on the block. I looked out in shock. *My goodness, it's a purge!*

House to house, they just went up and down the neighbourhood, killing women, men and children. It was the most brutal, scary and horrific thing I had ever seen in my life. I had never seen anything like this in my life. I just stood there staring out the window as I realised that they were getting closer and closer to our house, which scared me, not for my sake but for my mum's well-being.

Anna rushed down the stairs. "Jacob, do you see what's happening outside?"

"Yer, it's a purge of some sort. Quick, Anna! Rush upstairs!"

Anna nodded and rushed upstairs while I looked out the window in fear, keeping an eye on the gangs as they went house to house.

After they reached my neighbour's house, I quickly closed the blinds, and my anxiety kicked in. I turned and screamed out to Mum, who was moving at turtle speed grabbing the guns. "Mum, we have to move now!"

My mum then rushed into second gear, running around like a headless cock. I quickly rushed up the stairs and met up with her and crouched from an elevated position. Knowing that Mum was OK, I rushed down into the basement and deadlocked the door, preparing for the worst.

I grabbed myself an M4 and a Glock, while Anna grabbed an AR-15 and a pump-action shotgun. "Quick, Anna, we have to use anything at our disposal. Make anything you can use as a weapon."

We didn't have much in the way of bullets. We had two boxes of shotgun shells, six rifle clips and two boxes of bullets.

We both looked around the upstairs for any loose items like a fuel can. Thanks to the education I received in the military, I began to make makeshift Molotov cocktails using whisky, petrol and soap. We then used the couch as a barrier and hid underneath it. Our hearts sank into our chests as we heard a banging at the front door, and then we heard another round of banging until the wooden door at the front of our house came off its hinges.

Both Anna and I armed ourselves as the door continued to bang multiple times, over and over. Finally, with a crack, the door came off its hinges. I peeked my head up slightly as two guys stood in front of the front door. At first, I thought it may have been help, but no, it wasn't help. Quite the opposite. I saw the hangman nooses around their necks. They found us. Not thinking and ready for action, both Mum and I popped up from underneath the couch and opened fire, catching them by surprise. *Bang! Bang! Bang!* Bullets went flying everywhere. One of the bullets hit the guy on the right straight in the eye and the one on the left straight in the head, causing him to fall down the basement floor.

Two more thugs walked in, and we just continued opening fire, hitting one in the chest. We had been compromised. No point staying in the house, as this was an enclosed space with no way out, so might as well retreat.

We both rushed into my room, as my bedroom window was the closest to the roof, which would allow us to escape if we were overrun. When we arrived in my room, the first thing we did was push the bed frame up against the door. We could hear the men walking around downstairs, probably to check on their friends. I can't wait for them to find them.

Mum and I turned off the bedroom lights and placed our body weight on the door, but I looked around.

"Blast! We left our spare mags downstairs," I whispered to Mum, and she now had a look of concern on her face.

We both placed our heads against the door to listen to indistinct chatter. The people downstairs didn't sound happy.

They must have found their friends. Then we heard the stomping of footsteps coming up the stairs. Then *bang!* We could feel the force of the group kicking at the door. We tried to place as much of our body weight against the door, but it was no good, as they slowly began to breach through the door.

At that point, it was time to leave, so I signalled to Mum, and we both began climbing out the window and making our way to the roof. Once we climbed up on the roof, Mum and I looked in horror at the houses around us. Not only did they kill the people inside, but they had burnt their houses as well. So many houses were on fire that the smoke and orange embers covered the night sky. All we could do was watch. The Lower Levels had no fire brigade, so the houses just had to burn. There were so many fires, it was horrific.

Suddenly, we heard the door go flying across my bedroom floor as the men had broken down the door. At this moment, as I stood on the roof with my mother, I thought this was the end for us. This was where we die. I just hugged my mum for dear life, but then, we heard the bang from gunfire coming from my room.

Bang! Bang! Bang! I peered through the window to find two Klan members dead in front of the window. How did they die? Mum and I climbed through the window and back into my bedroom. The first thing we did was pick up the guns that were lying on the ground, next to the two dead bodies. Then, remaining cautious of any surprise attacks, we both made our way downstairs, where we found Ella waiting for us in the living room. We looked around to find five dead bodies lying motionless and stiff on the floor around her as she stood over them victoriously.

Ella turned around with a rifle in her hand. "Are you people OK?"

"Yer, we are fine, thanks," Mum said to her. "We owe you our lives."

"Thank goodness you guys are OK. I saw the horror outside. I thought the two of yous may have perished in the purge."

"Why did you come to check on us?"

"I am checking on everyone in this neighbourhood, and I saw you two on the roof, and I had to come help you. Yous are the only ones left."

"Well, thank you. It was pretty brave of you to come and save people you barely knew."

Ella smiled. "Come on. We have to get out of this neighbourhood. Yous are more than welcome to stay at our gun shop until this whole thing blows over."

The three of us proceeded to leave the house, and we made our way down the street towards the gun shop, which Ella so generously allowed us to stay in, as our neighbourhood was a war zone now. Burning buildings, dead bodies and blood spatter everywhere.

After entering the building, we looked out of the shop window to see Humvee after Humvee after Humvee heading to all different parts of the city streets, spreading the purge to more parts of the city. All of them were Klan vehicles, and all you could hear for miles were gunfire and explosions. It was urban warfare at its finest.

I then turned away from the window and closed the blinds to prevent any of them from seeing me, and Ella looked at me confused.

"What the hell was going on?"

I turned to her angrily. "It's a damn war out there."

Ella replied in a sarcastic tone, "Yer, no kidding, but why?"

Anna cut in and stated, "The houses. They seem to be targeting the houses."

"But why?"

Then, a light bulb went off in my head. "Of course, they want to target the houses to get the people out of them."

Ella cut in, "But why would they do that?

"To get the people angry, as this neighbourhood is a low-socioeconomic area, full of different ethnicities and races," said the strange man standing behind the counter.

I stood at attention and pointed my gun at the strange man. "Who are you, old man, and what are you doing here?"

Ella flung herself up and grabbed the gun out of my hand. "Stop! That is my father."

"No need to alarm yourself, my boy. I am Yandan Janeway, the owner of this shop."

Yandan stepped out of the shadow and into the light. He was an old but fit white man in his late 50s with a scruffy white beard, grey hair and a muscular build. Just like his daughter, he was a no-nonsense guy who didn't take crap from anyone. I stood there in absolute amazement. I mean, I had heard of her father, but I had never seen him before.

My mum then nudged me on the shoulder with her elbow. "Jacob, play nice."

I said in a sarcastic tone of voice, "I am always nice."

Mum just gave a 'hmm' sound, as if she didn't believe me.

Ella's father then said, while signalling his hand in a come-down motion, "Let's go down to the basement and camp out the night."

Mum, Ella and I followed him down to the basement, as the streets behind us kept exploding with noises of gunfire, screams of pain and cars roaring past. It was weird to follow some random guy into his basement, but what other choice did we have? Plus, it was safer than waiting up here to die.

Anna, Ella, Yandan and I were all sitting around the same couch that a day ago I had been bleeding out on in the basement, trying to get to know one another and trying to make the most of this awkward situation. We were discussing why the Klan were trying to get people angry. This was not like them. The Klan used fear tactics, yes, but not to this extreme. Their main focus was to control the streets. We all argued back and forth.

"It is a race war!"

"No! It is a rebellion against the corporate elites."

"No, it is—"

Bang! We suddenly paused, as we heard the sound of gunfire coming from upstairs; panicked, we all looked at each other.

"What was that? They must have entered the shop."

"I will go investigate," I said, volunteering to be the scout. I grabbed my rifle and a flashlight and silently made my way up the stairs. I quietly opened the basement door and found a dead Klan member on the floor near the shop door and a random guy in a black hoody, with his back turned to me, holding a rifle and looking for something in the shop. I passed the counter and slowly began to sneak up on the guy and *wack!* I knocked the hooded guy down to the ground with the butt of the gun and pointed my rifle at his head. "Turn around nice and slowly."

The hooded guy looked up at me from the ground. He removed his hood, and it was Edward, who had blood coming from the back of his head.

Angrily, he replied, "What the hell, man?"

"What the hell are you doing here, Edward? You nearly gave me a heart attack. I thought you were some random guy here to kill us."

"Give you a heart attack? I have a bump on the back of my head now because of you!"

"What are you doing here, Edward?"

"I saw you guys running past my pharmacy and decided to join, just to make sure you were all right."

I smiled. "Oh, you big softy."

I gave him an outstretched hand and lifted him up off the floor. Edward explained that he saw Anna, Ella and I running to the shop and was concerned. Also, he could use the company. Then Yandan ran up the stairs with Ella and Mum behind him, pointing a double-barrel shotgun at Edward.

Edward stood back in shock, putting his fists up, trying to act like a tough guy. "Let's see what you got, old man?"

"Yandan, stop, this is my best friend, Edward."

Yandan then pointed the shotgun down at the floor in a safe position. "Oh! Sorry about that. I am Yandan, the shop owner."

Edward gave him a wave. "Hi, I am Edward. I own the pharmacy down the road."

Yandan returned the wave. Ella also waved and introduced herself. "Hi, I am Ella. I also own this shop. Nice to meet you."

"Yer, I know you. I see you all the time. Jacob has told me so much about you."

I turned around and gave him a dirty look.

"You have?" Ella turned around to me, shocked, for which I gave a fake, awkward smile.

Before things could get more awkward, I decided to change the conversation and suggested that we go back down into the basement, which we all did.

Now we had Edward joining our little basement party, but at least things became less tense, as we all cracked open a bottle of Burban and shared it around with each other. But we had to be quiet, as gunfire and explosions roared up top, and any moment now, more men could burst in.

While we were all drunk, we shared a few laughs and some war stories, as everyone in the city had to serve in the military in one form or another due to the National Conscription Act. It turned out that Yandan dropped out of school at 14 and joined the army as a basic infantry soldier, fighting a few wars, and rose through the ranks to become a five-star general, even having the privilege to attend an offi-cer school in the Middle Levels. He eventually retired and, with the little military pension he had, opened this gun shop, which he ran with his wife until she died of cancer.

Ella also explained her story. It was her lifelong dream to become an architect. However, she grew up in the Lower Levels, so her dream was shot dead. She explained that she was always pretty good at math, science and engineering at school. She was even positioned to finish school and gain enrolment to attend university in the Middle Levels, but that changed once her mum got sick and she didn't have the money to survive up there, so she dropped out of school to help her dad run the shop. At 16, she joined the military and enlisted in the ADDF Air Force as an Iron Dome technician. It was her job to maintain and repair the air defence system that protected the border walls from incoming missile fire from rival cities. Ella loved it. She didn't have to witness any combat, plus she got to work with her hands, which she absolutely loved. Ella eventually left after serving her mandatory 4 years and came back to find that her mother had died of cancer, which broke her heart.

My mother, Anna, explained her story next. It had been her dream to become a teacher, but she also didn't have the money to attend university in the Middle Levels. Also, she married my father at 16 due to an unplanned pregnancy (me) to my father, who was a whopping 30 -years-old at the time, who she had met at a bar that she snuck into with a fake ID. She was dating him to piss off her parents, but it turns out, she fell in love with him. After I was born, she joined the ADDF Navy as an enrolled nurse, until she came back home to end up as a stay-at-home mum, but with my father passing away from a drug overdose, she had to take up a minimum-wage job at a supermarket to pay the bills.

Then it was my turn to explain my military service record as a marine diver, and then there was Edward. He was so lucky; the lucky duck only had to pick up a rifle to complete basic training, never even killed a man, never even saw what a battlefield looks like.

We all just sat drinking on the couch, where Ella had performed surgery, when I noticed Ella going into another backroom in the basement. It was a second bedroom. I decided to follow her, as I was concerned for her well-being. Ella was sitting there on the old rusty bed, drinking a beer in the dark alone.

I walked in and asked, "Can I join you?"

Ella just looked up at me. "If you like."

I sat there at the end of the bed, with Ella handing me a beer that she kept in the old fridge out the back. Ella and I sat there in silence, drinking our beers, when Ella was the first one to break the silence. "What was your dream?"

I stopped for a moment and looked at the floor. "I didn't have one. People like us can't afford to have dreams. You just got to take what you can get."

"But surely there was something that you would have done with your life if you had the chance."

I shrugged my shoulders. "I always wanted to help people, but I guess I did the opposite of that and became a soldier."

"Me too. That's why I wanted to be an architect, so I could redesign this hellhole into a more liveable place."

I smiled. "That actually sounded pretty nice."

Ella looked down at the floor depressed. "But I guess life had other plans."

She took a drink of her beer, and we both just sat there in silence, not saying a word.

"So, how's your boyfriend doing?"

Ella's face turned to anger. "Dumped me for some blonde barfly, the dumbass."

I replied with a half-hearted "I am sorry," trying not to smile.

Our moment was interrupted when Edward burst into the room. "Jacob, you may want to come see this!"

Ella and I both looked at each other and rushed out of the room. We both entered the main area of the basement to find Yandan pointing a gun at the head of my mother. My first instinct was to grab a gun and point it at him, but Ella grabbed the gun out of my hand and said in a panicked voice, "NOOO, don't shoot my dad."

I replied in a snappy voice, "He's got a gun to my mother's head!"

"Let me handle this."

Ella began to slowly approach her dad and said in a calm voice, "Dad, the war is over. You are home."

"Liar! You are all separatists who are trying to kill me. I will shoot every single one of you bastards."

As he slowly jiggled the gun, Mum held her eyes and slowly began to cry.

"Dad, it's me. It's your little girl. Please don't hurt that innocent woman."

Yandan snapped out of it and pushed my mum away and collapsed on the floor crying, "I am sorry, I am so sorry."

Ella rushed to comfort her dad, wrapping a blanket around his body. Yandan had been suffering severe wartime flashbacks, and the alcohol only worsened the problem. Years of warfare had taken a toll on him. Mum rushed over to me, hugging me and crying. While I was mad at him for pointing a gun to my mother's head, I really couldn't fault him for it. I mean, he was more of a victim than a madman, a victim of sorrow, pain and regret. I have been there. I knew what it was like.

Later that night, Yandan and Edward were sleeping on the floor, and my mum was sleeping in the other room due to her fear of Yandan. It was just me and Ella still up.

"Is your mum all right?"

"Yer, she is a bit shaken up, but she will be fine."

"I am sorry. He gets like that, sometimes."

"It's not your fault, and it's not his fault. I have been in his shoes. Mental illness is a pain."

We both just sat in silence. I wanted to keep the conversation going, but I was too tired, so I just got up and headed to bed. "Night."

"Night," she responded. "Hey Jacob."

I swung my entire body 360 degrees to face her. "Yer?"

"You seem like a good person."

I smiled and simply said, "You too. Night," and I walked into the other room and slept next to my mum, as there was limited space down there. That night, because of the alcohol in my system, I just blacked out and slept through the night.

The next day Mum, Edward, Ella and I woke up from our sleep to find Yandan upstairs staring at the state of the empty shop. The shop had been completely ransacked of all the guns, and the shopfront had been completely damaged, with windows smashed, rows broken and the counter completely destroyed. What made things worse was that small businesses in the Lower Levels had no insurance whatsoever. If the business was destroyed, then there is no way to financially recover.

Yandan began to cry, and Ella rushed to comfort him. Mum and I looked on with sadness in our eyes, and then Edward rushed out the door to check on the state of his pharmacy. Mum offered out a gesture of goodwill and invited them to stay with us at the house until the shop was repaired, as they couldn't survive down in that basement without running water and food. It was the least we could do as they had taken us in and rescued us. We owed them.

Ella, Yandan, Mum and I returned home to find, to our surprise, the house still standing in one piece. OK, yes, the house was a little worse for wear, but all the damage was repairable.

Later that afternoon, we all began working on the house. I started painting the house, and Mum began sweeping out the broken glass and bullets. Yandan and Ella began repairing the broken walls.

Ella turned to us while she and Yandan were sweeping. "Hey Anna, thanks for letting us stay here. We really appreciate it."

"No problem, Ella. It's the least we can do after you saved our bacon. So tonight, just rest. Tomorrow, we will help you repair your shop."

Both Ella and Yandan smiled at each other. "Thank you. You are good people."

"I am going to step out for a little bit, Mum."

"OK. Be back soon, Jacob."

I walked out of the house, as I needed a break. Also, I needed to get to work.

Even though our Level was rocked by a gang war, the company we worked for didn't care, and I had to go to work the next day.

I arrived at work, and I wasn't surprised at all to find the factory had not been damaged at all; I mean, not even a scratch. Those were the benefits of being a massive, private corporation and having a private security team and state-of-the-art protective gates and systems at their disposal. But what I saw made my blood boil; not only was the factory not damaged, but they added an extension to it. They had added to the side a gun shop selling better quality weapons at half the price of any firearm shop down here.

I knew they would do that. Anything to meet their quota. And just as Ella and Yandan had their business damaged, those greedy dirtbags were undercutting them too. While I wanted to walk away in fury, I couldn't. I still have to pay the bills. So I returned to my workshop to work on the latest robot when I accidentally bumped into my boss, and he dropped some papers. I bent down to help him pick up the papers when I turned them over to find plans for 'Operation Revitalisation'. I got a quick look at the plan when the boss snatched the papers from my hand and said, "Give me that! Get back to work!"

I looked at him in disbelief and grunted back to my workshop, swearing a few profanities at him under my breath. After a standard day of work, I returned home from work to find the house empty, dark and without power. I sat on the floor in silence when something caught my eye. It was a comic book lying on the living room floor. It must have been revealed after we moved around some furniture. The comic book was slightly damaged but was still intact, and it had a drawing of a man; not just a man, but a man in some sort of strange, weird-looking costume. The man in the costume appeared to be standing on top of a building looking down at the city. He was built like a rock; he had a blue cape and a red and black costume, with a red hoodie and a black mask covering his eyes, with blue superhero boots, a gold and black belt and black and red pants. I just stood there looking at the old comic book in amusement. I had never seen anything like this. It was an antique. It looked like it came from the 2022 era, and it had written in big, bold letters stretched across the top: The City Watcher.

The comic was covered in dust, and the ink had faded in the pages, but it seemed like a good read. I skimmed through the book, and it depicted the hero punching out criminals and helping people from disaster. I sat reading the book when I heard a voice from behind me, "That was my dad's favourite book growing up."

I turned around and found Ella standing on the stairs looking at me. My head swung around to face her. She explained that as a child her father would read that book to her at a young age to give her hope.

"It's a beautiful comic book. You were very lucky to have a father who would read it to you."

Ella stepped down the stairs and sat next to me on the living room floor. "Where did you get that?"

"I don't know. Is it yours?"

"No, must have been yours."

I looked at it. "That's strange. I don't remember this book at all."

Ella turned around to me and asked in a sympathetic voice, "Did your dad ever read to you?"

"No, my dad never had time for me. Whenever he had free time, he would always hit the drugs."

Ella replied, "I am sorry."

Then I asked, "Where's Yandan and Mum?"

"Out. Sorry, I tried to sleep in the basement, but it was just hurting my back, so your mum let me use her bed."

"Knock yourself out. Excuse me one minute." I quickly rushed upstairs, then rushed down the stairs and held up a bong. "Wanna get high?"

The hours passed by, and we sat there looking at the ceiling and told funny stories. After a while just lying there, I signalled to Ella to follow me. "Come on, I will show you something."

Ella was curious about what I had to offer, and we both left the house and decided to go for a walk downtown. After a 30-minute walk, we stopped and broke into an abandoned warehouse, climbing the roof, and we sat there and watched a hyperspeed train rush past. This was my favourite place to go. The city was truly beautiful up here, and Ella and I sat there looking at all the lights from the skyscrapers. Not saying a word, we both enjoyed the moment, taking it all and basking in the light's glow.

Then, after a brief minute of silence, we looked into each other's eyes. I was caught in her beautiful blue eyes, and I leaned in, and we kissed each other, but I stupidly broke the silence. "We should be getting back."

"Yer, let's head back."

We both laughed some more before returning home and heading to bed. Just as I was about to head to bed, I heard a bang. It was the front door being kicked in with force by Yandan making his way inside. I rushed down the stairs, and Ella rushed down with me. Yandan was covered in blood and holding a machete and a burlap sack. I looked in shock.

"What did you do?"

Yandan grabbed out of the burlap sack a decapitated head and threw the head on the floor. Ella vomited a little, and I was in complete shock.

"Who's that?" I looked further and realised it was my boss's head. At that point, I lost my cool. "What did you do?"

Yandan didn't say a word. He just looked down at the floor, but then, a question dawned on me, so I quickly ran out of the house and down the street, only to find the factory I worked for was on fire. Security guards lay dead on the floor. I just could not believe it.

I ran back home and demanded an explanation from Yandan. "Why did you do that?"

He shrugged his shoulders. "Simple. Because they were interfering with my business, and I couldn't have that."

"You took down that entire building by yourself?"

"I know a few things," he responded.

I just shook my head. "You have no idea what you have done! WeapCo—"

"Screw WeapCo. The time of big corporations pushing the little guy around is over. It's time to push back."

"You are going to get me and my family killed!"

"They are going to die anyway. They may as well die for a good cause."

"What! Have you lost your mind?"

"My mind is perfectly clear. Those fat cats don't get to just move in here and take whatever they want."

"That's not your call to make. Once WeapCo finds out about this, they are going to send an army after you and Ella."

"Ella knows the risk of doing business. If she dies, then she dies for the cause."

I had lost my temper at that point. "YOU DON'T GET TO DECIDE THAT!"

Yandan responded, "This is a war! You are either with us or against us!"

"No, I am not putting my mother's life on the line because you want to play hero."

"Fine. Then you are cowards. Come, Ella, we are leaving."

"Dad, they are our friends."

"NOW!"

Ella, still in shock, ran down the stairs and out the door, with her father walking out the door and slamming the now-repaired door. Yandan and Ella walked out of the house, leaving behind the decapitated head of my boss, a machete, and a burlap sack. *May as well clean up,* I thought. As I walked over to pick up the burlap sack, I felt something in there. *That's strange,* I thought, and I dropped the content of the sack onto the floor to reveal a file titled 'Operation Revitalisation'. I picked up the file and began to read it, and what I read shocked me.

Meanwhile, while I wasn't there to give an account of what was said, based on conversations I had with Ella, I learnt that Ella and Yandan had returned to their empty gun shop, with Yandan cursing around in fury, "Cowards, all of them!"

He tried to calm himself down by sharpening a combat knife. Ella was still trying to comprehend what had just happened, but he was her father, and she loved him and needed to be by his side, so she walked over to him, trying to understand the cause.

"How many people do we need to kill?"

Yandan stopped sharpening his knife. "As many as we need to save this shop."

"But how is adding more violence to the world going to solve anything? I mean, this neighbourhood is already filled with violence. Why add more?"

"Ella, those corporations are the ones causing this violence, ruining small businesses like ours. It's a dog-eat-dog world out there. I mean, look at what they did to this innocent neighbourhood. These corporations funded radical groups and terrorists to attack this neighbourhood, just to keep the profits spinning, killing innocent people, including my wife, your mum."

"How did they kill Mum?"

Yandan sighed and threw down the knife onto the coffee table with enough force to leave a dent in the wood. "Your mum didn't die of cancer. She was murdered."

Ella walked back in disbelief and shock. "You lie!"

Yandan sighed. "I wish I did. When the WeapCo gun factory first moved into town, they offered me $50,000 to close down my business, but I refused. Then they threatened me, saying that they 'hope nothing happened to me'. The next day, I was cleaning up the shop when I heard your mother's medical equipment had flatlined. She had died. At first, I thought that she had died of cancer, but after returning to the front of the shop, I found a man in a black suit from WeapCo standing there. 'You should have taken our offer. My condolences to your wife.' I was left in shock and disbelief. I wanted to destroy WeapCo, but I couldn't. I had experienced enough violence and wanted to live in peace for your sake."

Ella didn't know how to handle that news.

"I tried to live in peace and go about my business, but now that they have destroyed my business, I want revenge!"

Ella rushed and hugged her father, with Yandan grabbing his daughter's hand. "Ella, they need to pay for what they have done."

"Yes, Dad, whatever it takes."

Yandan smiled. "That's my girl."

Anna returned from work. "What the hell happened here?"

I responded, "Never mind that. Have a read through this."

I gave the papers to Mum, and she began to read.

"Operation Revitalisation was only Phase 1 of a much bigger plan. The plan is to fund the Crypts and the Klan to attack each other's neighbourhood to fuel fear and anger and buy more guns."

"That's horrible!" Anna said, shocked. "Then what is Phase 2?"

I had a look of concern on his face. "I don't know, but by the look of this plan, it couldn't be too good."

Anna then noticed the head on the floor. "What's that head doing there? And where are Yandan and Ella?"

"They went back to the gun shop. They are planning to start a war with WeapCo."

Anna looked shocked. "Are you going to join them?"

"NO! I have seen enough violence and killed enough people in my life. All I want is to live a peaceful life with you. Why is that so hard?"

There was some awkward silence in the room until Anna spoke, "Are you ready for some dinner?"

I looked down depressed. "I am not in the mood to eat. Goodnight, Mum."

I kissed her on the cheek and went up to my room to find Ella sitting in my room.

Ella was staring out the window, but telling by the look on her face, something was troubling her. I walked over and handed her a cigarette.

"Thanks."

We both just stared out the window, smoking our cigarettes. "How's the shop?"

Ella continued to stare out into the night. "We have nothing left. That attack has ruined us financially. All our inventory was lost, and we don't have the money to recover."

"I am sorry. How's your dad taking it?"

Ella stood looking out the window on the verge of breaking down. "Destroyed. He is ready to start a war with WeapCo."

I wasn't at all surprised. "Are you?"

"I don't know. I mean, he has a point. We have to do something. We can't just sit here and do nothing."

I tried to talk some sense into her. "It's a futile effort. You're both going to get yourself killed."

"I would rather die for something than live for nothing."

I couldn't stand that radicalised suicidal thought process, and I snapped at her. "That's your father talking. Don't die because your dad has some petty revenge plan."

But that statement sent her over the edge, and she stormed out of the room and angrily said, "I know what my goal in life is! Do you?"

Then she went down the stairs and walked out the front door. I stood staring out the window in complete shock, trying to figure out what had happened and what I had said to make her so angry.

Anna walked up the stairs and asked me, "What happened?"

"Nothing, Mum. It's all right. Just a misunderstanding."

Ella began walking home with tears rolling down her face, then stormed into the gun shop, kicking away the door and rushing down the wooden steps into the basement, where she found Yandan loading up a pump-action shotgun and preparing for an attack of some sort. There were blueprints and plans scattered across the floor.

Yandan got up off the couch and rushed over to Ella, who was clearly in pain. "What's wrong, sweetheart?"

"I am so sorry, Dad," she said, as she bawled her eyes out.

Yandan's paternal instincts kicked in, and like the good dad he was, he rushed over to hug his daughter, as she cried on his shoulder.

"I love you, Dad."

Yandan gave her a smile. "Love you too, my little princess. Sorry for putting you through this, but I am doing this for us, so that we can live a better life, together."

Ella wiped away her tears. "What do we have to do?"

Yandan looked at her and smiled. "I am glad you asked."

Ella walked over to the couch, and Yandan discussed the entire plan with her.

Outside a gun factory on the Middle Levels, Ella and Yandan were on a rooftop of the building next to the gun factory, scoping the factory with binoculars to assess the area and the security around it. They were dressed in heavy ballistic armour that covered them head to toe and were carrying various types of firearms. They have been carrying a Glock and two M4s strapped to their backs, which they managed to salvage from the WeapCo factory.

Ella stood there loading a handgun and asked, "What are we dealing with?"

"Five armed guys outside, two outside, multiple turrets and cameras. We go in, and we hit hard. And remember Ella, no mercy. Do it for Mum."

Ella nodded to him. Then they both put on bulletproof masks and rushed down the stairs of the building, crouching down behind an old, rusted-up car. Then they got up from behind the car and began shooting at the security guards who were standing outside of the building, cutting them down instantly. They rushed straight into the building, breaking out into a gunfight with the security guards. *Bang! Bang! Bang!* Bullets went flying everywhere. Finally, after killing all the security guards, they breached the factory and found a warehouse full of workers and robots assembling weapons at a rapid pace. All the workers and bosses looked in shock and fright at Yandan and Ella.

Ella asked, "What do we do now?"

"Move to the manager's office, take out the head boss and destroy the factory, but give the workers time to escape."

Ella nodded and began making her way to the manager's office. Ella rushed up the office stairs and kicked down the office door. In the office stood a balding, middle-aged man in a suit. He looked at Ella in shock and slowly started to back away as Ella reached for a combat knife and advanced towards him. The balding man backed far enough to hit his desk. He then grabbed a picture on his desk, held it up to her and begged her, "Please, I have a wife and kids."

Ella stopped advancing and looked down, contemplating whether to kill this man or to let him go free. Then, out of fear, the man rushed for the Glock underneath his desk. Out of instinct, Ella grabbed the guy's hand and stabbed him in the neck.

Yandan reached the office with a Glock in his hand to find the man bleeding out on the floor. He turned to Ella and said, "Good job. Now we must destroy the evidence."

He ran down the stairs, grabbed a can of oil, splashed it all over the floor and lit it with a lighter. Ella and Yandan then ran out of the warehouse as the place went up in flames.

Yandan turned to Ella. "We are done here."

He began to walk away, but Ella just stood there looking at the warehouse in shock and disbelief. Yandan yelled out to Ella, "Are you coming?"

Ella looked at the burning building for a few more minutes, and then they walked away.

Early the next morning, Edward and I, with no other option, had to go to the welfare office to gain some unemployment benefits, as we both had lost our jobs due to the gang war and Yandan killing my boss. Edward was pretty sad and angry. He was used to working for his money, and having to take welfare payments was demeaning in his mind.

"Bloody hell, we have been standing here for 2 hours. When is this line going to move?" He was clearly agitated.

"Relax, dude, it's almost there."

"Don't tell me to relax. I have no money, and the business I own is now up in ashes."

I looked at him in shock. "Chill, dude."

Edward looked down sad. "Sorry, it's just, this place is driving me mad. I feel like you can never rise in this place."

"I get that. Welcome to the Lower Levels."

Edward just looked down sad.

"I know what you mean. I don't know how I am going to help Anna. Sometimes, I think we are doomed to live in this miserable life."

Edward couldn't agree more. "So you really think that WeapCo is truly behind this?"

"It wouldn't surprise me. That's all these big corporations ever do."

"What are you going to do? I mean, there is no police force down here. Who is going to believe you?"

"Well, what can I really do?"

"Guess you are right. What about Ella and Yandan?"

"If they want to get themselves killed, they can knock themselves out."

"Don't you think you should try to help them?"

I sighed. "Na. I have seen too much suffering, and I have hurt too many people. I can't keep doing that anymore."

Edward gave me a sympathetic nod, and we both stood there in silence. "So, what are you going to do for work?"

"I don't know. You? How long will it take you to get back on your feet?"

"I don't know. Guess we will join the thousands of other people down here who are not working."

We continued to wait in line till an old, grey man in a black suit came out of the welfare building, escorted by two armed guards, and yelled out to the row of people. "Attention, everyone. Due to the recent criminal activity conducted by the people of the Lower Levels, the AD government will be suspending all welfare until further notice. We apologise for the inconvenience."

Edward and the thousands of people including myself waiting in line responded in shock, with the entire crowd letting out a 'What!'

The people in the crowd were not happy at all with that decision, and they all let out a stream of verbal abuse. 'That's rubbish', 'What, are you going to let us starve?', 'Upper Level snobs'. That shock turned to anger real fast, as the crowd began to riot, first storming the building and then taking it out into the streets. The crowd threw bricks and bottles and began turning over cars and lighting fires. The security guards outside the building were trying their best to keep the protesters at bay, whacking away as many protesters as they could with their batons, but it was no good. They were outmanned and were quickly overrun.

I signalled to Edward to get out of there, and we walked away slowly, slipping through the crowd to avoid the chaos. Tensions were already high in this place after the war, but to cut off welfare was an absolute stab in the back for these people. They needed that to afford the basic essentials to live, and now with the cut to welfare, the people had exploded out of fear for their families. It wasn't long until the protests spread across the entire Lower Levels, engulfing the streets once again into chaos.

Meanwhile, in a meeting room on the top floor of the WeapCo building sat 12 men in white suits. At the end of the large table, sitting in a large black chair, wearing a white suit, sat John Speer, the CEO of WeapCo. John was a well-educated, well-dressed business mogul. He was 40 years old but was in really good shape for his age, with black hair and brown eyes. People described him as a cold, ruthless business mogul who would do anything to get his way. John grew up in the Upper Level, having everything handed to him. He was incredibly intelligent, having attended the most prestigious school in these entire levels. John founded this company after his military service (with a small loan of $1.6 billion from his rich father), and with hard work, multiple defence contracts and a lot of exploiting and arse-kissing, he turned his company into an empire.

John sat there, rubbing a metal ball in his hand while looking at the holographic projection of the CCTV footage from the warehouse fires in the Lower and Middle Levels. He was not happy. He didn't like it when people interfered with his business. "Who are these people, and why the fuck are they messing with my business?"

One corporate egghead responded, "Sir, they are Yandan and Ella Janeway. We ran their files through background checks. Both were vets who ran a local gun business in the Lower Levels and were angry when we tried to undercut their business."

"Lower Levels?" John reacted in shock.

"Yes, sir."

"Are you trying to tell me that two sewer rats from down in the ghettos have managed to infiltrate not just one but two heavily guarded factories and destroy them, which has impacted my company and its profits?"

"Ah! Well, they are military trained, sir."

John slammed his fist on the table. "You're missing the point! How much did these vermin cost us in revenue and damages?"

"2.2 million in revenue, and 1 million in damages, sir."

At that point, John was furious. He stood up and threw his chair at the office window."

"3.2 million! Are you kidding me? These guys broke into my company and not only cost my company 2.2 million in revenue but have destroyed my precious weapon factories as well." He then calmed down and took in a deep breath. "People, I did not put in all this hard work and time to have my company run into the ground by some hood rats from the Lower Levels. People! Operation Revitalisation will be what puts this company on the map. Operation Revitalisation will secure our place as the biggest gun company in the world, and we would be able to manipulate and control any government and defence force, creating any wars we want. We would be a global superpower. Now, what are we going to do about these people?"

"Already taken care of it, sir."

"Excellent." John just picked up his chair and rejoined the meeting. "Now, to make up for the lost revenue, we are going to have to push up Operation Revitalisation."

"Yes, sir."

"Make these people suffer. I want their heads on spikes. Do what needs to be done."

John looked out the window, looking out past the concrete walls and over into the wastelands.

The WeapCo building had to be at least 100 storeys high. In this city, if you had money, you could build skyscrapers as high as you wanted. Anything goes in this city.

"That's the end of this meeting. Thank you, everyone."

All the staff members got up from their chairs, and in a hurry, they all scattered out of the meeting room and back to their workplaces, leaving John to stare out through the window thinking.

He stood there, rubbing the metal balls in his hand.

His receptionist Macy walked in. "Sir, you have your 12 pm meeting soon."

John sighed. "Thanks, Macy."

Macy wanted to walk out of there, as it was none of her business, but she stopped and asked, "Everything all right, sir?"

John paused. "Macy, why is it that when a simple, hard-working man like myself tries to build a dream, people have always got to interfere? Macy my vision was to rule this world, but did my father ever believe in me? No! He thought that I was greedy and selfish. Ugh! Nothing was ever good enough for that man. Well, fine, Dad. If I can't please you, then I will just have to please myself, and the only thing that would make me happy is if I own this entire world."

Macy looked shocked, and John walked out of the room.

CHAPTER 4

07-02-3025

After an intense day of rioting, the riots had simmered down, and the town was once again silent, though not for long.

Anna, Edward and I were sitting there at the dinner table, drinking glasses of wine, laughing as we stayed home enjoying the silent night, and eating some casserole Mum had cooked up. Edward and I were telling Mum about the riots at the welfare building and were cracking jokes. "Talk about a bad payday."

Then there was a knock on the door. It was Ella and Yandan. We greeted them and offered them to join us for dinner.

"We brought some pasta. Sorry for calling you cowards." Anna looked up.

"It's OK. Come and join us for some dinner."

So, we were all having dinner together when we heard a loud noise outside.

Vroom, bang! Vroom, bang!

I got up to look out through the front window and looked at the neighbour's house.

Vroom, bang!

I watched as my neighbour's house went up in flames. It was a missile. A missile had hit my neighbour's building. After witnessing that sight, I had to go investigate, so I rushed out onto the balcony, only to see a white flash of light disappearing up into the Middle Levels and then up into the night sky. It looked like an angel, and it moved so fast that I could barely see it.

Yandan, Ella and Anna followed me out onto the balcony and were left shocked to find not just the neighbour's house but multiple different locations containing shops and apartments full of people obliterated! All that remained were smoky piles of rubble. After the attack, groups of survivors, including us, gathered around the old town hall building. The people were completely confused and needed an explanation as to why a military drone had attacked civilian compounds.

The town hall was an ancient, abandoned building built in the early development of this town. The city didn't have the budget for a local government or legal representation, so the building just remains as a relic of what this city used to be: a government by the people and for the people. Now the only reason anyone came to this building was for the technology that ran through this building.

The people gathered around the Holonet projector to get some clues from the news as to what was happening, and an image of a white male in a suit with gel hair appeared on the screen. He was reading off a teleprompter of some sort, and he said the following: "Breaking news, an A20 lightstriker drone has been deployed down to the Lower Levels to wipe out ruthless insurgents. It was believed the attack was retribution for the factory attack caused by these insurgents from the Lower Levels."

The crowd was left mortified in disbelief. That was not what happened at all. The people all refocused on the Holonet projector.

"I am here with the commissioner of the Middle Levels Police Force, Commissioner John." Then the image of a middle-aged white man appeared on the Holonet. "Commissioner, don't you reckon this attack was a little excessive?" the anchor asked in a stern voice.

"Not at all. Look, we are not dealing with criminals in this matter. We are dealing with violent insurrectionists, and they must be stopped at all costs. The Lower Levels are completely anarchic places, and the people need to be dealt with like the rats they are!"

The crowd turned away in shock at that comment, and all Yandan did was shake his head in disgust.

Having heard enough, the people turned off the Holonet projector and quickly turned to anger, especially from the 'rats' comment. They began to scream out angry slurs: "Classic Middle Level losers. No surprise they attacked us. They probably ran out of their golden toilet paper."

Yandan then ran to the front of the crowd and stood on an old statue of some war general and whistled. He began to scream towards the crowd, "People! Once again, the people up above have shown us that they do not care about us, and once again, they think they are entitled to take from you, the working class! Well, are we going to let that happen?"

The entire crowd let out a 'NOOO', while Edward, Ella, Anna and I watched on.

"Those people first cut off our welfare, hired thugs to attack our streets, and now they attack us from the skies. You know what I say. If those people want a war, then a war they shall have. No longer will we destroy our own communities and hurt our own people. Instead, we will take our anger up with the people up above. Who is with me!"

The crowd all let out a cheer and roared in applause.

"The time has come for the Upper and Middle Levels to feel our wrath. They call us rats? Ha! Well, we will show them what rats can do. Are you with me, my people?"

The crowd erupted into roars of applause and began chanting, "Uppers Snobs! Uppers Snobs! Upper Snobs!"

"Prepare yourselves. Tonight, we mourn. Tomorrow, we go to war."

"Yea!" The crowd then dispensed in anger while chanting, "Down with the rich! Down with the rich!"

Once everyone left, it was just Mum, Ella, Yandan and I remaining. Out of concern, I went up to Yandan, hoping to stop this madness. "What have you done?"

"What I needed to. For too long, the rich have been pulling the strings, hurting innocent people and thinking they can get away with it."

"Didn't you attack their factories and kill their people?"

Yandan was not happy with that comment. "I did what needed to be done. WeapCo and the rich are a cancer on this city, enriching their own pockets while breaking down decent, hard-working people, like me, you, your mom." Then there was a pause, then he added, "My dear wife."

There was silence. A single tear rolled down Yandan's face, but that sadness quickly snapped back to pure anger. "Well, I say enough! Now I am going to rally the troops and take down every corporation in this city one by one if I have to."

I was in absolute disbelief. "Look, I get it, you lost people, but that's no reason to start a coup. People are going to get hurt in all this. There has to be another way."

Yandan shook his head, defiant to the end. "No! There is no other way, Jacob. You and your mother can hide and pretend like everything is normal, but we are no longer going to pretend."

I stood there in silence, then Yandan came up to me and pointed a finger at me. "Eventually you will have to take a side."

Yandan and Ella walked away while Mum and I just stood there in silence, not saying a word as we watched them walk away following the crowd.

Yandan's words really struck a chord with people in the community. The next day, I walked down the street to find across every storefront sign saying, 'Down with the Uppers'.

Yandan had let out a call to action in the community, and the Lower Levels had established him as a pseudo-leader. Every person I passed on the street was armed to the teeth. Hell, as I walked past my neighbours, they were sharpening a combat knife on their burnt front porch. On the way home, I passed

the subway station and saw crowds after crowds of radicalised people screaming at innocent monorail passengers to get
out. They were also chanting 'down with the Upper Levels'.
The people of the Lower Level seemed to have taken on lev-
elistic pride and resented anyone who came from up above. I
stopped to watch as the crowd attacked innocent bystanders,
people who were just trying to go to work or home, and all I
could think was, *Yandan what have you done! You are going
to cause a damn level war if you are not careful!*

Suddenly, violence erupted in the subway station, as
crowds began chucking bottles and bricks at people and began
entering the monorails, assaulting random people inside. It got
so bad that 20 officers of the Middle Level Police Department
(MLPD) had to come rushing down to quell the protesters.
The officers were standing in rows, armed with tactical riot
gear, electric shock batons and energy-projected shields. The
officers were doing their best to keep the crowd at bay from
entering the Middle Level and hurting other people.

The whole situation was getting serious because police
presence in the Lower Level was extremely rare, and having
the MLPD down there meant the rift between the Lower,
Middle and Upper Levels was boiling over, which meant
heads were about to roll.

Suddenly, one of the officers at the back of the row fired
a canister of tear gas, and the demonstrators quickly dispersed and fled in different directions, rushing back down
into the Lower Level.

Within 5 minutes, the subway station was completely
empty. I was the only one standing there. The officers looked
up at me and quickly told me in the nicest way possible to
'get the hell out of here!' I shrugged my shoulders. No point
arguing with the heavily armoured man. In a hurry, I left.

I tried to make as much distance as possible from the
subway station, trying to avoid any of the officers coming
after me, so, not thinking, I began rushing my way home. I
rushed until my heart almost gave out and still kept going

until I finally made it home, my dilapidated, slightly damaged and rustic building, where I knew the officers wouldn't find me. I walked in to find Mum and Ella, who now seemed to be friends, both in the living room sitting around on the newly furbished couch, drinking a couple of beers and talking about Yandan's stunt the other night. Both Mum and Ella seemed to be proud of him. I personally was not impressed, but there was no point getting involved in politics, so pretending like everything was normal, I walked over and kissed Mum on the cheek and picked up a full beer that was lying on the coffee table and sat on the couch next to Mum, trying to join in on the conversation.

Ella, while proud of her dad, had a look of concern on her face, so I decided to address the elephant in the room. "How is Yandan going, now that he is the leader of the Lower Levels?"

Ella's face quickly turned sour. "Not good. While I am impressed with his leadership skills, he's been acting weird."

"What do you mean by weird?"

Anna cut in. "Well, he hasn't been communicating with me, and all he does is spend time in the basement surrounded by random people I have never met before. He is planning something. Something big."

That can't be good, I thought. "Doing what, exactly?"

Ella's face looked at me in distaste at the idea of me judging her father, but since we were all friends now and she trusted us, she just came out and said it. "Terrorist plot of some sort." She took a sip of beer before continuing to explain. "He and his militia are planning to attack the main WeapCo Office in the downtown Middle Levels. He says it is retribution for what they influence in the Lower Levels."

I couldn't believe what I was hearing. "Bloody hell, Ella, that's suicide!"

"I know. WeapCo is all he thinks about now. He has become obsessed with WeapCo to the point that he is not even focusing on rebuilding his shop anymore. Yandan is even acting differently. He is so angry all the time, and I am afraid he is going to get himself killed."

We all just sat there not saying a word, as none of us knew how to respond to what we were hearing. I mean, I didn't know what was worse: the fact that Yandan was going to attack WeapCo directly, or the fact that Anna and Ella refused to stand up to him, particularly encouraging him with their silence and praise.

Suddenly, there was a massive bang, and through the living room window, we all saw a massive ball of fire coming from the railway tracks.

"What the hell was that!" Anna screamed out.

Without thinking, we all rushed outside to find the monorail completely blown off its tracks and the rails crumbling down in a ball of fire and black smoke. We had to go check to see if there were any survivors. Concerned for the well-being of the passengers, Ella, Anna and I all rushed out the front door and began making our way to the wreckage, only to find metal scattered across the road. What remained of the monorail was a complete fiery wreck. The three of us tried to search through the wreckage for any survivors, but there were none, only dead bodies, killed in the blast or upon impact. Most of them were still wearing seatbelts, and their skin and clothing were burnt off in the blast. All that remained were charred skeletons.

But what was worse was that I could smell them. I could smell the burning bodies, and frankly, I wish I didn't. Even I, a hardened veteran, rushed away from the scene and threw up. The scene was quite disturbing, as there were even children and pets on that monorail. That sight alone would mess anyone up.

After throwing up, I pulled myself together, and with blood pumping through my body, I began marching towards the gun shop, as there was only one person responsible for all of this – Yandan!

Yandan was down in the gun shop basement trying to relax by polishing a rifle when I barged through the door, grabbed him by the neck and threw him against the wall.

"How many! How many people did you kill?"

Yandan struggled to talk. "It doesn't matter. These people mean nothing in the long run. It's not like they cared about our neighbourhood, anyway. They were to send a message."

That is absolute madness, I thought. "Those were innocent people just taking a ride on the monorail. They weren't involved in anything. Why kill them?"

"So what if they were innocent? What about the men, women and children who were killed by those airstrikes? Were they not innocent? This attack was to send a message that we are not going to stand by and let those Upper Level snobs impose their rules on us anymore."

I was still confused.

"Those people up there are not innocent, as they line their pockets while we all suffer and die. It's their ignorance and selfishness that allows companies like WeapCo to rain down here, so no, they are not innocent. They are just as guilty as WeapCo is."

Yandan was going off the rails. I had to talk some sense into him. "Yandan, this has got to stop!" I threw him to the ground, and Yandan got back to his feet.

"This attack is just the beginning."

I thought I could deter him. "How many more are you going to kill, Yandan? Hundreds? Thousands?"

"I would kill millions if I had to. These rich bastards need to know that they can't just step on anyone they please. They think they can ignore us. Well, we will be a massive problem, so they won't be able to ignore us."

"Killing all these people and committing these attacks will make you no better than them."

"They kill us on a daily basis, poisoning our planet. I mean, look around. They nuked our planet just to make bank. And I'm the bad guy for wanting to change the world?"

I just shook my head. "You don't get to justify one evil with another."

"Don't be a hypocrite, Jacob. How many people have you killed?"

That comment really stung. "I have killed people, you are right, and I live to regret it, but killing won't bring back your shop or your wife."

Yandan's face went red, and he grabbed me and shoved me to the wall and pushed me towards the stairs. "Get out!"

I had had enough. I went to the staircase and began to walk away, but before I went up the stairs, Yandan grabbed my arm.

"Boy, you got to learn that down here, it's a war, and you must choose your side."

I refused to fight, so I took away my arm. "I will not be a terrorist."

"Fine, you have made your choice. Stay away from my daughter, and stay away from my shop, or I will beat your arse!"

That comment angered me. I was only trying to help. I stormed up those stairs and through the front door.

CHAPTER 5

After I had left, I heard Ella asking Yandan. "Dad, what happened?"

Yandan got off the floor. "Nothing, Sweetie, just a little misunderstanding. No biggie."

But suddenly, they heard loud noises from outside.

"What was that?"

Yandan and Ella rushed out to find armoured Humvees, tanks and at least 100 fully armoured soldiers marching down the street, holding plasma rifles. I also looked behind me and watched as tanks rolled down the road. Then, a speaker blasted from one of the tanks with an announcement.

"Attention! This is the PF from AD city. This level is under martial law. Curfew will be in effect. Please remain in your homes, or you will be prosecuted."

Yandan was not taking this and stormed down to the basement to grab a gun.

Crowds of people gathered around, and one of the bystanders outside decided to approach the peacekeepers. "You can't do this to us. We have rights!"

The hoard of soldiers began to approach the man. "Get back!" yelled one of the soldiers, hitting the bystander to the floor with a baton.

The peacekeeping force was a group of Tactical Response Units from the MLPD and the AD Army's National Reserve Division. This was in response to the subway explosion.

One person had been arrested, and Yandan opened fire on the crowd, with Ella providing backup fire. Suddenly, the protesters erupted at the peacekeepers, and fighting commenced. The rioters quickly turned to combatants, as they all took up arms and began firing at the troops. They were fighting from everywhere: on the top of buildings, from windows, behind cars and under sewers. It was a firefight, as bullets and laser bolts went everywhere. I watched in horror; the fighting quickly escalated, as tanks began to open fire on buildings, and some of the buildings in the downtown district were going up in fire and exploding.

Buildings collapsed, and debris was lying everywhere. The fire from buildings was so bright that the skies were dark red. I didn't know what to think. Suddenly, *bang!* A tank shell went straight into the gun shop, obliterating the storefront. Out of panic, I rushed as fast as I could to the building and scraped through the rubble, looking for Ella and Yandan. After searching for a few minutes, it was obvious to me that they were dead, but then I heard a voice coming from underground. "Down here!"

It sounded like Ella's voice, so I placed my head down near the shop floor.

"Down here!" the voice repeated. They were trapped underneath, and I needed to get them out. I ran to the dead soldier's body and grabbed his grenade launcher.

"Stand back!"

I blew a hole into the basement roof. Yandan and Ella coughed and blew away the smoke from the blast. They looked up at me. "Need a hand?"

The two of them smiled, and I reached out a hand and helped lift them out of the basement.

"Thanks, Jacob."

"Don't thank me just yet. We still have to get out of this."

Ella looked around. "Where do we go now?"

I looked around at the chaos that unfolded, and then I had a light bulb moment. "Let's get back to my house, as it will be safe there. But we need to grab Edward first. His district is being hit hard, and he won't survive without us."

Both Yandan and Ella nodded in agreement, and we all picked up some guns lying on the floor and began making our way down the street towards Edward's apartment. After dodging calibre bullets and plasma fire from all directions and the explosion of buildings and cars, we finally reached Edward's old, dilapidated Pasadena-style apartment. Edward was certainly inside, but he wouldn't be easy to reach, as the building was under siege by the peacekeeping force. It was a mess; dead bodies were lying everywhere throughout the building and outside, fires raging on different levels, and all you could hear from the building was the sound of gunfire and explosions. We had to be ready for anything, so we all reloaded our guns and began to enter the building.

We slowly moved into the lobby of the building, only to find the elevator destroyed; it looked like the soldiers had destroyed the pulley system, and the elevator had fallen 50 feet and crashed down to Ground Level. Ahead of us, there had to be at least 10 soldiers on the stairwell shooting up at different apartments from the staircase, using the walls as a cover from the gunfire. We all slowly began creeping up behind them, and we opened fire at them, which caught the soldiers off guard, as they quickly turned around and returned fire at us. It wasn't our smartest move, as we were quickly outgunned; there was no point standing out in the open. We quickly took cover behind anything that we could find. The soldiers were covered head to toe in body armour, so it would take a few shots to take them down.

The soldiers were striking us; we were ambushed from all directions, and we could barely move, let alone fire. Through persistence, we managed to take out four of them, but the intensity of their gunfire pushed us back outside into the foyer. One soldier came near the doorway, so like a bull, I charged at him and rammed him into the doorway, which caused him to drop his gun. While I was engaged in the fight, Yandan distracted two of the soldiers but not long enough for one of the soldiers to point his gun directly at my head. Dang! I was going to die. Out of nowhere, Ella charged at the soldier and knocked him to the ground. The soldier I had tackled kicked me directly in the face and got to his feet; it was time for hand-to-hand combat. After a few back-and-forth attacks, I pulled out the combat knife he had in his utility belt and stabbed him right in the neck. However, luckily for him, the body armour he was wearing covered his neck, and while it caused him to step back in pain, it didn't kill him.

Out of anger, the soldier front-kicked me onto the concrete path out the front of the building, leaving me defenceless on the floor. The soldier was about to pull out his secondary weapon when I kicked him back out of adrenaline and went for the stun grenade on his utility belt. I grabbed the grenade, placed it next to the helmet and boom! Flashes of white sparks and smoke quickly escaped the grenade capsule and engulfed the soldiers, causing him immense pain, as the sparks blew his eardrums and burnt his face. The soldier stepped back in shock, holding his ears. I kicked him back and reached for the knife on the floor, then pulled off his face covering and stabbed him in his throat. The soldier fell on the ground dead.

I looked over at Ella, and she was struggling; the soldier had gotten the upper hand and was beating her while she was on the ground. She was struggling, trying to block every attack. I had to help. I picked up the nearest plasma rifle, aimed it at the soldier and zoomed! The blue plasma bolt flew out of the gun and hit the soldier straight in the head, killing him instantly. I walked over and offered Ella a hand up.

Yandan rejoined us. He had taken care of the two other soldiers. After regrouping, we all began to make our way up the staircase, passing the dead bodies of soldiers and combatants lying motionless on the floor with bullet shells scattered everywhere. The staircase was a complete wreck, and apartments had been raided and burnt. We ran up four storeys, and on the final storey, we found at least 10 soldiers and 10 civilians armed with rifles engaged in a close-quarter firefight, with Edward smack bang in the middle of it. We had to help him, or he would die. We rushed in and ambushed the soldiers from behind. It was intense. Fighting in an enclosed space was not pretty; people were coming out of every apartment, hiding behind doors and inside apartments for cover.

We quickly opened fire on the soldiers, as they realised, we were behind them and began to return fire. The fighting was so intense that we had to retreat down a level. While we took out two of them on the stairwell and I managed to throw one down an elevator shaft, a soldier on the staircase shot Yandan in the left shoulder. Yandan yelled out in pain, asking us to keep going. Pissed off, he grabbed the soldier's gun and shot him in the chest.

"Yandan, are you all right?"

"Yer, it's just a scratch. Not my first rodeo, kid."

All plasma projectile weapons have a severity-control modulator that controls the intensity of the plasma projected. Luckily for him, the plasma shot severity was low, so the wound was cauterised, and he wouldn't bleed out, but it did mean that he had a small, precise hole through his shoulder, limiting movement throughout his left shoulder. After taking out the soldier on the stairwell, we ran back up the stairs and found all the soldiers on the fifth floor dead. I looked around at all the dead bodies, leaving me completely shocked.

I looked around the hallway. "Hey, Edward, are you all right?"

Edward walked out of one of the apartments covered in dust and quickly readjusted his glasses. Edward wasn't aware of what was happening, so he turned around and looked at all the dead bodies. "Why? Why are these soldiers doing this?"

"Because they have instigated martial law in this place."

"Martial law! Really? That is not a good sign." Edward paused to contemplate what that meant. "Where are we going to go now if the entire city is under martial law?"

"I don't know, but we can't stay here."

"The best thing we can do is head to my place; it is the safest option. I have to check to see if my mum is safe."

He gestured to me, "Lead the way."

We had to get out of there quickly before more people showed up. The walk back home was relatively peaceful, as the peacekeeping force was mainly stationed in densely populated areas of the Lower Levels like downtown and the apartment blocks. The outskirts where my house was located was quiet. Plus, most buildings were abandoned during the race wars, so hardly anyone was there.

Once we arrived at Mum's house, she unlocked the door and pointed a shotgun at our head. Then she realised that it was us and hugged me and said, "Thank God. I was so worried about you. I thought you had died."

Anna, Ella, Edward, Yandan and I began boarding the windows and doors.

Anna explained that after coming home from work, she saw the troops rolling in; it started relatively peaceful until the soldiers began to open fire at the protesters. She ran as fast as she could home, and because she didn't know where I was, she rushed back into the basement, only thinking about me and my well-being. She then turned to me and slapped my shoulder in a sort of angry way.

"Aww!"

"Where were you?"

"I was out taking care of something, saving this dumbass over here."

"Hey, I resent that!"

Yandan walked through the door, nursing his shoulder. "Ugh, my shoulder is killing me."

Anna sighed, her eyes still resenting what he said, but she had to suck it up. It was a crisis, and, in a problem, we have to help our fellow man. But Yandan wasn't grateful; he was bitter.

"Why are we hiding out here when we should be fighting?"

I replied, "What! Do you want to get slaughtered by the 100 troops outside?"

Yandan replied, "I just feel we should be out there defending our home, our community. This whole thing smells of WeapCo."

I snapped at that point. "No! These forces are the government's response to your orchestrated terrorist attack on the subway."

"WHAT!' Anna screamed in shock.

Yandan just shook his head. "I will never apologise for standing for what is right."

"Oh, rubbish! This is about your pettiness and anger."

"No! This is about power. Those Upper Level scum think they can push us around and keep us down. All I want to do is settle down and run my shop with my daughter in peace, but they have to keep pushing us. Not just me, but everyone down here. I mean, look at this place. They have turned their back on this place for years, letting it turn into this shithole and for what? Profits. Do you know what I have learnt living in this place, Jacob? If you want anything in this world, you have to fight, no matter what. I intend to bring down not just WeapCo but all of the giant monopolies out there. No longer will the little bend knee. Now is the time to fight back."

Yandan then brushed past all of us. "If you need me, I will be resting in the basement."

Both Anna and I looked at each other in disgust. "Who said he could sleep down there?" Anna whispered in a bitter tone, thinking what he did was so rude, and she stormed up into her room, leaving Edward, Anna and me in silence.

We watched out the living room window as what seemed like millions of troops were called in to reinforce the levels, occupying the roads and streets with tanks, Humvees, Rocket launchers and all sorts of military vehicles. The sky was filled with drones, floating helicopters and UAVs. All we could hear from outside was gunfire and explosions and the tread of tyres on the broken roads.

"This isn't a peacekeeping force; this is a damn invasion force." Ella looked out in shock, watching building after building fall.

"Maybe we should get away from the window before any of the troops spot us."

She nodded her head. "Agreed!"

We all walked away from the window.

Later that night, I lay in bed, drinking whisky and smoking a cigarette. I lay there reliving old memories, as if I had nothing better to do. I was remembering the only good childhood memory I had with my dad before he became a crack addict.

My father had a tragic life; his father would often beat him and his mother to a bloody pulp. He put up with that for 16 years, before running away and joining the army as a commando. After years of service, he married my mum and had me primarily due to an unfortunate condom accident. The two of them settled down, and he got himself a job as a factory worker producing farming equipment for the biosphere farms on the Mars Federation. He and Mum got rich quickly, as the manufacturing, building and automotive industries were booming.

After World War Three, technology was set back by 100 years; human labour came back with high-paying union jobs and excellent wages. However, as the city grew bigger and bigger, and as technology was recuperating, robots were reintegrated into manufacturing. Therefore, human labour dried up, and my father began to work longer and longer hours with less pay. Losing his job took a toll on him, and he began to develop all sorts of mental health issues, eventually descending into drug and alcohol problems. Also, losing his job caused him to lash out at Mum and me.

I didn't have a lot of good memories of my father. I didn't even get to see him when he died. But one good memory was when I was 10 years old. I was walking with my dad when he was in one of his good moods. We were walking down the street, eating black chocolate ice cream, and we walked to the border walls. At one of the walls, there was a unique lookout point reinforced with radiation-proof glass, and you could look at the fallout wastelands. The wastelands were deserted and empty; it was beautiful. It was peaceful and relaxing compared to the rest of the city, which was loud and chaotic.

"How's school going?"

I turned around with my face full of chocolate ice cream and told him a funny story about how my friend decided it would be funny to jump off the school roof, but he landed in a garbage bin the wrong way and broke his arm. It was pretty amusing, and we both started laughing. "What a dumbass."

Then, he wrapped his arm around my neck and hugged me. "Love you, son."

Sometimes, I would replay that memory repeatedly when I was alone, even to this day; I still teared up at that memory. I wished life would have been different and my father had been happy and healthy instead of what he turned into. I mean, why does life have to be so cruel sometimes? We could have done much more together if he hadn't lost his job or mind.

I heard a knock on the door and shot up from my bed, wiping away my tears. Ella popped her head through the door. "Can I come in?"

"Please do."

Ella paced around the room. "Nice place you got here."

My room was decorated with a blend of an 80s teen bedroom and a twenty-first-century boy's room, full of posters, movies and books. Ella was investigating my room, but she stopped to notice a display case with my military medals. "Nice medals. Did you get that on the Australian Front?"

"Yep, and I also served during the Jap-Sino-Russian war."

Ella nodded, continued to investigate my room and noticed a photo of my mum and me standing in a military uniform after graduating from basic training.

"Aw, that's cute."

"Thanks. I got that before I was deployed; it was when I was young and hopeful."

"No father?"

"No, he was too busy in and out of shady business deals to fuel his drug addiction."

Ella's face looked a bit sad. "I am sorry."

Ella continued investigating my room and noticed a strange object on my office desk. "What's that?"

"That's an ancient iPhone."

She studied the thing, trying to figure out what it was. "What's that?"

"It's early 2000s technology. Here, let me show you."

I got off my bed, went to the bookshelf, scrolled through it, found a song and clicked play. "I'd Do Anything for Love" by Meat Loaf started to play. It was my favourite song. Ella began vibing to the music, and we both started to dance. Ella slipped, and I went in to grab her, and we both locked eyes briefly. She looked into my big blue eyes, and I looked into her lovely blue eyes, and slowly, not thinking, I leaned in to kiss her. At first, I thought she would slap me across the face, but no, she kissed me back instead. We went back and forth, exchanging saliva with each other. Then things got a little heated. I ripped off Ella's white top, revealing a white bra, and Ella ripped off my shirt, and we both made our way to the bed. We did all sorts of freaky stuff, and after 2 minutes of sex, we went to sleep.

The following day, both Ella and I woke up half-naked, so we slapped on some clothes and walked downstairs to find Anna cooking blueberry pancakes and Yandan and Edward eating them and making small talk with each other. I walked down.

"Morning, guys."

Anna replied, "Morning, Jacob. Morning, Ella. You too seem to have gotten a good night's sleep."

We both smirked at each other. Yandan noticed our smirks, pieced the picture together and wasn't impressed.

"Ella, if you are finished 'getting acquainted' with Jacob, how about you and I head back to our shop to get cleaned up?"

"What shop?"

Yandan looked down at his pancakes sad.

Ella and I joined the table for some pancakes and some orange juice. No one mentioned anything, as there was silence in the room, but something was off; there was silence, which was weird. All of last night, there was nothing but gunfire and explosions.

"Why is it so quiet today? Where are the troops?"

Yandan looked down at the pancakes angrily. "According to intelligence, the troops have occupied all the Lower Levels. Yer, who would have fought that millions of dollars' worth of military hardware could take down lower-class people armed with outdated weapons."

We all looked at each other. "So, what will they do with us now?"

Yandan sighed. "The troops have enforced a mandatory lockdown. Only essential workers are allowed out. The troops have been driving up and down, patrolling the neighbourhood in their overpriced cars and their tanks. Yep, legal tyranny at its finest."

"So, what are we all going to do then?"

"Well, isn't it obvious, Daughter? We are going to fight."

"Oh, not this shit again, Yandan. Haven't you learnt that fighting has gotten us nowhere?"

Yandan slammed his fist on the table. "Jacob! They have an occupying force at our level, and what? You want to sit around and do nothing."

"If we wait, we can—"

"No!" Yandan cut in. "If you and your mum and your wimpy friend want to sit around and play happy little family, then go ahead, but I am going to fight."

Once again, he stormed out of the house with Ella following him; I just shook my head. "That moron is going to get himself and this community killed."

Edward replied, "Oh well, just some people's minds can't be changed."

Ella and Yandan were sneaking around the backstreets, avoiding the patrols and drones.

"Bloody cowards. Don't they understand that this is war, and wars are won by fighting, not by cowering in their houses?"

"But maybe they have a point. I mean, haven't we done enough?"

Yandan quickly turned around, facing Ella directly. "You're not getting soft on me, are you, Ella?"

"No, Dad, I am just saying that maybe we need to stop and think for a second. I mean, they have a lot more men and weapons than we do. How are we going to beat them if we barely have equipment from this century?"

Yandan responded, "I have been in contact with the rest of the community. We are all going to meet in the Sewer Levels, and that is where we will reveal our plan of attack."

They waved in and out of backyards until they found a storm drain. Yandan signalled to Ella, "After you, my dear."

Ella climbed into the sewage system, and Yandan followed.

They finally reached the end of the brown tunnel after crawling through the dark, dank, smelly, rat-infested and possibly allishark-infested sewage system. The sewage system convened into one spot where all the sewage ended: the filtration system. In the filtration system, there had to be at least 1,000 resistance fighters who were fed up living under martial law and had now turned into resistant fighters. The sewage system was the only place the soldiers would never think to look. The internet was a wonderful thing, given the power one text could achieve; within minutes, Yandan could call on a resistance group of a thousand people with one mission in mind: to take down WeapCo.

WeapCo was the primary beneficiary of this city's defence force, accounting for roughly $1 trillion towards the Defence Budget. Therefore, the company practically had a say in what wars this city fought; it was a 'circular' system. Nothing turns profits more than a good war. But the problem was that there were no foreign wars to fight in, as of this moment, as the economy was holding firm. With no foreign wars, nothing sold weapons faster than a civil conflict, so with the aid of the media and connections in ParliaCongress, the corporate eggheads pushed for a civil war by exploiting the situation with the social service cuts and provoking fears about the riot within the Lower Levels as a way to sell weapons to both sides, which would, in turn, increase the profits of WeapCo. Everyone involved wins. The media gained viewers, and the politicians gained votes for providing law and order to the city and then going behind the people's backs to fund gang lords that supplied drugs to the Lower Levels, in turn fuelling more chaos, therefore increasing the need for more protection via military spending, and around and around it went.

The system worked, but not for us. The media won, the government won and also housing and construction won, as they pushed the Lower Level out of their homes, freeing up more space for skyscrapers and for gentrifying the neighbourhood, which pushed up rents and inflation. But Yandan was not going to take it anymore, and neither were the people. The crowd was standing around talking and waiting for Yandan to talk. Then, Yandan stormed up to the front of the crowd and stood above the crowd with Ella by his side.

"People, this martial law is just another attempt by the Big Corpo actors and the weak-spined government to try to keep us submissive like sheep. But no longer. They roll their tanks into our streets, occupy our skies with aircraft and kill our women and children, and for what? Profit. Now, I would like to thank you all for coming today, but action needs to be taken. If we are going to take action, now is the time. Who is with me?"

"I am!" The crowd all turned around to face me.

Yandan stopped his speech and paused. "Nice of you to join us, Jacob. Change of heart?"

Out of concern for their well-being, I had begun to tail them down to the Sewer Level.

"I have been thinking that you're right. This is our home. If we are going to live here, we must defend it. Can you forgive me?"

I didn't believe half the stuff I was saying; the truth was that I was worried for Ella's safety. I guess I loved her in a way and was afraid that she would go down Yandan's rabbit hole of insanity, so I may as well follow the group to ensure nothing happens to Ella. In a way, I had also grown fond of Yandan and didn't want him to get hurt.

Yandan approached me, jumping down from the platform and walking over. I took a step back, as I thought he was going to attack me, and as he got close to my face, I closed my eyes, waiting for him to punch me. Instead, I opened my eyes and found an outstretched hand. "I knew you would come around."

The crowd, including Ella, began to clap.

After the encounter, Yandan let go of my hand and walked back to the platform to talk to the crowd, while I just joined as another faceless number in the crowd to listen to Yandan confess his plan of attack. But as I looked around at the crowds of neighbours, friends and former co-workers, I noticed a familiar face. I didn't believe it. I walked up to him and tapped him on the shoulder.

"Edward!" Edward turned around and greeted me.

"Oh hey, Jacob, long time no see."

"What are you doing here?" I was in absolute disbelief, as I didn't expect to see him here.

"Like everyone else, I am here for the gathering." That was weird.

"But you said you don't believe in this rebel stuff, and you don't use technology except when you're in the pharmacy, so what are you doing here?"

Edward looked guilty, but before I could get a solid answer from him, Yandan interrupted and said, "Can I have everyone's attention once more?"

We all turned around to face him. Now, I was more concerned than ever; that behaviour was weird for Edward. It seemed suspicious of him and gave me major red flags. I guess everyone was buying into Yandan's Ideological way. However, I chose to ignore it, as Edward was not the main concern.

"All right, everyone, here is the plan. It's time. Ella, go grab the board."

Ella ran down the stage, pulled up a classroom whiteboard and turned it around to the plans of the WeapCo building with blueprints and pictures.

"So everyone, here is the plan. We have to infiltrate the WeapCo building and take down the CEO, John Speer, and the board members behind the company. To do so, we will have to climb up to the Middle Levels, which is going to be a lot harder now that the peacekeeping force is down under. The troops have blocked the subways to the Middle Levels, so we need to bypass their blockade. Once we are up top, we will storm the main building, bypass the high-tech equipment, take down the 5,000 private soldiers they have at their disposal, climb up 100 storeys, and when we finally reach the top, we take out John Spear."

Everyone looked at each other in concern.

"Easier said than done," one person said. He was kind of right. The plan did seem elaborate.

"So, here is the plan. Gather all the men and women you can, gather weapons and equipment and sleep tonight, because tomorrow, we take down WeapCo!"

The crowd broke into cheers, but I was more concerned than ever; it was one thing to call on a protest, but his plan was a call to action. This was more volatile than ever, and more people would die.

After the speech, the crowd broke up and headed back up to Ground Level to prepare for the mission tomorrow. Just as he was about to leave, I approached Edward. I asked, "Hey Edward, everything all right?"

"Yer," he replied. "I am just a little stressed from the pharmacy burning down and the martial law thing."

I nodded in agreement. "Hey, Anna and I have Taco Tuesday tonight, and we found an old copy of *Martian Attacks* in a bin outside our house. Want to come over? Grab some beers and join us."

Edward gave me a slight smile. "Sounds good. You go, and I will follow you."

I began to walk away slowly, but I looked back and noticed Edward doing something weird; he took a photo of the whiteboard on his phone. *Why would he need to take a photo of the plans? Oh well, it's none of my business.*

After some homemade vegetable tacos, a couple of drinks and a few billies later, Anna, Edward and I sat there watching the TV, and we were all pretty zoned out, as all of us were baked. The gang was laughing and carrying on when Anna got up.

"All right, I think I am going to hit the hay."

"All right, night!"

"Night, Anna."

So it was just Edward and I on the couch talking. It was silent for a minute until Edward broke the ice with a question. "You know how we talk constantly about getting out of here?"

"Yer."

"Well, if someone gave you a chance to get out of this shithole, would you take it?"

"Well, yer, I guess so? That was a bizarre question, Edward. Where did that come from?"

Edward just shrugged. "Nothing, just curious."

Edward had a guilty look.

"Edward, are you all right?"

Edward just sat silently. "Anyway, I might get some shuteye. Night."

"Night, I guess."

Then Edward began to head up the stairs, but he dropped his old phone as he headed to sleep in my sister's room. I quickly turned over to grab the phone. "Edward, you dropped your phone," I called out, but he was out of earshot for him to hear me.

Out of curiosity, I looked through the phone, and on the lock screen was a message that read: *Don't forget our deal.*

I looked at that message in concern, which raised red flags in my mind.

"What deal? What is he up to?"

I then put the phone on the coffee table and headed to bed, because tomorrow was the attack, and I didn't have time to think. I couldn't stop thinking about the message on Edward's phone. *What is Edward up to?*

But it wasn't just Edward; I was also concerned about this whole plan in general.

Are we going to attack a heavily fortified skyscraper with a small militia army at its disposal? This is going to be suicide. I didn't really want to do this, but oh well, this wasn't really about me.

CHAPTER 6

Ly mind was racing from the potential assault that
was bound to take place the next day, but if I was
going to prepare my body for a fight, then I needed sleep.
Unfortunately, sleep was where my demons were at their
strongest. After I fell into a deep sleep, my mind began dream,
and it was a very weird dream as well. The dream involved
me being strapped down to a gurney and a doctor in a white
coat walking around the room and screaming at me, "Wake
up, Mr Turner! Turner! Can you hear me? Nurse, the patient
is non-responsive and in a deep-comatose state."

In the dream, I couldn't move at all. All I could do is lay
there and look around the room, which was mostly a blur,
but from what I could make out of it, it was sort of an old
mental hospital. But I had never been to a mental hospital
before in my life. Hell, I didn't even know what a mental hospital was, but somehow, my subconscious knew what it was,
and it felt familiar to me like I had been there before.

"JACOB, WAKE UP!"

Then I opened my eyes, as Anna busted into the room.
"Come on, Jacob, no time to sleep. We have work to do."

The morning was such a rush. We didn't have time to
sit down and enjoy a family breakfast. We just packed. Any
weapons, body armour and military equipment we could
carry, we packed. Me, Edward and Anna, all armoured up
and armed to the teeth, we began to make our way back
down to the sewer to join the rest of the crew. Avoiding the

patrols, we made our way to the main area, where we all had met the last time. Everyone from last time was there, loading weapons and packing ready for the assault. The crowd had turned into a well-regulated militia, armed to the teeth. Everywhere you looked, there were assault rifles in every hand, and everyone had body armour and military helmets on. Some had libertarian badges on, like the Potsdam Flag.

Yandan, who was dressed in his general attire from his time in the military, busted into the room and called for everyone's attention. "Listen up, everybody. Thank you for coming today. Today is the day we make history. Today, we take down WeapCo and send a message: Don't mess with the Lower Level."

The crowd all held up the weapons in solidarity and let out a 'Yea!' and chanted, "Freedom! Freedom! Freedom!"

Yandan yelled out, "All right everyone, gather around, here is the plan of attack."

The group then focused on Yandan telling his strategy of attack.

"The first strategy is to sneak through the subway station, then make our way through the Middle Levels towards the lobby of the WeapCo building, and finally take out WeapCo. All right, everyone, let's begin."

The crowd let out another 'Yer!', and they all began to make their way up towards the Ground Level, chanting, "Down with WeapCo! Down with WeapCo! Down with WeapCo!"

The crowd snuck around the streets, passing patrols and drones, stealthily killing any troops that may slow them down. The crowd had split up into two groups in order to get into the subway without notifying the peacekeeping force, but what was most concerning was that there were hardly any patrols; there were no troops or drones. Where had they all gone? As of last night, this place was swarming with them. It was incredibly suspicious that there were hardly any patrols around. But there was no time to focus on them. We had a siege to carry out. Edward and I and about 100 other fighters were all part of group A. It was our job to scout ahead and capture the subway station. Ella and Yandan where part of Group B.

After martial law had been declared, the subway station had been completely closed; no trains in or out of the station. The only thing in the station were drones scouting out the area with blue laser scanners. After we reached the stairs to enter the subway, two guards stood there patrolling the area with plasma rifles, pacing around the staircase. Edward, the crowd and I were all crouched behind old, rusted, flightless cars, trying to figure out a plan to take out the security drones. We worked out that I would sneak into the subway station alone as to not alert any patrols. I slowly walked up the stairs, but before I could enter the platform, I realised there were two guards marching down into the subway station from the Middle Level. I coughed slightly, just as the guards were marching on the subway platform, up and down the platform, goose-stepping as they passed each other. It wasn't smart to rush into this situation half-cocked. I had to take his time. Like a cobra, I needed the right moment to strike.

I remained crouched, breathing slowly and focusing my mind by breathing in and then out, in and out, in then, *woosh!* I saw the guard walking past, so I quickly bolted up the stairs as fast as a cheetah and grabbed one of the guards, knocked him out and then quickly bolted into one of the waiting rooms before the drone arrived. Quickly! I had to move before the other guard came. I rushed behind the waiting room door, jumping back into combat mode. Just like before, I stood there waiting in attack mode, crouched down in the dark like a cat ready to pounce.

Then, I could hear the guard walking past. The squeaking from the standard-issue military boots on the subway floor was a dead giveaway. That was my cue to get ready. As the guard made his way to the waiting room, I quickly grabbed him, pushed him to the ground and *boom*, knocked him out by hitting his head on the concrete floor. But I was too busy concentrating on the guard, and I completely forgot the drone. It quickly turned around, its eyes went from blue to red, and it began to enter the waiting room. I could hear the drone's 'buzzing noise' that sounded eerily familiar to a swarm of bees. It entered the room, scanning the dimly lit room, using its now red laser to scan the seats looking for life signs.

Luckily, at this point, I was hiding behind a vending machine, waiting for the laser to pass. Then, as the drone turned its back to scan the room again, I ran as fast as I could to grab it before it could turn around. The drone was wheezing around the air, letting out all sorts of sounds, and then it armed up and began firing plasma bolts, shooting blue bolts all over the place. I had to take it down before I got hit, so using the knife I kept in my back pocket, I ripped open the back panel covering the robot's circuits and cut the red and green circuits, which left the drone disabled and motionless on the floor. Then the other two drones entered the waiting room. Just as the drones were about to open fire, out of instinct, I rolled over to the knocked-out soldier, grabbed his plasma pistol and shot the two drones in the eye, leaving them disabled and destroyed.

After taking out the drones, I peered my head out through the door to see if there were any more enemies, but surprisingly, there were none, which was quite strange. *This is the only security guarding the area. How can that be? Where did all those soldiers go? This is all a bit suspicious.*

But there was no time to focus on that. I had a job to do. After taking out the only security guarding the station, I scoped out the remaining subway area to see if there were any more enemies in this place. I went into the darkened subway station, where the light barely reached. It looked like something out of a horror movie. It was like I was staring into the abyss. There were no people here. It was weird seeing a train station without people.

Suddenly, as I signalled to the others to approach, it finally dawned on me. My intuition had finally kicked in.

This was a set-up. My goodness, it was obvious; the lack of security. They were luring us into a trap. I had to alert the others about this. But before I could alert the others, I turned around to find Edward staring blankly down into the streets, barely looking at me. This was weird.

"Edward, I have something to tell you."

"What, Jacob? What is it?"

There was something different about Edward's voice. It sounded fake. "I think we are being set up. I have to alert the others."

Edward ushered me near the tracks, looking a little panicked. "Woah, slow down. What makes you think that?"

"Edward, why do you think we barely passed any of the peacekeeping force? And why do you think there is barely any patrol in this station? This is most obviously a set-up. WeapCo knows we are coming and—"

I stopped because I was too busy focusing on Edward's face, and I didn't even notice his body. I looked down at his torso and saw a revolver pointed right at my ribcage.

Edward began to cry. "I am sorry."

Bang! He pulled the trigger, shooting a bullet right in my rib cage before I could do anything. In shock, I walked back, clenching my chest and trying as much as possible to fight through the pain. Blood was pouring out my chest at a rapid rate, and as much as I wanted to get back at Edward, I couldn't. I lost all strength, and I began to collapse into unconsciousness.

The last thing I remember was falling off the train platform before landing on the streets below. I heard a sharp bang coming from the impact, but I couldn't see anything.

A rusted old car had broken my fall, but I could most definitely feel the impact, as a sharp pain coursed through my body. The impact had made me bleed from the mouth and made breathing almost impossible for me.

But as my sight was slowly fading away, I could see Edward, who was staring at my body, with a small tear sliding down his right cheek. "I am sorry, my old friend."

Then, I collapsed completely into unconsciousness, lying there on the car, motionless. I felt like I had died.

Edward walked away from the scene and headed back to the staircase, where he met up with Ella, Yandan, Anna and the rest of the group.

"Where's Jacob?" Yandan asked.

"He had to take care of some business."

Yandan and Ella both stared at each other.

Ella looked at Edward. "What type of business?"

"He didn't say. He just got up and left."

Anna's face was in absolute disbelief, and she felt a bit suspicious. "That doesn't sound like him."

"That's what he did."

Yandan was angry. "Coward! Well, we won't back down." He signalled to the rest of the group. "Come on, everyone, we have a job to do."

Yandan then gave a hand gesture, and Ella, Edward, Anna and the entire militia began running up the stairs into the subway station. Edward was worried that one of the fighters would look over the railway track and see Jacob's dead body, but no one bothered to look. Everyone in the group was too focused on the task at hand. After making their way into the dark train station, they then all began to rush up the stairs into the Middle Level. Like soldiers storming the beach, they rushed up in surprisingly perfect unison. They all merged from the darkened subway up into the brightly coloured city. They ran as fast as they could from the terminal and out into the Middle Level Streets.

The Middle Level was completely different to the Lower Levels, not as good as the Upper Level, but much better than the Lower Levels. There are skyscrapers and flying cars everywhere, well-maintained apartment buildings, restaurants and cafes, gyms, hospitals, statues, gardens and community centres and sunlight, or in this case, moonlight. These people were so lucky to be born here, as most people in the Lower Levels barely got to see glimpses of the sun or the moon down there.

The militia stopped charging for a second and slowly started to walk around the city streets, putting their weapons into standby mode. The people they passed started to cross the streets after they saw the guns in their possession and looked at the crowd in shock as they walked past. It also didn't help that they were covered head to toe in body armour.

Then five flying MLPD patrol cars arrived on the scene and descended from the sky, landing at the Ground Level. Officers all panicked, and they jumped out of each of the cars and scrambled to find cover, pointing their guns over the bonnet of the cars. "Freeze! Drop your weapons."

The group of fighters then started to open fire on the crowd of police officers, with the police officers returning fire. However, as the police only had pistols and the group had semi-automatic rifles, the officers were quickly outgunned, and within 5 minutes, the police officers began to flee. One of the officers called for backup on his radio before running away into the streets.

Then the group, elated from their victory, began to follow Yandan to the WeapCo building. They marched past the shot-up police cars and down the road. The crowd of bystanders all ran away or back into their houses in fear of getting hurt. The group made their way down the road to the building, walking for 15 minutes before finally approaching the Goliath-sized building. The building stretched so long that it touched the sky, expanding over 100 feet and with a width expanding as far as a football stadium. The building was a very industrial, modern-style skyscraper with a red W Logo located at the top of the building. The crowd looked up at the building in amazement and fear at how enormous the building actually was in person. However, realising the importance of the mission, they snapped back into fighting action; nonetheless, they were all a little scared of what could be waiting inside.

Yandan stood on the steps outside of the WeapCo building. The hundreds of fighters all gathered around to listen to

Yandan. Yandan obviously had been practising his oratorical skills. "People! Now is the time. Tonight, we will take back our streets and our freedom. ATTACK!"

The crowd then held their firearms in the air and chanted, "YER!"

Suddenly, the group charged the building, rushing into the building with Yandan leading the charge. But, as the crowd entered the building, to their surprise, there were 2,000 active soldiers in the building. The soldiers ambushed the crowd from all sides on the balcony of the reception and the ground floor. The soldiers consisted of the entire peacekeeping force from the Lower Levels and WeapCo's private security. It turns out that Edward had tipped WeapCo off, which gave the troops the chance to move their entire forces to prepare for the attack. Then, the troops opened fire on the crowd, cutting down at least 30 soldiers in the first 5 minutes. The surviving crowd members all hid behind reception desks, bins, anything they could find that would give them cover from the fire.

The militia tried to return fire, but at this point, it was futile. It was like throwing a bucket of water in a rainstorm. After a small firefight, the troops completely outgunned the militia, forcing them to flee. Anna, Ella, an injured Yandan and the remaining 200 crowd members tried escaping the building outside, but they were quickly sealed off when 100 floating police cars descended quickly down to Ground Level, with hundreds more of police officers getting out of their cars and aiming their guns at the militia. The militia had been surrounded from all sides with nowhere to escape or run. Nothing to do, the crowd all tired and injured had to put their hands up in surrender, throwing down their guns on the concrete pavement in defeat. Then the police officers and soldiers tackled the crowd to the ground and restrained them all.

CHAPTER 7

10-02-3025

I didn't know what was going on. All around me, there was nothing but darkness. Darkness everywhere. It was both peaceful and maddening all at the same time. But it was in the void of the unknown that I began to see. I began to see flickers of light, and I heard a voice calling me in my head. The voice was unrecognisable to me, as I had never seen, heard or met this person in my life. Then, the voice went from a faint whisper to a loud roar.

"Wake up, Jacob! Now is the time to wake up. WAKE UP!"

The voice scared every nerve in my body, and it caused my bloodshot eyes to open straight away and caused me to cough out blood.

I am alive.

I didn't know how, but I was alive. Unfortunately, my pain also returned, as I barely had any strength to lift myself up. I really didn't want to do anything, as my entire mind, body and spirit were weak, and I just lay there. While I loved the idea of just laying here and dying, I couldn't, as my family and friends needed me. So, fighting through the raging river of pain that was coursing through my body, I used the last of my strength to roll over, and I fell off the car and landed directly on the ground.

"Aghhh! Great, just bloody great."

I was in tremendous amounts of pain, and now my damn nose was broken. I sighed and lay there, thinking about how my life had turned out. And honestly, this had to be the lowest point in my life. I was in pain, I had been betrayed by my best friend, and now I was left to rot on this dirty, broken road about to die.

"Why can't something good happen for once in my life?"

Then a miracle happened. I looked around on the ground and saw an unused anapen just lying underneath the car and still within date. My only chance at surviving. As a last-ditch effort, I crawled towards it and injected it straight into my hip. I was still in massive pain, but I had the energy to get up from the floor and move again. After getting up, I began to hop on my damaged foot back to the house.

After an agonising hop home, I finally made it home, and I had to quickly remove the bullet in my rib before I bled to death.

Bleeding out on the floor, I collapsed near the kitchen sink. To survive, I had to rely on my military medical training to extract the bullet from my rib cage.

This was a technique I learnt in the military. First, I needed to pour some salt into a water bottle. Then I would attach a makeshift drip into my right vein. Next, I would reach for the first aid kit that was underneath the sink. But before I began cutting into myself, I had to sterilise the equipment, and the easiest way to do that was with a bottle of whisky. Quickly. The clock was ticking. With my body slowly getting dizzy from the blood loss, I began to extract the bullet from my rib cage. It wasn't easy, and it stung, but after digging in and out and flinching a couple of times, I found success! I dropped the bloody bullet on the floor.

Now that the hard part was over, I had to seal the wound up. Using some fishing line and a needle, I began stitching up the wound. I took a large sip of some Jack Daniel's to numb my mind from the pain. Weak-headed, I lay on the kitchen floor, trying to overcome the pain. Eventually, I blacked out, but nonetheless, I would be able to survive, though I would need some time for healing.

After performing surgery without anaesthesia, I woke up the next morning in severe pain and needed something to numb the pain, but without a doctor or hospital to go to, I would most likely die. With no other option, I had to go to Edward's old pharmacy and grab the secret drugs he had hidden in his safe. After pulling myself off the kitchen floor, I began to climb down the street, passing all the destroyed buildings and the constant peacekeeping patrols that were beginning to patrol the Lower Levels in full force again. Funnily, not one of them assisted to help me.

I did eventually receive help from two survivors of the WeapCo siege, who cowered out just before the group stormed the tower. They spotted me limping down the street and approached me. "Jacob, is that you?"

"Oh, hey Kim and Courtney, where are Anna and the rest of the squad from the victory at WeapCo?"

They looked at each other and gave me a look of sympathy. "We need to talk."

What a significant stroke of luck. Kim and Courtney were a couple who ran a secret underground hospital, as they were both doctors from the Upper Levels who had lost everything in the economic collapse and had started up a free but unlicensed medical clinic. Guess the universe is kind sometimes. They escorted me down into the underground basement and placed me on an old hospital bed. The two of them examined me up and down, looking at my wound and assessing my stitches. They gave me credit for my medical stitching, and they asked me how I got like this and why I wasn't part of the assault. I explained to them what had happened with Edward and how he sold us out. They weren't impressed, as they called him a bastard. But I was still confused.

"So girls, where are Anna, Ella and Yandan?"

They both looked down in sadness and in a depressed voice explained how the peacekeeping force was waiting for them and they were all captured. At this point, I became extremely angry by this revelation and at the fact that my friends and family were in danger and that Edward put them there. After losing my friends and family and having my best friend betray and try to kill me, something in my mind had just snapped. I was overcome with an intense, internal anger that I could not control; it made me feel like a werewolf or a vampire craving blood. I had only one mission in life: To kill Edward! After Kim and Courtney stitched me up and gave me painkillers, they sent me out onto the streets, and I began to pace as fast as I could with my limp to the one place where I knew I could find Edward: the pharmacy.

Meanwhile, the treacherous Edward was being marched up by two heavily armed security guards inside the WeapCo building up to the CEO's Office. Inside the office, John Speer was sitting at his desk, rubbing metal balls in his hand and staring out his window.

"Sir, we brought him to you."

John kept staring out the window for a few more minutes before spinning his chair around. "Of course, send him in."

Edward entered the room, and the security guards left.

"Congratulations. Your tip paid off, and you are going to be a rich man."

Edward should have been happy; he was rich again. Instead, he felt guilty. "What have you done with the people?"

John then looked back out the window. "They have been moved to an undisclosed location."

"OK fine, what about Anna?"

John swung his chair back and stared down at Edward. "None of your concern."

"That's not part of the deal!"

John just kept staring out the window. "Do you want your money or not?"

Edward contemplated taking the money. He had lost everything, so he may as well take it. "OK."

John slid the silver briefcase across the table. Edward opened the briefcase and within it contained $1,000,000 in cryptocurrency, the main currency in this city. Edward took the money and left the office. He just stared down at the briefcase full of money. He couldn't believe that after years of suffering, he was finally rich again. Edward should have been happy, but deep down, he wasn't, because he knew he didn't deserve that money. But nonetheless, he had no choice now. Grabbing the suitcase, Edward marched out of WeapCo and began walking back to the pharmacy, getting ready to pack up and move back up to the Upper Levels.

After an agonising hop, I finally made it. I peered through the broken window to find an abandoned pharmacy with nothing inside, as this place had been destroyed by the riots. The shop lay decrypted, as shelves flung across the store and random products and medications laid all over the floor. The dispensary desk had been completely shattered, but what was strange was that the light was on around the corner. Edward was definitely in there, as the rest of the shop was completely dark and barren.

I slowly pushed open the still-intact metal door to avoid the bell notifying the person inside that I had entered the building. I crouched down and passed through the destroyed shop shelves while nursing my wound and limping on my damaged foot. I finally reached the source of the light to peer into the office to see Edward in there. He was packing his bag with clothes to move back up to the Upper Levels. Sitting on the pharmacist's desk behind him was the suitcase full of money. Edward was packing his bag while drinking an entire bottle of Jack Daniel's and crying. He was talking to himself in guilt.

"What have I done ... I have betrayed my friends, my community. I got the closest thing to a mother to me killed, and I murdered my best friend." He said, taking another drink.

Anger boiled in my blood, and I stood in front of Edward, ready to take him down.

"Hey Edward, turn around."

Edward turned around in shock. "Jacob!"

I went straight up to him and socked him in the jaw, making him collapse on the floor with blood coming out of his mouth.

"Jacob, you're alive!"

"No thanks to you. How could you do that to me? To Anna!"

Edward collapsed into tears. "What do you want from me, Jacob? A rep at WeapCo offered me money for insight into Yandan and Ella, so I did it for us."

"FOR US?" I was flabbergasted at that statement.

"Yes, for us. I was hoping for you and Anna not to join so we could split the money, but after you joined the militia, I had no choice. Come on, Jacob, if they had offered you that money, would you have taken it?"

"No! Because as much as I hate this place, I would never put this community, my friends and my family at risk." I shook my head. "You were my best friend. We took you in and treated you like family, and then you go and try to kill me and put my friends and mother at risk."

Edward looked down in shame, not even bothering to get back up. "I am sorry. I didn't want to hurt you and Anna, but you both were at the wrong place at the wrong time. If I could have told you, but—"

"Save it. I should kill you where you stand."

Edward then whimpered in fear at the thought of dying. I contemplated killing Edward right then and there. However, I couldn't kill him. Despite my anger, it would have been beneath me to kill him, no matter how much he deserved it. I just looked down at the floor. "But I am not going to. Congratulations, Edward, you got your wealth back. Take it and go."

I grabbed the briefcase with money and threw it at him, hitting his torso with enough force to cause him to flinch. Anyway, I wasn't here for him. I had something more important I was looking for. I turned to Edward. "Now where is the vial of Xenogren?"

Edward then got up off the floor. "Here, I will get it for you."

Edward then proceeded to use his key to unlock the pharmacist's safe on the floor of the office and handed me two vials of green-brown serum and said, "Here. Be careful with this stuff. It is dangerous and expensive."

I snatched the vials out of Edward's hands and began to walk away. But before I left the shop, Edward called out to me. He had a sad look on his face. "Hey Jacob, I am sorry."

I looked up and down at Edward with a saddened look. "Me too, my old friend."

I walked out of the shop, slamming the door and leaving Edward in the dark shop.

I then turned and headed into a corner to inject the Xenogren. Xenogren is an incredibly potent drug made from the essence of radiated tree bark found outside in the wastelands. The effects of the drug mutate human genes for 24 hours, giving them incredible inhuman abilities. However, it is incredibly dangerous and extremely expensive. One vial costs up to $1 million. So if I was going to use them, it would have to be done properly.

Walking behind an alley, I grabbed a dirty needle on the ground and injected the Xenogren straight into my veins. My veins turned red, with my blood feeling like it was on fire. It was the most painful experience ever. I could also hear the snap of my bones morphing and snapping back into place. I pulled up my shirt to see the stitches near my rib cage disappearing back into the skin as if they weren't even there, and my eyes shot blood red as if they were staring at the sun. My brain felt like it was on overdrive, and then I heard a noise. I heard a scream. I recognised the scream. It was from my mum; the source of the sound was located 1,000 miles away, near the end of the border wall.

Out of anger, I let out a painful scream and began running non-stop towards the border wall. The speed at which I was running was incredible. I was running as fast as a cheetah, and I could feel the wind blasting my face. My body heating up from the speed, but I couldn't feel it.

I reached this abandoned warehouse. Right behind the old, somewhat abandoned warehouse was the border wall which separated the city from the wastelands. I stood there staring at the building, thinking why I was here. Then I heard it, the scream from my mother. She was in there. I had to help her.

Ella, Yandan and Anna were inside the building. They had been tortured, beaten and bloodied. All three of them had cuts and bruises, were sleep-deprived and had had their limbs beaten and broken. The three of them had been sitting tied up in metal chairs, as a bunch of masked thugs bashed them with baseball bats and other blunt objects. Behind the thugs was a table full of medical devices used for torture. One of the thugs picked up a knife, ready to cut into one of them.

"I am going to teach you three a lesson to stay in your lane and not interfere in business."

Then the thugs all ganged up and began to beat them all to a bloody pulp. All three of them could barely keep their heads up.

After hearing the screams, I used my incredible strength to kick down the locked metal door with such a force that the door went flying from one side of the warehouse to the other. The Xenogren increased my aggression and bloodlust, so all I could think about was ripping their throats out. I rushed to one of them, picked him up by the neck with one hand and crushed his skull like a trash compactor would. Then, two thugs rushed at me, but I picked both of them up and threw them against a wall, snapping their necks on the impact.

Suddenly, three more men rushed into the room, holding plasma rifles in their hands. They began to shoot plasma bolts at me, but the bolts had no effect on me. My skin was practically impenetrable to their weapons. I slowly walked to the other side and threw an old assembly bot at all three of them, knocking them down and breaking their backs. The enemies had all been incapacitated, so I broke Ella, Yandan and Anna out of the restraints. Unfortunately, they had all passed out from the trauma and blood loss. I grabbed them and threw all three of them over my shoulders. I walked outside with the three of them, and like a kangaroo, I jumped high into the air, and 10 minutes later, I landed on the porch of my house.

Time was of the essence. I used my heat vision to cauterise their exposed wounds. They moaned in pain from the heat. I again picked them up and threw them over my shoulder. I had to move quick, so I began running, but not fast enough to burn the skin off their bones, just at a moderate pace. I ran towards Kim and Courtney's underground medical clinic, hoping they would be able to stitch them up and nurse them back to health. I reached the door of Kim and Courtney's house and knocked on it slightly so as to not break their door down.

Dr Kim rushed up the stairs to find me, placing Ella, Yandan and Anna on the floor, injured and passed out. I pleaded to Kim to please help them. Kim then gave a look of despair and sympathy towards us. She then yelled out to Dr Courtney to assist her. Courtney then rushed down the stairs and gave us a concerned look. Coming to assist, she picked up Ella, Yandan and Anna and escorted them down into the basement and onto three separate medical beds. Then, with nothing to do, I took up a seat and watched as Kim and Courtney performed surgery. All I could do was wait as I wasn't a doctor and I couldn't do anything, but man, it was hard. It was hard to watch friends and family struggle with no way to help them.

After 10 hours of surgery, I had to step out because I suffered from withdrawal syndrome as the Xenogren began wearing off. The withdrawal symptoms on Xenogren were intense. The symptoms included constant vomiting, headaches, nausea, muscle aches, paranoia and difficulty breathing for up to 4 hours. Near the end of the withdrawal, I began to vomit green slime. Then suddenly, something went wrong, and I collapsed on the floor. Courtney and Kim would have come to check on me, but they were busy focusing on the intense surgery of the three people.

Meanwhile, I was lying on the floor, slipping into a temporary coma because of the drugs. In the coma, all I could remember was I was standing on a beach. But what was weird was that I had never been to a beach before. Hell, I didn't even know the word 'beach' existed. Hell, I had never seen blue water before. The water in this place was green. I was standing in the water, looking at the dark blue sea and looking up at the bright blue sky. I looked around, and all I could see was sand, mountains and some rock caves. It was a bizarre place. Then, another question came to my mind. 'Why am I standing on this beach?'

CHAPTER 8

Trying to figure out what was going on, I looked around to investigate the place.

I walked out of the water and onto the sand, feeling the strange sand particles brazing over my exposed feet. All I could hear was the sound of sandy winds blasting around, waves crashing on the shores and some weird white bird chirping and flying overhead. I couldn't feel anything, and as I looked down at my hands, they were clean, with not a scratch on them.

I went for a walk and decided to climb up the green, grassy mountain and went for a look around. After reaching the top of the hill, I looked out and saw this old wooden structure connecting two mountains together, and as I looked to my right, I could see some weird, white metal object that had three long steel beams rotating around on a circle. It was strange. I had never seen this place before, except, wait – yes, I had. But how could I recognise this place without ever being there?

As I climbed up the mountain, I looked at the top, and I could see beautiful farmland hidden behind the mountain. But as I was taking in the scenery, my mind was bombarded by a massive migraine, and I fell to my knees. I began to experience strange flashbacks. But they weren't the flashbacks I was used to; no, they were flashbacks of me behind the wheel of a red Mustang car, driving past this exact place and looking out the window in amazement. I seemed to have been accompanied by this strange woman. Who was she?

The woman was of African American descent with beautiful black hair and blue eyes.

Then I snapped back to the beach-looking place. Confused, I decided to go for more of walk to look around. Out of nowhere, I heard the voice of a female. "Jacob, I think I love you. Jacob, would you still love me if my hair fell out?"

Then I heard a bark from a dog, a car horn and a frightening scream. What the hell was happening? Then, the environment around me changed, the sky turned grey, and it started to rain heavily. I quickly turned back to the ocean to see the water getting wild. The ocean was storming, and the waves were crashing heavily onto the sandbank. I watched in horror at what was happening, and then I saw it in the distance: a weird, dark object. It was calling my name.

"Jacob!"

I froze in fear. I didn't know what to say. Then the object began to walk closer and closer. It was starting to resemble the figure of a child, and it called my name again.

"Jacob!"

I watched as the figure walked on water and approached me. Then it called my name again.

"Jacob!"

Then I could see the figure. It was a boy. I had never seen this boy before in my life, but somehow, I recognised him. He was a small, white, 9-year-old boy in Spider-Man PJs. The boy had brown hair with a buzz-cut haircut. I rubbed my eyes in disbelief. This hallucination was quickly turning into a nightmare, and the boy was standing in front of me with blood pouring out of his eyes and talking in an unrecognisable voice.

Out of curiosity, I decided to slowly reach out my hand, like a person about to touch a snake. I was concerned, as the child was bleeding from his eyes. "Hey, kid, are you all right?"

The boy then screamed at me, "Jacob!"

He began charging at me. Out of fear, I slipped and fell back, tumbling down the mountain, and landed face first onto the ground.

I got up, and the ocean scenery was gone, it was replaced with a grey hurricane-like view. I couldn't see anything. All I could hear were rapid winds, constant thunder and heavy rainfall. I covered my face from the heavy rainfall and continued to look around and found a black-tarred road with yellow markings. It was a highway of some sort. With nothing left to do, I continued to walk, and then I saw a sign. It was a white sign attached to metal poles. It read 'Welcome to Yellow Creek'.

"Yellow Creek? What's that?"

Then I heard a car horn and the scraping of car tyre treads on the road. Then, suddenly, a red car appeared out of nowhere with its high beams on, burning my retinas out. Then the red car rushed at me, barking its horn. I bolted as fast as I could down the road with the car following behind me. Then I stopped in pain. My head was hurting again. I looked up, and I was standing in front of a sharp turn on a mountain. Then, I heard screams, a sharp scream coming from a boy and a girl, and then a 'Jacob!' and a cry.

I woke up in shock, back on the floor of the hospital basement, near a bucket I had been vomiting in. My body was drenched in sweat. Must have been an adverse effect from the Xenogren.

Dr Courtney came in the room drenched in blood. "Are you all right?"

"Fine. How did the surgery go?"

Courtney then let out a sigh. "We need to talk."

This can't be good, I was thinking.

Courtney dragged me aside as she needed to give me her honest medical opinion. "Yandan and Anna will make a recovery. They both have sustained serve injuries, both internally and externally. But with enough bed rest and a few weeks on painkillers, they would be fine."

"What about Ella?"

"That's who I wanted to talk about. Ella has sustained severe damage to her heart and will need a heart transplant. Without a healthy heart, she will die."

My facial expression changed to despair. "Are they awake?"

"The anaesthesia will wear off in an hour, but we will keep Ella under sedation for a while. I am sorry, I wish there was more we could do."

I put my hand on her shoulder. "No, you have done all you could. Thank you."

Courtney and Kim then headed upstairs to sleep. I decided to sit bedside next to Anna and Yandan to wait for them to wake up bedside.

After an hour of sitting next to them, I heard a cough coming from Anna, and then her eyes slowly woke up, and she coughed some more. I hugged her, with her flinching in pain.

"Mum, you're alive. Praise the Lord."

"Son, is that you?" she asked, while rubbing my cheeks. Then Anna reached in to hug me, and she cried. "I thought I would never see you again."

I returned the hug in kind. I sat there drinking a coffee, explaining what had happened. I explained how I took drugs to save them from the warehouse, and I told her about Edward's betrayal.

"Bastard! How could he do that to us?"

The betrayal still stung; I rubbed my head. "He is a greedy dirtbag."

There was an awkward silence.

"How did you end up in that warehouse?"

Then she laid her back on her pillow and began tearing up. "The siege failed, and the police and the peacekeeping force took us under arrest. However, being from the Lower Levels, we were not worth the time to end up in the courts or the prison system. Who knows what happened to the rest. All I know is that Yandan, Ella and I were the main organisers of the siege, and the people at WeapCo knew that, so they wanted to make us suffer through torture. WeapCo gave us over to those thugs, who tortured us and beat us to bloody pulps until you came.”

“How long was I in there?”

“One day. Luckily, the Xenogren allowed me to track you down, or I fear you could have been there longer. Are you all right, Mum?”

I watched as she began to cry. “I thought we were going to die.”

I hugged her and kissed her on the head. “Don’t worry, Mum, you are safe now.”

She shed a single tear and gripped my shoulder hard, not wanting to let go.

Suddenly, a hospital curtain swung back, and Yandan was just lying there on a hospital bed.

“Hate to break up the lovely reunion, but how the hell did we get here?”

We both looked down in silence.

“Yandan, we were betrayed. Edward sold us out. WeapCo knew we were coming.”

“Shit! I can’t believe it. That little bastard got all those people—” Yandan paused in silence, coming to a realisation. “No, it was me. I led those poor people to their deaths. Those innocent people. All because of my grudge and my bitterness. Ugh, Jacob, all I ever wanted was a better life for me and my daughter.”

Yandan then slouched back in his bed.

“Huh, look at me, Jacob. I am just a bitter, tired old man who now has nothing but his daughter.”

Yandan looked around.

“Where is my daughter?”

Looking sad, I grabbed his hand and sadly explained that there was something wrong with Ella’s heart and that without a heart transplant, she would die.

Yandan looked sad and defeated at the thought of losing his flesh and blood. Contemplating, he knew what he had to do.

"Take mine."

"Are you sure, Yandan?"

Yandan sighed. "My time is up. My daughter is the only thing in the world that I care about. She should not suffer because of my mistakes. I have tried to give her everything but have given her nothing. The least I could do is give her a second chance at life."

There was a silence.

"Yandan, thank you!"

"Tell Courtney I volunteer my heart."

I didn't know what to say. I mean, what a gesture to give your heart to save a loved one. It was honestly loving and admirable.

"I will tell Courtney straight away."

But before I rushed off, Yandan stopped me. "Jacob, I just want to say thank you for saving us. I am sorry that I got your mum hurt. You're a good man."

I then nodded in sympathy and left the room, trying not to make an awkward moment.

After I had told Dr Kim and Courtney about Yandan's decision, they moved Yandan and Ella into the surgical room. Yandan was still conscious and awake, compared to Ella, who was completely asleep and knocked out. Just as Yandan was about to be sedated and prepped, Yandan held the hand of his daughter. "I am sorry, my darling. All I wanted to do was create a better world for you. I love you."

The chemicals put him to sleep, knowing that he would never be waking up again. The things a father would do to save his child.

While Ella and Yandan were under the scope of a knife, I got to spend time with my conscious mother again while she nursed her wounds. I knew it wasn't appropriate, but I gave her a cigarette so that both of us could share one together, as I thought I would never see her again. As we sat there smoking our cigarettes, I couldn't help but enjoy this little moment we shared together. Almost losing someone really puts things into perspective for you.

We just talked about Yandan and how noble of an act this was and what it meant for Ella, agreeing that both of us must be there for her. Then we sat there in silence, smoking our cigarettes. I also told Anna about the dream I experienced when withdrawn from Xenogren.

Anna laughed. "Must have been a powerful trip you experienced."

I replied with a laugh and finished off the cigarette. Then Anna was feeling tired, so she went to sleep, with me falling asleep on a chair next to her. I sat there holding my mother's hand as she slept.

I had nearly lost her once. I did not want to lose her again.

CHAPTER *9*

Courtney stormed into the room, removing her surgical gloves. I stood up in surprise and rushed towards her. "How are they?"

"Ella will recover, but—" Her voice dropped, and she had a sad look on her face. "Unfortunately, Yandan passed away at 2:00 am. I am so sorry."

I rushed to hug her as she cried on my shoulder. After a moment of grief, we both pulled ourselves together.

"Where is Ella?"

"Down the hall, still on the surgery bed."

"Is she awake?"

"Yes."

I walked into the surgery room to find Ella barely awake in a hospital gown with a scar down her chest, looking so weak. I confronted her slowly. "How you feeling, Ella?"

"Great," she said, coughing. "Never better. Well, thanks for busting us out of that warehouse. How did you do that by yourself? Did you make them suffer and bleed? I hope you did. Dad and I were barely holding on at that last moment. By the way, where is my dad?"

Ella then locked eyes with me and noticed the sad look on my face, and I approached her slowly and grabbed her hand. "Ella, I am sorry."

Ella then went from happy to sad, yelling, "No! No!"

She burst into tears, with me offering her a hug. Ella and I just hugged each other for a while, and then I helped escort her out of bed to let her see her father's dead body. Ella held her father's hand and gave him a hug.

Courtney, Kim and I placed Yandan's body on a hospital bed, and we began to wrap Yandan in white bed sheets, wrapping him up tight like a mummy. We decided to give him a Viking burial. We all took him outside, stacked up some wooden pallets and placed the body on the wooden pallets. Then, in two wheelchairs, we wheeled up Ella and Anna to watch the ceremony. I then joined Ella, Anna and Courtney, as Kim read out passages from the Bible. After 15 minutes of reading a passage from the Bible, Kim asked, "Any final words?"

Ella stepped in. We all stood there with Kim, signalling Ella to go on. "Dad, I could never thank you for what you did for me. Since Mum died, you made sure to bend heaven and earth to help me. I will always remember when we had a break from service and went to this radiated beach on the coast of Old Taiwan. I sat there crying, and all you did was hug me and tell me that you loved me. I will never forget the words you uttered to me when I was at my most low: 'Ella, the world may take everything from you, but the one thing the world cannot take away from you is who you are as a person. Your mum was a lovely woman, but her time is up. It is now up to you to not let her death be in vain. Change the world and chase your dreams.'"

There was a brief pause, as tears began rolling down Ella's face.

"I love you, Dad."

She gave him a kiss on the bed cover, covering his face.

Ella walked away from her dad. Out of concern, I threw a hand over her shoulder to comfort her. Then Kim lit a match, and we all watched as Yandan's body went up in flames. We stared at the fire.

Listening to what Ella had said got me thinking. Maybe it was time to change the world. Maybe Yandan was right. Maybe it was time to stop taking a backseat in life. Maybe it was time to start changing this city for the better. I needed to be the change the city needed. But now was not the time for vengeance. Now was the time to mourn.

After the fire was extinguished, the alley was left completely dark, and Yandan's body was left in complete ashes. Ella and Anna were completely tired, both physically and emotionally. After consulting with Kim and Courtney, we concluded that it was safe to take them home. Thanking them for the tiresome hours of work, I gave them something better than currency, my gratitude. Giving Courtney and Kim a hug, we began to wheel Ella's wheelchair back into the darkened, lightless street. We may as well give her a place to stay. It was the least we could do. No one deserves to be alone.

This city was quite beautiful at night, and now thanks to the peacekeeping force, it was quiet as well, the only good thing that came from this occupation. However, it wasn't all a good thing. We had to be careful, as the peacekeeping force was out in full force, and since the WeapCo invasion, they were not holding back. It was completely totalitarian down there. We couldn't walk down the street at night, as troops patrolled throughout the night.

Anna, Ella and I witnessed an 80-year-old man being assaulted. We didn't know him, but he was picking up groceries late at night when he was approached by two peacekeeping officers who asked him for his ID, as there was a curfew out, and anyone out this late needed an appropriate reason to be. The old man refused to give ID, so the troops threw him to the ground and started beating him to a pulp. It was an awful scene. I couldn't help but wonder how they could beat up an old man. What cowards. The peacekeeping force may say they want to help us, but they didn't. It was just a slogan they said to justify terrible actions. Honestly, that's all the government did. They said they wanted to help, but they didn't. They only cared about their own interests. I mean, what had they done to help? Nothing. All they had done was destroy businesses, kill innocent, hard-working people and

take away their help and leave them to die. Where's the help?
I couldn't see it ...

After witnessing that horrible incident, something inside
of me began to boil. I mean, I hadn't felt that way in years.
All I did was try and live my life, try to be a normal Joe, try to
live in peace. But where had it gotten me? My friends killed,
my family hurt and my home swarmed with soldiers. Well, if
life isn't fair, I will make it fair. Screw peace. Like my father
used to say, "If you want peace, prepare for war!"

After 10 days, while Kim and Courtney were not confident in Anna and Ella being discharged, they saw no other
option and discharged them both. I pushed Ella, with Anna
in the wheelchair next to her, back to the house and put them
to bed. It was so sad seeing them in a state like that. It made
me sad, especially seeing my mother, who was now scarred,
tired and broken. It truly broke my heart inside. I always
pictured my mother as a smart, strong person, but seeing her
like that, I couldn't comprehend it.

After putting the two broken souls to bed, it was time for
my bedtime ritual of smoking, drinking and staring out the
window. But as I picked up the cigarette and lit it, I looked
down at the cigarette, and something dawned on me. I realised that it was time. I can't just sit around poisoning my
body. If I wanted to change the world, I needed to get back
to fighting state. I grabbed the cigarette and threw it into an
empty trash bin. But why stop there? If was going to go on a
health kick, then I needed to get into shape.

As quick as I could, I ran down the stairs and out the
front door. But as I walked out the front door, it dawned
on me. *Oh, brilliant,* I thought. If I was going to start something, then I knew the perfect spot. I marched in fury. I was
a man on a mission; a mission to return to the sewer system
where we all met up with Yandan and the freedom fighters.
I had a theory about something. I believed that the peacekeeping force didn't find the secret spot. I just retraced my
steps, jumping over fences, dodging past patrols and head-

ing back down into the sewer. After reaching the treatment plant, I was caught by surprise. Honestly, it was all there, even the whiteboard with the plans. It was all there. My theory was right. The peacekeepers never found this place. Hard to believe that with all the fancy equipment, they couldn't find this place, an ancient system that had been around for decades, something you could easily find with a map if you actually put in the effort.

I just stood there, looking at the plans repeatedly, thinking about how to take down WeapCo. But it was going to be hard, as Ella and Anna were out of commission, and the remaining freedom fighters were either dead or too chickenshit to fight again. I guess it was all up to me. Time for Plan B.

After reviewing the plans, I left the sewage system. I needed to gather supplies. I knew one place that offered state-of-the-art weapons and equipment for free, and that was my old workshop: the weapon factory. With a bit of backtracking out of the sewer, I made sure to sneak through downtown, making sure to avoid the drone patrols and the troops goose-stepping up and down the pavement. I stopped to watch them. The way they held their guns and walked certainly evoked the tyrants of old. After a little light gymnastics workout and a few aches that I would definitely feel tomorrow, I finally arrived at the charred remains that were once my workshop. The only thing that surprisingly remained was the fence that gated the place. Guess it didn't really do a good job, though. What was most surprising was that my ID pass still worked to let me through the gate, as the giant metal fence retracted. I marched into what remained of the factory to salvage anything that I may be able to use.

After an hour of rummaging through building debris, I was able to salvage some high-tech calibre-proof body armour, military-standard stun sticks, an A100 plasma rifle, gauntlets, a grappling hook gun and a calibre-proof face mask. However, I couldn't remain here for long, as I heard armoured vehicles pulling up to the wreckage site. It was peacekeeping soldiers. They must have heard me rummaging through the rubble and decided to investigate.

I packed everything I could into a duffle bag and got out of there. There was no time to waste, as I could see the light beaming around the building, searching for remains. One soldier got spooked. "Hey, what was that?"

Both of them turned around to identify the strange noise. It was most likely a possum-rat, but I saw it as an opportunity; not wasting any more time, I jumped into the nearby sewage duct and began crawling my way through the sewer. After arriving at the lair, I hid the equipment and weapons in secret spots where no one else could find them, especially not any of the peacekeeping force.

What a night!

Now, I needed some rest. My eyes were bloodshot red, and my mind was starting to come down off the high. I stumbled up the stairs of my house a little sleep-deprived and tired, but I finally felt like I had achieved something. I was about to crash hard on the couch when I heard my name being called from upstairs.

"Jacob! My feet are hurting. Come rub them for me."

Then a voice called from the other room. "Jacob! I need to use the bathroom."

This was coming from Ella's room. I let out a sigh, pulled myself off the couch and began walking up the stairs.

"Coming!"

I walked up the stairs, jokingly thinking, *Boy, I wonder what it would be like to live near that beach in my hallucination. Probably wouldn't have to deal with yelling girls.*

I then ran up the stairs to go to the girls' aid. I put in the hard work, and now was the time to rest and relax. For tonight I needed to act.

The girls were finally asleep, and I was well rested on at least four hours of sleep. After making sure my girls were safe and sound, I headed out into the night and back down into the sewers. I needed to modify my armour to make it combat-ready. I spray-painted the armour black and red and attached a hoodie to mask my identity from surveillance technology. After a bit of engineering and building, I decided to start an intense workout. If I were to take down a powerful organisation, I first had to get into fighting shape. Also, if I were to take Xenogren again, I would need to work out to get my body prepared for the withdrawal process that accompanied it, though I guess I could enjoy the beach again.

The workout consisted of running back and forth in my cell 100 times, 100 push-ups, 100 sit-ups, 100 pull-ups, 2 hours of Kav Bitz Kar Do training, an hour of weightlifting training from an old gym set I found in the trash and, to finish it off, 30 minutes of yoga and gymnastics.

"Woah, I am a bit famished."

After a 5-hour workout, I was tired, hungry, angry and sore, so I decided to detour through the sewers and went to the local supermarket to grab a protein drink of some sort. I went to the shop Armamart, which was a small shop run by a lovely Armenian couple. They were both in their late 50s and had run this shop for 30 years.

After stopping in to pick up a protein shake, two peace-keeping officers barged in and shoved me aside.

"Hey, watch it, pal!" I yelled out, but they ignored me and began to confront the elderly couple. The officers were screaming at the elderly couple for having this shop open 24 hours when martial law dictates that shops must close at 7.00 pm sharp. They began belittling them, treating them as garbage. The Armenian couple screamed back at the officers, and the situation escalated, with one of the soldiers going behind the counter and throwing the elderly man to the ground, with the other soldier pinning the elderly woman to the floor. Then, the officer kicked the elderly man in the face, with the elderly woman screaming in terror. I was mortified, standing there watching it unfold. Normally, I would have ignored it as that was the convention of things, but I was not going to let this happen.

I had to act fast. Not thinking, I grabbed an old Uncle Sam mask that was hanging from an aisle and quickly charged at the officer who had pinned down the elderly man, effectively knocking the officer to the floor, and began punching him. The second officer swung his body around and was in complete shock at the sight of his co-worker on the ground. In a hurry, he tried to reach for the firearm in his holster, but the elderly woman grabbed a glass bottle and smashed it over the officer's head. The officer was stunned for a few seconds but snapped out of it and slapped the elderly woman across the face, causing her to fall to the floor. Poor woman. However, it did give me the opportunity to take out the officer, as I grabbed the gun from his knocked-out co-worker and shot the officer in the torso, which sent him flying into the smoke rack. Thanks to the body armour the officer was wearing, it didn't kill him, but it did keep him down for a bit longer.

Then, out of instinct, I turned the gun on the officer on the ground and shot him in the head, executioner style. Luckily, the gun jammed, so I just knocked him out with the butt of his gun. It was brutal but fair.

The elderly man pushed the officer off, and I rushed to the aid of the elderly woman, offering her a hand up. The couple was grateful that I helped them out and said that they would clean up the bodies and that I should go before more arrived. I nodded to them. "Thank you."

I rushed out of the shop to a nearby alley. I stood there in the alley, looking down at the gun, and I couldn't stop laughing. I mean, what a rush! But what was more important was that it felt so good to help those people and to whip out some justice on those thugs. What happened in that shop made me realise how important my mission is. Someone needed to stand up to people like that, and I would make sure to deliver that justice. But first, I had to make sure that my family was all right. I'd better get home and make sure that Ella and Mum were all right.

I grabbed the mask and the gun and threw it into the bin and began making my way home, as I heard more forces pulling up to the shop.

I was on cloud nine. I was feeling happy, excited and glad. Finally, I had made a difference in someone's life. While it may have been a minor change, it still felt good. But that mood suddenly changed when I unlocked the door and found Edward sitting on the couch, drinking a cup of coffee, while I just stood there in complete shock.

Edward stood up and placed his coffee on the coffee table. "Hey, Jacob."

My happiness then turned to anger as I quickly swung the door closed and began to walk up to Edward. "Look, Jacob, I know—"

Before he could finish his sentence, I sucker-punched him straight in the jaw, which caused him to fall to the floor. While on the floor, he side-kicked my knee, which knocked me off balance, and now I collapsed onto the floor. Then he got up and kneed me in the nose, knocking me back to the floor. He was about to approach me when I grabbed an empty glass near me and smashed it across his face, before tackling him into a kitchen storage cabinet. In response, Edward elbowed me in the jaw, before grabbing the collar of my shirt and throwing me over the couch. At that point, I was so mad and wasn't holding back.

I returned with a punch to the face, but Edward saw it coming and blocked it. Still, I caught him off guard by front-kicking him into the dining room table, breaking it on the impact. Both of us took a quick, minute break, and then we continued to fight. We both went into it, heavily throwing punches and kicks and then simultaneously we threw a punch and knocked each other out simultaneously. Both of us fell to the floor unconscious.

We both then got up, sore and tired, with Edward asking, "Jacob, are you ready to talk?"

Still angry but too fatigued to fight, I simply said, "Yer, I guess." I was confused. "Edward, why are you still here? You got your money."

Edward was sad at this point. "Look, after you shot me in the shoulder, I did a lot of thinking, and I realised that I couldn't leave you and Anna. I love you guys. You are family to me, and what I did was wrong. I never wanted to betray you. I am so sorry."

I was a lot calmer, yet I still held a lot of resentment, so I had to ask, "Why did you betray us, Edward?"

"I didn't want to betray you and Anna. I just wanted to regain what I lost all those years ago, what my parents lost. It wasn't just about the money. It was about restoring my family's name. It was about my dignity. So when I was invited to WeapCo by John Speer, he said that if I gave him intel on the potential attack on his company, he would give me $1 million. When I sold the land and the Xenogren, I would be able to move back to the Upper Levels. So I told him everything that Yandan and Ella had planned. But I made him promise not to hurt you and Anna, to which he agreed. It's obvious now that he broke his promise to me."

I just shook my head. "A billionaire lied. Shocker!"

Normally, Edward would find my sarcasm amusing but not at this moment. "Don't you judge me, Jacob! I saw an out, and I took it. An out from being poor, hungry, depressed and having no opportunity. Come on, Jacob, let's face it. If you didn't sleep with Ella, you would have done the same thing, and you know it."

"Edward, you shot me. You were like a brother to me, and you shot me."

Edward just smirked. "Well, you shot me in the shoulder, so I guess we are cool now."

"Edward, you got my mother hurt, you got Ella hurt, and because of you, her heart was damaged, and her father had to give him his. How can I trust you now?"

Edward just sighed in disappointment. "You're right. I may have done your family wrong, but I now realise that you are my family, and I wouldn't trade it for the world."

I couldn't help but sigh.

Tears began to roll down Edward's eyes. "I know I did you wrong, and I can never take back the pain I caused you and Anna, but I am truly sorry."

I started to cry too. "You were like a brother to me. How could you betray me like that?"

There was an awkward silence, and Edward was the first one to break it. "I am so sorry, and I will never betray you again. I promise." Edward reached down near the couch and handed me his silver briefcase full of money. "Take it; it's yours."

I was so happy. While I still needed some time before I could ever trust Edward again, him giving me a suitcase full of money was a start.

I took a breath and then got up, as our fight caused a bit of a mess around here, and someone needed to clean it up. "Edward, if you want to get on my good side, grab a broom."

Edward got up and joined me in helping to sweep up the floor. "So, Jacob, are we good?"

I turned around to him while sweeping the shattered glass off the floor. "It's going to take some time. Edward, Anna and I are still quite furious at you, but we will see. Time heals all wounds, so let's leave it at that."

Edward gave me a simple nod and began sweeping.

After our fight, Ella came down the stairs, still quite weak from her transplant surgery but better enough to walk again, thanks in part to medication that, while considered outdated, was still far more effective than medications made thousands of years ago.

"Hey Jacob, I am feeling like—"

She paused as she saw Edward sweeping up the living room floor. Anger overwhelmed her, and she reached for the handgun on the cabinet near the stairs and pointed it at Edward. "What the hell are you doing here?"

I had to intervene. "Ella, he is here to make peace."

However, Ella was completely dumbfounded. "Make peace? He is the one who got us in that situation in the first place."

Edward quickly snapped back at Ella. "It was your father's plan that got this whole town in this situation. I mean, they were just working-class people, but you turned them into terrorists. And look where it got them and your father."

Ella wasn't having it. "It would have worked if you hadn't sold us out."

"No, it was doomed to fail. They would have found out eventually. They have resources and technology at their disposal."

"Oh, you are such a coward, Edward."

"I am the coward! You dragged innocent people, including Jacob and Anna, who I cared about, into fighting some silly war because he damaged your shop. I mean, your dad thought he was the next Che Guevara, but you're just a bunch of bitter, angry people who use innocent people to settle your scores, because you can't fight your own battles. Who's the real coward?"

"No, we should just sell out the community like you did. I should just kill you."

Edward shook his head. "Good, kill people. That's all you are good at, you brute!"

"I am going to make you pay for getting my father killed."

"Hey, you did that yourself."

Ella at this point was over the conversation. She pointed the gun at Edward, ready to shoot, with Edward crouching down to not get shot.

I was over this. "Hey, stop it you two. Look, I know we are not all on the best terms, but we need each one of us. We are all in this together, regardless of our past mistakes. We all have a common enemy now."

Ella was furious. She threw the gun to the floor and walked back into her room, slamming the door behind her.

"Come on, I will get the basement set up for you," I said, with Edward nodding in agreement. We marched down into the basement.

"How's your shoulder holding up?"

"All right. Using my pharmacy training and my military medical training, I was able to patch up the wound. How did you get Anna, Ella and Yandan out of that warehouse, Jacob?"

"The Xenogren."

"Shit, Jacob, be careful with that stuff. That's a very potent drug. You're lucky you didn't die."

I laughed a little. "I know, man, the withdrawals were a pain."

"I am not surprised. There's a reason it is banned in all nine cities. Even the fittest athletes have ODed on that sort of shit."

Curious, I asked, "Hey Edward, you wouldn't happen to know if that drug causes hallucination by any chance, do you?"

Edward looked puzzled. "Not surprising. The side effects of that drug are not yet known. You're one of the rare ones to survive."

I hadn't known that the drug could have killed me, but oh well, no point dwelling on the past. I had more important issues. "Hey listen, do you mind taking care of Ella and Anna till I get back?"

"Sure. Where are you going?"

"I have to take care of some business."

"Well, Godspeed then, I guess."

I walked up the stairs and out the front door, ready to continue my mission. Having Edward back was a significant helping hand, as he would be able to take care of Ella and Anna while I went out and plotted to take down WeapCo.

My first mission was that if I was going to get anything done, I needed to get the peacekeepers out of the Lower Levels. The people of the Lower Levels were struggling under the tyranny of the peacekeeping force. The peacekeepers are supposed to be upholding the peace, or at least that's what their motto says, but all they had done was terrorise the community, acting as judge, jury and executioner, killing citizens without a trial or due process. Since they had arrived, they had killed hundreds of people, most of whom were innocent, hard-working people. They had ruined local businesses and caused irreparable damage to the local economy. Well, enough was enough. It's time to take out the peacekeeping force from this place once and for all. But I couldn't just rush into this. If I had to take them out, I would need to come up with a plan, and I knew where to start. Throughout the Lower Levels, they had installed six Military Mobile Communication Centres (MMCCs) around the city. These portable communication centres controlled the entire communication network for the troops, with each of them costing millions of taxpayer dollars. So if we took them out, the troops would have no communication amongst each other. Divide and conquer – the oldest trick in the book.

The first location was near Yandan's old gun store. The MMCCs were expandable shelters fitted on the back of trucks. These bad boys were fitted to withstand ballistic fire, shrapnel, mines, lateral blast attacks and electro-magnetic attacks. The centres are equipped with state-of-the-art technology, the best money could buy, all of which was bought directly from WeapCo at inflated prices. These centres were heavily armed and guarded, so getting in would be very tricky, but I had a plan.

After squeezing in through the gap in the floor of the gun shop, I managed to get into the basement. After waiting for the 10 patrolling troops to pass by, I made my move. Once I couldn't hear the marching of military boots, I quickly crawled out of the crack and bolted behind a car. Next, I would approach the heavily armoured MMCC in absolute silence. I needed to find a way to take out those troops and distract the plasma turrets. Then a light bulb clicked in my head. I'll see if the car is working, and if it is, I would ram it into the MMCC.

With a plan in place, it was time to act. Crawling quietly around the car to the driver seat, I checked to see if it was unlocked, and just my luck, it was unlocked. Crawling into the unlocked car, I quickly sat in the driver's seat and looked through the sun visor and the glove compartment, but no luck. Guess I would have to try and hotwire the car. I was relying on techniques I had learnt in electronic class at high school to get by. After fumbling with multiple different wires, trying to connect red and black and hearing sparks, I heard a vroom from the battery starting up. Success! But I had to act quickly, as the soldiers turned around and began to shoot at the old car with their plasma rifles.

Looking around quickly, I placed a heavy bag of clothes on the accelerator pedal and began listening to the roaring of the engine as I pulled the handbrake, which sent the car flying. It went charging down the road, like a bull charging towards a bullfighter. The car knocked down 10 soldiers, either killing or severely wounding them; I didn't have time to check. The car was about to hit the MMCC when the plasma turret on the top of the MMCC sprang into action with its little red robotic eye, shooting 10 plasma bolts at the car. One of the bolts hit the engine of the car, disabling it and causing it to stop. While the car didn't even dent the MMCC, it did distract the turret. I quickly grabbed one of the plasma rifles from the fallen soldier and ran behind the car.

The turret detected my movement and sprang into action, with its red eye looking right at me. I turned to the side of the car, aimed quickly at the turret, and shot a blue plasma bolt right into the eye of the plasma turret, causing the turret to shoot out blue sparks everywhere and deactivate. Meanwhile, inside the MMC, two young reservist officers from the Middle Level (who were obviously using this job to pay for their law degrees) snapped out of their chairs in shock and quickly grabbed their pistols that were near their cans of energy drinks and empty pizza boxes, hoping their 10 hours of firearm training would come in handy. Holding the gun at the door, they were shaking in fear because they had obviously never killed anyone, as they were only reservist with barely any combat experience.

I blasted the door lock on the MMCC and entered the room. The officers quickly threw their guns to the ground and surrendered. I entered the highly modernised control room, which was full of computer monitors and military-grade equipment everywhere. I was standing there pointing the rifle at the officers, trying to figure out what to do with these soldiers. One thing that surprised me was the communication coming through the radio channel: "Control, this is artillery. Preparing to fire practice rounds, over!"

Artillery? They brought artillery down here? This is an urban area full of families. This isn't a war zone. My goodness.

But it may be a blessing in disguise. Instead of having to take every individual MMCC down, I would be able to hijack their artillery to take all the MMCCs out in one night.

I turned around, pointing the guns at the inexperienced officers, who were clearly about to piss their pants.

"That radio comm, where is it from?"

Both the officers just stood there in silence, not saying a word.

Then, I pointed the gun at the ceiling of the MMCC and fired a warning shot up into the ceiling, making the two officers jump in fear. I was beginning to lose my patience, so I barked again, "Where is that artillery located!"

One of the officers fearfully explained, "They're doing training near the abandoned warehouse."

I knew where they were referring to. It was the old steelwork factory that my dad used to work at. I knew where to go, but one question remained: Morally, what to do with the soldiers? I could kill them, but they are just young kids. I could let them go, but then they would inform the Peacekeeper force. Thinking hard, I came to a decision, "All right, guys—"

I was interrupted by one of the officers pleading for their life. "Don't kill us, man, please ... We won't tell anyone, we promise."

I started up again, "All right, guys, here's the deal. Get in the cabinet behind you, and I am going to lock it. If you survive, you will have your life. If you don't, then you die. Now get in there, NOW!"

The two soldiers fearfully ran into the cabinet, and I locked them inside.

Now was the time to get busy. I then began shooting at the console of the MMCC, causing all the wires and circuits underneath the board to be exposed, and sparks went flying everywhere. Then, I opened the door and went outside and grabbed one of the jerry cans located near the electrical generator. I grabbed it and went back inside, pouring the jerry can of petrol everywhere. The entire room was covered in colourless fuel and smelt of petrol. Now, it was time to light the fuse. Running outside, I quickly grabbed a lighter out of one of the knocked-out soldiers' pockets and rushed back into the MMCC control room. But, as soon as I lit the match, the automatic sprinkler system kicked in, wetting the entire room and leaving me and my clothes soaked. I stood there looking at the wet room with a frown on my wet face. Plan B, I guess. I ran out of the MMCC and back to one of the knocked-out soldiers. On him, I found a state-of-the-art thermal implosion grenade.

I rushed back to MMCC, pulled the pin and threw the grenade inside. The grenade sucked in some oxygen before the light on the cylinder grenade turned orange, letting out an orange pulse of thermal energy. I was standing outside when I saw the entire MMCC go up in flames within a matter of minutes. Now was the time to flee.

As for the officers in the truck, the cabinet they were in was covered in stainless steel, but the truck was on fire, so I would leave it to the imagination to determine if they got out alive or not.

Once the truck was on fire, I fled behind a burnt-down shop of some sort. I couldn't tell what kind of shop it was meant to be.

Spotting the charred remains of the MMCC, I could see the military Humvee rush to investigate the fire, and I could see at least 10 drones, the same design as in the monorail station, swarming the night skies, using their red scanners to investigate the fire. After all the drones swarmed the MMCC, now was the time to flee.

After bolting down to the industrial area, I found the area completely crawling with troops and military equipment. It was finally starting to dawn on me: this whole thing wasn't about keeping the peace or enslaving the Lower Level; this whole war was a training exercise in urban combat. The peacekeeping force was trying to train the next generation in urban warfare, preparing them to take down forces that may threaten this city and flex their military might to the public and spend taxpayers' money. The only problem was that they didn't care how many people or property they damaged, because, to them, the Lower Levels were worthless and a perfect place to train. It was kind of sick and pissed me off even more. This isn't some military exercise; this is our home, and the people they are killing are someone's sons and daughters. But now was not the time to think about the injustice; I had to act fast.

Suddenly, I heard a bang sound coming from the factory, and as I looked up, I could see this metal object flying through the night sky, leaving behind a yellow streak from the missile. The object then disappeared out of view. I needed to investigate further.

Peering through the hole in the barbed wire, I could make out the artillery; it was an M150 High Mobility Artillery Rocket System which was equipped with a Long-Range Hypersonic Weapon, a 6-million-dollar weapon. That bad boy could take out city blocks from here all the way to Asia. Very powerful weapon, a bit excessive to use in a training exercise for urban warfare.

Peering through the fence, I could also see six unfired rockets just lying on the ground, waiting to be loaded into the launcher. There were at least four guards, from what I could make out, patrolling the area and at least two inside the truck itself. But I wasn't sure I had to investigate further. After scoping around the fence area, I couldn't see much of a difference. I had to make sure to remain crouched to not alert the troops. I got through the main entrances to find two soldiers with plasma rifles guarding the entrance to the artillery.

Then I heard an '*fffff*' sound coming from the chamber containing the missile, and I looked and saw the missile shoot up from the chamber with flames and into the sky. It disappeared into the night sky along with the residual smoke trail from where the missile had launched. But it didn't disappear for long. I could hear from a few blocks away a boom coming from a few shops downtown and a mushroom cloud rising from what remained of the shop. I had to act fast before the troops fired the remaining missiles.

I leapt into action, grabbing a blunt metal pipe that was conveniently placed next to this burnt-out car beside which I had been crouched down, watching as one of the soldiers in the truck hopped out to load the missiles into the launcher.

The instant he stepped out of the car, *whack!* The soldier went down, and I shot the other soldier through the chest with a blue plasma bolt from the knocked-out soldier's side pistol. Luckily, though the soldier still had armour on, he collapsed to the ground motionless and stiff on the ground, possibly stunned or dead. Either way, it did the trick.

Two other soldiers came rushing towards the scene to investigate, but they only found trouble in the form of me, who was jacked up on adrenaline, charging directly towards them with a plasma rifle loaded in my hand. I could tell that these troops had little to no combat experience, as they had missed every shot. I mean, I could literally see the blue plasma bolt flying past my head. I guess it was time to show them what a real battle-hardened veteran could do. I rushed towards them like a rhino, at which they took a step back in shock. Then, I slid under the first soldier's feet, knocking him down to the ground, and with the flex of my right hand, I shot the second soldier in the head with the blue bolt that shot straight into the night sky. With the second soldier, I smacked him with the butt of the plasma rifle and then turned the gun on him, and *bam!*

Two other soldiers behind cover returned fire at me. Now, if they were well-trained, I would have been dead by now, but they were rookies, so I was safe. Getting up, I returned fire, taking them out with ease. In a way, I kind of felt bad for these kids. I mean, they were just young boys; they didn't know what they were getting themselves into. I didn't want to kill them, but they attacked my community, and I had no other option. But there was no time to think of that, now! It was time to hijack this missile launcher and take out the remaining MMCCs.

Now, with all the crew dead, I got into the missile launcher. However, it suddenly dawned on me. I didn't know how to operate this launcher. I was a radiation diver marine, not a missile launcher operator. I looked at the dashboard of the launcher confused. I guess I had to wing it. I pressed the biggest button I could find, and miraculously enough, I managed to fire a missile out of the cylinder. But there was one problem: I didn't load any coordinates into the system. Shit! Now there was a hypersonic missile flying through the city.

Suddenly, I heard a massive *BOOM* coming from outside. The missile had hit a random target within a matter of minutes. I peered out the window of the truck and saw a massive hole in the middle of a random skyscraper. I was mortified. That was never the target. Suddenly, the 20-storey skyscraper caved in on itself, and within a matter of seconds, the building made of steel and concrete completely collapsed. The whole building plummeted to the ground, covering the entire Lower Levels and Middle Levels in the debris of smoke and leaving a crater of rubble where the mighty tower once stood.

I was lost for words. I just stood there in absolute shock and dismay at the destruction I had caused. After hearing the sirens from police, ambulance and fire vehicles rushing to the scene, I had to get out of there before they investigated.

I got out of the truck and bolted from the scene of the crime, running as fast as I could down the main street. I was shocked and in horror at what I had done. I hoped I hadn't killed anyone.

As I was running down the road, I looked overhead at flying vehicles, both military and emergency services, flying to the scene of the explosion. Luckily, they were too high up to spot me running on the road away from the scene of the crime, but I could see the drones from destroyed MMCC coming straight towards me to investigate the missile launchers.

Quickly, before they spotted me, I looked at the ground and noticed a sewer hatch. I lifted the hatch and jumped down into the Sewer Levels. The drones flew straight past without even looking at me and began scanning the missile launcher. While down in the sewer, I could hear the remaining peacekeeping soldiers' vehicles all rushing to the scene. I could look up and see tyres driving past the sewer hole. Tonight, I unfortunately failed in my mission, and I felt bad because not only did I fail, but I also got innocent people killed. I didn't know if it was 100 or 1,000 people I had managed to kill.

After nearly an hour of walking through dirty, disgusting sewer water and having to endure the terrible smell of human waste, I finally made it home. I pulled up to the front door of my house tired, covered in blood and sweat, and of course, my pants were covered in sewer water and smell of shit. But what was worse was that I couldn't wrap my head around the fact that I may have killed thousands of people. Also, I think I may have made the military occupation in the Lower Levels worse. But I guess that is something for another day. After opening the front door, I noticed that everyone was asleep; Edward was on the couch, and Ella and Anna were in bed.

Boy, I was tired and full of guilt at what I had done and really needed some sleep. I needed to forget about this horrible day and just zone out. However, as I entered my room, I noticed something strange lying on the floor of my bedroom. It was a hardcover book, but what was a book doing on the floor of my bedroom? I picked it up to investigate, and it was *I, Robot* by Isaac Asimov.

What? I never owned this book. Hell, I barely even read books. But something strange happened as I flipped through the book, and there were no words in the book. The entire book was just blank sheets of paper. I thought nothing of it. I brushed it off as weird, and I didn't bother to read it and just chucked it on the floor. But when I went to turn out the lights, I noticed that the book was gone, nowhere to be seen. Weird!

I just ignored the entire situation. I had had enough excitement for one day and just went to bed, hoping to forget the world.

CHAPTER 10

The next day, I couldn't stop but feel guilty about the people I had killed and the destruction I had caused. Out of curiosity, I decided to sneak up to the Middle Levels to investigate the destroyed building, leaving Edward to take care of the girls. I tried to take the subway, but it was swarming with the peacekeeping force. With no other options, I decided to take the long way around. I walked to the nearest skyscraper that was placed directly next to the subway line, and I climbed up one of the subway pillars and hopped directly onto the rail. The tracks were not electrified, thank goodness. However, it was probably advisable not to look down, as it was pretty high up. I was nearly 10 feet off the ground.

After following the tracks around, I scaled down the subway pole and landed in an artificial park in the Middle Levels. The park was beautiful, full of fake plastic grass and holographic trees everywhere. There were even simulated bird noises. I couldn't help but stop for a minute to look at the park. If only it was real … It was just like the air I breathe, fake.

After walking through the pack, I began to make my way to the Central Business District to investigate the rubble, when I witnessed protests accruing on the streets with at least 100 people walking down the street holding signs and making noise with their microphones. It was a small protest;

they were anti-war protesters by the look of them, protesting the "peacekeeping" force down in the Lower Levels. It was strange to have protests up here in the Middle Levels. Honestly, I was surprised, as I thought the Middle Levels were too busy drinking their lattes to care what goes on in politics. The protests up here were certainly not like the ones down below, as we are violent. The one up here was not violent at all; not a single gun or Molotov cocktail in sight. In fact, they were quite peaceful. All they did was protest. I just stood there looking confused. *What the hell is going on? Why are they protesting? Since when do the people up here care about us, the people down below?*

Out of curiosity, I ran towards the nearest Holonet projector and watched the news report. On the Holonet News, a white guy and a white girl in fancy suits were projected on an obviously fake-looking newsroom backdrop. The anchorman was the first one to speak.

"You have heard it today, folks. Our reserved forces are destroying our city. Late last night, a missile accident resulted in the destruction of an insurance building, killing five night workers. The insurance company is furious and demanding legal action."

The female anchor cut in while showing the CCTV footage of the missile destroying the building.

"That's right, Bill. It is believed that reservist and former employee Max Dawson went mad after being sacked from his job, and with his history of mental illness, he snapped and killed his colleagues. He then fired the rocket at the insurance company in retaliation for his firing, killing the remaining people in the building. Let's hear what General Heathson has to say on the matter. General, good morning."

A balding old grey-haired general in his 40s appeared on the Holonet.

"Good morning, Ally. The army is deeply appalled by the actions taken by Dawson, and my heart goes out to the families of those victims. The Department of Defence will be conducting an internal investigation into the matter."

I stood there with a grin on my face. What a perfect unintentional scapegoat to get myself out of trouble. But after hearing the news and looking at the protest, I began to cultivate a new plan of attack to get the peacekeepers out of the Lower Levels. It would be impossible to take out the soldiers by a physical insurrection. No, the best way to get them out would be through the system. I would have to take them out from the inside, through the government.

Before I headed back down to the Lower Levels, I may as well escalate the situation before it cooled down. I snatched a bullhorn out of one of the protesters' hands and stood on top of a car and used the mic to signal to the protesters.

"People! Are we going to let the stinking government spend our hard-earned tax dollars on a military force that does nothing but destroy our buildings and take away our jobs?"

The massive crowd cried out, "NOOO!"

The mood of the crowd started to rile up into anger.

"People! How is it that this military force managed to destroy an entire skyscraper and get away with it? Did they pay for it? Did they say sorry? No! They just gave you the same bureaucratic rubbish they always gave us. We are conducting an internal investigation. We are looking into it. Blah blah blah … Are we going to take it?"

The crowd then, even more furious, let out a cry in unified anger, "No!"

"Then let us rise up and tell them to stop wasting time on military exercises and repair our building."

That did the trick. The crowd quickly turned on the police, throwing bottles and rocks. The protesting went from peaceful to violent in a matter of minutes. It got so bad that riot control police had to descend down into the crowd, armed to the teeth, and firing sound disruptors and tear gas into the crowd (now it felt like a protest in the Lower Levels). But that only fuelled the anger of the crowd even more, as the protesters descended into trashing shops and flipping over cars. I found the whole experience satisfying. It was like winding up a toy car and watching it race around the room. I pickpocketed some random protester's holophone, threw my hoodie above my head and vanished into the crowd, disappearing like a ninja.

Oh well, at least I have an idea of what to do now. If we can't beat them, then we may as well join them. If we can't use physical force, then we must create a political force powerful enough to get the troops out of our city.

Vanishing without a trace, I headed back down to the Lower Levels and took refuge in the shop run by the Armenian couple.

The couple greeted me with a smile. "There he is, the superhero! Come, come, browse at whatever you like."

They were super nice to me. But while I was here only to take refuge, a light bulb went off in my head. "Is your CCTV camera working?"

They both looked at each other and responded with a simple "Yer."

"Can I look at the footage of that night?"

The Armenian couple both agreed and took me to this dank, run-down room in the basement and showed me a clearly outdated yet still adequate monitor that housed the shop's security cameras. The monitor was clearly twenty-first-century technology, but hey, I can work with this. The footage was heavily pixelated, but it still showed the peacekeeping force beating the Armenian couple, which is what I needed. This footage clearly showed the peacekeepers abusing their power.

I wonder what would happen if I were to put this on social media?

After somehow managing to hook the modern technology of my phone to the antique technology, I transferred the footage straight to my stolen phone, and onto social media it went. I scrolled through the phone and found this new social media site – Tik-Instraverse – and I captioned the footage as *#PeacekeepingBrutality*, and onto the internet it went. I never really got this whole social media thing, with all the stupid dances and stupid videos (though the cat videos were funny), and I didn't know what a pronoun was, but social media would make for a powerful political and communication tool. The Lower Levels can barely afford food, let alone expensive phones. I still couldn't understand why more people aren't political and trying to help our cause. I mean, they have entire archives of knowledge at their fingertips, and they waste it texting and sending pictures. What is worse is that our level has to deal with outdated books and poorly funded school, which angers me even more, because they want to keep us stupid. But no time to think about that. If it gets these bloody fascist pigs out of our communities, then I would play along.

The footage had only been up on social media for an hour, and it has already been viewed by 10 per cent of the world's population and has been shared over a thousand times. That footage may have been provoking, but it still wasn't enough. If I was to cause more chaos, I would need more footage. Luckily for me, I knew just where to look.

After I was finished with the monitor, I thanked the lovely Armenian couple, bought a Cola and ran out of the shop and down the street towards the apartment blocks. The apartment blocks may have been old, but I presumed there would have to be some camera footage or some old CCTV camera in there somewhere. After passing the constant peacekeeping force patrols, I reached the apartment block. The apartment block was still damaged from the fight. Holes remained in the wall, and yes, the bodies had been cleaned up, but the hallways and stairways were damaged, and the doors of some apartments were barely holding together with duct tape. The people, having no choice, had to move back into the apartments, because they couldn't afford to go anywhere else and couldn't pay for the repairs. I walked up 20 flights of stairs and scoured across the different floors, but to my disappointment, there was no surveillance of any kind in this place. It was time to go to plan B. While

I could not use camera footage, I could however use first-hand witnesses.

In a mad dash, I ran towards the occupied apartment blocks in the hope that someone would tell me their stories. Some were hesitant to speak out of fear of repercussion, and some were downright rude to me. However, I managed to hear and record the story from four people who witnessed and fought that night. One story was from a 40-year-old African American woman, who recounted that on that night, one of the soldiers shot her in the shoulder, which knocked her to the ground. However, instead of providing her first aid, the soldier kicked her in the face, knocking her teeth out and breaking her jaw.

Another victim came forth. It was from a Hispanic man in his 20s. He recounted that he was in a firefight with the soldiers, and one of the soldiers outgunned him. With no other option, he threw down his gun to surrender by kneeling down on the ground. But instead of being handcuffed, which is a standard protocol, one of the peacekeepers pulled out his knife and stabbed him in the back. The man managed to survive, but unfortunately, he was left paralysed from the waist down. The man teared up about the encounter. Unfortunately, this wasn't the saddest story I heard that day.

A lovely Filipino lady told me her story. The lady wasn't even fighting that night; all she was doing was hiding behind the door of her apartment, trying to avoid the gunfire. From behind the door, she could recall peering out through one of the peepholes. While peering out through the hole, she saw this young boy – who was only 10 years old – running up the stairs, trying to retreat from the peacekeepers. The boy's gun had run out of ammo, so he threw the gun and tried to run. Unfortunately, two soldiers caught up with him, and one managed to grab him. The boy retaliated out of fear and punched the soldier in the face. This angered the soldier, so in retaliation, the soldier grabbed the boy by his left arm and left leg and began to swing him around rapidly, and then *bang*, he hit the boy's face into a brick wall with such force that it crushed the boy's head, killing him instantly. The Filipino woman was left traumatised by that situation.

The saddest story came from a young Caucasian girl who was 16 years old. The girl lived on the first floor and was spending time with her boyfriend after school when the peacekeepers began the siege into the apartment. In her apartment, the woman and her boyfriend approached the door in fear. But then, *bang!* A peacekeeping soldier broke down the door and punched and stabbed the woman's boyfriend. After recalling the events, the poor lady broke down into tears. It was a terrible thing for someone so young to witness.

These poor people had been through hell at the hands of this so-called peacekeeping force. While it sucked having these people recall these terrible stories, it was necessary, as it needed to be told and shared with the world. Everyone needed to know what had really happened that night. After hearing these stories, I thanked these people, gave them a hug and posted it all to social media for the whole world to see.

After posting the stories to social media, I returned home to find Edward with Ella and Anna, who were both feeling much better, sitting on the couch watching TV. Yep, nothing had really changed. While I still felt a bit of tension between Ella and Anna towards Edward, everyone was on good terms. Edward got up from the chair.

"There you are. Where have you been?"

"Oh, just taking care of some chores."

Edward had known me for years and wasn't buying it. "What are you really up to?"

There was no fooling Edward, so I sat down on the couch and showed Ella, Anna and Edward the stolen phone.

"Where did you get that?"

I sat down for 30 minutes and explained my plan and what the next move was. Ella and Edward both looked at me with a little bit of contempt, with Anna looking at me in concern.

"Jacob, what are you doing here, man? You're not a politician. What are you hoping to achieve here?"

I calmly explained that I was fighting back against this brutal occupation and that the only way to do that was through political division. But being the stupid me, I accidentally slipped that I shot the rocket at the apartment building, which Anna was not happy about.

"Wait, that was you? You attacked the building? People died in that building, Jacob!"

I tried to justify my action by explaining that it was an accident, and yes, people got hurt, which I felt guilty about, but it did some good. Isn't that all that matters?

"So what! People die down here all the time, and no one bats an eye. Yet when one building gets destroyed, the entire system goes haywire!"

Ella was not impressed. "Jacob, my dad tried to stop them, and he died for it. What makes you think you will do any better?"

"Simple! I have a way. We can chase them out of this city not through violence but the will of the people."

Edward was sceptical. "Jacob, you don't know what you are messing with. WeapCo has money and influence in ParliaCongress. Your efforts would be meaningless. You are just one man."

"I have to try, Edward. The soldiers don't belong down here, and we all know it. You tried that once, and where did it get you?"

"What, are you going to betray us again?"

Edward wasn't impressed. "THAT'S NOT FAIR!"

Anna did her best to try and defuse the situation. "Look, I get it, Jacob, you want to help. But Jacob, think of what you will lose. Me. You will lose your friends and family."

"I know, Mum, but I have to do something. Yandan was right. No one is going to help us down here. We are on our own. If we are going to survive, we have to fight back." I then hooked up the phone to the old TV and signalled to them all. "Just look."

The footage and stories I had posted to social media had caused an uproar in the Middle Levels. The protest had escalated even further, causing looting and rioting. There was even news footage of protesters throwing Molotov cocktails and police responding with tear gas and rubber bullets. The protests up there were so bad that they had to move the peacekeepers from the Lower Levels all the way to the Middle Level, which was extremely rare. The crowds were chanting, "Down with fascism, down with fascism," and "Hey, hey, ho, ho, police brutality has got to go."

The footage I had sent through had gone viral not just in this city but across the world. It was so intense that the media had gone into a complete frenzy, and it was causing headway in the higher-ups. All the ParliaCongress members had to each prepare PR statements to save face.

Ella, Anna and Edward were impressed. "Look guys, I know you are scared, and we lost so much last time – friends, family – but there is still work that needs to be done. We need these soldiers out of our communities, but I can't do it alone. I need you guys. So, who is with me?"

Edward got up off the couch. "Count me in."

Ella and Anna both joined in. "Us too!"

I smiled. "All right, let's do this thing."

"So, Jacob, what's the plan?"

CHAPTER *11*

Igathered the gang around the dining room table. Edward was eager to help. "Jacob, where can I help?"

He was trying to suck up to me to make up for the betrayal, but I may as well take his help.

"Edward, you have a private school education. Can you teach me how bills are made in this city and what the political system is like?"

Edward smiled. "Follow me. We are going to the Capitol Autonomous Zone."

Ella, Anna and I scratched our heads in confusion. "Edward *what* is that?"

None of us had gone up to Upper Level, let alone visit the Capitol. Edward rolled his eyes. "Just follow me."

In a hurry, we all walked out the front door.

After walking up to the Middle Level, the four of us walked for nearly an hour until we finally reached the Capitol Autonomous Zone or CAZ for short. CAZ was a small, designated area located in the centre of the city and was completely autonomous for legal reasons. Within CAZ stood a building, the Capitol, which covered an area of 3,600 sq m and housed around 10,000 representative seats for each district of the city. It was a massive building which is divided into two sections: the House of Representatives (the Lower

Levels) and the senate (Upper Levels), with each section housing 5,000 representatives.

After we had entered the building, we were all amazed at the size and grandeur of the building. Anna, Ella and I looked around in amazement at the paintings of famous presidents and the amazing architecture of the building with its marble statues and giant pillars. Edward wasn't that impressed, as he had been here multiple times on field trips. He was our personal tour guide, explaining the history of ParliaCongress to us. He was well-versed in how the system worked, so he explained to us that the current system in this city was a combination of the old British parliamentary system and the old American representative government system, whatever the hell that meant. Edward explained to us that legislation is first introduced into the House of Representatives, and if approved, it is then voted on in the senate and then is introduced to the president. The president has the power to either veto the bill or approve the bill and turn it into law. This whole system was confusing, but I guess we had no choice but to play along. We sat in the viewing area on the top balcony, as the room quickly filled with thousands of politicians all dressed in their fancy suits with their gel-backed hair. What started as excitement quickly turned to boredom, as we all quickly learnt that politics was as fun as watching paint dry. It was just two hours of them talking about budget deficits and going back and forth at each other with questions. Oh, thank goodness it was over. We all walked away from that session disappointed and bored out of our minds. I hadn't realised how complex politics really was. This was going to be tougher than I thought.

All walked out of the Capitol, sad and disappointed. We were way out of our league. We were taking on a Goliath system, and we were just nobodies. But then, something caught our eyes as we all made our way down the steps of Parliament – or should I someone – our David to this Goliath system.

We all couldn't help but look at the political figure who was advocating out the front of the Capitol. She was a young ParliaCongresswoman who had to be in her 20s. She was African American-born, bold and ambitious, and around her stood a crowd of at least 100 people, all of whom were holding banners and posters and cheering and chanting her name. Her name was Alienize Lier. But what was amazing was these young women weren't advocating for war or lower taxes; no, quite the opposite, she was advocating to get the peacekeepers out of the Lower Levels. I didn't realise people cared about our level. We all stepped down from the steps and joined the crowd of supporters who were advocating for her and watched as she spoke like a naturally gifted orator and had a remarkable way with words. I was in love with her passion and her drive. She spoke more like an entertainer than a politician. I could listen to her for hours and hours. Alienize was the person the Lower Levels needed, a hero, and we needed her on our team.

Once Alienize finished, we made our move. We followed her back to her political office, as we needed her alone. After following her for 30 minutes, we watched as Alienize entered her office and observed her through the window. The first thing she did was approach her desk and open up a cabinet underneath her desk and pulled out a bottle of whisky, pouring herself a drink and coughing the drink down as if it was cough medicine. She seemed burnt out and tired. It must be so frustrating to work hard constantly and never go anywhere or really change anything. It can feel a bit futile and pointless. But the reason she wasn't getting anywhere was because she didn't have us. Alienize may be our only hope at getting rid of the peacekeepers, so I wrote on a note saying 'Come to Pernenci in 30 minutes', knocked on the door, slipped the note under the office door and we all ran away, as we didn't want her to see us stalking her. This whole thing was childish but necessary, as we didn't know what security measures she had.

We all sat there waiting at Pernenci's, an Italian Restaurant in the Middle Levels, hoping she would take us up on her offer. Luckily, it was a weekday, so no one was really in the restaurant. We had the place to ourselves. We sat there for nearly an hour, but we all lost hope, as we knew that someone as important as her would visit nobody. Giving up, we all finished our glasses of complimentary wine and headed home. But then we saw the headlights of a floating car rushing past the restaurant window. It can't be! Was it her?

Then the ParliaCongresswoman entered the restaurant with a black dress with an official city flag on her collar.

The first thing Alienize did was to approach the Italian restaurant owners and greet them, as they seemed to know each other personally.

The couple greeted her. "Alienize!"

"Hello Marco, Hello Gabriella. It has been a while."

They talked for a couple minute, and then she asked, "Do you guys know who sent this letter?"

The couple pointed to our table, and she said goodbye to them and approached our table. *Oh my goodness, she was coming over.* We all did our best to look professional.

The ParliaCongresswoman then sat at the table, confused as to who we were and what we wanted from her.

"I got your message." Alienize was not an easy woman to fool. We had to maintain professionalism.

"Sit down. We have much to discuss."

Alienize was curious about our proposal, but she didn't look impressed. "Look, I am busy, so get to the point."

As she slowly began to get out of her seat, Ella cut in.

"Sit down and listen to us! We may be the only thing that can help your political career."

She sat back down. "Speak! And make it quick."

I explained to her my ingenious plan. At first, I thought I lost her, but she hung on to every word. I finished with a question. "Interested?"

I was a bit concerned. I thought she was going to get out of her seat, but instead, she directed the waiter, "Order us some pizza and some wine. We have so much to discuss."

After some glasses of red wine and some meatlovers' pizzas, she shared how she came from working as a waiter at this very restaurant to gaining a scholarship to study law and political science at a prestigious university in the Middle Levels. In exchange for her openness, we also shared our story, telling her about Yandan, the attack on WeapCo, the riots, the peacekeeping occupation and the use of social media to spread the message about the unjust occupation.

Shocked, the ParliaCongresswoman looked at us impressed. "Wow, you people have been through a lot."

"Will you help us?"

Alienize then picked up a glass of wine and thought over our proposal. "OK! But it is not going to be easy. Are you willing to take this fight to ParliaCongress?"

Now we were all excited and determined, and we all unanimously said, "Yes!"

"OK, come to my office tomorrow at 9.00 am." She then got up threw some cash onto the table, drank her last glass of red wine and walked out of the restaurant.

We all just sat there smiling at the victory we had achieved that night.

The next day, we all approached the office to find that it was completely different than it was last night. It was full of staffers, rushing and chatting on the phones. Then, Alienize came out of her office and greeted us. "Ella, Anna, Jacob and Edward, welcome! Please follow me into my office."

Alienize gave us a tour of her electorate office and then escorted us into the office. After entering her private office, she explained the political system in more detail.

"OK, politics is a two-party system, with the two main parties being the Monarchist Party and the Democratic Party. The Monarchist Party is a right-wing party that supports wars, free markets and lower taxes, whereas the Democratic

Party is a left-wing party that supports liberal ideas of higher taxes for the rich and more funding for social support."

I cut in. "Yer, we know that. We all watch the news. But how do we get peacekeepers out of our level?"

She nodded her head. "Fair enough. So most within the big party are bought by the defence industry, which includes key players like WeapCo and Wacco. So, to get the peace-keepers out of the Lower Levels, we would need to target the smaller independent parties and get them into power, like me. Independents are less likely to be bought by defence mongers and would give a chance, but it's not going to be easy."

I looked over at Edward, Ella and Anna. "OK, what do we have to do?"

"That's what I like to hear. The midterm elections are in a month. I think we would be able to get the bill onto the representative floor, but you'd have to play your part. We need all Lower Levels, as they are a decisive element in the next election that few people realise. If we can get the independents in the House and senate, we would be able to create a 'Hung Parliament' and thus get our bill passed into Parliament. Sound simple enough?"

We just looked at each other in confusion as to what she was going on about. Even Edward was confused by the plan, but wanting to know what we talked about, we all just agreed.

"Sure! Sound simple enough."

"Great! You all do your part, and this bill will easily get passed."

"Thanks!" We then proceeded to leave her office as she went on filing paperwork.

After leaving her office, we needed to gain supporters, and what better place to do it than the local pub. The local pub was where all the Lower-Level people would go after work or if they were unemployed. It was the most profitable business in the Lower Level and the only business to stay afloat in this place. However, it was also a perfect place to find Yandan supporters who had gone into hiding after the

WeapCo ambush. We all headed to the local pub. Ella and Anna talked to all their girlfriends from work and school, and Edward and I talked to all our former workmates, army buddies and friends from school. After buying them all so many drinks and hearing so many boring work and school stories, we told them all about our secret meeting down in the Sewer Levels. They were all a little bit reluctant at first and fearful of retaliation from the peacekeepers, but after some metaphorical arm-twisting, we managed to convince them all to join in the campaign.

Later that night, Anna, Ella, Edward and I did the usual avoid to the peacekeeping patrols and snuck into the Sewer Level, as we were ready for our meeting. Tonight, we were expecting to only have a small crowd, but to our surprise, there was a massive crowd. Almost the entire Lower Level showed up to support us. We weren't expecting this many people. Hell, we didn't think this many people believed in our cause, but they did. It goes to show that despite the peacekeepers' attempts to keep us down, they had failed. Now we had to seal the deal.

I stood up there and spoke.

"People, we have to act now to secure our future and get the peacekeepers out of the levels."

Unfortunately, I had no charisma and wasn't a natural-gifted orator like Yandan was, and I was beginning to lose the crowd. The people began to chant out, "Go back to work" and "Don't tell us what to do." My speech wasn't met with a positive reception.

One of the protesters screamed out, "That's what Yandan said, and he got our people killed. Why would we all listen to you?"

The crowd chanted in agreement, "Yea."

Then another person screamed out, "Haven't you got enough of us killed?"

The crowd then started booing and throwing stuff at me, as Ella, Edward and Anna all watched in horror. Anna couldn't stand there and watch me struggle anymore, so out of anger, she grabbed a shotgun and shot up into the ceiling of the meeting area and then went on a rant.

"Shame on you people. How can you all just cower like rats? I mean, did you all forget that they killed Yandan and are terrorising our community? They beat us, rob us, and we do nothing. Look, I know you are all hurt, and we are all suffering, but we need to remember who the real enemy is: WeapCo. WeapCo is terrorising our community using these 'peacekeeping' thugs because they want to divide us up. Are we going to let that happen?"

Anna managed to regain the crowd, as they returned to our side and screamed out in unison and support, "NO!"

I was honestly amazed at how quickly she turned the crowd around. She reminded me a lot of Yandan. It was amazing, but Anna wasn't finished.

"We cannot divide. We need to unite and vote not just to get rid of the invaders but to gain our freedom back. And the only way to do that is by taking it up with the government. So let's go up there and give the government a piece of our mind. Let's give our community a voice!"

The crowd then repeated what Anna said, "Give us a voice! Give us a voice!"

They all walked out the meeting area with their fists held high and chanting. We had done it. We had gained the community's support. Well, I shouldn't say 'we'. More like Anna did it. I was surprised and proud that Mum had that fire in her belly. She could have made a great politician. Still, it was going to be hard to maintain support, as people were afraid of the peacekeeping force. If this whole thing went south, the people would face the repercussions, and it could mean more people dying. But while it may be hard, if this plan was going to work, we needed to come together as a community.

Our campaign was in full swing, and everyone had their part to play. It was Ella's job to reach out to voters who did not attend last night's meeting at the local shops and supermarkets. Anna would hold secret rallies to spread the word for more support, while Edward reached out to the blue-collar workers in the industrial areas. My job was to reach out to as many people as possible through social media. I have to admit; I was getting used to this social media thing.

The first week was hard. No one outside of our community was listening to our message and our pleas. But within 2 weeks, people were starting to slowly turn around, as across the city, I could see poster signs saying 'Give us a voice' with graffiti art of the peacekeepers depicted in a not-so-pleasant light. Our voice of opposition began to grow louder and louder by the day, and more and more people were beginning to join our cause. Our campaign was starting to reach people in the Middle Levels; hell, even the Upper Levels were starting to notice our cause. Another bonus was that more stories were being shared about what had been happening under the occupation. The stories I heard were despicable, as I heard all sorts of stories about sexual assault, police brutality and even war crimes. Those were the least disgusting. Some of the stories keep me up at night.

The community pride in this place was astounding. Even in the face of legal tyranny, we grew nothing but stronger together. I even heard rumours that the Crypts and the Klan were joining forces to aid our cause. Eventually, it boiled up to the point that despite the backlash and heavy resistance, the community formed another protest. The protest started out peaceful at first, but it wasn't long before the peacekeeping force escalated the protests into violence by using live rounds and mustard gas. The peacekeeping force opened fire with military-grade equipment, killing dozens of people, of which I shared footage on social media. The Peacekeeper activity could no longer be hidden, as they were gaining worldwide attention from multiple cities. Even media companies were sending down journalists to attend the front line of the protest, which was a massive win for us.

In solidarity, the people from the Middle Level began peaceful protests of their own. Just like that, the peacekeeping force made another critical mistake. They began to attack people from the Middle Levels. It was OK to attack people from the Lower Level, but to attack people from the Middle Level, hell was about to break loose.

Social media was flooded with footage of the peacekeeping force attacking citizens, and people quickly took to media sites condemning the forces. Even politicians condemned the forces, and of course, governments from other cities used the protests to condemn our city's government. But the most remarkable thing to come from this whole mess was that for the first time, the class rift between the Lower and Middle Levels was disappearing, and the city was coming together in support of our cause. Yes, we still faced opposition from rival political parties, but we were definitely going to get our bill passed.

Unfortunately, the protests took it too far, as rioting got out of hand and police and military bases were burnt, vehicles and equipment were vandalised, soldiers and police officers were attacked, buildings and shops were burnt, and the city quickly turned to pure chaos. Businesses went into a complete shutdown, the markets took a nosedive, and the government was in complete disarray and shock. Unfortunately, all good things must come to an end. Support quickly flooded back to the peacekeepers, as social media was now flooded with people condemning our protests, and more reinforcements came down to gain control of the protests. Just like that, we were back at square one.

Oh well, it was fun while it lasted. Guess we would have to come up with a new plan.

CHAPTER 12

The protests were finally stopped by the peacekeeping force, and the city returned to its normal state. Unfortunately, it wasn't looking good for our case, as the riots had ostracised our cause, which couldn't have come at a worse time. Alienize was about to introduce a bill into ParliaCongress that would be revolutionary for our cause. The bill was known as the Give the Voice Act, which would give the people of the Lower Levels the power to vote in the next election, as in earlier elections, the Lower Levels weren't formally recognised, thanks to legal loopholes and a lack of awareness. But if we wanted to get future bills passed, we needed this bill to pass. This was our time to change the tide of power for our community.

Ella, Anna, Edward and I were all sitting in the electorate office watching on the Holonet News as the ParliaCongress session unfolded. Normally, ParliaCongress sessions took too long and were tedious, but for this one, we were on the edge of our seats. And when all hope seemed lost and we thought we were going to lose, success! The bill passed, as ParliaCongress roared into applause. We won! After the sitting, Alienize took Ella, Anna, Edward and me out for drinks to celebrate. After shooting a few rounds, courtesy of the ParliaCongress budget, she thanked all of us for the team effort.

"All right, everyone listen up!" We all stopped drinking and concentrated on Alienize. "This is perfect. Now our plan is on track, but while we may have gained a victory, we have to make sure not to slip. We cannot lose this election. If we lose this election, we lose everything. But tonight, we take this victory and celebrate by drinking!"

Spoken like a true politician. We drank until we couldn't drink no more. Boy, our heads were sore the next morning, but today was a new day. We had our moment to celebrate, and now we have to get back to finishing what we had started.

After recovering from my hangover, I gathered everyone around the dining room table, with the exception of Alienize, as she was back in her electorate office.

"All right, everyone, thanks for gathering around. Here is the plan that we have all agreed to. Step 1, get the peacekeepers out of the Lower Levels, and of course step 2, take down WeapCo. But first, we have to prepare for the upcoming election. The election was supposed to be this week but was pushed ahead another week due to the riots."

The peacekeeping patrols were back again, but they were significantly reduced to prevent any negative media attention, thank goodness. Because having fewer troops hanging around gave the community the chance to open up again, shops were open, children were playing in the street, and people were gathering and heading to restaurants again. This place was also beginning to feel like a community once again. But there was a scene that I had never seen before in this community: political gatherings.

I passed the street towards the old town hall where months ago, Yandan had preached to take down WeapCo. Now, the halls were full of election officials setting up the polling booths and getting ready for election night tomorrow. I could see crowd after crowd of people gathering to listen to independent candidates pitch their ideas and ideologies to people in the hope that they would cause real change.

It was amazing. For the first time ever, we felt as if we had a chance to voice our opinion in government.

After grabbing the medicine, I headed home to rally the gang. Now was the time to campaign. Ella and Anna went and preached alongside as many independent candidates as we could. The people responded to Ella because of her dad's influence over the community, and they responded to Anna as she was a natural-born politician and a figure in the community. So the girls had to be the face of the cause. Edward with his Upper Level knowledge was sent up to the Middle Level to rally as many people as he could to support our Lower-Level candidate. I did what I do best: Take to social media and spread more political anarchy. The gang and I were out all day and all night trying to spore up more votes for the candidates. It was tiresome, but it was worth it, as the big day came around: the midterm elections.

Today was our only chance. If we wanted these peace-keepers gone, we needed to win today. Just as Ella, Anna, Edward and I were heading towards polling booths, we wit-nessed the most disgusting display of intimidation I have ever seen. While waiting in line at polling booths with thousands of other people, we noticed that the peacekeepers were stand-ing outside the polling booths. The soldiers were armed with guns to intimidate voters into voting in their favour. It was unconstitutional and disgusting.

One of the soldiers turned to one of the random people standing in the line and said, "I will be checking your vote, so you better vote right."

What I saw today sank the peacekeeping force to a new low. They were engaging in political coercion by trying to intimidate voters into voting for the big parties. It was truly sick, but there was nothing I could do. All I could do was shake my head in disgust.

After entering the booth and casting my vote, I sat in the voting centre and watched the election result on the holograms they had on display in the voting centres. I sat on the metal reclining chair and watched as the people of the Lower Levels came in like swarms of locusts to a cornfield. It was amazing watching democracy at work, and despite the aggression from the peacekeeping force outside, the people were not deterred. In fact, it encouraged them to fight back even more.

I had done my part. Now that Ella, Anna and Edward had finished voting, we sat there watching the news until the polling places closed. The news was boring, as all it consisted of was a boring anchorman pointing to a coloured map with coloured polls, talking about numbers and statistics and predicting what would happen. Nonetheless, I couldn't wait to see the result of this election.

After watching the news for hours on end, I fell asleep until I woke up and the polling booths had all closed.

The polling booths were all deserted. Even the peacekeeping force had gone home for the night. The only people left were me, Ella, Anna, Edward and the polling staff. Nothing left to do, we helped them to pack up the polling booths and count the endless amount of ballot papers. We all helped until the results were finally all counted, and the news projected the results. At 12 o'clock, we all ran towards the holographic projectors to see the results.

The results concluded that out of 5,000 seats in the Lower House, the Monarchist Party had won 2,000 seats, and the Democratic Party had won 2,000 seats. But then the news that we had been waiting for all night came in. The independent candidates that we had endorsed had gained control of 1,000 seats in the ParliaCongress, which included Alienize winning back her seat. After hearing the results, we all let out cheers of joy and hugged each other in delight. Another victory! Our luck was beginning to change. We had created a Hung ParliaCongress, which meant that we could present more bills to ParliaCongress. Finally, we were a step closer towards getting the peacekeeping force out of our level.

Unfortunately, our independents didn't get into the senate, but we would cross that bridge when we got to it. Right now, we had won a victory tonight, so we celebrated. After the results were called, we all headed back home to party: another fun night of drinking and dancing to random hip-hop music. While in an intoxicated state, we all just sat on the couch, laughing and telling stories. We were even engaging with Edward, who we were hesitant to engage with because of his betrayal, and tonight, we were all in good moods. We told funny stories and shared war stories, but we also talked about what this victory could mean for us. After my alcohol buzz faded, I decided to go to bed, because tomorrow would be a new day for the Lower Levels.

Over the following week, not much had changed. After a week of sitting and waiting, the day had finally come. This was the day when ParliaCongress would vote on a bill to extend the peacekeeping exercises. I was hoping that the bill would get cancelled in ParliaCongress because of the multiple independent candidates coming from the Lower Levels. I was so excited to see this bill get killed in ParliaCongress and to have the peacekeepers finally leaving the Lower Levels. I walked up through the subway station with a spring in my step, singing a tune in my head. After stopping off at a little caravan coffee shop to quickly grab a cup of coffee, I headed into the CAP and entered the Capitol building to watch the session in progress. I climbed up the enormous stairs, sat in the viewing area and watched as all the ParliaCongress members sipped down their coffee and attended their seats.

Then the House Speaker stood up on the podium and said, "The five-hundredth session of ParliaCongress is now in session. Members from the Lower Levels have something to say!"

Then the independents all stood up, with one white man in a black suit saying, "We have, Ma'am. Today is the vote to extend the unjust, overused military exercise that is damaging my community and does nothing but waste taxpayer money, kill innocent citizens and destroy jobs. Please I beg you all, please end these exercises now!"

The independents and some members from the Democratic Party began clapping. I burst out in applaud. That was the interesting part. Now came the boring part. There came some nonsensical PR from the other side that was clearly funded by WeapCo. This whole tirade went on for 2 hours, but now came the moment of truth. Voting time!

The House Speaker then stood up again. "Voting is now open on the extension of the Military Exercise Bill."

She banged her gavel on the podium, and the members all rushed into a frenzy to vote on the bill. All 5000 members were focusing. Now I was interested, watching the monitor and witnessing all the votes be counted. The votes were flooding in!

The Monarchist Party all voted in favour of bill, all 2000 of them. The Monarchist Party were bought by WeapCo, the defence industry, gun companies and mining lobbyists, so it was no surprise that they voted for the extension of military exercises. On the other hand, the Democratic Party all voted to oppose the military exercise. But don't be fooled, they were voting against the military exercise not to save the Lower Levels but only to fund other projects that they wanted, such as free healthcare for the Middle Level or renewable energy projects that they had a stake in.

Now that the two major parties had voted, it was up to independents and Alienize. My heart was pounding at the prospect of winning, and for the first time in my life, I was confident that we were going to win. After a lot of thinking from the independents, they finally cast their votes. Out of 1,000 candidates, 500 remembered where they came from and voted against the military exercise. However, the other 499 members let the power get to their head and were obviously corrupted by WeapCo's influence and voted for the extension of the military exercise.

The ParliaCongress was at a standstill. It was a 50/50 split. The only person who could break the tie was the vote from one ParliaCongress woman, Alienize Lair. I was thinking, *Oh, we have this vote in the bag. I know for a fact that she is going to vote in our favour. I just know it!*

Then, she got up and said, "The representative from the Middle Level ..."

Here we go! Say it!

But instead of saying what I expected, she said, "... abstains her vote."

CHAPTER 13

"The representative from the Middle Level abstains her vote."

I was left in complete shock, and for the remainder of the session, I stayed in a state of disbelief.

"What had just happened?"

This whole plan came from her, and when it was time for her to step up, she cowered away. I was pissed. All that hard work and for nothing! We worked our assess off, slaved day and night to get those votes. We finally got a chance to have a say in government, just to have it wasted on another corrupt politician.

Because of the abstained vote, it was up to the vice president of American Division City to cast her vote. The vice president, a lady in her 40s, stood out of her chair. "The vice president votes in favour of the military exercises."

Because the vice president voted in favour, the bill was a pass and was sent to the senate, which I knew was going to be passed due to the majority of them being from the Monarchist Party. In essence, the peacekeeping force was not going anywhere. I was so furious that once the session ended, I stormed out of the building in fury and down towards Alienize's office.

I stormed into the office building, banging the door aside in fury, and screamed at the top of my voice, "ALIENIZE, HOW COULD YOU DO THAT TO US?"

Alienize came out of her office and gestured to me, "Get into this office, now!"

I marched into the office with fury and took a seat. "I demand answers for this betrayal."

"Look, I know you are angry—"

I gave her a dirty look and responded in disbelief. "Angry? I am furious! I mean, this was your plan. This whole thing was set up by you, and when the time came, you stabbed us in the back."

"Look, WeapCo has influence over my family, Jacob. It's not like I can just say no. What would you have done?"

"We would all have put our lives on the line to save our community. I mean, we looked up to you, and you promised us change, and what did you give us?"

Her expression then went from a look of concern to carelessness. "Sorry kid, that's politics for you."

That comment shocked me to my core. "So this whole thing was just about yourself?"

She just shrugged her shoulder. "See, now you get it."

"Congratulations! You're just another liar and hypocrite, just like the rest of them."

I couldn't take anymore, so I just stormed out of the office in disgust and disbelief. My anger turned into disappointment and sadness. I had let everyone down: my community, my friends, everyone. How could I face them after I encouraged them to fight back and put themselves in danger for some silly cause, just to lose and possibly make the entire situation worse?

Devastated, I started making my way back home but not before stopping off at the local bottle shop to pick up a bottle of whisky. This loss had really hit me hard. I thought that I could make a change, but I guess I was wrong. The world is just rigged against us. Guess I will be nothing more than some random hood rat, designated to die at the barrel of a gun or on some factory floor. To think Yandan and all those people died for nothing. What was the point of it all? I gulped down the entire bottle of whisky and drunkenly walked down the street, cursing the world and cursing Alienize for betraying us. I mean, how could she do that to us? We were so close to achieving a breakthrough. I get that she had to care for her family, but, oh what's the point of even trying anymore?

Depressed and defeated, I pulled up to the front door of the house and entered the living room.

Anna got up. "We lost, didn't we?"

I could barely look at her. "I am sorry."

I then walked up the stairs into my room and slammed the door shut. I began to throw random objects against my room, and I even flipped over my office table. I was mad and sad all at the same time, and I felt like I was a failure. Worst of all, I felt like a nobody.

The next morning was a wet and cold day; guess the weather manipulating machine was generating a rainy day today. I decided to head down to the shops to see how the community was holding up under the extension of the peace-keeping force.

It was just as I expected; it was back to the way it was when the invasion began. Constant patrols on the roads, drones patrolling the skies and peacekeepers beating up innocent citizens. It was so sad. I tried to make a difference, and all I did was make it worse. No more. I was giving up this whole crusade and just lay low. Heading down the street, I stopped by the local Armenian couple's shop and asked for a job. They offered me a job for long hours, dirt-low pay and no benefits at all, but they offered me free smokes, so I guess my luck was starting to turn around. For the next 10 hours, I bagged groceries, counted pennies for old ladies and took ridicule from the community for letting them down, coping names like 'sell-out' and 'false prophet'.

All of a sudden, two soldiers barged into the shop drunk. Those two soldiers were at the end of their shift, and they were drunk off their heads. They came into the shop, pushing over aisles, and as the Armenian man asked them to leave, they grabbed a beer bottle and flung it at the Armenian man, knocking him to the floor. The Armenian women screamed in horror, and all I could do was stand there and clench my fists. I really wanted to fight them, but I hesitated; it would only get me into more trouble. After my shift, I decided to swing by the local bottle shop and grab a bottle of wine. I felt useless, a failure, and the community hated me for it. I tried to wave to some former co-workers, but they snubbed me and pretended to ignore me, going as far as to cross the street from me.

After finishing the entire bottle of wine, I walked back home and up the stairs into my room, trying hard to maintain my balance and not fall over.

After stumbling into my room, now was the time I would begin the real drinking; I sat near the window, poured myself a glass of whisky, lit a cigarette and just looked out at the city, watching the military vehicles patrol up and down the streets. Sitting there, all I could do was sit, drink and laugh my pain away.

I heard a knock on the door. "Don't knock. Come in."

Ella entered the room in her pyjamas. "There you are. I was wondering where you are. Where have you been?"

I just sat there drinking. "Working. I got a job, as what else am I supposed to do down here?"

Ella looked at me shocked. "OK, but what are we going to do about getting the peacekeeping force out of the Lower Levels?"

"Nothing."

"So what, you are just going to give up?"

I snapped back at her. "Ella, look around! We tried to make a change, and all we have done is lose people and make the whole situation worse."

"That's no reason to give up." She then sat down next to me by the windowsill and grabbed a smoke, which I lit for her. In an empathic voice, she grabbed my hands. "Look, I get it. We hit a major setback, and yes, the system is against us, but we can't give up. We have to try again, because if we give up, then we have lost. So shut up, sober up, because tomorrow is a new day and a new chance to try again."

She then put out her smoke and left the room. After she left, I sat there smoking my cigarette and thinking. *She is right, now isn't the time to cry as the battle is still raging on every day.*

I threw down my cigarette and drink. Now was not the time to drink myself to death, because today I had a mission. But as I got up, I felt dizzy. Well, OK, maybe tomorrow. I then collapsed on my bed asleep.

The next night, after my shift at work, I snuck down to the Sewer Levels to get my suit. I didn't have a backup plan to get the peacekeepers out, but I knew where to start – taking down Alienize Lier.

After retrieving my suit and grabbing my grappling hook, I grappled up to the skyscraper overlooking Lier's office. I couldn't take her down with all the security guarding the office. I had to wait for when she was alone. For the next hour, I just watched her through binoculars, waiting for her to leave. I was so bored and felt like a creep just watching some politician in the rain in a sweaty, heavy body armour, but she had to pay.

The past hour felt as if I was back at work. The time was going so slow. All she did was answer phone calls and sign random papers. The only thing I was thinking was, *Come on, leave already.*

Then, the time finally came. All her staff had left, and she was ready to leave the office. But then, something caught my eye. A man in a black suit walked into the office and began to approach Alienize. This could be interesting. I needed to get a closer look. After shooting the grapple wire from the skyscraper, I used the gun to slide down onto the roof of the office. As I was sliding down the wire too fast, once I crashed down and hit the roof, I knew it was going to hurt tomorrow, but that wasn't important. Pushing through the pain, I stood near an exposed vent and listened closely. Getting a closer look through the vent, I saw Alienize sitting at her desk and the guy in the black suit talking angrily to her.

Then I heard the conversation. "Unacceptable. You promised us a guarantee that the bill would be passed."

I had to get this on film, so I grabbed my phone and began recording the conversation.

"When we funded your campaign, you were supposed to protect WeapCo's interests and ensure that these military exercises continued."

She betrayed us for WeapCo! She toyed with us for her own political gain.

"I got the bill onto the senate floor. What more do you want from me?"

The man in the black suit banged his hand on the desk. "On a close call! When you took those million dollars from us, you were supposed to convince all the independents to vote in favour of the bill, and only half voted for it!"

"Jacob and his team were more convincing than I thought. He managed to change their mind."

I couldn't see much, but from what I saw, Alienize was looking nervous.

"Are you telling me that some nobodies from the Lower Levels nearly put our entire operation at risk? What if they interfere with the bill in the senate?"

"I can assure you that these losers will not interfere with the bill. It will pass, and your investment will be saved."

The man in the suit then pointed to her. "You better deal with these people and get that bill through the senate, or I swear, your daughter won't live to see 10."

The man slammed the office door and walked out of the building and back into his limo. I was lost for words. She used us to settle her own personal debt with WeapCo, and not only had she put herself at risk but also her daughter. If I wasn't angry before, I was now.

Grabbing the grapple line, I swung through the window and smashed through the office.

"You false prophet! You promised the people of the Lower Levels change and freedom, but you only benefitted your own pocket!"

Alienize got up from her desk. "Jacob! Is that you?"

Out of anger, I flipped over her desk and pinned her to the wall. "We believed in you! We put our trust in you! Only to put it into the hands of WeapCo. How could you?"

Alienize's face went red from the lack of oxygen. "You don't understand. I cared about the cause, but they threatened my daughter, and I needed the money to get my political campaign off the ground."

I shook my head in anger. "And in exchange, you sold your soul." I then laughed and threw her to the ground. "But don't worry, once this voice recording goes online, your voters will see you for who you truly are. Say goodbye to your career."

I then walked out the front door, leaving Alienize on the floor.

After leaving Alienize's office, I stopped by the lair to drop my suit back. Once I opened the front door of the house, *whack!* I was hit in the head by a flying fist and fell down the stairs onto the concrete pavement. Then at the entrance of the front door stood the man in the black suit from Alienize's office. I quickly jumped up into a combat stance. The man in the suit with aviator sunnies clenched his fists. "Where's the recording?"

"In my pocket. Come get it."

The man laughed, took off his sunnies and cracked his knuckles. "This is going to be fun."

The man then charged down the stairs and tried to throw a punch at me, which I ducked and landed a rib blow. The man was big at 6'4" and 82 lb, so the blows didn't affect him at all, but they did make him angry. He kicked me with a front kick, which knocked me to the ground. Then he picked me up and tossed me onto the balcony. He marched up the balcony, but luckily, while lying on the floor, I picked up a beer bottle and threw it straight at his head. The bottle disorientated him, causing him to lose balance. This was my moment. I got up and jumped at him, landing a double kick into his chest, which caused him to hit his head on the pavement. I then managed to land two punches to his head with him lying there and bleeding.

"Where's my family?"

In response, he let out a sinister laugh. "You better look up."

I looked up and saw a peacekeeping soldier standing over me. He must have snuck up on me while I was busy fighting this guy. Before I could even respond, the soldier hit me with the butt of his rifle, disorientating me. Then two more soldiers came over as backup and started beating me up with batons. The man in the suit got up while I was lying there barely conscious and kicked me in the face, knocking me out cold.

I woke up, but I couldn't see anything; all I saw was darkness, and all I could feel was the blood on my face and the cloth of the mask over my head. Also, I could feel two hands grabbing me and dragging me along the floor because I didn't have the strength to stand up. I was scared out of my mind. What was going on? Where were they taking me?

I could feel the people pushing me onto a metal chair, and then they pulled off the cloth mask. It was night-time, and it looked like I was on the roof of a skyscraper. It was a very tall skyscraper too, as I could see the top of the border wall and the dome that kept out the radiation. It was another rainy day. Looking around, I saw two peacekeeping soldiers. Out of anger, I snapped at them, "You better let me out of this chair, or I am going to kill you all."

But the threat didn't work. One of the soldiers punched me in the head. "Shut up!"

"Do you know who you are messing with?"

A sinister laughter came from the doorway. I looked over, and it was John Speer, the CEO of WeapCo himself, standing there laughing at my bloody state.

"This guy got some fight in him. I expected nothing less from you."

I looked at him and smirked. "Well, well, well, look who it is, Lucifer himself."

John's face turned from confident to angry, and he sucker-punched me in the face. "You little smart-arse, you and your friends have been ruining my business."

"You're ruining my home and my community!"

John just shook his head. "I could kill you, and no one would even give a rat's ..."

"If you kill me, I die a martyr, and more people like me will rise up."

John smirked at me. "Martyr? That's rich coming from a ghetto rat."

I could have snapped back in anger, but I decided to give a smart-arse comment, "I may die, but you know what else is going to die? Your bill in the senate. I have friends who are determined enough and are willing to fight tooth and nail to see you destroyed."

At that, John laughed even harder. "I run a Billion-dollar company and have resources at my fingertips. Do you really think you can intimidate me?"

"Yes. While you may have money and influence, I have a voice and a standing in the Lower Levels. They look up to me. If my friends and I were to tell them not to buy any more guns from WeapCo, how much profit you would lose?"

John then snapped his fingers, and the two soldiers moved me to the edge of the building. "No, my hood rat friend, you will not say another word, and you will not die a martyr." He then came up close to me and whispered, "Because no one will listen to a man who committed suicide!"

He stood upright and kicked me in the chest. He kicked me with such force that it caused my chair to tilt back and fall off the skyscraper.

"Ahhhhh!" I let out a massive scream, as I began to fall 100 storeys to my death, tied to a metal chair.

I could see my life flashing before my eyes; spending time with Mum and Dad together as a kid, my first kiss with a girl at one of my friend's house parties, my time in the military and losing one of my friends in a firefight and driving down the street with my wife and son.

"Wait, wife and son?"

But before I could answer that question, snap! What a terrific stroke of luck! It turns out, the skyscraper next to WeapCo was undertaking construction, and my metal chair caught on the hook of the crane. How lucky is that? If that crane hook didn't catch me, I would have fallen to my death. While I may have survived the fall, I was still tied up in the chair, and I didn't know how to get down. The blood was rushing to my head, and looking down 50 storeys was giving me such vertigo. Also, the metal chair wasn't strong enough to hold my weight, and I could feel the chair slowly starting to lose its structural integrity. There was nothing I could do but look down and fear for my life.

But I had to respond, or I'd die. Focusing my mind, I had to figure out a way to get out of this. I observed the crane and realised there was a crane operator asleep in the crane control room. If I could get his attention, maybe he would let me down.

I wiggled and wiggled hard trying to free any part of my body, and yes, my arm may have gotten free. I looked through my pockets, and the only thing I could find was some loose change. I grabbed the coins and threw them at the window of the crane control room, but no luck. The crane operator didn't budge. What was worse, I heard a sound from the crane. The chair wouldn't last very long. I swung back and forth like a pendulum, trying to grab onto any piece of the crane I could, and with a stroke of luck, I grabbed onto a piece of the crane. But the chair's back snapped, and I was left hanging onto the crane piece. Luckily for me, the rope was loose enough that I could wiggle out of the chair, and the chair fell down to the ground.

I was still left there hanging from the crane, and my hands were getting tired and sweaty. I guessed this was it. This is the end of my story. This is how I die. I closed my eyes, and my grip finally gave way. Even with the adrenaline coursing through my veins, I couldn't hold on any longer. I began to fall and hoped that I would go to heaven when I finally stopped. I opened my eyes and looked up to see that the crane operator had woken up and grabbed my hand just as soon as I had let go of the crane. I then grabbed the crane again, and with our combined strength, he lifted me onto the crane and attached a vest and a harness around me. I breathed heavily and let out a sigh of relief. Thank goodness for that. I thought I was dead for sure. Luckily, that crane operator woke up in time, or else I would have been splatted all over the pavement.

The crane operator looked at me shocked. "What the—? How did you get there?"

I breathed heavily for a couple of minutes and looked up. "Let's just say I have had a bad night."

I then thanked him by giving him a handshake and made sure not to slip off the crane in the rain. Then I heard a strange sound; I looked up in the sky and saw a military drone. Guess John is pretty thorough and wanted to make sure the job is done. The military drone's red eye then spotted me and engaged, preparing to open fire. My only thought at this point was to run. I then unattached the harness and began running. The drone opened fire, shooting blue bolts across the crane and hitting the crane operator, causing him to fall 50 floors and crumble like a balloon of red water when he finally hit the ground – if I could see it, but I was 50 floors up; my sight to the ground was obscured by clouds.

I felt sorry for that man; all he did was help me, and now he was dead. But I couldn't stop now. If I did, his sacrifice would be for nothing. I quickly bolted to the elevator, as it was the only way down the crane. I pulled the lever, and the hyperlift shot me down to Ground Level at 50 m/s. After reaching the ground on the Middle Level, the first thing I did was kiss the ground. But I couldn't stop for long. The drone quickly spotted me on the ground and began descending down from the crane, shooting at me with blue bolts. I quickly ran into the construction site, hiding behind concrete slabs and using whatever I could to shield me from the blaster bolts. The drone got closer and closer to me. I had nowhere to run. I was trapped behind a concrete wall, and after looking around, I saw a sledgehammer. The drone's red eye peered through the wall, and using the sledgehammer, I smashed the drone in its big red eye. The drone then floated around disorientated and began flying around in circles. I went in for a final swing and whacked the drone's propeller, causing it to hit the floor. I finished off the drone with another hit by the sledgehammer.

I breathed heavily, catching my breath from the constant swinging. Now that I was on the ground, I had to get home and find Ella, Anna and Edward to make sure they weren't in danger. But I had to be careful. John was after me, and he had soldiers and advanced tech at his disposal. First, the drones recognised my clothes and face. Looking around, I noticed the puddle that was the crane operator. I knew this would be horrible, but I had to get rid of these clothes, or else the drone would recognise me. Approaching the puddle, I picked out the operator's clothes. After putting the clothes on, I threw my clothes into the puddle and walked out of the construction site.

I had to remain out of sight. The city was full of facial recognition technology and advanced surveillance technology. Also, the police and military were in the pocket of WeapCo. I had to get down to the Lower Levels quickly, as down there, the technology was so outdated that it would be the best place to conceal my identity. It was going to be tricky getting back down to the Lower Levels. The entire level, including the subway systems, was monitored with drones and peacekeeping forces. Now that WeapCo was invested in taking down the Lower Levels, they paid the military an extra billion to double the forces and even hired private military contractors. But I had to say I felt a little flattered; all these extra forces for me and my family. Guess we had really had an impact on John's profits. But another internal question was coming to mind. *How was spending all this money on peacekeepers and private contractors making the company a profit?*

Oh well, I guess their accountant would have to figure it out. I didn't have time to discuss business. I had to get back down to the Lower Levels. But then, another idea came to mind: power.

If I could manage to take out the city's power grid, I could disable all the technology long enough to sneak down to the Lower Levels without being detected by the surveillance technology. But there was only one problem. The power grid was powered by the nuclear reactor located outside the border wall in the wasteland. This was going to be tricky. First, I would need to get to the left end of the border wall. That's nearly a 5-hour trek from here, and to do that without getting caught was going to be impossible. But I had to start somewhere. Searching through the nearby dumpster, I managed to find a slightly torn-up hoodie, perfect for concealing my identity from outdated CCTV cameras. Then I began walking down the street, making sure to turn my face around cameras. I managed to steal a Halloween mask that was designed to resemble a sort of Mexican skull mask. Unfortunately, this outfit made me stick out, so even without the facial recognition not being able to detect my face, the CCTV cameras set off many red flags, alerting nearby police forces, and now they were after me.

Police patrols after patrols rushed around the city looking for me. I quickly had to get off the streets, but where would I go? I looked around for 5 minutes and found an electric charging station. The electric charging stations were like old-fashioned petrol stations, as they also acted as convenience stores. This is the perfect way for me to get my hands on vehicles, food and supplies. I didn't have any money to pay for these supplies, so unfortunately, I would have to resort to something I never thought I would do: rob. I sighed and felt guilty. I couldn't believe I had to resort to robbing, but desperate times called for desperate measures.

Looking around for a weapon I could use, I ravaged through the nearest abandoned shop and found a vintage Smith and Weston Model 610 revolver. The gun was a bit outdated but would do the trick. I barged into the charging station. "Give me your money!"

The 20-year-old console operator stuck his hands in shock. "Don't shoot. Please, here, take the money. Here, let me just reach for the cash."

The console operator was slowly reaching for the register, but then I realised, *They don't have a register. He would have to electronically transfer the money.*

The clerk then raised his hands to reveal a quadruple barrel shotgun, and *bang!* The clerk tried to shoot at me, but I ducked in time behind an aisle. He called my bluff. This gun isn't even loaded. *Blast!* The clerk then fired another round, blasting a hole through the shelf. I had to move, running across the aisle while crouching to avoid gunfire. I had got to the front of the counter. Looking at the aisle, I grabbed a can of soup and threw it into the air, which the clerk shot. Quickly, while he was reloading, I had to move. I got up and charged the front counter, and before the clerk could shoot up the reinforced blast shield covering the front counter, I jumped over, grabbed the clerk's gun and butted him with the back of the gun, knocking him out cold. I grabbed the gun and slung it over my back. Next, I grabbed a bag and started packing the bag with food, drinks and any spare shotgun shells that the clerk had stored under the counter. As I looked around, I noticed that under the counter, the red light was flashing. Oh no! The clerk had managed to click the silent alarm during the shoot-out. *I must get out of here quickly.*

However, just as I was about to leave the shop, three floating police vehicles pulled up to the electric charging station. Out of the cars, six police officers exited and began to hide behind the cars, pointing their guns at the shop.

The leading sergeant in the first car close to the shop demanded through the microphone, "This is Middle Level Police. Drop your guns to the floor and come out with your hands up."

I remained under the counter, because if I put my head up, they would shoot me at sight. Panicking, I quickly looked around to see if there was anything I could use. I decided to peak my head up just a little to see what the police were up to. I could see the leading sergeant signally to two of the officers with his fingers to enter the building. *I must act fast. Quick, Jacob, think! Think! Think!*

Then a light bulb clicked in my head. I knew just what to do.

The first officer approached the front entrance, armed with a police-issue blaster, and the second officer was sneaking behind the back, armed with a double-pump shotgun. Acting quickly, I went out the back and climbed up the top of the shelf, grabbing a bottle of Fanta-Cola and hiding on top of the shelf. Just as the female officer breached the backdoor, she began to scope through the room. I leapt off the top shelf, tackling her and knocking the double-pump shotgun to the floor, which disorientated the officer for a couple of minutes. As I got up off the floor, the male officer began to fire a few shots at me, also signalling on the radio for backup. *I have to get out of here.* Luckily, the female officer had given me a way out of the building. Moving quickly, I rushed towards the other side of the room and collected the double-pump shotgun before running out the door. Unfortunately, as I was leaving the building, the male officer managed to land a shot on me, with the blaster bolt piercing my left hand. My left hand now had a hole through it, which hurt like hell, but I had to push through. After leaving through the backdoor, I searched through the dumpster to find some cloth that I could wrap around my hand.

After nursing my hand, I quickly climbed up the maintenance ladder and onto the roof of the building. After reaching the roof of the building, the female officer exiting the building pulled out her standard-issue bolter blast and shot a blue bolt at me, which missed my head. She then proceeded to climb the ladder. After she got to the top of the ladder, I kicked her right in the hand, causing her to fall off the ladder and hit her head on the floor. It didn't kill her, it only knocked her out, but it was enough to enrage her partner. I crouched behind the 'charging station' sign to prevent getting shot by the officer outside.

The male officer climbed up the ladder, and I could see the anger in his eyes; he wanted to kill me. The officer rushed at me with blind rage, charging at me like a bull, and he managed to tackle me like a footy player. The tackle flung my gun across the roof of the station, and the officer began to strangle me. I was losing air, but the adrenaline was rushing through my veins, and not thinking, I grabbed the baton off the officer's utility belt, extended it, and whacked the officer across the head, which disorientated him for a second. The officer then reached for his firearm, when I hugged him like a bear, kicked him in his knee, and pushed him to the ground. The force of the impact caused his firearm to fly across the roof. I rushed to grab the shotgun while making sure to keep it low. After grabbing the shotgun, the officer grabbed his firearm and pointed at me. "Freeze. Drop your weapon!"

I slowly raised my hand and began to approach the officer. The officer demanded I drop my weapon once again. Once I was close enough, I turned the gun to the roof and shot a hole through the floor of the roof. The hole weakened the roof and caused it to collapse, with us falling through. The officer and I then hit the counter, landing on two different sides of the counter. The impact knocked the officer out, and while it didn't knock me out, it did hurt my shoulder really bad.

After I got up off the floor, another male officer barged through the station and fired a shot at me. I ducked, and the bolt hit the cigarette cabinet. I rushed towards the button that shot up a blast-proof glass within a second. The glass shot up just in time, as it managed to intercept three blaster bolts from the officer, leaving dents in the glass. I rushed towards the door of the counter to lock it just as the officer rushed to enter. The officer then kicked the door down, to which I responded by punching him in the head and pulling out his stun gun. *Zap!* The stun gun discharged two bolts into the officer's ribs, sending an electric shock through the officer, causing him to spasm on the floor.

I searched the officer's belt and grabbed car keys from his back pocket. My ticket out of here. After rushing out the back door, I noticed that there was nobody guarding the police car at the back. The sergeant must have gone inside. But just as I was rushing towards the car, the sergeant who was hiding behind the car door tackled me to the floor of the station. I karate-chopped the officer's neck lightly, which caused him to flinch back in pain, and it winded him for a while, as he gripped his throat in pain. I rushed towards the car, hopped in and powered up the car. But just as the engine started, the sergeant got up from the ground and charged towards the door of the car. Just as I was about to lock it, the sergeant flung open the door and tried to pull me out of the car. But I was determined not to get out of the car, so with as much force as possible, I kicked the officer straight in the chest, knocking him out of the car. I slammed the door and locked it.

Still, the sergeant wasn't backing down. He got back up off the floor and began to discharge his gun from the holster. I quickly pulled the gearshift to F for flying and flew away from the station. However, just as I was pulling out of the station, the sergeant fired three bolts at me towards the car while I was mid-air. The first two bolts missed me completely, but the last bolt hit the back window, shattering it instantly. One of the bolts just slightly missed my hand.

On the ground, the sergeant fired some more shots, but at that point, he was completely out of range, and the blast just went flying into the night sky. I looked in the mirror and watched as the sergeant put his gun back in its holster and began to call on his radio and rushed into the station to check the remaining officer's status. Now, I normally don't like hurting people, especially police officers, as they were people just trying to do their jobs. But I had no choice, as this was about survival. I had to focus on my mission and took control of the car and began flying to the power plant.

CHAPTER 14

The car just shot into the sky at a hypersonic speed, ducking and weaving through the skyscrapers and subway tunnels. Sitting in the driver's seat, I used the tablet in the car to set the car to 'autopilot' and plotted a course to the nuclear power plant.

I heard through the radio: "Attention all units! Attention all units! Be on the lookout for a stolen police car piloted by a Caucasian male in his 20s. He is considered armed and dangerous."

They probably knew my face and my identity by now, so I quickly had to look around for anything I could use. Looking through the glove compartment of the car, I managed to find a state-of-the-art first aid kit. I took the bandage off and saw the big hole in my arm; I could almost vomit. Opening the first aid kit, I sprayed the green foam into the hole, and within seconds, the nanites in the foam had repaired the hole. I could barely tell it had even been there. My hand was fixed, but my shoulder was still hurting. Unfortunately, there was no cream that would fix that up, so I searched through the first aid kit and found pain suppressor pads. After ripping off the backpatch, I placed it over my shoulder, and while the pain was still there, I could barely notice it. Now that my wounds were taken care of, I had to look for a weapon of some sort.

As I looked back at the blown-off back window, blue and red police sirens were trailing behind. I had to get out of there. Turning off the autopilot, I switched it to manual and quickly flew down into the Lower Levels. I had to lose them. I looked through the back window to find three police patrol vehicles tailing my trail with their lights flashing.

From one of the police vehicles, a microphone blared with the voice of a male police officer, "Descend your vehicle to Ground Level, or we will open fire!"

I began to panic. How was I supposed to get out of this one? I decided to try a risky manoeuvre by spinning the car around in circles clockwise. Two of the police vehicles followed and eventually crashed into each other, leaving behind a smoking, burning pile of rubble falling to the ground. But unfortunately, the police car in the back was smart. Its driver didn't follow his other colleagues through the circles and was still hot on my tail. One of the officers in the police car winded down his window, pulled out his gun and opened fire at my car. The first blue blaster bolt missed my car completely, but the second one hit my car's rotor, causing the car to spin out of control. I was starting to get dizzy. This car was about to collapse into the ground. Thinking quickly, I climbed to the boot of the car and grabbed the triple barrel shotgun and a parachute. I opened the boot and jumped out of the car. I fell for a few feet until I ejected the parachute and landed on the roof of an abandoned steelwork factory. I hid behind the roof until the police patrol disappeared. I had to get to the power plant. Though it may be pointless now, I still had to try.

I looked in the distance and saw the peacekeeping patrols heading towards the wreckage of the car. Drones and troops were going to be patrolling this area soon. I needed to flee ASAP. I climbed down the ladder of the steelwork factory and ran for it before the forces arrived. I jumped over barbed wired fences and ran through back alleys until I finally reached my house. I couldn't stay there long, because once John figured out that I lived there, the peacekeeping force would be targeting this place. So in and out I went, dodging the drones and patrols. I managed to slip through a broken window in the basement (thank goodness Anna never repaired that window) and landed in the basement to find a handgun pointed at my head.

I turned around to find Ella pointing the gun at my head. After she noticed it was me, she asked, "Jacob, where have you been?"

Ella then turned her head around and screamed, "Guys, it's Jacob. He's alive."

Then out of the spare room in the basement, Anna and Edward ran out and hugged me. "Jacob, oh, thank goodness you survived. We thought you had committed suicide."

I looked shocked and questioned that comment. "Suicide?"

Ella, Anna and Edward explained that two peacekeeping officers had come to our front door and told them that my body had been found on the pavement outside the WeapCo building. The officers then explained that John Speer had claimed that I barged into his office holding a gun and, out of depression, jumped off the WeapCo building.

I looked at them angrily.

Anna then went on to say that the peacekeeping force had gotten worse. They had begun to open fire on civilians, so out of safety, they had to hide in the basement.

"What happened to you, by the way, Jacob? You look like you have seen a ghost."

So I set the record straight how the peacekeeping force kidnapped me and took me to John and how he pushed me off the roof, where a crane caught my fall and that I had to battle police officers just to get here.

Ella, Anna and Edward looked at me shocked. "Jeez, what an ordeal you have been through. That bastard! How could he even try to do that to you?"

Ella cut in, "Wait, why are you going to take down the power plant?"

"Because taking down the power plant would take out the city's power grid, which would cause more anarchy and create more riots, which would divert the forces from the Lower

Levels to the Middle Levels. Also, WeapCo has surveillance everywhere, so if we can temporarily take down the surveillance technology, we can take down John and his evil company.

Ella then gave me a look of concern. "Jacob, I don't like this. It's one thing to rally people for a campaign, but to destroy the city power grid, that crosses a line. I mean, that's terrorism, Jacob!"

"For the greater good, Ella. I mean, people like WeapCo have taken everything from us. It's time to teach people like them a lesson that they can't push us around."

Ella had a scared expression on her face. "Jacob, listen to yourself. You're starting to sound like dad. Haven't we lost enough?"

My face then turned to anger. "Because your dad was right. If we want to change the world, we have to fight! We tried doing things the peaceful way, but now, we need violence."

Ella then looked at me angrily. "Who are you, Jacob?"

"I am a fighter. What are you? Fine, if you don't want to help me, I will do it myself."

I headed upstairs to my room, changed my clothes, grabbed a handgun and snuck out my bedroom window to avoid the peacekeeping patrols and the drones. After doing the usual of jumping fences and running across the back alleyway, I walked for 12 hours, stopping only to pee and eat. My body was sore, and I hadn't slept, as I had been on the run. I was so tired, but I finally made it to the entrance of the nuclear power plant. The entrance was embedded within in the wall itself, and there was a giant steel gate that led to a secret hypersonic train system that took scientists and plant personnel 2 hours away from the city to a radiation-sealed and heavily guarded power plant located within the wasteland. But thanks to the hypersonic train, it only took 2 minutes.

It was going to be tricky to get through the gate, let alone into the power plant, and I was wondering how I was going to get in there.

Then, I guess another stroke of luck hit me. A nuclear scientist who looked exactly like me, but with glasses, began to approach the gate. I noticed that around his neck, he had a security pass on. If I could grab that pass, I would be able to enter the facility. Just as the man was about to scan his pass, I threw a hoodie over my head and rushed like a cheetah, grabbing the man and throwing him to the ground. I didn't want to kill this guy, as he was an innocent scientist, so I used a sleeper hold on him that only knocked him out for a couple of hours. Then, stealing his glasses, coat and security pass, I grabbed his body and threw it into the trunk of an old, abandoned, rusted-out car. I approached the gate with my glasses and outfit on, scared that something was going to happen. Watching the scanner line trying to read the barcode, I feared that it was going to signal security and guards were going to come rushing out, but the scanner went green, and I heard mechanical clicks and warning sirens go off as the gates began to retract back into the wall.

I stood there in amazement as I saw into the compound how massive and modern the place was. After entering the compound, I could see scientists rushing around everywhere. In the middle of the compound was a hyperlink train, and every 15 minutes, I could hear the *woosh* coming from the train's speed as it left the station and the boom from the sound barrier breaking as the train left the station. I had to stay out of sight. I didn't know what sort of facial recognition or computer software they had in this place. While in costume, I kept my head pointed to the floor and only looked up when necessary. I looked around and noticed a group of scientists heading into a changing room; I decided to follow them.

Heading into the changing room, I noticed there were red hazmat suits hanging on hooks. The suits were required when heading into the power plant, as they were radiation-proof. While the plant was sealed off from the wasteland, the scientist was still around radioactive material that could be potentially lethal in the wrong hands. After putting on the suit, I hopped onto the hyperlink train and headed towards the power plant. It was incredible to see the wasteland, as I had never left the city, and I chose to sit close to the window to get a glimpse of the wastelands. Because the train was fast, I only got a brief look at the wasteland, but still, it was beautiful. The dark green skies and the emptiness of the land were somewhat tranquil. But there was something strange I noticed briefly out in the wasteland. It appeared to be a skeleton in a hazmat suit walking around with some wolf-like creature. What the—? But before I could get a better look out the window, the train pulled into the power plant docking bay. The train doors swung open to reveal a slightly old but still operating power plant comprised of two cooling towers, a PWR nuclear reactor that was contained inside a spherical containment building, and the entire power plant that was self-contained within a sphere, similar to the one that contained the city to keep radiation out. What I was amazed about was how far out this building was in the wasteland. I didn't think anything could survive this far out, but I guess I was wrong.

One of the things that concerned me though was the radiation in this place. Attached to the right side of my suit was a Geiger counter. It was giving off a reading of 100 mSv, which was somewhat safe, I thought; I didn't know that much about radiation. Oh well, I just assumed it was fine.

Not knowing too much about this place, I decided to follow the group of scientists as they were being led by the leading scientist, a white woman with glasses who was probably in her mid-30s. I followed the group but made sure to conceal my presence by remaining in the back. The group of scientists I was with were not scientists yet but nuclear physics students from some Middle Level university on a tour of the facilities. The leading scientists up the front of the group were talking about the history of the place – how it was formed 10 years before the formation of the megacities, and for the past 510 years since 2490, this place had been the main source of power, excluding the solar wind farms for the city. She also explained the function of each building, from the cooling towers to the water-cooling system. Then I saw it, the nuclear reactor core. The reactor core was held within the containment building, which I could see behind through reinforced glass. That is where I could see the core of the reactor. The leading scientists explained that the core was an early twenty-first century pressurised water reactor, though the core was said to be replaced with a high-tech fusion reactor by 3040.

The leading scientists went on to explain how electricity was generated. "The nuclear fuel in the reactor pressure vessel is engaged in a controlled fission chain reaction, which produces heat, heating the water in the primary coolant loop by thermal conduction through the fuel cladding. The hot primary coolant is pumped into a heat exchanger called the steam generator, where it flows through several thousand small tubes. Heat is then transferred through the walls of these tubes to the lower pressure secondary coolant located on the shell side of the exchanger, where the secondary coolant evaporates to pressurised steam. The transfer of heat is accomplished without mixing the two fluids to prevent the secondary coolant from becoming radioactive."

All this science talk was going straight over my head. While I found the science interesting, this topic was a bit above my education level. But it was fascinating to hear this talk about how the nuclear reactor works. As the lead scientist was going on about the reactor, I was starting to have my doubts about taking over this place. Ella was right, it was one thing to engage in some political fights, but to destroy something that brings electricity to the entire city was crossing a line. I thought for a minute and decided to cancel the plan and just head home, placing my gun deep in the pocket of my pants.

As I tried to sneak out, the door to the containment building opened, and two heavily armoured officers came rushing through the door, pointing their state-of-the-art automatic blaster bolt rifles at me. These officers weren't with the local

PD or the peacekeeping force; they were FBI special agents. They were different from the police, as local PD wore blue uniforms while these guys wore light green uniforms and were armed with exoskeleton suits, state-of-the-art blasters, calibre-proof body armour and automatic weapons. I was in major trouble now. If FBI special agents were after me, then I was definitely considered a terrorist now.

The officers screamed at me while pointing their guns, "Get on the ground now!"

There was no point fighting these guys. They were well-trained and well-equipped. With nothing to do, I complied, getting on the ground with my hands behind my back. One of the officers then came to pat me down while the other remained with his gun pointing directly at my head. The officer patting me down found the gun on me and threw it to the other side of the room.

"We picked you up through the facial recognition camera out the front of the gate. You didn't think you could sneak past us, did you? Punk! Get up!"

The officer then proceeded to zip-tie my hands before the other one came to pick me up off the ground. While I was glad they caught me just in time before I did something stupid, I couldn't get captured; a punk like me from the Lower Levels couldn't afford a lawyer, which meant there was a 100 per cent guarantee that I could get the death penalty. So as a response, I elbowed the soldier's neck, which caused the officer to flinch. But the second officer used his magnified strength from the exoskeleton and threw me across the room like a rag doll. The officer was careless, though. He threw me into one of the control panels. They both came over to me to pick me up and escort me out of there, but a loud red siren began blaring in the room.

The leading scientists and some other professional scientists came rushing into the room, while the FBI agents stopped in their tracks.

Oh, this can't be good, I thought to myself.

Then the lead scientists screamed out in panic, "Coolant pressure has been lost in the core!"

The FBI agents probably did that when they threw me into the console.

The team of scientists rushed and began typing rapidly to try to fix the problem. The FBI officers were too distracted by the disaster to notice me. Using the chaos to my advantage, I sneakily rushed out of the building with my hands zip-tied behind my back.

Over the speakers, an alert went out through the entire power plant. It was a warning system.

"The plant was going into meltdown, and everyone needs to get out now."

Oh no, I have messed up now. I quickly bolted towards the hyperspeed train, hoping to get out of there straight away, but so did everyone else. All the scientists, officers and university students were all dashing towards the train. The train was quickly filling up with people, and the train was packed like a can full of sardines.

The line to get onto the train was incredibly long. There had to be at least a hundred people waiting to get on that one train. I waited for a bit, but from what I had heard and what I had learnt from history, any accident involving nuclear activity is never a good sign, based on what had happened in the wasteland. The train was the only way back to the station; there was no other alternative but to break through the Dome and enter the wastelands. The wastelands were an incredibly dangerous and radiated place, but I guess so was this place, and I didn't want to burn in a radioactive fire. Guess I am going to have to enter the wasteland. After quickly running back into the contamination area, I grabbed a new hazmat suit and a metal pipe and broke a piece of the Dome glass and started running into the wasteland.

The wasteland was barely visible. The only thing I could see was the green fog covering the entire area. The ground was just like how it looked out the window, full of sand and dirt. I couldn't see anything. Even the railway tracks were invisible. The only thing I could see was the sky, which was completely dark green and thundering.

I better hurry back to the border wall, as the fog and the cloud indicate that acid rain is coming my way.

Another problem was worrying me. Looking down at the Geiger counter, I could hear a ticking sound on the counter. I noticed that the Geiger counter was climbing rapidly from 100 to 200.

I must run now; otherwise, I would die from radiation poisoning.

I turned around and started running straight, breathing heavily through the breathing apparatus.

It was kind of amazing being in the wasteland. I was probably one of the few people to have entered the wasteland in over 500 years. I ran for 30 minutes when I heard it. *Boom!* My heart just sank in its chest. I turned around and saw a giant fireball in the shape of a mushroom shoot straight up into the air. Luckily for me, I was out of range of the radiation, but the blast knocked me off my feet and sent me flying a few miles. Then I saw it, the border wall, but I flew straight into it. I hit my head on the border wall, and it caused me to fall to the ground. Luckily, the impact wasn't strong enough to kill me. While disorientated, I decided to lie down in the wasteland for a little bit, just until my head stopped hurting.

The hit to the head must be causing me to hallucinate, as now I was in a twenty-first century car. I was driving in a forestry area of some sort with "Lost Highway" by Hank Williams playing through the radio. On the passenger side was an African American female who looked to be in her 20s. I had never seen this girl in my life, but she did seem to know me, as she was talking to me about all these random things, about how she was turned down being a sergeant because of that bitch Rosanne, and whatnot. I looked down at my own self, and I was wearing a blue tuxedo.

Wait, that girl does look familiar, but where do I know her from?

The female then leaned over and gave me a kiss on the cheek. "Don't forget, this banquet is important for me and my career, so boys, be on your best behaviour."

Wait, boys?

I looked in the mirror and saw a young 10-year-old boy sitting in the back seat. He then spoke, "Mum, can we stop off at McDonald's after the banquet?"

"Maybe, if you are good."

I was about to say something, but then I heard a sound. It was the sound of the Geiger counter. It informed me that the radiation was increasing. Hearing the sound, I snapped back out of it and woke up back to reality.

I looked down at the Geiger counter to see that the radiation had climbed to 1,000 mSV. *Oh no,* I thought, *I must get out of here now or I am going to die.*

I looked around and saw an old maintenance ladder built within the wall. It must have been one of the original walls used during construction. I jumped into action and began climbing the ladder. It was incredibly long and old, and there were no safety features, so if I fell, I would die. I had to climb fast. After reaching the halfway mark, my head started to feel dizzy, and being incredibly high up, I was beginning to suffer from vertigo. My entire body was shaking and becoming stiff, but I had to persevere. I used all of my strength to keep climbing. After climbing 100 feet, my body was vertically dead. The ladder snapped but was still attached to the bolt.

I guess this is where I die.

Just as the ladder was about to collapse, an air defence technician noticed me. He rushed to my aid, offering me a hand that I grabbed just before the ladder collapsed and fell to the ground. He used all of his strength to lift me over the wall and looked at me in amazement.

"What the hell are you doing up here?" he asked.

I took a glimpse over the border wall, and through the Dome glass, I got to see the city. I made it, but what was more incredible was the sight of the city from atop the border wall. Seeing skyscraper after skyscraper, I felt like God looking down at His creation. But what captured my sight was the massive dome that covered the entire city, and in the middle of the dome was the weather-regulating machine. Because the world was radiated, and the weather was too harsh outside the walls, the weather-regulating machine was necessary. It was a fascinating device, as the machine artificially generated weather to make the city more sustainable. Plus, it decontaminated oxygen from the wasteland so that it was breathable within the dome.

I could sit there for hours and watch it go; it was truly remarkable, as it was currently generating a storm with the machine, generating gallons upon gallons of rain from nothing but thin air. Seeing it pour down onto the city was a once-in-a-lifetime opportunity.

After looking out through the dome for a long period of time, my nausea kicked in, and I collapsed onto the floor of the border wall and began to vomit. Guess I wasn't over my vertigo … or was it something else?

A nearby defence technician rushed over to help me up. "You all right, mate? Here, let me give you a hand."

The defence technician then gave me a hand and helped to lift me off the floor. He reached into his pocket and scanned me up and down with his radiation detection device. "You might have some radiation poisoning. Here, let me get you to the sick bay."

The only problem was that this was a defence facility. If they took me to the sick bay, the military would report me to the authorities.

"No!" I screamed. "Just get me back to the Ground Level."

"OK, I will get the elevator."

He then flung his arm around my shoulder and carried me to the sick bay, but I had to stop him as I had to get one last look at the Iron Shield Defence System. The Iron Shield Defence System was a high-tech, state-of-the-art defence system costing over $100 billion to create and $1 million a year to restock. This machine was an air defence system, rocket launcher, mortar, and early warning detection system all in one. Not only could it defend against short-range and long-range rockets, artillery shells and missiles but could also act as a defence against a ground invasion from opposing cities, primarily by firing rockets at tanks and other military vehicles, while the mortar fire took out ground forces.

There had to be at least 10 of them scattered across the entire border wall that provided a 360-degree defence. On top of that, there were 10 military-grade drones guarding each of the iron domes.

The air technician then dragged me along the ground and put me onto the elevator. As I looked at the wasteland, I saw something that shocked me to my core: the nuclear power plant was now in ruins, and all that remained was a crater. All those people on the train, gone! The power to the train line was cut, which trapped all the people inside the power plant. My goodness.

Vroom! The elevator shot down to the Ground Level at the speed of a bullet, but I really didn't care. I was in complete shock and dismay at what had happened to the power plant. I was physically destroyed and could barely move at all. I didn't know if it was the radiation poisoning or the PTSD from killing hundreds of people.

I walked down through the streets of the Lower Level, crawling on the dirty ground. In the artificially generated rain, I collapsed in an alleyway by the side of a dumpster. My heart was pounding out of my chest, and my head was rushing around in circles. I could hear a loud ringing in my ear from some unknown device. I didn't know what that sound was, but all I knew was that it was painful as hell. However, what was even stranger was that I heard a voice call out to me.

"Jacob, is the treatment working?"

Out of an unknown subconscious reflex, I simply blurted out, "Dr Moon."

Then I snapped out of it, as I heard military vehicles roaring towards the power plant. Vehicles were occupying the streets and the sky, as they all rushed towards the scene of the incident. The walk home was bleak. The good thing was that all the military forces were at the entrance of the Hypersonic Station, so I didn't have to worry about the peacekeeping force. But it was a dark walk home, as the wind farms didn't work at night, and with the power plant out of commission, there were barely any lights or power working anywhere. While I had achieved my mission, I wished I hadn't, as I couldn't stop but feel bad. I mean, I killed them. All those people. I had become a murderer.

I had never seen the city this dark. It was kind of creepy in a way. The people of the Lower Level were taking full advantage of the darkness and the lack of the peacekeeping force by doing what people did best during times of complete anarchy: commit crimes. Storefront after storefront was shattered, and people were rushing out in all directions with all sorts of items, not that there was really anything valuable down here anyway.

During the chaos of the night, I even witnessed the Armenian couple's shop that I used to work at being robbed by some unknown assailants in black hooded masks. The group had run away with food and drinks of all sorts, and the windows of the shop were smashed to pieces, while the couple just looked out in horror. Such a shame. They were decent, hard-working people. I should have gone over there and helped them, but I was too sick, too shaken up and too tired to do anything. I went home instead.

I just passed through the burning city and watched as all the once-peaceful community members turned into animals. But it wasn't just the Lower Level that was suffering that night. The Middle also went into a complete frenzy. The Middle was experiencing heavy rioting. Cars were burning, shops were vandalised, and police clashed heavily with protesters. The rioting in the Middle Level was worse than in the Lower Level; it was so bad that they had to transfer the peacekeeping force up to the middle, which rarely ever happened. What was even rarer was that the higher class were also participating in the anarchy. The city was coming apart at the seams, all thanks to me.

I walked up the stairs to my house and was about to unlock the front door with my keys when Ella violently opened the front door and began to scream at me, her fingers pointing. *"Did you do it? Did you kill all those people?"*

I was speechless, and I just stood there.

"A thousand people you killed, Jacob, and for what? Your silly pride?"

"I didn't mean to kill those people, I swear."

But that didn't defuse the tension at all; in fact, I think I may have made it worse.

"Well, congratulations. A thousand people have died, the city has gone up in flames, we are without power, and you have become my father."

Ella couldn't even look at me anymore. She stormed down the stairs.

"Ella, wait!"

"Stay away from me!" She stormed out the door and back into the streets.

I felt like an absolute disgrace. All I wanted to do was help rebuild my community and my home, but instead, I had become a terrorist and a failure, while John Speer sat there in his mansion probably laughing at me.

I entered the house to find Edward and Anna sitting there, barely looking at me or acknowledging me after the awkward encounter with Ella. With nothing better to do, I headed upstairs to my room and just sat near my windowsill. I had a pounding nausea and a sore head, but still, I just sat at the end of the bed thinking, *What have I done?*

It was moments like these when I wished my father was there. I mean, yes, he may have been a drunk and an abusive bastard, but when I was younger, he was the voice of wisdom. One thing he said to me that stuck with me my entire life was when I was fascinated with superheroes. He said to me, "Son, costumes, superpowers and money don't make you a hero. It's your deeds, generosity and sense of community and compassion that make you a hero."

My dad, when he was in a stable mind, taught me some valuable lessons that I could carry on into my adulthood. Yes, while they were brief, they were valuable. I could never forget one moment when I was 10 and I had accidentally kicked my mother's cat. Instead of hitting me, my dad escorted me downstairs and gave me a can of tuna. Then he told me to feed the cat the tuna, which I did, and he told me to pat it, which I did. The cat rubbed up against me and purred at me. My father sat me down and put his hand on my shoulder. "Son, with a little love and a little bit of time, all wounds can heal."

After smoking my cigarette and downing my whisky, I threw up into my wicker basket and went to bed to hopefully sleep this whole thing off.

The next day was no better. The city was falling to pieces, as all the levels were fighting with the National Guard, the peacekeeping force, the police and, now thanks to special orders from the ParliaCongress, the military. The entire city was now under martial law. Buildings and businesses were burning at the scenes. The government was scrambling to save face, using any PR statement they could to save votes and pretend they were on the side of the people. Even the president came out and called for peace. Meanwhile, the markets were in free fall, and rival cities thought they could take advantage and fire rockets at the city.

It was anarchy, and everyone was losing, except of course for WeapCo. Not only were they supplying weapons to the military, upper class and middle but had also set up mobile gun shops in the Lower Level. WeapCo was making money over fist, and the city was burning, all thanks to me. I felt like a fool. I was no hero. My friends had abandoned me. My family couldn't even look at me. And my enemy, WeapCo, had won the war both financially and morally.

Over the past 3 days, I fell into a deep depression. I had been depressed in my life, but not like this. All I could do now was drink and sleep. I could barely keep my eyes open anymore, and I was done with life in general. This whole system, the whole city, I was done with it all. Time to go. Saddened, I decided to kill myself.

I walked down the stairs, passing Anna, who could barely look at me, and Edward, who – even though he had betrayed me – still could barely look at me.

After walking out of the house and onto the street in the rain, I was planning to jump off one of the skyscrapers and end it all. But as I was walking down the street, my last bit of will kicked in, and I decided to stop into one of the local chapels in town. I walked into this old brick chapel with a cross on the top and surrounding the chapel were these mega-skyscrapers, which were a stark contrast, as the modern, complex skyscrapers encompassed this small, rustic brick chapel.

Walking into the chapel, I could see glasses depicting Jesus and the Virgin Mary. Inside the chapel were wooden chairs, and in the front of the room were wooden tables. At the front of the chapel was an altar that was covered in white linen and lit with candles.

I had never been to church before, so I just sat down in one of the wooden rows of chairs and pretended to pray like I knew what I was doing, but I just looked like an idiot. I was thinking to myself that this whole thing is useless. But then I heard the thump, thump of boots treading on the wooden floorboards, to which I turned my eyeballs sidewards to see a blonde-haired woman dressed in a white habit come and sit next to me.

At that point, I turned my head fully around, and the blonde woman smiled at me. "What's troubling you, my son?"

I tried to keep my composure, but I exploded into tears from the guilt of what I had done, for which the minister hugged me and comforted me.

The minister and I then got up from the chair and started walking around the church's artificial garden, and I confessed it all – how I accidentally caused the power plant meltdown, killing innocent people, and how I let my hatred and anger cause me to withdraw from my relationship with my family, friends and community. I then turned and asked her a simple question. "What should I do?"

The minister, instead of looking at me in disgust, looked at me and smiled.

"Oh child, you are of a poor soul." She then patted me on the back and told me her story of how she became a minister.

The minister – her name was Alissa – was originally a prostitute who became addicted to crack cocaine, until one day, her pimp kicked her out, and she wandered around the city, hopeless and in disappear, until she sought refuge at a local church. It was through the church that she managed to break her addiction to Coke and became a born-again Christian. It was through her long and hard journey that she managed to complete a theology degree and rebuild her life as an ordained minister.

She then turned and looked me in the eye. "You see Jacob, you are human, and you need to forgive yourself, but you also need to be willing to forgive others? John, yes, may not be a good guy, but if you don't forgive him for what he has done to you, it will destroy you inside and cause you to destroy yourself." Alissa then quoted to me a Bible quote from *Colossians 3:13:* "Bear with each other and forgive one another if any of you has a grievance against someone. Forgive as the Lord forgave you."

I looked at her and thanked her for her time and walked out of the gates of the church and tried to contemplate what she had said to me. Forgive John? He kidnapped my family, tortured them, killed my friends, destroyed my community and killed thousands of people in this city and around the world. And what? I had to just forgive him? Screw that.

Also, how the hell could I forgive myself? I had killed so many people. What's worse is that I didn't even know the exact number of people I had killed, which was scary. But I had to try to think about what the minister had said to me and try to forgive myself. I decided to head down to the Sewer Level and do some soul-searching.

As I was crawling down to the sewers, the entire Sewer Levels were flooded, which had never happened before. These sewers were built to hold the equivalent of a river down there. Even my hangout area, my suit and all my equipment were completely underwater. I wasn't worrying about soul-searching anymore. Instead, I was curious as to how long it had been raining in this city, as it had got to the point that it had flooded the entire Sewer Level. It was raining when I fell from the tower and also when the power plant exploded. Hell, I saw the weather machine generate the rain, and it has been raining today. I better go investigate this, because the weather machine was supposed to prevent the weather from being too constant.

There was only one place that I needed to go now, and that was to the city's water reserve. This was a massive water dam that provided the city with fresh drinking water. There was no way in hell that it could possibly flood, but what I saw shocked even me. I headed up to the water reserve to find it at full capacity, which was supposed to be impossible. But to my surprise, it was at full capacity and was on the verge of overfilling. What scared me, even more, were the cracks in the dam wall. And they weren't small cracks but massive ones. Now, I know I don't have an engineering degree, but dams aren't meant to have cracks in their walls.

Oh no! This isn't good. The dam was already at full capacity, and it was still raining. If the rain didn't stop now and the dam broke, it would cause a flood in the Lower Levels. I needed to go talk to the defence technician about the weather machine and tell him to turn it off. But before I left the dam wall, I saw a plaque on the wall of the dam, and it read: "This Dam Wall was constructed by Devil Gates Construction, a Subsidiary of WeapCo."

WeapCo! Why am I not surprised? I needed to investigate further, so I snuck into the dam and confronted a construction worker, who was just sitting there with his steel lunchbox and eating a sandwich.

I asked him, "Is the concrete secure? There seem to be some cracks in the walls."

The worker looked at me like an idiot and gave a slight laugh. "Ha, concrete. You're kidding, right? This place isn't made of concrete. No, the big bosses are too cheap for that. They just used some fake concrete that they brought off some local company. Pretty ingenious, if you ask me."

I stood there shocked. Wait, this dam isn't made with real concrete? But if it is not made of real concrete then?" I paused a minute more to think, then I panicked and thought, *Oh no, this Dam is coming down.*

Time was of the essence. I had to act fast. Out of instinct, I ran towards the town to warn the people of the upcoming disaster.

When I arrived in the city, the people were just rioting in the streets, smashing buildings and fighting each other. I jumped on top of a car and screamed to the people to listen to me, but I was met with no response; they all just went about their business.

I screamed a little louder, "Hey guys, I need you all to listen to me!"

There was barely a response from the crowd. It was hard to hear over the chaos unfolding around me. This time, I had to scream from the top of my lungs. "LISTEN TO ME!"

Now I had their attention, and within a matter of seconds, the crowd of people turned around to face me.

"Now that I have your attention, we need to get to a higher ground. It is not safe down here."

But the people were not willing to listen to me, as one woman cut in, "Why should we listen to you? It was you who got us into this mess with you and your family's silly crusade."

Then an older lady cut in. "Yer, Mr Righteous. If it wasn't for you and your criminal friends, we wouldn't be in this mess."

Then other crowd members joined in, jeering at me. The comments soon got mean, and they started screaming out, "Thanks for killing our friends, you jerk!"

The people were no longer listening to me, and to be honest, I didn't blame them. I would be angry too, as we promised them change, and instead of giving them change, we only further escalated the situation.

Then, an emergency Holonet was broadcast over every hologram projector. *Thank goodness, finally, I had some evidence telling my side of the story.*

But no, that was not what the Holonet projection was for. Instead, the broadcast was from the Department of Homeland Security. All hologram projectors in the nearby area flashed red, and then a message appeared on the hologram: 'Attention, people! Attention, people of American Division City! There is an escaped convict on the loose!'

Oh, this could not be good! I thought, as I felt a rush of anxiety coursing through my body. *Not now! Not when the dam was about to collapse and this entire level was about to flood.*

"Former Sergeant Jacob Turner, age 27, wanted on charges of theft, grand theft, robbery, assault, assaulting four police officers, damage to property, fraud, conspiracy to commit terrorism, grievous bodily harm, mass murder, resisting arrest, conspiracy, trespassing, murder, damage to government property, entering an unauthorised military zone, entering the wastelands without a permit, possession of illegal firearms, political espionage, crime against the environment, terrorism and treason. He is considered armed and extremely dangerous and is wanted dead or alive for a reward of $1,000,000 in crypto.

Suddenly, the crowd all turned away from the Holonet broadcast, and they all stared directly at me like a pack of hungry hyenas who had just spotted their prey. Then like a scene from a zombie movie, the crowd swarmed the building I was standing on as they began to approach and climb from every side of the building. I had no way out of this mess. I looked around to hopefully find a way out, but there was none; my luck had run out.

Then at least a hundred people started crowding me and kicking me to the floor. I was hurting all over my body, and I could feel every hit. I could feel the crowd throwing me off the roof onto the ground. My mind was in a daze, and I could hear that strange voice calling out to me, "Jacob, Jacob, you there?"

The crowd continued to pelt me with kicks and punches, until a boom rang through the air. I could only get a glimpse through the legs of the different people. However, in my bruised state, I could make out a shadowy figure holding some sort of object approaching me while it was pouring rain. The people moved to one side as she approached closer and closer. I could not keep my eyes open for long, and I collapsed into a state of unconsciousness.

I was breathing heavily, but my vision was still a blur to me. Slowly, I started to regain my vision, and I was back at my home. I heard a voice call out from me in the kitchen. "Rough night?"

I knew that voice; as I shot my head up quickly, I saw her. Alienize!

She had saved me from the crowd, but she wasn't looking like herself. She looked run down, with her suit all creased and ruined. Also, her face was a complete mess, with tears running down her face. By the looks of her, she was drunk.

I looked confused as hell at what she was doing here. She was sitting at my kitchen bench drinking a glass of Hennessy with a half-empty bottle next to it and a single-pump shotgun lying on the table.

"I guess you could say that. What are you doing here?"

She then let out a fake smile. "Same as you, I guess, barely trying to survive this whole carnage in this mess you created."

I was still puzzled by this whole thing. "How do you know where I live?"

She then let out a small smirk. "Well, City Watcher, after our small little encounter inside my office, I tracked you down, thanks to the help of a few connections from the CIA, and I managed to gain your address."

I began to pick myself up from the living room floor. "Well, thank you for saving my life, I guess."

Then the mood changed. Alienize let out a small chuckle. "Oh, don't thank me just yet. You see, when you encountered me in that office and posted that video online, I lost everything. I lost my voters, I got impeached, I lost my career, I lost my daughter, and thugs from WeapCo are chasing me down for money. Now I have nothing! I am homeless and living on the streets.

I looked at her blankly. "Serves you right for screwing us over."

She then nodded in agreement. "Maybe. But do you want to know something? The world isn't a fair place. It is a mean and cold place, and I am a mean and cold person who will do anything to get what I want."

My sympathy went out the window for her. "Well, bully for you!"

Alienize downed the glass of Hennessy, and her eyes stared directly at me with lustful anger. "The only reason I saved you from that mob was so that I could kill you myself for what you have done to me."

I stood up. "Yer, well, I would like to see you tr—woah."

My speech and my balance started to fade, and I collapsed onto the floor again, barely able to move or speak.

She then laughed, got up from the table and began loading her shotgun with a single shell. "I drugged you while you were unconscious. Don't worry. you will be dead long before the drugs wear off, anyway."

Alienize began to walk into the living room where I was lying on the floor, barely able to move or speak. "I woke you up so I could see the fear in your eyes when I kill you." She then pulled the choke on the shotgun and pointed it directly at my head. "Goodbye, Jacob! Once I am finished with you, your friends are next."

Bang! I heard a shot ring out, and out of reflex, my eyes quickly shut, and I could feel blood splatter over me.

I kept my eyes closed and waited for my body to shiver from the bullets. But there was no pain. In fact, I couldn't feel anything. I open my eyes, and in front of me, I could see Alienize looking down at the bullet hole in her chest. Her face went white, and the wound began to bleed out. She then collapsed on the floor dead. I turned around to the staircase to find Edward standing on the staircase holding a handgun in his hand with the barrel still smoking from it.

Edward then turned to me and ran down the stairs. "Jacob, are you all right? I didn't even hear her come in."

He rushed to me to lift me up off the floor. I shrugged Alienize's dead body off of me, but I was still drugged and a little bit dazed and sore. I still couldn't stand. "Boy, you look the worse for wear."

"No kidding, Sherlock. Where's Anna and Ella?"

"At the gun shop with Ella."

I smiled for a bit, probably due to the drugs, but then my mind snapped back into action, as the drug started to wear off and I remembered that I had to warn people about the incoming flood.

"Edward, the dam wall is about to collapse. We need to warn people."

Edward thought I was still drugged, as I was rambling like a madman. "Jacob, I didn't hear a damn word you said."

I sighed. "But Edward!"

"No, Jacob, you need to stay here, because everyone in this entire city wants your damn head."

"Edward, the dam wall!"

"No, Jacob. Look, I don't know why you think the dam wall is going to break, but for your own safety, we need to go into hiding."

Suddenly, a Molotov cocktail went flying through the window, and within seconds, it splashed lit fuel all over the living room, and the entire room went up in flames. Edward tried to put out the flames, but it was futile as the house was pretty old, and the living room just went up like a dried-up Christmas tree. Instead of worrying about some old house, Edward and I just ran up the stairs, hoping to escape the fire. We went into my bedroom to find that the entire house was surrounded by people who were out for my head. Downstairs, I could hear the front door being kicked in and windows being smashed by objects.

Edward turned to me. "Jacob, how are we going to get out of here?"

It was hard to think, as I was still dazed from the drug, but I had to try, else we would die. There was only one way out. It wasn't safe, but it would have to do. I signalled to Edward. We lifted my bed and pulled out a handgun, opened the bedroom window and began to open fire on the crowd, not to hurt them but only to scare or disarm them. After the crowd backed off a little, Edward and I crawled out on the window ledge and onto the roof of the house.

Yep, standing on the roof of a burning building. Good move, Jacob! Now we are stuck on a building that is going to implode on itself within a matter of minutes. Smart move, Jacob.

I could literally feel the heat radiating off the burning building, and I could see the smoke rising from downstairs and out through the wall. But what was worse was Edward and I had nowhere to go; people surrounded all angles of the building, and there was no way to jump onto the nearby rooftops without falling and breaking something. Edward and I were quite scared, and we knew that there was no getting out of this.

Out of fear, Edward turned around to me and hugged me. "I love you man. Sorry for trying to kill you."

I hugged him back, as I also thought we were going to die. "Love you too, brother."

We just stood there and hugged while the entire house began to burn down. Then another miracle happened. A warning siren ran out through the city.

"Attention, citizens of American Division City. This is your government broadcasting an emergency warning announcing the commencement of Article Four of the Emergency Response Act. I repeat Article Four is in effect. A class four (natural disaster) emergency is imminent. Please evacuate to the tallest building in the area and follow directions from government officials. Your government thanks you for your cooperation."

After hearing that message blare out through the city, people began screaming and scattering all over the place, trying to get to safety and completely ignoring us.

It looks like my prediction was correct, but I was too late to warn them. The warning did provide enough of a distraction to make the people completely forget about Edward and me.

Just before the building collapsed, we jumped onto the ground. Now that the people were gone, it was much safer. And just our luck too, as within minutes, our house collapsed into a burnt pile of rubble. It was a sad sight to watch our house go up in flames. I had grown up in that house. My dad and mum fought hard to keep that house. It was the only thing in my life that was constant, and now it was gone!

Edward then signalled to me. "Come on! We must reach Ella and Anna at the gun store."

But as we walked on the sidewalk, Edward and I both looked at each other as the Lower Level was filling up with water from the Sewer Level. It was going to be a massive problem, and it was just a bad omen for what was to come.

Edward and I rushed down the nearly flooded street to the gun shop, when we heard coming from a loudspeaker: "Due to technical difficulties, we advise all citizens to evacuate to higher levels."

That's not good. The machine started generating heavy rain and wild winds to the point that it was generating its own artificial hurricane, which was only going to accelerate the flooding. What's worse was that the people fixing the machine could not turn it off, because if they did, we would die. That machine was the only thing generating oxygen into this place.

After hearing the message, I tapped Edward on the shoulder. "Come on, Edward. We have to go."

He nodded in agreement, and we both rushed off. Edward and I were running as fast as we could, but it wasn't getting us far, as the winds were pushing us back, and the streets were flooding up fast to the point that the water was beginning to flood the sidewalks. The winds were getting stronger and stronger to the point that we were nearly getting blown off our feet. Edward and I were completely soaked from head to toe from the rain, and we were walking into this situation without being able to see anything. This was bound to be a bad situation.

The weather machine was changing rapidly by the minute. The winds were getting stronger to the point that garbage cans and any loose items were being blown around rapidly, and the water was filling up to our knees. There was nothing I could do. I had to keep going, because if I didn't reach Ella and Anna soon, they would be underwater within the next hour.

Suddenly, as we were walking through the flooded streets, a 2-ton car came blowing down the street towards me and began pushing me down the street. The harrowing winds were pushing the car down the street with me trapped behind with nowhere to move. Then, boom! The car came to a complete stop. Luckily for me, the car became trapped on a loose traffic light coming out from the ground and stabbing into the tyre, stopping the vehicle temporarily.

I must move now, or that car is going to crush me.

I swam for it, hoping to get out of the way of the car, but the current of the water kept pushing me down the road with nowhere to move. It felt like swimming in rapids, and it didn't help that the streets were filling up rapidly with more water.

My only option was to dive into the dirty water, where there was no visibility. But hopefully, with my diving experience, I may have a better chance down there than up.

Ducking down into the water, I heard a screeching sound coming from the car, and then *snap!* The car broke from the sign and began hurtling down the road towards me.

Shoot! I better get moving or else this car was going to entrap me again.

I swam as fast as I could, but I was not fast enough to get out of the way of the car. Then the car hit the side of a building, which changed its angle and trapped it along the building. Another stroke of luck. The current kept pushing me down the road until my foot got caught in the grates of a sewer. I couldn't move. I couldn't get it out. What was worse was that the water was past my head. I couldn't move. It looked like I was going to drown to death. I could hold my breath for 4 minutes because of my military training, but after that, I was dead meat.

I did everything to get free from the grate but no luck; my foot was trapped deep, and I was running out of air to the point that my vision was beginning to fade. Also, my lungs were filling up with water fast. Now, I had been through this situation before. I thought, *This is the end.*

I was not willing to give up. Still, after being trapped underneath the water for 4 minutes, I began thinking that I was going to die, as I couldn't breathe, and my vision began turning black. Then I heard a young male voice scream at me. "Dad!"

Then I heard a splash, as a shadowy figure dived into the water just as I collapsed into unconsciousness.

I felt a slap, and a rush of pain went across my face. Then I felt another slap go across my face, and my eyes shot open. It was Edward, who was drenched and breathing heavily. Edward looked me straight in the eye, and he was saying something, but I couldn't recognise what he was saying, as my eardrums were blocked with water.

I tried to focus on what Edward was saying, and slowly, the water from my eardrums was draining out, and I could make out some of the words that he was saying. Finally, I woke up completely, as Edward gave me mouth-to-mouth resuscitation. Then finally, I began to cough up water from my lungs, with Edward patting me on the back, and I could finally hear again.

"Jacob, are you all right?"

I barely recovered from nearly drowning, but the rain and the wind were waking me up quickly. "Sure, never better."

"Come on! We have to go."

I got up and began running with him. This time, we would take the rooftops.

We jumped from rooftops to rooftops. Normally, there would be fear of falling, but the level was pretty much flooded, so there was no chance of falling to our death. However, it wasn't an easy task, as the wind currents were incredibly strong. The wind kept pushing us back, so we had to fight twice as hard to keep moving forward, which was hard for me, as I had nearly drowned to death.

After jumping from rooftop to rooftop, we finally made it to the ruins that used to be the gun shop, but I couldn't see Ella or Anna anywhere. Then it suddenly occurred to me where they could be: in the basement.

So quickly, I jumped off the rooftop into the icy water and began to dive down, deep into the dirty flood water. But then I saw a blurry shadow swim straight past me, and I heard a *foosh* sound coming from the water. I didn't know if that was my brain playing tricks on me or what, but I had to rescue Ella and Anna quickly before the floodwater drowned them.

I swam down to the floor of the gun shop and peeked through the hole, but I couldn't see anything. Running out of oxygen, I swam back to the surface for air. Then I noticed something. It looked like a lizard tail of some sort that swam behind me and then out of sight. *Oh no, that can't be good.*

I hightailed it to the surface, with Edward lifting me out of the water and back onto the roof. "Is there anyone down there?"

"No, I couldn't see anything. I will have to go back down there."

"Are you crazy, Jacob? There is no one down there. Quick, let's get out of here."

"No! Edward, if there is even a chance, I will have to go back down there!"

Edward pulled me by the shoulder. "No, Jacob, I am sure Ella and Anna have already made it to safety. Look, let's just get to the safe zone and figure it out from there."

But I knew for sure that they were down there. I shrugged Edward off and jumped off once again into the flood waters to go rescue Ella and Anna. I swam back to the gun shop to search the basement for any survivors. I surveyed the basement through the crack, but no luck. I couldn't see anything down there. If I was to check, I would need a closer look.

I searched underwater for an entrance into the basement. Bingo. I swam down the stairway and into the now-underwater basement. I entered the basement with objects floating everywhere, and I still couldn't see anything. But then it dawned on me. There was another room in the basement behind the stairwell. Quickly, I swam into the room to find that there was no one in the room but a bed and a few objects floating all over the room.

Then, I felt something on the back of my neck. Out of a reflex, I turned around and saw Ella swimming there, and she signalled me to follow her. I swam behind her, and she led me into the bathroom, where inside I saw an upside-down bathtub, and I could see that Anna was under it, using it as an air pocket to keep them alive. Ella and I both swam under it to use it to catch our breaths. I was so happy to see Ella and Anna alive. Both Ella and Anna hugged me.

"Thank goodness you are alive! We thought we lost you."

I returned the hug. "The feeling was mutual."

After we all stopped to catch our breath, Ella turned around. "All right. Jacob, what is the plan?"

"All right, this was some clever engineering creating an air pocket, but it is not going to last. Edward is in the closest building next to the gun shop. So I would suggest that we all swim as fast as we can up to the surface and don't get caught. Agreed?"

Ella and Anna both nodded.

"All right, then let's do it."

All three of us ducked under the bathtub, and we all swam as fast as we could back upstairs. We waved through all the floating objects upstairs. Ella was swimming in the front, while Anna was swimming in the middle, and I was lucky to last at the back.

Swimming out of the gun shop, I thought for sure I saw a lizard tail. But then again, I had suffered so many blows to the head that it was probably nothing.

CHAPTER *15*

Anna, Ella and I were all swimming in unison back to the surface. It was a rush against the clock, because if we didn't swim fast, we would drown. Of course, I felt sorry for the people, but I did have to admit, it was kind of beautiful down under the water, seeing all the buildings underwater. I don't know, it resembled that of Atlantis, our very own underwater world. But then the mood quickly soured when I saw the dead bodies floating throughout the water – with some floating in cars, some floating up to the surface and some still within the buildings. In all, I could see at least a hundred dead bodies lying within the flood waters.

Ella and Anna had made it to the surface, and I was still trailing behind, but suddenly I turned around and saw a half-alligator and half-shark creature come rushing towards me.

It came with its jaws snapping at me, but it managed to miss my head by a few inches. The allishark then circled me ready to strike again. I watched as this 7-foot-long scaly green half-alligator and half-great white shark creature with red eyes, a dorsal fin, a long lizard tail and a long green snout that had at least four rows of teeth, as it began circling me.

The only thing I could do was swim there and keep an eye on it to make sure it didn't try to attack. Then, at break-neck speed, the creature went for an attack, just as my back was turned. Luckily for me, I turned around fast enough to sucker punch the bastard in its scaly nose. The monster retreated a few feet, but its eyes were hyper-focused. It bared its dinosaur-like teeth and let out a loud screech. "YAAAA!"

The behemoth then swam at me, ready to attack me once again. The only option was to swim into the wreckage of the old building. The monster tried to lunge at me again, but I was ready. I swung my fist once again and punched it right in its jaw, but the monster was incredibly durable, so a few punches to the jaw were not enough to kill the thing. To survive this, I was going to have to find something to kill it with, and I would have to do it fast, because I was running out of oxygen pretty fast.

Hightailing it, I began the mad swim into the wreckage of the gun shop, as I could feel the oxygen bubbles slowly escaping my lungs. I swam and I swam. Then, out of reflex, I kicked the beast in its face which caused the monster to loosen its jaw so I could get loose from its jaw. The blood pouring from my boot was only fuelling the monster's blood-lust even more.

The monster trailed behind the blood trail, and it paused for a moment until it then began swimming even faster towards me. But luckily for me, I was almost there at the gun shop. Just as the monster was about to snap at me again, I ducked inside, with the monster getting stuck within the large shards of glass that were sticking out from the shopfront. The monster's face wiggled around while it was bleeding from its jaw. It was injured and trapped temporarily, but that was not enough to kill the monster. It could at least buy me enough time to find a weapon or object to slay the beast. I had to act fast, because if not, I was either going to drown, bleed to death or become monster chow.

I looked around the wreckage of the gun shop, but just my luck, there were no guns. But once again, luck popped its little head around, as I looked at one of the shelves, and there it was: a military-grade filtration device, designed to breathe in water both clean and radiated, high altitudes and in outer space. This was perfect, but just as I placed the filtration device on, the monster broke loose from the glass and began to charge at me once again. Luckily, I managed to enter the gun shop basement just as the monster closed its jaw. I looked around the basement, and luck won again as I managed to find a thermal nuclear grenade. This grenade could destroy a tank within seconds and was as hot as the sun when lit. This would be perfect for taking down the monster.

The monster caught a glimpse of me and started slowly squeezing through the hole, but it got stuck within the hole in the basement roof. The monster let out a monstrous screech, as it revealed its razor-sharp jaw and rows of jiggered teeth.

I grabbed the grenade and armed it by switching the switch, causing the lights on the grenade to turn orange. I had to act fast. I only had a short period of time before the grenade would go off. I grabbed a stick and stabbed it into the jaw of the monster. I only had seconds before the stick snapped. Swimming as fast as I could, I threw the grenade into the mouth of the monster, just as the monster's jaw snapped down, breaking the stick with such force that it caused wood chucks to fly everywhere.

Everything paused for a minute, then boom! The monster's head exploded, which caused blood, brain tissue and muscles to fly everywhere around the basement.

The corpse of the allishark floated there, lifeless and unmoving, with the entire basement covered in blood. Pushing the corpse of the allishark out of the way, I began swimming through the crack in the basement roof and back to the surface, but it was becoming incredibly difficult. Also, I had been underwater for too long, so I was losing precious oxygen by the second, and I didn't think I could last anymore. My eyes began starting to see dots, and I was feeling extremely nauseous. Halfway there, I thought that I was definitely close, but in the far distance, I saw them fast approaching at rapid speed. Two allisharks were closing in hot, and what was worse was that I didn't have the strength to fight on. The last thing I saw was the sharks about to attack before I fainted into blackness. The last sound I heard before I fainted into unconsciousness.

I had just died, and I had become monster chow, as I could feel nothing but emptiness. Then I began to cough, which was followed by another cough. *Coughing? Dead people don't cough.* Then, my eyes began to open slowly. I tried to scope the environment, which looked like a hospital of some sort. Then my eyes shot fully open to reveal that I was in a mobile medical centre, which was a makeshift military hospital created by the army for natural disasters. Thanks to Article Four of the American Division Constitution, the government is obligated to help the city in the event of a natural disaster. So active military personnel and the peacekeepers came into the Lower Levels to evacuate all citizens, and they even sent down divers to rescue any trapped citizens, which is what saved me from the allisharks.

Now, I was lying in some random medical bed, and I had to endure that annoying beep noise that kept going off every 5 minutes.

Then a middle-aged military doctor pulled back the curtain covering my bed. "Good morning, Patient 455590. How are you this morning?"

"Honestly, Doc, I am not feeling the best."

The doctor gave a chuckle. "Ha! Yes, I am not surprised. Do you work around radiation?"

"No!"

"Well, I don't know how, but we also detected some radiation in your blood."

It was probably from my time in the wasteland.

"Not to worry. We have given you a course of nanite injections. Just follow it up with some Raderase pills, and you will be fine."

"Thanks, Doc."

The doc walked away to check up on some more patients.

After he left, Ella, Edward and Anna came to check up on me. Anna was the first one to speak, just after giving me a hug and a kiss.

"Love! Thank goodness. You are all right?"

Edward then cut in. "What happened? We thought we lost you. After we resurfaced, the American Division Navy picked us up in their vessel, but you were nowhere to be found. What happened to you?"

"Well, Edward, do you remember when we were kids, you used to tell myths about the allisharks in the sewer?"

"Yeah!"

"Well, let's just say they ain't a myth. They tried to kill me."

"Oh, my poor baby!" Anna came in to hug me, followed by Edward.

"Come here, you big unit."

The only one to not hug me or say anything to me was Ella, who entered the room to see my status and left. I guess she was still angry that I was responsible for killing those people and shutting down the city power supply, for which I could not blame her.

Agh! I hated the feeling of the nanites. It felt as if bugs were crawling within my skin and I couldn't scratch them out. But I didn't know what hurt more, my physical pain or the emotional pain from Ella not talking or even looking in my direction. But how could she forgive me when I couldn't even forgive myself? This whole situation was caused by me.

It turns out that when I destroyed the power plant, it ruined the software of the weather-generating machine and caused it to pour excessive rain. So not only had I robbed the people of power and killed innocent people but now I had caused a massive flood which had destroyed the city.

Man, I guess I am just as bad as John; maybe even worse. I don't know how I can live with myself.

You see physical pain may last temporarily, but the pain that you have hurt innocent people or the people you care about is a pain that lasts forever. That pain never truly goes away, but I guess I will have to live with it and move forward and try to find forgiveness, not just from Ella but from my family and my community.

The process was going to be long and strenuous, but that pretty much-summarised life in general. Because as much as the saints and preachers in life want to preach about rejecting sin and evil in our lives, the reality is that we are all sinners, and every single person on God's green earth has demons we all try to run from. But how we handle our demons differs. Some drink, some have excessive amounts of sex, some work out, some preach, but the one thing we all have in common is that we all try and hide behind smoke and mirrors. So, enough. I was no longer going to hide. I was going to have to confess the truth.

I am not here. I am a killer!

Gathering my strength, I was able to walk again and after hours of the nanites doing the job within my body, I was feeling like my old self once more. But there was still work that needed to be done. Picking myself up from the medical bed, I threw on some fresh, clean clothes that had been donated by a local homeless shelter and began walking to catch up with the gang.

After walking past the hundreds of hospital beds full of sick and dying people, I flung open the hospital door only to be met with a strong gust of wind that pushed me back off my feet for a bit. But as I gazed out of the door, I could see all the people of the Middle and Lower Levels all huddled together in a refugee camp that was stationed in the subway station of the Middle Level and that was constantly surrounded by soldiers and medical tents. There were people with towels and bottles of water while they all took refuge from the storm. The Lower Levels were completely devoured by floodwater to the point that it was almost invisible under dirty, muddy stormwater.

It saddened me to see all the people, as they didn't know the future and didn't know what awaited them when they returned home. But even in the darkest moments, people can surprise you. People were helping one another, giving each other blankets, clothes, bottled water and medical supplies. It really was amazing I mean to see people from all races, all ethnicities and all incomes together looking after each other.

The storm had died down slightly due to multiple defence teams working to contain the weather generator, so there were glimpses of a rainless sky. Every hour, navy patrol boats loaded citizens both alive and dead into the refugee camps. It was only a matter of time before the rain would start up again. I needed to find my family and quickly, because even the government officials didn't know how long they would be able to contain the people within the subway station. Already, after the temporary hiatus from the constant rainfall, the rain was starting up again and was pouring down heavily. But what I feared the most was what awaited. The dam wall was already at full capacity and with all this heavy rainfall, I didn't know how long it would take for the dam walls to come down. Once that happened, then this city was in for a much bigger disaster than anyone could anticipate.

Then I saw them – Anna and Edward – huddled together in blankets in a subway tunnel. I rushed towards them. "Edward! Anna!"

They couldn't hear me over the constant chatter coming from thousands and thousands of people talking to each other and all of them screaming over each other.

"Edward!" I yelled as loud as I could to get their attention. This time did the job, as Edward turned around and looked in my direction.

"Jacob!" Anna and Edward then turned around to face me, with all of them also ducking and weaving through the people.

Then Edward rushed towards me and gave me a massive man hug. "Jacob, thank goodness you recovered."

"My sweet boy, I am so glad that you are all right."

"I am all right, Mum" and I hugged her to ease any concerns she may had.

I turned to both Edward and Anna. "Where's Ella?"

"Ella volunteered to help the navy in finding more survivors during the storm."

"Yep, that sounds like something Ella would do."

But suddenly it dawned on me. I got so carried away from meeting them again that I forgot the most important fact of information that a disaster was coming. Unfortunately, Ella was dead smack in the middle of the storm, because when that damn broke, it would be bad news.

After giving Anna another hug, I said, "I am sorry, Mum, but I have to go back out there. Ella is in danger, and she needs me!"

Anna's face went to concern again. "Son, you can't go out there. You have barely recovered from your surgery. You could die!"

I placed my hand on her shoulder. "Mum, I need to do this. I have caused so much damage to this community, and I need to go help Ella."

Edward cut in and said, "I am in."

To that, I replied with a simple "Thanks, man."

Now was not the time to talk. Now was the time to act.

I signalled to Edward to head over to the nearest sea vessel, as I would catch up, but not before giving Anna a kiss on the cheek. Off I went towards the end of the subway station. We both approached a floating naval gunner ship which was being used to help rescue people. Approaching the crew of naval seamen, I screamed out, "Hey! Do you guys need volunteers?"

The captain of the ship came out and looked us up and down. "Do you guys have military experience?"

"Yes. I was a former rad diver, and Edward has officer training."

The 50-year-old captain nodded to us. "Fair enough. Jump on board, slap on some naval gear and give us a hand."

We jumped on board, went below deck, slapped on the gear and returned to the deck to watch the boat zoom off into the neighbourhood.

Edward and I stood on the edge of the boat, looking at all the submerged buildings and the floating debris lying on top of the floodwaters. I have to say, looking at the community like this made me feel sad, especially looking at all the dead people floating on top. It was too dark to see anything, as the clouds had made the environment pitch black, with the only thing keeping this place alight being the emergency red light that the city dome generated in instances of natural (or in this case artificial) disasters. Suddenly, I and the crew of naval sailors investigated the sea to find a green shark fin sticking out through the water and swimming past us. Then we heard a creaking sound coming up from the water, and an allishark jumped onto the boat and let out a loud, shrieking sound. Luckily for us, the automatic turret on board let out 10 plasma bolts a second at the creature, killing it instantly and leaving its corpse to lie there on the deck of the ship.

We looked over the bow of the ship to find at least five creatures swimming towards the ship. The first thought that came to my head was of dread, but everyone else didn't look concerned. However, I knew we were in trouble, as the turret on board was built for anti-aircraft purposes. It wasn't built to take on underwater creatures.

Sirens signalled all over the ship, and the captain yelled, "Battle stations!"

All the sailors and volunteers rushed to the nearest gun locker to grab a plasma rifle. At least 50 sailors rushed towards it, as they realised the severity of the problem. The turret wouldn't be able to hold off the creatures, so they all grabbed their rifles and then returned over the bowels of the ship and began pointing them at the creatures. All the people were lined up in battle formations, clocking their rifles and getting ready to take down the creatures.

Then the laser turret kicked into action, letting a vroom sound, as the automatic turret let out a blast of laser bolts while spinning around 360 degrees at rapid speed.

While the turret was effective at deterring the creatures for a few seconds and severely hurting a few of them, it could not kill them, as the creatures have the capability of diving underwater, and unfortunately, this model of automatic turret couldn't pierce through water, giving the creatures an advantage against our laser rifles and turrets.

Suddenly, the crew opened fire into the water, hoping to hit a few of the creatures just as they were emerging from the water and about to attack the crew. While they all managed to hit some of the creatures, there were too many of them to be contained in the water. At least 10 managed to dive onto the deck of the navy ship, and the bloodbath began. Blaster bolts and body parts went everywhere.

I managed to signal to Edward to get down below deck, as the crew engaged into a firefight with the creatures. However, while some of the crew managed to take out some of them, at least five from what we could see through the door, there had to be at least 20 dead bodies lying with blood splattered throughout the deck of the ship. Edward and I sat there behind the door of the ship for at least 5 minutes listening to the shrieks of the remaining creatures onboard. Then suddenly, the blaster fire stops. Edward and I looked at each other in concern, and Edward turned to me. "Are they all dead?"

I gave a shrug of confusion and slowly began to peer through the door when I saw a bruised up, bleeding allishark crawling on its four legs past the door, barely noticing us. But as I was slowly closing the door, the creature slowly turned its red lizard eye towards the door and noticed us, letting out a screech, and they came rushing towards the door.

"Crap! Quick, Edward, Run!"

The injured allishark pierced through the steel door as if it was made of cardboard and let out another shrieking noise and then began to charge at us with full force. Luckily for us, on land, these creatures are incredibly slow compared to when they were underwater, which gives us a massive advantage. Edward and I bolted as fast as we could, ducking and weaving through cables and pipes below the deck of the ship, just as the creature began cutting through them and getting closer towards us. It looked like we aren't getting out of this one. Then, as we ran into the boiler room of some sort, I looked up at the blast door and signalled to Edward to stand at the control panel. Edward rushed towards the control panel and put his hand on the lever.

"Edward, don't pull that lever until I say so!"

He nodded in agreement. Then, the creature turned the corner and started crawling at us at a moderately faster pace, letting out a shrieking noise before it began charging at us.

Closer and closer, the creature approached us, and finally, I signalled to Edward, 'PULL THE LEVER!'

Just as the creature was about to lunge at us with its jaw wide open, a blast door shot down and decapitated the creature, forcing its head to roll on the floor. Edward and I looked at each other and laughed.

"Whoa, that was close."

Anyway, no time to be a smart-arse. Quickly, I rushed to close the rad-proof doors and magnetically sealed the doors as to buy us some time before the allisharks killed us. We looked around the room for a way out of here, but no luck. This room was incredibly sealed and covered in steel. I couldn't sit here and wait for us to die, so I kept looking for anything, any little crack or hole that could give us an escape.

Suddenly, as we waited for the allisharks to bust through the doors, we heard some strange noises coming from outside the rad-proof doors. The sound we heard was shrieking coming from the allisharks, followed by the boom of the auto-laser turrets, then and again the screeching from the creatures. Edward and I were looking at each other trying to contemplate what the hell was happening right now.

We then heard a knock at the door. Confused, I asked, "Who's there?"

Instead of another bang at the door or anything, I heard a human voice respond, "This is Colonel Hufford. Open up!"

Edward and I let out a massive sigh of relief. "Thank Goodness!"

We pressed a button to open up the blast doors. In front of us stood the same old, greying captain who had welcomed us onto the ship. The captain was standing there with at least five heavily armoured navy seals standing over the corpses of five allisharks whose bodies lay motionless on the floor, with blood and blast marks scattered all over the wall.

The captain asked, "Are you all all right?"

Edward and I shot each other a dirty look. "Great! Never better!"

But I was confused. "I thought you died when the allisharks took over the ship."

The captain let out a laugh. "Ha! You think those sewer rats would be enough to stop the AD Navy? Now, if you boys are done messing around, we could use your hand upstairs."

Edward and I followed the captain up the stairs to find the body of at least five more of the creatures on top of the other dead allisharks. They lay motionless on the deck, with sailors sweeping them off the deck and back into the flood waters. That was a really close call, as I thought we were going to set off a little nuclear weapon, but thank goodness, the captain had a plan of his own.

The captain explained that after the allishark jumped on board, thanks to some intense firepower, they held off a swarm of the allisharks on the roof. However, the attack took out a significant portion of crew and volunteers, so the ship was basically running on a skeleton crew of a few dozen sailors, which was going to make rescue and recovery significantly hard.

Nonetheless, we had to try and help as many people as we can. The captain turned around and gave us commands, "If you boys are done playing with lizards jump into the life rafts and begin looking for struggling survivors."

Edward and I just stood there looking at each other in shock. It had been a long time before we had been given commands, but the captain then clapped his hands. "On the double!"

Out of our military instinct, we yelled back, "Yes, sir!"

We both looked at each other and gave a bit of chuckle at the thought of taking commands again. Then we all jumped into the old, outdated, electric-powered life rafts that looked as if it had seen better days.

After unhooking the rope from the boat, we saddled off and rushed into the path ahead. It was going to be incredibly hard now, given the fact that we had got a little distracted with the allishark attack. Plus, we took too long, and it was now pitch-black night sky down in the city with stormy and harsh weather, and we had nothing but old, ineffective spotlights that looked like they were salvaged from the wastelands.

Despite stuffing around for a few minutes trying to load our equipment into a boat that was constantly drifting back and forth in the wind and was being smashed against the ship with rough waves, we managed to get onto the raft in one piece.

Wanting to get out of there, we pulled the cord on the motorboat, and after a few pulls, we got the engine running, and we sailed once again. Edward took over steering the boat engine, and I oversaw the boat light, hoping to spot any sign of life out there. We had to be going at least 10 knots, as we were not too sure what may have been lying at the bottom of our boat. On the bright side, at least we had an antique bolt-action rifle by our side to keep us company on our journey that was going to repel an allishark (not). Hell, by the look of this thing, it wouldn't even be able to repel a giant cockroach.

We were having no luck at finding any survivor and at this rate, Edward and I were beginning to question if there were even any survivors out there to help. The only thing we were able to find were destroyed, flooded buildings and dead corpses that lay above the water from the damn. I must admit, seeing the occasional dead body wasn't enough to trigger my PTSD, but when you have seen at least 100 bodies in the past 24 hours, it severely starts to trigger flashbacks from my time in the war. But poor Edward had it worse. He was getting seasick. It turns out Edward didn't like water, despite training to become a naval officer. He could be a funny bloke sometimes.

After searching the flooded city for 5 hours, Edward and I were starting to worry that Ella and the remaining crew she went with were probably dead by now. But I couldn't give up, because if there was at least a chance they may be still alive, then I had to keep looking.

Edward, on the other hand, was getting tired of searching and was cynical at the idea of Ella and the crew being alive. "All right, let's turn this ship around and let's go home."

"No! We have to keep searching Edward."

"Jacob! We have been searching for nearly 5 hours now. Ella's probably made it back to the refugee camp. The same with any survivors. I mean, look around. There's no one around."

But I was determined and stern. "Edward, if there is any chance that there is at least one survivor, then we must not give—"

I was interrupted by a flash of light that caught my attention. Puzzled, I turned to Edward. "Edward, did you see that?"

Edward turned around and saw a flash of pink smoke emerging in the distance. Despite the rain damping the brightness of the light, it was still visible in the distance. In a hurry, we manned our stations, Edward on the engine and me on the light, we floored it towards the pink light. Vroom! The little motor engine drifted us to the location of the pink flare, but the light was starting to fade back into the black and rainy sky. We hurried fast, watching as the boat tore through the water. But once the flare fully died down, we saw her! We saw Ella holding a pink flare waiving it in the air to gain our attention with at least 20 survivors from all different classes of society who were lucky, because the water levels indicated that if they hadn't been found within the next hour, they would have been underwater. The survivors were standing on the roof of some old, dilapidated warehouse factory. The poor buggers looked drenched and were all hurtling together for warmth as the rain continued to bucket down around them. In front of the warehouse stood another naval rescue boat that looked as if it had snagged on a building and was beginning to sink into the waters below. We began to float closer and closer towards the roof, hoping not to snag our boat on any piece of roof or debris that could damage the ship.

After safely securing the boat to the side of the building, Ella threw down a rope so that we could climb up to meet her on the roof.

Honestly, it was great seeing Ella in one piece, even though she was drenched from head to toe.

"What happened to your ship?"

"I managed to save all these people, but I couldn't save my ship from a sharp roof edge."

Edward looked at her in surprise, "Is *everyone* all right?"

"For now, I manage to save 20 people, but these people are hungry, thirsty, have lost loved ones and need a place to go, urgently!"

Edward and I then stared at each other. "There is a rescue ship about 30 minutes out from here. We will get you out of here."

"Well, you better hurry. The water level is rising."

"All right!" I then commanded Edward to radio to the naval ship and tell them to send a ship over. Edward then nodded his head and ran down to the ship and began to radio them. While we waited, I felt that now would be a good time to talk. "Ella, can we talk?"

"You want to talk now, Jacob? While we are standing on top of a nearly flooded rooftop?"

I grabbed Ella's Elbow very slightly as to not hurt her but to grab her attention. "Look Ella, I know that you can never forgive me for destroying that power plant, but ..."

Ella interrupted me, not looking impressed that I brought this up now. "Jacob, you killed those people, and now you have put this entire community and this entire city in jeopardy, and you expect me to what just forgive you?"

I then looked her dead in the eye. "Look, I know that you can never forgive me. Hell, I can't even forgive myself.

What I have done is absolutely terrible, and what I have done to this community … I will never forgive myself. But I just want to say that you are right, I crossed a line that I should never have crossed. I played the hero trying to fix everyone's problems, but the reality is that I only created more problems for the city, the community and my family. I know that now, and I want to atone for my sin. That is all I will say."

Ella just stood there for a moment. "Jacob, I—"

Edward climbed back up the rope and interrupted our moment. "Guys, I radioed the rescue ship, and they should be here any moment."

Ella and I stood awkwardly looking at each other for a few minutes. "We should really get these survivors prepped for the rescue ship."

"Yes!" She then paused to brush her hair away from her right ear. "Let's get out of here."

Edward, Ella and I helped the 20 people slowly down the rope and onto the little boat. The boat was much heavier now, and I wouldn't have been surprised if it sank, and yet, its structural integrity held despite its age. Still, it was now much slower, and what was worse was that it had no defences besides those antique rifles. A boat with no defences that was full of defenceless people was slowly sinking into the water obviously spelt trouble, especially because this flood was full of allisharks who were hungry and ready to make us their lunch.

The city was filling up fast, and we had to move quickly. Edward pulled the cord, and the boat went chugging along the flood water, slowly but surely until we could finally see, in the darkness of the night, the rescue ship.

"Yes!" We made it. Despite our fears, we made it to the rescue ship in one piece with no causality or anything going wrong.

After docking our boat near the ship, we did the same thing as we did before, escorting people from the boat onto the rescue ship with a ladder. Also, the captain came over the deck to offer all of us a hand.

Once, all the survivors were on the boat, he called out to us. "Having fun down there? Come on you lazy buggers, don't just sit there. Help our guests out."

We both let out a little smile, but then I felt something in my gut. The hairs on the back of my neck were standing up. This was too easy and too quiet. My instinct was telling me that something was going to happen. Where was the danger? The ship was now fully crewed up with people, as those who could work helped around the boat, whereas those who couldn't help just went underground to dry off.

The captain returned to the deck of the ship. "All right, listen up everyone. You are all now safe aboard this ship, so let's get you people to safety!"

The crowd then let out a cheer and a sigh of relief. Even my anxiety died down as we were in the clear. The captain yelled out across the deck, "All right, Jerry, radio to any other remaining ships. We found survivors and are returning to port!"

But then, a sense of dread rushed over the captain and crew as Jerry, the radio operator, broke the news. "Sir, we are not getting any response from any of the other ships!"

The captain's face turned into an expression of shock. "What do you mean you haven't heard anything from any of the other ships?"

The radio operator then repeated what he said a few moments earlier. "Sir, we haven't received any communication from any of the other ships."

Just as things couldn't get any worse, another radio operator sprung out of his chair. "Sir! The refugee camp is being overrun by allisharks!"

Everyone on board was now scared and concerned. What was happening? Allisharks have taken over the refugee camp? How was that possible?

Then we heard a shrieking sound coming from over the deck, but it wasn't just one; there had to be multiple different creatures producing the sound. My heart sunk in its chest. Instantly, I rushed over to the side of the deck, and the others had the same idea. I thought it may have been nothing, but I could not be more wrong, as I could see slight movement in the water ahead, speeding fast through the water like bullets, leaving nothing but air bubbles to escape the surface of the water as they rushed ahead. Sticking out through the water were green dorsal fins. It was an entire school of allisharks heading towards the ship.

This is going to get really ugly very fast! How are there so many of these creatures?

What makes the allisharks dangerous is not the fangs or their claws but their ability of parthenogenesis, meaning they could reproduce rapidly if there was enough food supply.

The crew on board were terrified. The ship had barely survived the first wave, and from the looks of the fins, there were more allisharks than before.

"Holy hell!" The captain, who was now in a panic, screamed out, "Battle stations!"

Red lights and sirens blurred throughout the ship, with the entire crew preparing to man their stations, just like with the first wave.

The crew outside went towards the nearest gun cabinet. It didn't matter how outdated those guns may have been; if it could fire, they would use them. Even the volunteers and the refugees were picking up arms. Everyone in this city has some sort of military training, and everyone on this boat was not willing to die on this bucket of bolts; hell, I sure as hell wasn't.

The captain stood in the middle of the deck, taking up his rightful position. *"All right, He-man or She-man or whatever type of man you are, be ready! Now is not the time to cower in fear. Now is the time to fight to see another day. Everyone, be prepared to engage."*

The ship remained silent for a few seconds, the only sound being from the waves crushing on the side of the ship. Then suddenly, the sonar operator called out, "Five seconds till impact!"

The crew all lined up in battle formation over the deck of the ship. We heard the shrieking sound from multiple different allisharks and then nothing! Not a sound. There was a long pause. We all stood there gripping our rifles, waiting for them to attack.

Nothing was happening. "Maybe they swam past us?"

Suddenly, an allishark leapt out of the water, its jaw wide open, and as it was about to land in the middle of the ship, the high-powered laser turret cut that it to shreds. It began! More and more allisharks leapt out of the water and let out a massive shriek as they began to extend their massive jaws and began to land on the deck of the Ship.

The creatures were quickly dispersed, thanks in part to the turret and to all of our combined firepower, but we were quickly running out of ammo, and the creatures just kept on coming. Two more launched on the ship, then another five. Like the first wave from a few hours ago, the deck quickly filled with gunfire, both from laser fire and calibre fire. But with all the firepower, the allisharks slowly managed to land and completely overrun the deck again. Human body parts and allishark remains splatted all over the ship, with bullet shells and blood spreading all over the deck in another brutal scene. The captain couldn't do much but stand there and watch in horror at the carnage that unfolded before his eyes.

The laser turret was running out of plasma, and our crew was dying by the dozen. Edward and I couldn't do much, as what could we do, really? The captain knew we couldn't just sit there and do nothing, so he signalled to the driver to turn the ship around and to head back to the subway station.

Suddenly, as the ship was turning around. An allishark jumped on to the captain's deck and bit into the captain's shoulder, causing him to fall to the floor. The creature let out a shriek, and out of instinct, I grabbed the standard-issue officer plasma pistol from the naval officer next to me and unloaded three shots into the allishark, causing the creature to fall backwards, out of the ship's deck and into the water. The allishark may have been killed, but the captain was severely wounded. The captain was lying on the floor of the deck, bleeding all over the floor. It looked like the allishark's jaw had hit an artery in the captain's shoulder. Unfortunately, without medical treatment or medical supplies, the captain was going to die. After 1 minute of coughing up blood, the captain collapsed on the floor dead. We had no captain to take command of this ship, so we were pretty much just sitting ducks in the water. But I for sure was not going to sit ideally and watch as the entire crew die. I stood in the centre of the ship, and with no other higher-ranking officer, I took 'de facto' command of the ship.

"Driver, begin charting course towards the subway station."

"Hang on! You're not a military officer. Why should we take order from you?"

"Do you have any other suggestions?"

The driver then paused for a moment. "Plotting the course back to the subway station."

The officer and the crew knew I was not a qualified captain, but they knew that I was the captain this ship needed to get us through this invasion. The ship was still being overrun by the allishark herd, but how would we get out of here? Then an idea hit me. I then turned to one of the officers. "Officer, tell the crew to pour the fuel onto the deck of the ship."

The officer gave me a concerned look. "But sir—"

"Just do it!"

The officer didn't have faith in my idea because he didn't know what I was planning, but it was our only shot. He nodded in agreement and radioed to the crew to pour the fuel onto the deck of the ship, and within minutes, fuel covered the surface of the ship. Then I approached the broken window. "FIRE AT THE FUEL!"

The turret gunner programmed the automatic turret to fire a laser at the oil, which caused a spark on the deck of the ship. Within minutes, the entire deck went up in flames.

The remaining allisharks went up in flames, with some of them jumping back into the water in the hopes of easing their pain, while the ones that were not so lucky burnt alive on the deck. The crew cheered in response to the allisharks fleeing. However, I reminded the crew that we were not out of the woods just yet, as we may have gotten rid of the allisharks, but we still needed to get back to the subway station. Thank goodness this ship was made of metal, or else we would have burnt up with the rest of the crew.

My plan worked, we burnt away the remaining allisharks, and fortunately, none of the crew was hurt, as they all got under deck in time. Once everything had calmed down, it was time to get this ship moving.

"Man your stations! We need to get to the subway station."

The crew nodded in response, and while they may have been exhausted, they also knew that we needed to get there, so within less than 5 minutes, everyone was back at their station and we were making course, but only to find the subway station completely submerged underwater, and within it, another herd of allisharks.

There were more fins than I could count. The allisharks were merciless, cold-blooded creatures, and they had managed to slaughter all the wounded people in the medical bay and at least half of the soldiers guarding the refugee camp. It was horrifying as their bodies laid floating upside down throughout the water. The sight alone sickened me to my core, and what was worse was that I didn't know where my mum was or if she was alive. The morale of the crew was at an all-time low. We had all lost hope and were grieving, as many had lost sons, daughters, sisters, brothers and loved ones.

We had just given up. We were out of ammo, out of supplies, and frankly, we didn't know where to go.

It is over for us! We may as well—

"Hello! Hello! Does anyone copy?"

"Where did that come from?"

"Sir! Our radio is picking up a signal!"

"Hello! Hello! Does anyone copy?"

Thank the Lord, there was hope after all. Not wanting to lose the signal, I rushed over to the radio and picked it up immediately.

"This is Jacob aboard the naval rescue ship, over!"

There was no response. *Oh no, I lost them.*

Then static came through the radio. "Jacob! This is an emergency!"

There were survivors, I had to act quick. "Where are you? Over!"

"At the old Anglican Church between Wolf and Gabel Street, over!"

There were survivors outside of the subway station. The crew was still saddened at the loss of the people in the subway station, but there was cheer too, as there was at least some hope.

"Coming to the church, over!"

We now only had one mission, and to be honest, it was better than waiting for the allisharks down below to eat and kill us. I signalled all crew to set sail, and off we went.

We pulled up to the old Anglican Church to find half of it submerged underwater. The remaining soldiers were on the top of the church. But by the looks of them, they were barely holding ground, as the allishark herd was encircling the church. The soldiers were low on ammunition, and the refugees were low on supplies, and telling by the looks of the church, they were not going to be able to hold out for much longer.

I guess it was up to us to help. Thankfully, in that time, the nuclear reactor down below created enough plasma; not a full clip, but enough to use the turret again for a short burst. Not for long, as the turret required more time to fully recharge. Not wanting to waste any more time, I commanded the turret gunner, "Fire at the church!"

The plan was that if we could divert the allisharks, then we would be able to pick them off, an old divide and conquer strategy.

I didn't even have to signal this time, as the turret gunner happily commanded the turret to fire towards the herd of allisharks, with the burst killing at least ten of them. But it only made them angrier, as the remaining allisharks came charging at us, with at least five of them staying at the church. Now they were coming towards us, but it worked; we got them away from the church. The only problem now was that they were heading towards us in large numbers, and we barely had any ammunition to fight them off. The creatures then let out their infamous shriek and began to charge the ship. The remaining crew on board didn't need orders, because they already knew what was coming.

I signalled to the driver to pull us out a bit, but as we were backing out from the subway to get us some distance from the allishark herd, we got caught on the roof of one of the abandoned industrial buildings next to the subway track. No way out, and with a herd of allisharks, I guess the only thing we could really do was fight like hell and pray to God we get out of this one.

After the first allishark leapt out of the water and onto the deck, the fight was back on for the third time today. But the fight didn't last long. We could only fight for 5 minutes before the crew was forced to flee downstairs and into the kitchen and resting areas, locking the blast shield behind them. The allisharks have overrun the entire ship, and it wouldn't be long before they overran the lower decks. Edward and the remaining crew just stood there behind blast door and the exposed window. We all knew that our fate was sealed.

However, Edward, the quick thinker that he was, turned to me with a plan. "Jacob, get me to the fusion core controls."

I pointed him to the fusion controls but was dumbfounded at what he was doing. "Edward what on earth are you doing?"

"I remember some of Fusion 101 from my time in the naval academy. They taught us to never increase the temperature above the maximum heat threshold, or else it would heat the entire ship up. So if we could increase the temperature, then we would be able to conduct the heat into the metals that surround the ship and burn the allisharks alive, like we did with the fuel, only riskier."

But one of the scientists on board was cynical. "But that would also kill the crew on board!"

"No! There is no metal in here, as this room is aligned with a special non-conductive polymer, so we will not be affected."

I was scared as hell, but this is our only shot. "Do it!"

"Jacob, quickly, get everyone down to the lower decks, or else they are going to fry!"

"On it!"

Getting them below deck was going to be tricky, especially considering all the allisharks aboard, so I had to find some way to distract them. Then an idea dawned on me. Without thinking and without fear, I grabbed a flare gun from inside the first aid kit, approach the broken window and shot a flare directly in the middle of the hoard of allisharks, with a red puff of smoke discharging from the canister. The allisharks swarmed towards the light. I then opened the door, and the crowd of people from downstairs quickly rushed up back onto the deck. While some of the allisharks began to chase the crowd of people, fortunately, most of the allisharks began to swarm towards the light. Quickly, I signalled the driver to activate the emergency energy shield (EES). The EES was an emergency chrono-shield that encompassed the deck in a 5-metre shield. Anyone who approached it would be frozen in suspended animation for a short period of time. The ESS was built to last only one hour and was to be used in incidents of a possible enemy invasion, but I thought for sure that this was as perfect a time as any. But this was a one-shot deal.

I flicked the switch, and a vibrating sound emerged from the ship; I decided to walk towards the broken window to investigate, and after looking out, I could see the allisharks. They were stuck just inches from approaching the lower deck. The shield would keep them at bay, but not for long, so we had to hurry. But because there were massive numbers of allisharks, they began to slowly move again. Just as the survivors signalled to me that they were in a safe distance with simple thumbs up, I called to Edward to turn on the machine, and within seconds, the nuclear energy began to course through the ship.

I walked over to the window once again to see the entire deck heat up a bright red and the creatures bursting into flames. It was truly a refreshing sight to see. After 2 minutes of feeling the heat radiating from the ship and the smell of burning flesh from the allisharks, I signalled to Edward to turn off the machine. The allisharks were reduced to nothing but ash and charcoal.

After waiting at least 20 minutes for the ship to cool down, I signalled to the survivors to return to the ship. They all hopped aboard, and we began to dock at the subway station. I got up off the boat and began to make my way towards the church to find the church surrounded by dead allishark bodies. Our plan worked; the soldiers managed to handle the allisharks. After docking, I jumped off the boat and landed on the church roof where I began to survey the people, looking for my mum, hoping she was alive. Then I found her! In a burst of excitement, I began to rush towards my mum. She is alive! I ran as fast as I could and wrapped my arms around her, with her doing the same. "Thank God you are all right. I was so worried about you. I thought something bad had happened to you!"

"I am all right, dear. It's OK. Nothing bad has happened to me, dear. Are you all right, though?"

Even the strong man that I was, I cried at seeing my mother healthy and alive.

"Yer, Mum," I said, with tears rolling down my eyes, not wanting to let go. "I am fine. Been through a terrible ordeal, but all right. Love you."

I then wrapped my arms around her. "Come on, let's get you on the ship and get you to safety."

The crowd from the church flocked into the one ship, which was now at full capacity with at least a thousand people onboard. But now was not the time for a headcount. Now was the time to reach the checkpoint.

Thanks to the intel from the people on the church, the AD Army has commandeered a football stadium located in the centre of the Middle Level. Hopefully, heading there would give me and everyone on this ship a dry and safe place to rest and recuperate.

But when we thought we were safe, I could hear in the distance a loud cracking noise coming from the dam wall.

"Oh no!" I turned my head and looked at the dam. Slowly, the concrete started to fall off the dam wall, just as water was slowly starting to drizzle out of the damn wall in large volumes.

"Oh no! No! No!" I yelled to all the crew to get this ship moving and to get to their stations. The dam wall cracked even more, and an even bigger piece of the wall fell off, and just like a house of cards, the entire dam came crashing down. I looked in the distance as an entire tsunami of water came falling like a bull running through cardboard at such a rate that it reduced the cement to nothing but rubble. I watched in a panic as the entire Middle Level was slowly being consumed by the dam wall.

My anxiety had kicked in, luckily. We got the ship moving, so I signalled to the driver in layman's terms, 'GET US OUT OF HERE, NOW!'

The engine roared, and the ship shot out from the church at such a speed that it left a massive white trail behind as we shot though the water like a laser, parting the seas away. But it wasn't fast enough as the roaring rapids of dam water came belting towards us. The flood water was as high as skyscrapers and as wide as two football stadiums.

CHAPTER 16

"Floor it! Floor it!" I screamed at the top of my lungs, as the engine roared like a bull. Behind us, the behemoth of water was consuming buildings mercilessly as they began to disappear, never to be seen again. All we could see was the water fast approaching us.

"We need more thrust!" I demanded of the driver, as the water was pulling us into a rip. "Quick! We need to exhaust the nuclear fusion engine."

But Edward was concerned, as exhausting the engine may cause the ship to become hot again. But with the amount of water approaching us, I was sure it would cool the ship down. Edward did exactly that, and I could see the engine behind us shooting us at a speed so fast that it broke the sound barrier. However, the water behind us was gaining speed too, as more and more debris was collecting into the tsunami. Also, if we didn't find a way to get out of this then, we would soon be consumed by the water.

Unfortunately, the speed of the ship wasn't enough to break free off the hold of the water, and we were sucked into the flood water. The water basically absorbed the entire ship and carried us along the water surface, as we could do nothing but watch in hopelessness as the water edged us closer into the border wall. All we could really do was watch in horror.

The only thing I could do was warn the passengers to brace for impact. The poor people rushed down below, and the ones that couldn't had to hold on for dear life. The water propelled us at such a speed that it practically ripped off the thrusters on the side of the ship and turned the ship onto such an angle that equipment and even people began to fall off the ship. Then in an instant, BANG! The ship hit the border wall, which instantly destroyed the entire ship and left it as nothing but rubble from the buildings. All the people, including Edward, Ella, Anna, myself and what remained of the passengers, were now underwater. I opened my eyes but could barely see anything, as the dirt from the pieces covered my eyes. Just like that, I was trapped underwater.

The only thing I could see was water everywhere. Entire buildings were submerged under the water, along with debris and dead bodies floating underneath the surface. My ability to breathe was running out fast, as my lungs were quickly filling up with water, and I couldn't last much longer. I had to quickly make haste up to the surface of the water.

Using my strength, I pulled with my legs and arms, trying to make a mad dash up to the surface to survive. I had a long way to go. It felt like I had to swim to the heavens. All I could see in front of me was nothing. My lungs were in such pain from the lack of oxygen that I felt like my chest was collapsing in on itself with every time I took a breath.

This entire situation was something that had never happened in this city's history. The entire city was flooded; the Middle and the Lower and even the Upper Levels were completely submerged in water. I was literally swimming past skyscrapers.

The surface seemed almost impossible to reach, and I could feel my eyes starting to shut down. *Come on, Jacob. Push through the pain and keep going,* I kept saying to myself internally, and I pushed myself harder than I ever did, to the point that my body felt like breaking down, and I could literally feel my body screaming internally in pain. My brain, oh goodness me, my brain was starting to black out again.

All this passing out could not be good for my health, really. Around me, all I could see were the thousands and thousands of dead bodies that once made up this city, and what was worse was within the pile of floating dead bodies was the lovely Armenian couple. How sad. Two great people whose bodies were now lifeless corpses who were just slowly floating up to the surface of the water. But what was truly beautiful was the fact that in their final moments, they were holding hands as husband and wife.

But now was not the time to grieve; now was the time to survive. Still, survival seemed impossible, as all I could only see was darkness up above me.

But then a miracle occurred. In the distance, I could see a light, a shiny white light that shined through the darkness of the water, and what was weird was that in this moment, I felt lighter and felt as if I was saved. I was lifted up as if I was floating through the water.

Then, coughing hard, I had made it to the top. I looked around, and the entire surface was covered in rough and dangerous water with waves crashing and smashing into skyscrapers. Up above, rain and wind blew the water around the city, with only the big skyscrapers barely visible, with nothing below but water. My entire body was drenched, and I was completely tired and had no energy to move.

I looked above up at the dome to see over the wall into the wasteland, and in the distance, I could see the bright white sun gleaming through the dome and into the water that surrounded me in its glow. It was invigorating in a way; the light made me feel so warm, even though the waters were as cold as all hell.

But I couldn't just stay there and drown. I looked around for something to cling on to, and in the distance, I swam to the nearest floating billboard sign. I hung on to the sign until I was able to regain my breath and my strength. But in this weather, I felt that it was going to take a while for me to regain my strength. I breathed heavily and began to cough up water from my lungs. Then I looked over into the far distance, and a crowd of people who were barely holding on to a building were slowly beginning to be pushed back out into the open water.

I wanted to only care for myself, but I knew in my heart that I couldn't let those people drown, so I swam as fast as I could using what little strength I had, and I helped save them. I swam to the roof of the building and hopped onto the rooftop of a 50-storey skyscraper and rushed over to the crowd of people that were barely hanging. One by one, I began to lift all the people, from the young to the old, onto the roof of the building, while the rain began to bucket down and make my hand more slippery to hold on to.

But in the end, I managed to pull at least 30 people onto the roof of the building. However, as I began to look around, I could see all over the city, people were clinging to rooftops and cars, grasping for dear life and hoping to not end up the many few people who lay below.

Despite being tired, I knew I had to help. I Jumped off the rooftop and began to swim towards one person who was clinging to a car, then to another who was clinging to a billboard, then another who was starting to sink underneath flood water. One after the other, I swam and tried to save as many people as I was physically able to. In the end, I couldn't save everyone. Most of the people drowned or were swept up in the waters before I could save them. But out of many people that died, I did however manage to save from my count at least 10 more people.

I swam those people to the rooftop, where all the other people were trying to camp out the stormwater, but the rooftop wasn't going to last long, as the floodwater began to slowly rise again, and the roof was slowly starting to become submerged within the floodwaters.

But their timing could not have been any better. A military helicopter shined its light on us and all I could do was smile and let out a wave of distress. Then a rope slowly dropped from the helicopter, and two soldiers in harnesses abseiled down to the roof. One by one, I helped the soldiers to harness up the citizens into the helicopter, and finally, it was my turn to go up into the helicopter. I looked down as the floodwater consumed the roof that I had been standing on only a few minutes ago. The entire city was consumed in flood water. The only place that was remotely safe was the tallest building in the city, the WeapCo building. The helicopter dropped me and the survivors on the rooftop, with the remaining million people who also sought refuge.

All I could really do was just stand there on the overcrowded rooftop, where there was little to no room at all to move. I didn't recognise anyone who was at all familiar except for one. In the distance, I looked through the crowd of people and saw him: John Spear, the CEO of WeapCo himself, standing on the roof with the rest of the commoners. I really wanted to go up to that guy and punch him in the mouth, but now was not the time for violence. After all, we were all in the same boat, as we were all wet and cold and needed to wait out this disaster. All I could really do was stand and wait for the storm to pass. But it was amazing seeing the community coming together; everyone was giving each other bottles of water and food, and even John himself was talking to people from the Lower Levels. I guess despite our class, race, religion, colour, creed or sexual orientation, at the end of the day, we were all just everyday people. I guess disasters can either bring out the animal or the humanity in people.

After waiting nearly 24 hours, the military finally switched off the weather machine. Finally, no more rain. It was an incredible sight to see. After they managed to switch off the weather machine, the entire military, with the help of citizens, managed to drain and dispose of all the water into the wasteland. Now was the time to head home and help to repair the community. While the water may be gone, the entire city was a complete wreck, and there was a lot of work to do.

Edward, Anna, Ella and I all put aside our petty feuds and got to work. Everyone in the community worked tirelessly, some including myself worked 12-hour days, repairing any and every building in the city. Within 5 months of hard work from the millions of people, we manage to get the city, while not the way it was before but in a condition that made it liveable. Those times were rough, living in and out of tents and eating nothing more than canned beans; hell, my face is totally rocking the Jesus beard, and I stank to all hell. But finally, I was able to return home.

But then it dawned on me. The house had been left destroyed by the fire, and the only thing that remained was an empty block of land. When Mum pulled up to the block of land, she broke down in tears at the loss of her house. Everything that we worked for and everything she fought for was gone! It was devastating witnessing my mum break down in tears, but in this moment, all I could do was to hold her hand. "Don't worry, Mum, we will rebuild. We are survivors."

The next morning, Mum and I got to work. The work was going to be tough, as we had to rebuild this house frame by frame, but we tried to make the most out of this situation. We went to the industrial factory that was offering free building materials and supplies, and with a bucket of paint, wood and a work radio, we got to work. I had to admit, despite losing everything, we were in high spirits. Edward and Ella entered the house holding a carton of beers and some burgers and chips from the local food truck.

"Food is here, guys!"

That really brought a smile to me and Mum's face. "Mmmm, smells good."

Ella then slapped my hand away as I tried to pinch one of her chips. "Ahh!"

At that, she just laughed. "Wait till we plate up, Jacob."

"OK, Mum, jeez."

While Ella and I were on much better terms, there was still that strain in our relationship. Anna got up. "All right, everyone, lunchtime!"

We all jumped with glee. Anna and Ella plated the burgers, and Edward and I poured the Cola. Finally, we were a family again. While yes, we were all tired and sore from having to rebuild the house, but I must admit, it was great to have a few laughs again with all of us.

Just as I was about to fall asleep, Ella came running down in nothing but her PJs. "Hey Jacob, are you ready to talk?"

My head shot up from my pillow. "Sure. It's a nice night out. Do you maybe want to go for a walk?"

I jumped off from the floor, slapped on my pants and T-shirt, with Ella turning her face as to not see me in my underwear. Then I grabbed Ella's hand, and we went for a walk down the street.

For the first time in this level's history, there was no gunfire or crime, as everyone was too preoccupied with repairing the city to go out and commit anarchy. It made the night walk even more magical. Walking down the cement pavement and passing all the depauperated and flood damaged buildings, while at the same time holding Ella's hand made the night all the more special. Then, as we walked for a few minutes, Ella decided to break the silence.

"Do you maybe want to grab a coffee?"

"I would love to but, I don't have any money."

"Don't worry, I brought my wallet. It's on me."

A blissful walk and free coffee with the girl of my dreams … My life was finally starting to turn around.

We pulled up to this beautiful makeshift coffee van that was built into a vintage caravan. The shop was probably the only thing making money in this entire street, and it certainly showed, as the van was decked out with white LED lights and was decorated in beautiful shrubbery and plant life.

Ella and I pulled up and a young man who looked to be in his early 20s and was rocking the hipster beard asked; "What will it be, my friends?"

I looked at Ella, as she was the coffee expert. "Two flat white, please. And put it on the card."

We walked in silence for a couple of minutes and taking a sip of my barista coffee, I broke the silence, "Look Ella, I just wanted to say—"

"No, Jacob, please, I owe you an apology. I know all you were trying to do was help this city and to help fulfil my father's legacy, and it was wrong for me to say all those horrible things about you."

I couldn't dismiss my actions. "No Ella, you were right. Look, Ella, I know that I crossed a few lines and committed acts that were unspeakable. I am aware of that. But I am a soldier and a worker. That's who I am. That's who I was destined to be, and that's all I will ever be. I am just so tired of losing everything, while all the evil people in the world get everything and take everything from everyone. It just takes a toll on you over time."

Ella and I paused. She then looked down at her coffee cup in despair. "I get it, Jacob, I really do. This whole world is built to keep people like us down at the bottom. But Jacob, I know the world isn't black and white, and sometimes, we lose track of ourselves to the point that we don't recognise ourselves. We have to remember that if we lose our values and our morals, then we truly have lost everything."

Ella and I collapsed onto the artificial grass in the park located on the Middle Levels and stared up at the dome that surrounded the entire city.

"I agree. I know I have sold my morals and values to the devil. But Ella, WeapCo has taken everything not just from me and you but from our community, and they continue to take from us and poison our city."

Ella just sighed. "Two wrongs don't make a right, Jacob."

I looked back at her. "No, but I need to at least try to make the rights that have been wronged."

I wanted to add something back, but all I could do was look into her beautiful blue eyes, and with my hand, I brushed her hair away. "I forgot how blue your eyes are."

She looked back into my eyes. "And I forgot how blue and innocent your eyes were."

We both stared into each other's eyes for a few seconds, and then we both rolled over and looked back up into the sky.

The power was still out, as they were still repairing the nuclear reactor, so without the lights, it allowed us to see into the night sky and look at all the beautiful lights that shined up the night sky.

"Have you ever seen lights like that before?"

"Sometimes, we all get so busy in our lives that we forget to enjoy the little moments like this."

Ella gave out a small laugh. "All right, Aristotle, no need to get all philosophical."

"I am serious. I mean, we are always so working our arses to the bone that we sometimes need to just look up into the night sky."

Ella then paused to take in the beauty of the stars. "No matter what walk of life you are in, you can always look up at the night sky."

"Wow. I never knew you felt that way."

"Hey Ella, do you ever miss your dad?"

Ella, looking sad, lied down and looked up into the night sky. "All the time. I mean, he was always there whenever I needed him. He was my rock, and I was his, but now that he is gone, I just don't know who I am or what it is I am meant to be. I mean, who am I, Jacob?"

"Who do you want to be?"

We just sat there in silence, as a once-in-a-lifetime meteor shower rushed past the night sky.

After a romantic night, we both got up and walked back home, ready for what the next day would hold. I laid my head onto the cold cement and tried my darn hardest to get some sleep. It was peaceful, until I heard a whirring sound coming from outside. It sounded like tires scrapping on the road outside. *Oh no, that can't be good.*

Out of instinct, I shot up from the floor and to see what was unfolding. Immediately, I ran up the stairs and back into the living room, with Anna, Edward and Ella waking up to the noise.

"What's happening?"

Curious, I opened the newly constructed front door to find military vehicles returning down to the Lower Levels.

It looks like the peacekeeping force was done playing the humanitarian role and was ready to get back to fulfilling the role of an occupying force back in the Lower Levels, even though there hadn't been a single crime reported in the area since the rebuild occurred. Tanks, trucks and helicopters all drove and flew past our house in waves, ever constant. Soldiers began marching the roads and were going door to door again checking up on people.

Anna and I were furious. This community had already been through enough, and we all did more than our fair share helping to repair the city, so why were we suffering? I guess nothing ever truly changed in this city. Political and social institutions may make quotes like 'we are all in this together', but the reality is that nothing ever changes. We have and always will be at the bottom, and nothing is ever going to change that. I just thought that the flood would lead to the rebirth of this city and cleanse it of all its problems, but the reality was that this city would never change.

Watching the tanks and truck roll past made my blood absolutely boil. It made me angry and sad at the same time, but what could we really do? We had no power or prestige, so we just stood outside on our front porch and watched as the military equipment rolled on past our house. While it made us angry that we were once again under military occupation at this moment in time, it was something I couldn't control, so I just stood there and appreciated the people in my life that I cared about. I leaned my head on my mum's shoulder. "Love you, Mum."

"Oh Jacob, you have always been the strong rock that your father never could have been. Please don't ever think you have to try to prove yourself to me. I would always love you, even if you didn't make the world a better place."

After our lovely hug that night, we both went back to our beds, fearful of what the next day was going to hold.

The next morning, we got up out of bed, and it was just like it was before the flood, as troops once again patrolled our streets. Just as we were only trying to look around, two peacekeeping officers slowly began to approach us with their guns held close to their chest. Seeing the soldiers beginning to approach us, I thought they were going to attack me or ask for my papers, so not wanting to be caught off guard, I decided to get ready to fight by getting myself into a combat stance. However, the soldiers just walked past me. I was confused and weirded out. Usually, the soldiers were quite awful to the people down here. But now, they were somewhat friendly. I mean, I actually noticed that the soldiers were interacting with the community, as I saw two soldiers having a coffee and chatting with some locals, and in the corner, I noticed a group of soldiers playing ball with the local kids. It was honestly an amazing sight to see the soldiers getting along with the community.

Hell, some of the soldiers were helping around the community, painting houses and helping old ladies with the groceries. I guess all it took was a flood or a natural disaster to show the humanity in people.

However, just as Anna and I turned a corner, we both noticed a news crew, with the cameras pointed at a podium. The chief of the reserve army got up to the podium with pre-prepared speech in his hand.

"Agh!" I sighed. This wasn't about community spirit. This was all just a PR stunt to keep the military occupation going. Man, for a second there, I thought things were actually getting better, but Anna was not having it. It was one thing to commit horrible actions, but to then cover up and lie about it? To Anna, that crossed a line. She stormed up to the stage with fury.

"Excuse me, but who do you think you are to send these troops down into our community like this?"

"Hey, listen, lady, why don't you take a seat and—"

Just as the chief was about to finish his statement, Anna cut in. "No, you listen here. We repaired your buildings, repaired your roads, repaired your gardens, all for free, and never asked for anything in return, and what do we get? You send troops down into our homes, and you let tanks roll down our streets. Is that the thanks we get?"

The chief gave a single cough and readjusted his tie in discomfort. "Look, lady, I will explain the full plan in a minute if you just go and sit down."

Furious, Anna grabbed a copy of the plan and ripped it up, sending the paper shreds flying through the sky. Then, Anna tried to throw a glass of water at the chief, but two peacekeeping officers restrained her, as they slowly began to drag her away from the podium. All the while, I may add, the whole thing was being broadcast across the entire Holonet News for the entire city to witness. I then leapt onto the stage and punched the chief straight in his face. While it wasn't hard enough to kill the guy, it was enough to cause him to stumble backwards and fall off the stage. Two more peace-keeping officers approached me with their stun sticks. At that point, I ran through the media team as fast as I could, when smack! I felt his hammer fist strike my chest with such velocity that it knocked me off my feet and caused me to hit my head on the pavement and bleed out of my mouth. I lay there coughing up blood, while the other two peacekeepers came over and flipped me on my back before zip-tying my hands.

Now, standard police practice was to pick me up and throw me into the back of the police cruiser, but they decided to have some fun; two of them held me down while the other one shocked me half-voltage with the stun stick while they just laughed. They did it for 2 minutes before they were done.

I could feel the bolt burn through my skin. All three of them picked me up and threw me into the back of a military police cruiser. Because I was zip-tied, all I could really do was lay there in this dark, bright white police cell and cry.

Of course, I had an electrical burn blistering my skin and burning my insides. It sucked. Then I heard a large thump from the two police officers getting in their vehicle, and I heard the loud sound of the engine being turned on. I could feel the wheel start to accelerate.

I couldn't really do anything in this cell. There was nothing in here to pick free (standard police protocol), and I tried to kick the door, but it was magnetically sealed. Guess all I could really do was lay there. Then suddenly, smash! My entire body was sent flying into the right side of the cell, and then I fell face first on the floor of the jail cell. Something had smashed into the side of the truck, and unfortunately, I could not move my body, as my hands and feet were tied. All I could really do is wiggle.

Then the police cell door opened. I peered up my head and saw two masked men in some sort of Halloween mask enter the cell. One of the men walked behind me and flicked open a switch knife, and I honestly thought he was going to stab me. Instead, he freed me from my bonds and escorted me to my feet.

"You all right?"

I recognised that voice. That was my neighbour from down the street. He used to babysit me years ago. The man helped me to my feet, and I looked out through the carrier. *Great, another riot.*

It looked as if I was on the Middle Levels, as the entire place was on fire. Black smoke brimmed from cars, trucks and buildings. Cars were turned over and flipped upside down and as protesters clashed with police in riot gear. The police were equipped with tear gas and barking dogs to keep the protesters at bay, as the crowds dispersed and then re-emerged from the tear gas.

The city was coming apart at the seams. I ran into the main street of town that was now tarnished with garbage, primarily from the garbage bin that had been chucked at the police cars. I looked out above at the protesters who were now being sprayed with water cannon by police and being pushed back by horses.

What the hell is going on?

I stopped and noticed a Caucasian male with a skinny plastique, and a towel wrapped around his face rushing towards the protests. I ran up to the man. "Excuse me, but what the hell is happening here?"

The protester was shocked at that question. "Didn't you see the news? Some dude rushed the stage in protest of the military occupation and—" The protester stopped mid-sentence. "Oh my gosh! You're him? You're that guy?"

I paused and looked at him with a face of disbelief. He signalled over another protester, and he confirmed my identity; "Oh yes! You're that guy who rushed the stage! Hey, can I get your autograph, man?"

The guy then handed me a black marker, expecting me to sign his body like we were at some concert. I signed his body very quickly and rushed towards town square. Then I found Ella. She had a bullhorn in her hand. "We will no longer kneel before a corrupt force that is solely run by outside interest."

The crowd all screamed, "Yes!"

"How many women and children have to be beaten for you to leave? We are people, not sheep, to be controlled, am I right?"

The crowd let out another chant and screamed in unison, "Yes!"

"Now I would like to introduce you to a special lady. Please, everyone, give it up for Anna Turner!"

The crowd all broke out in applause. Anna then walked and stood up on the statue all dressed in a nice suit that covered the bruises from the police throwing and shoving her around. She walked up to the statue and gave Ella a hug, and Ella passed her the bullhorn. She began to give a prepared speech from her pocket. I just stood there in shock. "Mum, what are you doing?"

Mum stood there with a sheet of paper in her hands. She raised the microphone up to her mouth and read her speech.

"People of American Division City, allow me to open your eyes to the truth. For months now, our city has been under siege by the irresponsible greed of those up above. For months now, they have rolled tanks, planes, drones and soldiers down our streets, through our churches and through our kid's school. We help to rebuild this city from the ground; yet we are the ones that do not get to sleep in peace? Does that sound fair to you, people of ADC?"

The crowd, holding up their signs and their fists, let out a loud "No."

"So we are the ones getting bashed and bruised while they fire missiles into our level. Are we going to stand there and let that happen?"

The crowd then let out another loud "No."

"That is why I personally am running for as a representative from the Lower Levels to bring justice and equality for all my people so that no more of your hard-earned dollars are spent funding these pointless military exercises. Can I count on your vote, people?

The crowd then let out a loud, "Yes!"

After a minute, they all disperse to either go home or to join the protesters in their protest. I approached Mum, who had jumped off the statue and was now talking to Ella. I honestly didn't know what to say. "Mum, what happened? You're running for political office?"

I never thought that Anna of all people would run for political office. Mum then looked at me and gave me a hug.

"Jacob, my boy, you're all right. You have got to stop disappearing on me, my boy. I was worried sick about you!"

I returned the hug. "Mum, what's going on?"

She then grabbed my hand. "I will tell you later. Come, let's go home."

Ella, Mum and I walked back home as the protest continued behind us. "What do you mean you're running for political office?"

Mum then took a deep breath in. "OK, remember when the police officers tackled and stunned you?"

I looked at the throbbing wound on my back. "Sure, how could I forget?"

"OK, well, that footage of you being stunned while restrained went viral across social media and the Holonet News. Jacob you are a hit, and I thought why not use that to our advantage, just as you did."

Ella then cut in. "The military is already under scrutiny for their poor performance in the flood rescue, and when footage of an unarmed man being stunned went viral, it caused the people to explode in rage on all levels."

Anna added, "We thought we could use that anger to fuel a new political movement, one that was under our control."

I was amazed. "Guess we are going to have to wait another 4 years before any of us get elected."

"Actually," Ella replied, "no, we won't. They announced it today that they are holding a referendum. Because many of the politicians drowned in the floods, it left a vacuum within the legislative branch. Plus, with the death of Alienize Lier, there are left multiple spots open in ParliaCongress."

"Hey guys, there is one thing that still bugs me."

Ella and Anna didn't look impressed. "What?"

I was curious to know. "What did the peacekeepers do to you? Were you arrested?"

Ella and Mum both looked at each other and smirked. "That's for me to know and for you to find out."

Then they both burst out in laughter. Well, it's probably best I didn't know how they escaped. But what I was most impressed with was the relationship between Ella and Anna had seemed to have developed. They had formed a sort of sisterhood, one would say. It did make sense, considering the time they had spent together. Not really knowing how to respond to that, I shrugged it off.

"All right then, girls, what's the plan? Let us head home, and we will work on a game strategy together."

CHAPTER 17

27-08-3025

Ella, Anna and I gathered around the kitchen table ready to formulate a plan.

"So, what's the plan, girls?"

Anna cut in. "Not yet, Jacob. We have to wait for Edward to arrive."

I didn't say anything. I just nodded in response.

Then Edward barged through the door with his eyes all watery and his shirt covered in capsicum spray. As he walked in through the door, the aroma from the capsicum spray made all our eyes water.

"Sorry I am late, everyone. I was just having my eyes burnt out and my back beaten by the riot police."

Anna nudged at me. "Jacob, get Edward some milk."

I acknowledged her, went straight to the fridge and got a 1 L bottle of milk and poured it straight over his eyes. "Better?"

He breathed heavily. "Yes!"

"All right, now that you boys are done clowning around, come and sit down so we can go over the plan."

Edward and I pulled up a bar chair to the dining table and sat there in silence, drinking our beers as we listened to the plan.

Anna started first. "All right, everyone, he is the plan. The Emergency Election is being held within 2 months. Now, according to the news, the Reservist Military Spending Bill was rejected at the senate, giving us a chance to revoke the bill. That's the good news. Here is the bad news. A majority of the senators and legislators were killed in the flood, which gives the people fighting to get the bill passed a majority in both houses. So it is our job to get those numbers. Does everyone agree with the plan?"

I shot my hand straight up in the air. "Question. Why are you running? I mean, you don't exactly have the qualification or the experience to be a legislator."

Ella shot me an angry look. "Jacob, your mum is the best chance we have to get the bill quashed. We need someone who has a positive image in the community and hasn't committed any crimes."

Fair point, I thought in my mind, but then another question came to my mind. "But, I am a wanted felon, remember? So won't they think of my last name and associate it with your name?"

Anna then took a sip of beer and looked down at the countertop. "Yes! This is the hard part. Jacob, you are going to have to go to jail."

"Hahahahah, good one, Mum!" But I noticed that her face wasn't shifting. She was dead serious. Then it dawned on me. "NO WAY! HAVE YOU GONE NUTS? YOU WANT YOUR ONLY SON TO GO TO JAIL?"

Anna shot up from her chair in defence. "Jacob, I know it's hard, but if we are to have a chance at getting any bills passed, we need to win over the Lower Levels. So we need to show them that I am not associated with you. By you going to jail, I can denounce your actions, and it could give me a fighting chance at becoming a legislator."

"Woah, woah, hang on a second. I thought the people considered me a hero for getting beaten up by the cops?"

Ella cut in. "They don't consider you a hero, they consider you a martyr for getting beaten by the police, but they will never trust you for political office after what happened at the nuclear power plant."

I let out a sigh. "That was an accident!"

Anna interrupted to try and stop a potential showdown. "Regardless, we can't have a person on our team who's got criminal charges out for terrorism."

"But Mum, I am from the Lower Levels. If I got to court, I am stuffed. We can't afford legal representation, and the court system doesn't look kindly on people from the Lower Level. So the best punishment I would get is an execution, and that was them being generous, as the alternative is that they could send me into the wasteland with no radiation suit."

Ella weighted in. "Jacob, don't worry. Now that your mum is running for political office, the worst they can really do is keep you in a cell until the elections are over, and then they execute you."

"Jeez, thanks!"

"Jacob, don't worry, we will work out a plan to get out. You will not die, I promise. Please, Jacob."

I sighed again. "AGH! FINE, I will go to jail."

Anna gave me a hug and a kiss. "Thanks, Son!"

"But you better get me out."

"We will. Don't worry, Son."

I didn't respond. I just sat there drinking my beer.

Anna then turned her attention to the rest of the gang. "All right, everyone else, here is the game plan! I want you all to go out and campaign hard. I expect to there to be billboards, posters, whatever is needed to win this campaign, not just for me but for the others. We need the numbers. Does that sound like a plan?"

"Absolutely, it does"

Then we all put our hands in a circle and lifted them up rapidly, "GO TEAM!"

The next day, I rocked up to the steps of the Middle Level Police Department, District One Police Station, armed with nothing. I walked in through the sliding door to the police reception.

"Good morning, everyone. Lovely day to get arrested, don't you think?"

The officer behind the reception desk and the two officers who were just entering the building, plus the others in the back who were sitting at their desk, all sprung up from their chairs and pointed their guns at me.

"FREEZE! GET ON THE GROUND, NOW!"

No point arguing when I had a gun pointed at me. I threw my body to the floor of the police department, and the two officers who were just behind me kneeled on my back and neck, twisted my arms behind my back, and slapped cuffs on me.

The officers then picked me up and escorted me, where they took 3D imaging of my entire body and gave me a black jumpsuit with a box on the side that had the numbers 56899546 sketched across the white box. That all I was now, just a number, a single piece within the industrial prison complex.

I was sitting in my bland, colourless cell with reinforced shock-proof glass, wearing metal cuffs that dug into my hands and feet. I watched the officers and lawyers walk by. Then an old, obese officer opened my cell and chucked me an old holographic projector. "You get one phone call or one text. Your choice."

The officer then locked me in my cell, which is a sound-proof cell. I picked up the phone and dialled in her number, 0478964877, and the phone began to ring.

Then I heard, "Hello?"

"It is done. I have turned myself in."

"Good boy. Thank you for doing this for me."

"You better get me out of here!"

"We will, I promise you. I love you."

"Love you too. Stay safe."

We both hung up the projector, and I returned mine to the warden and sat back in my cell, watching the Holonet News that was projecting in the far corner of the office, as lawyers and the police walked by. Don't worry, I will be out of here in no time.

One week later, I was lying on the floor of my cell. One of the officers gave me a tennis ball to throw at the wall to kill the time. In the far corner, I noticed a faint picture on the Holonet News. I was in shock as my mum was standing on a podium dressed in a sharp blazer and a nice suit.

"Hey, can you turn the picture up?"

Surprisingly, he did. *Hah!* I thought to myself. *Normally, when I made a request for a pizza or a burger, he told me to keep my mouth shut or I would get a kick in the arse. But no, he turned the volume up, so he must be in a good mood.*

I watched as my mum got up to the podium. "Firstly, I would like to condemn the actions of my son, Jacob Turner, for the atrocities he has caused. He has brought great shame to his family. And if it wasn't for me convincing him to turn himself in, he would have killed again. I hope he gets the help he deserves in there."

A part of me wanted to cry at that statement, but I knew it was all staged, so I just sucked it up and took it as it was.

"Ladies and Gentlemen, I—"

Bang! A plasma bolt went flying into her left shoulder, and Mum went flying back from the impact, and the feed cut out.

Mum! I need to know she is all right.

CHAPTER 18

It's a busy, hot, sunny day on the Middle Level. The podium was all set up for Anna to speak, with camera crews from all different news outlets targeting their cameras directly at the stage waiting for Anna to speak. The stage was lined with banners that read 'Vote Anna'.

Behind the scenes, Anna was talking to her manager, Fred. They were going over about what to say in her speech. Meanwhile, Ella and Edward were also organising things behind the scenes, checking the lighting and the equipment. All the while, Anna was drinking a bottle of water and trying to gear her up, saying to herself in a mirror, "You got this, girl. You got this."

Then, after Ella and Edward were finished behind the scenes, they joined her in her trailer. Once Edward and Anna entered, they all gave her a hug. "You all right?"

Anna let a sigh of distress. "Yer, I am fine, but I am nervous as hell."

Ella cut in. "Remember, confidence is key!"

Edward added, "And remember, just look at the camera and smile!"

Just as they had finished, a stagehand came in. "Showtime!"

Ella and Edward gave her a final hug. "Best of luck!"

She excitingly left her trailer and made her way to the left side of the stage, where she lingered for a bit. Then, just as the announcer announced her name, the crowd roared in a fury of applause. Anna walked to the podium with pride and confidence, waved to a crowd of hundreds and blew kisses to the news crew to show off. She unrolled her prepared speech, took a deep breath and began to read. "Hello, everyone. Thank you for being here today. First, I would like to condemn the actions of my son, Jacob Turner, for the atrocities he has caused. He has brought great shame to his family. And if it wasn't for me convincing him to turn himself in, he would have killed again. I hope he gets the help he deserves in there. Ladies and Gentlemen, I—"

Anna's body was sent flying backwards across the stage, and she was slammed into a back wall.

Fred, Edward, Ella and her security detail all ran on stage. A second shot came ringing from a high rise across the street, as a red plasma bolt went flying past them, barely missing Anna and hitting the back wall. The colour of the plasma bolts mattered, as red indicated that the bolt was powerful, which was mainly used in sniper rifle, whereas blue meant low intensity and required less power, which produced more speed and was mainly used in plasma rifles and turrets.

"Quick! We need to protect Anna!" the security team yelled out, as they rushed to form a circle around her so the sniper could not get a clear shot of Anna, while Edward and Ella crouched in between the guards, trying to pick Anna up and escort her backstage.

Anna lay there motionless. Ella and Edward were shocked and were still trying to comprehend what had just happened.

"Gosh, I hope Anna is all right. Please be all right!"

With a gasp, Anna shot up, taking a deep breath in. Ella and Edward could not be more relieved. "Are you all right?"

"Yer. I am all right. Luckily, I am wearing a standard-issue plasma-resistant suit. State-of-the-art for all political figures."

She tried to get back up but couldn't, as the impact of the bolt have caused significant damage to her shoulder.

"Edward! Go to the building and find out who shot her."

Edward nodded to Ella and ran out from behind the stage and into downtown to find the building.

Meanwhile, police and ambulances arrived at the scene of the crime. Ella felt powerless in this moment. All she could really do was comfort Anna as much as possible, while Anna just held Ella's hand. "You are going to be all right, Anna. Just hold on!"

Edward ran for 5 minutes and eventually arrived at a construction site. That surprisingly was the same construction site where Jacob's life was saved by a crane. But this time, there was no crane and more construction as the building stage was nearly completed.

Edward noticed a flight of stairs, and in a rush, he sprinted up the steps to confront the man who had tried to kill his best friend's mum. After rushing up 20 flights of stairs, he got to the 20th floor and noticed a figure dressed in camo gear and wearing state-of-the-art body armour, lying prone and looking through the lens of a laser bolt sniper rifle.

The shooter sprung up and turned around to face Edward in shock. He didn't think Edward would arrive so quickly and was caught unprepared, as he quickly tried to turn the gun to fire at Edward. But before he could, Edward grabbed the sniper rifle barrel and pointed it down at the ground, just as the figure was about to pull the trigger.

Bang! The plasma bolt shot through the cement floor, which caused the laser to shoot through the floor and the structure of the concrete to collapse, which caused both of them to fall to the 19th floor.

Edward and the shooter both got up at the same time. Both were sore, yet they were determined to fight. The shooter reached for his sniper once again, but Edward knocked the shooter's gun out of his hand, causing it to fall out the window and hit the ground floor below. Edward was more than capable of holding his own, as he was a Kav Bitz Kar Do master.

Punches and kicks went flying back and forth. The shooter clearly was an elite soldier, as he knew how to use a sniper rifle and was a master in Kav Bitz Kar Do.

Back and forth they fought, both exchanging blows and both arming up with weapons from whatever resources they could find. The shooter armed him with a sledgehammer he found on the floor, while Edward armed himself with pieces of cement.

The fight got intense, as the shooter tried to swing the sledgehammer around, but Edward ducked and whacked him across the face multiple times, causing the shooter to move back in pain and caused his mask to fall off, showing Edward his face. The shooter was a white male with brown eyes and was bald with tattoos across his face.

Edward was about to come in for another strike, but the shooter obviously knew parkour from his military training. So the shooter swung his entire body 180 degrees in the air, putting his weight on his left hand, while bringing both his feet in. As Edward approached him, he projected his feet, performing a double kick and sending Edward flying backwards.

While the force wasn't enough to hurt him, it did cause Edward to fly off his feet and hit the ground. Just as the solider reached for a combat knife in his right shoe, Edward swept his leg, causing him to trip over and land on his back, and the knife fell out of his hand.

Then, Ella came bursting into the room with a laser pistol in her hand, firing three blue plasma bolts at the shooter.

While the first two shots missed, one did manage to hit the shooter's shoulder. While he was wearing body armour, but the impact of the shot sent him flying through the window falling to the streets below. They both looked out the window to find him, but he wasn't there. He disappeared, which was impressive considering he fell 19 storeys.

Ella and Edward rushed back down to Ground Level, only to find nothing, not even a crater. But as Edward looked, he saw him, the shooter, hanging from a steel beam, and he jumped down between Ella and Edward, causing them both to be knocked over. Ella quickly reached for the gun and opened fire. She managed to fire one bolt, but it only skinned his shoulder on the right, and the bolt went flying past him.

The shooter went for a punch, but Ella dodged in time to avoid the punch, just as his fist hit the ground, leaving a dent. This guy must have cybernetics, because he was incredibly strong and incredibly durable.

Ella was about to get up from the floor when the shooter kicked her straight in her chest, sending her flying back and hitting a wall. He was fast approaching Ella, but Edward managed to get the guy in a chokehold to hold him at bay temporarily. They both used their strength to push him to the ground, and he just lay there on the ground. They both approached him slowly and stood in front of him, looking at this balding 40-year-old man with a Black Sun symbol carved into the tattoos on his forehead.

The Black Sun was a far-right radical group. They were anti-immigrant and extremely nationalistic. The shooter just lay on the ground, but Edward was angry and tired from fighting. He went on all-interrogation mode on him. "Why did you try to kill Anna?"

The man spat blood at Edward's face, just as Edward tried to throw another punch at him.

Then the shooter let out a chuckle. "John wants you and that woman's head."

"WeapCo was behind this. We figured so."

He then laughed. "Oh no, WeapCo was only one part of the puzzle piece. The person who hired me was the pres—"

The shooter looked shocked, as a tick sound from his armour went off. He then just laughed. Ella and Edward bolted out of there and rushed behind cover, as it sounded like a bomb was about to go off. But luckily, the shooter didn't account for the fact that the body armour would contain the blast, so the blast just imploded on itself, causing him to become nothing but a skeleton from the head down.

"Blast! He died before we could get any information out of him!"

"Edward! Quick, we have to get out of here."

In the far distance, police sirens began blaring towards the scene. The neighbours must have heard the gunshot or the explosion.

"Edward, meet me at the Middle Level Hospital!"

Edward nodded, and just like that, they both ran in separate directions. Ella jumped over barbed wire fences, and Edward ran up the stairs and jumped over to the next building top. All the while, the police officers were fast approaching the scene.

Both Ella and Edward met up with Anna at the same time, who was in a hospital gown and had successfully recovered from the plasma shot. They both hugged Anna, who flinched a little at the pain from the laser bolt wound. A robotic nurse was there scanning her wounds, not even paying attention to the people hugging Anna, as this type of robot had no empathy.

"Are you all right, Anna?"

Before Anna could answer, the robot cut in and said, "Patient Z6 has suffered from a gunshot wound and has tissue damage in her shoulder and some trauma to her head and back, but the patient is free to leave."

Thank goodness for state-of-the-art hospitals. Some of the perks of being a soon-to-be elected official were good hospital care. They picked up Anna and slowly wheeled her out of the hospital room and into the backseat of Fred's floating limousine car.

The group sat in the backseat, watching the Holonet News, with Fred explaining to the gang that the whole assassination attempt had boosted her in the polls by 20 per cent, putting her ahead of her incumbent and adversary, Ron.

Ron was a corrupt far-right politician who was clearly in WeapCo's pocket and was Anna's number one adversary. If he was to get elected, there was no telling what that man could do to the Lower Levels. His policies included loosening gun laws to allow kids as young as 12 to buy firearms, no government support and an increase in military spending and occupation. He was trouble, but thank goodness that Anna was ahead of him in the pools.

Anna, Edward, Fred and Ella were all in the backseat trying to have a few drinks.

"Are you all right, Anna?"

She let out a sigh. "Fine Edward, it just—" There was a pause. "I don't know. Maybe I made a massive mistake running for political office. I mean, I've been shot, people think my campaign is a joke, and what is worse is that I gave up my son to the authorities."

Anna let out another sigh. "Maybe I should just give up on this campaign and use the money to bail out Jacob."

Ella looked shocked. "No! Don't you dare. Look, don't worry about Jacob. I am sure he can handle himself in prison. Look, I get it, it's tough, but think of all the good you can do! Anna, you just have to look at the bigger picture. The impact you could make for the community would be enormous for the whole Lower Levels."

Anna let out another sigh. "I know. I just hope Jacob is handling himself in that place."

Edward then let a mild chuckle. "Ha! I am more concerned about the other prisoners' safety than Jacob's. That guy never stays down for long."

Everyone in the car, except for Fred, let out a chuckle at the thought of Jacob being hurt in prison, as everyone knew the type of guy Jacob was.

Then suddenly, ram! Their car was hit from behind by another car, knocking all of them to the floor.

Edward was now panicked. "What the hell was that?"

Ella got to her feet and looked out the back window. "I think you know what it is!"

The car then reversed back, and at full speed, hit their car again, this time causing a massive dent in the car and causing the boot to implode in on it.

The mysterious black car then reversed from the damaged boot and pulled to the side of the car. Edward looked through the tinted black window.

"Guys, I think we need to get down!"

The black car's window winded down to reveal a mysterious figure who looked like the one that tried to snipe Anna, with the same tattoos and everything.

The figure pulled out a sonic blaster and, with a pull of the trigger, released a sonic boom headed straight towards the car. The blast was loud enough that it damaged their eardrums. While it didn't damage the car, it did cause the glass to shatter, which is what they wanted, as the entire car was calibre and laser resistant.

Then the car sped up and turned its body to the side so the right side was facing the car. Two other thugs flung up their old M134 Miniguns as Ella looked at the front windscreen.

"GET DOWN!"

Everyone dropped their entire body to the floor of the car as fast as they could and placed their hands on their heads. The turret barrel spun around at a rapid speed, and 6,000 rounds per minute went flying into the car, cutting through the passenger-side door, the driver's seat and the driver, leaving nothing but half a chair and a body in its place. They were all lying on the floor as the bullets went flying through the windscreen and out the back window so fast that it was as if a thousand sparks went flying through the car. They almost looked like lasers. But thank goodness they weren't an inch lower, or else everyone would have died.

After nearly 2 minutes, the turret stopped firing, as they had run out of rounds. The figures shut the passenger-side door and flew around to the right-hand side of our limousine to check for survivors. They thought they had done the job, when Ella shot her head up, quickly jumped over the glove compartment and sat on the driver's lap to get their car as far away from their attackers as possible.

"Time to put the pedal to the metal!" She quickly put her foot on the pedal, which caused the car to go zooming at a rapid rate, blowing past the attacker's car as it rushed at Mach 1 down the highway. Ella was trying to not be grossed out by the fact that she was sitting on a dead body, but she just couldn't. Nonetheless, she had to get the others to safety first. Edward then hopped into the passenger seat, forcing Anna to be stuck in the backseat with wind blowing through the exposed window. Luckily, these cars were built with inertia-proof shielding so the wind would not cut her to pieces. Ella pulled the wheel closer to her chest, causing the car to fly downwards, as she hoped to lose their pursuers in the Lower Levels, ducking and weaving through power lines and railway tracks. Still, it wasn't enough to lose the mysterious car, as it was tailing right behind them.

Suddenly, the mysterious car rolled down the right-side passenger window, and one of the mysterious figures popped his upper body out the window and opened fire with a blaster pistol. The figure managed to fire a blast at the car, damaging its mirror. But the figure tried again, trying to fire another bolt at the car, this time hitting the passenger-side door and leaving a massive dent in it. However, just as the figure tried to fire a fourth shot at the car, Ella quickly manoeuvred the car to the left, which caused the attackers' car to fly off-course and head downtown into the Lower Level. One of the attackers leaned out again, but this time, he was unlucky, as there was a railway pole and let's just say he was out of action.

The old factory was fast approaching. "Holy hell! Ella, pull up! Pull up!"

Ella, out of reflex, quickly pushed the steering wheel inwards to shoot the car into an upward trajectory. However, the attackers' car was not quick enough, and it crashed into the old factory. It was remarkable watching the car crash through the wall of the factory and come out the other side all torn up, its propellers shot to hell. They all celebrated in victory and let out another cheer. Finally, they managed to get the car off their tail.

But the military was still conducting military exercises, so the automated anti-air launcher picked up their flying car zooming past its radar, and within seconds, a missile projected itself out of the launcher, and through its thruster, the missile propelled forward at hypersonic speed towards their car.

Ella looked out through her window. "Everyone, bail out!"

They all opened the door, which was just sticking out through the inertia-proof shielding, and just before she left, Ella grabbed the inertia-proof shielding device. The inertia-proof shielding device was a device standard in all floating cars because the car travelled at hypersonic speed. If they jumped without it, they would be cut to shreds. It was a device like a phone and was built like a little black box on the top of the driver's side.

Ella pulled the device off its holder and told everyone to jump, which they all did, and they all took a leap of faith. They all let out a loud scream, but luckily, they were high up, and they all landed on a random skyscraper. Now, another handy thing about the device is that it prevents force and fall damage, so Ella, Edward, Fred and Anna landed on the skyscraper unharmed. The group just stood there are the car flew up into the air. The missile managed to hit the back, knocking its back propeller, and the car began to fall, landing in some unknown spot in the city, as they couldn't see it through the skyscrapers.

They all stood there catching their breath, as they were still in a bit of shock from what had just happened. They could see the smoke trail from where the missile had travelled in the sky, and there was black smoke appearing from the impact of the car.

They were pretty sure the firefighters would take care of it, as they heard sirens from fire trucks rushing towards the scene. They all just stood there for a couple more minutes to allow their hearts to slow down. Then, they took the stairs back down to the Lower Levels. They were all a little bruised and tired, especially Anna, who had only a couple hours ago survived a plasma wound, but they just nursed their wounds and began walking home alive.

After walking home in the dark, they pulled up to the front door exhausted and drained from the fighting that wasn't supposed to happen that day. Ella, Fred, Edward and Anna all collapsed on the couch, completely drained of energy. None of them could even get up to have a beer. Anna hunched over on the couch, rubbed her eyes, and as bluntly as possible, she just simply started the conversation with, "Far out!"

Ella let out a sigh, "Yer. What the hell were they trying to accomplish?"

"Same as the guy in the construction site. They were members of the Black Sun."

"Yes, but why would a far-right group go to all that trouble just to kill one legislator."

"Isn't it obvious? They are trying to take me out because they know that I would be a threat to the military bill."

"Well, duh, Anna! But what I mean is, who is funding them and giving them all this equipment?"

"Isn't that obvious? WeapCo? Defence Contractors? I mean take your pick."

"Well, they certainly did a number on us today."

"Ha! You can say that again. We might as well check the news."

Anna grabbed the remote that was lying on the couch and flicked on the Holonet projector to watch the Holonet News. After the projector turned on, the first thing to project on was the face of her adversary, Ron Kurkey. The dude was clearly part of Black Sun by the small tattoo on the back of his neck. Also, he was clearly in the back pocket of WeapCo, as he was seen at every WeapCo event, drinking wine with all the executives. According to Ron's bio, he only served 18 months in the military, where he got an alleged spinal injury (the doctor was paid off by his dad), and after that, he got a job in his dad's banking firm, despite not holding a bachelor's degree, where he 'worked his way to the top' and eventually changed careers to politics. The first thing he said when the Holonet projected his face was a lie. "My condolences are with Anna and his family for these horrific attacks. I pray for a speedy recovery for her and her friends."

All Ella could do was roll her eyes. "Oh, shut up. He was so clearly behind those attacks!"

"Oh, absolutely no doubt about it!"

But Fred, still the same optimist, stood up holding his electronic tablet to show us the latest statistics. "Don't worry, guys, we can still recover from this. We are still two points ahead of Ron. If we campaign hard and begin upping our game within the lower and the lower-middle communities, we could easily win this election."

Anna let out a sigh. "Excuse me," she said, then got up from her chair, grabbed a cigarette and began walking up to her room. She lay on the bed smoking a cigarette, contemplating her choice to run for political office.

Ella knocked on the door. "Can I come in?"

Anna let out another sigh. "Yer, I guess so."

Ella, looking concerned, sat on the end of the bed and asked, "Are you holding up all right?"

"I don't know. I mean, I am in immense pain, I sold out my son to the cops, I have put you and Edward in danger, and I am so exhausted, and it is only the start of the campaign. I just don't know what to do."

"But you're doing great. I mean, yes, you may have put us in danger and sold out your son, but you're leading a strong campaign, you're two points ahead and you got the

Lower Level communities looking up to you. You can't give up now!"

"Yes, but come on, you and I both know that we can't compete against Ron. He has too much power, too much influence, and I am just some mum from the Lower Level with little money and no power whatsoever. I mean, I just want to live a normal life."

Ella snapped back at that ridiculous comment. "But you're not built for a normal life, Anna. I mean, look at you. You're Ella Turner. You not only managed to overtake a billionaire's son, but you managed to survive a car chase and an assassination attempt, all in one week. Anna, I know you are exhausted, but you are at a point where you can make a real change in this place, because you have the integrity and courage to face anyone who stands in your way."

Anna just lay there smoking, but Ella could tell that she had cheered up a little bit more. "Hah! I guess you're right!"

"Girl, you got this. Anyway, you are in a lot of pain, and I am tired. I am going to hit the hay. Night."

Anna just replied, "Night."

As Ella shut the door, leaving her to just lie on the bed and smoke, something in Anna's had changed; her attitude changed from sad to curious.

After finishing her smoke, she grabbed her official work tablet and began scrolling through it for the old archives of past presidents from the old United States of America. Something caught her eye. It was old news footage of John F. Kennedy, a historical president from times past. Watching a video from him was like looking at a cave painting. That's how old he was. But what he said had an impression on her: "Those who dare to fail miserably can achieve greatly. Leadership and learning are indispensable to each other. Ask not what your country can do for you; ask what you can do for your country. A man may die, nations may rise and fall, but an idea lives on."

The quote, that speech, really struck a nerve in her. She felt so inspired by what he said. Yes, she had no idea who this person was or what he accomplished, because she failed ancient history in school, but those words really seemed to resonate with her and what she was going through. She may have been failing, but she felt that she had a duty not just to her level but to her city. For years, she had watched corrupt officials and shady businessmen ruin her community, kill her people and ruin her family, and frankly, she had had enough of having to hide and run and try to live a normal life. She was a fighter, and she wanted to fight back. And if she failed, she would fail trying. Tired and sore, she went to bed that night determined.

The next morning, she walked down the stairs in a nice, clean-cut suit with an American Division City flag badge pinned to her collar. Anna was defiantly roaring with energy. "So, why are we all looking so tired? We have an election to win!"

Ella, Edward and Fred stood up and clapped in applause.

"All right everyone, gather around. Here is the campaign plan!" Fred, the campaign manager, stood around the coffee table, holding the work tablet in his hand. "Now, here are the current results from the polls. You are currently just two points ahead of Ron, but that's OK, because we still have a chance to win this!"

Fred then switched the projection of the polls to the district map. "Now you have a majority of the votes in the Lower Levels, whereas Ron has a majority of the votes in the Upper Levels. So if we are to win this, we have to target the Middle Levels, as that is currently a swing level. Now, a majority of the time, they normally vote for the Upper Level candidates, but with the flood and the riots, it is split up the middle at the moment."

Fred then switched the tablet from the district map to the game plan. "Now Edward, you grew up in the Upper Level, correct?"

"Yes!"

"Great! Use your family connections and influence to try to win some of the voters and investors in the Upper Level to fund the campaign. Ella, you and your father grew up in the Lower Levels, right?"

"Correct."

"Great. Go up to the Middle Level and bring some friends and campaign hard. Hand out flags and posters and volunteer at soup kitchens if you have to. Do whatever it takes! I will do some social media campaigning. Now Anna, get prepared and be ready. The first debate is tomorrow. We have a lot of work cut out for us."

Anna was not deterred. "Ready, team?"

Everyone put their hand in a circle.

"Go, team!"

In the next couple of weeks, Ella, Edward and Anna hit the campaign trail hard. Everyone knew what they had to do, and they did it. Edward went to so many fancy lunches and dinners that he managed to gain 5 kg in 1 week.

However, Edward managed to shoot Anna's approval rating up by 10 per cent. Meanwhile, Ella and Anna rocked up everywhere in the Lower and Middle Levels, appearing in supermarkets, shopping centres, movie plazas, cafes, aged care centres, and building sites. Wherever the people were, the team went there with a 'Vote Anna!' badge or a simple handshake and a short speech. Their combined campaigning shot her approval rating up by another 10 per cent. Fred had the easiest job out of all of them, just on the couch, on his phone texting his fingers off while under an air conditioner. Poor guy. But even by doing that, it shot her approval up by another 10 per cent.

Then, every night, they would come home to the Holonet to find a smear campaign against her with the ad going something like this:

"Inexperienced, immature and a woke leftist, is that really someone you can put your faith in?"

While these types of ads may have angered Anna, she was not going to let them keep her down, as she was determined to win this election. Also, they had ads of their own:

"Ron claims to be a family man, but did you know that he has had an affair with two others? Can you really trust this man to run the level if he can't even run a family? Vote for Anna Turner."

Or "Do you really want a terrorist in ParliaCongress? Vote for Anna."

They continued this strategy for the next 2 weeks, and she managed to poll 10 points ahead of Ron. It was a significant victory so far, but they still had two more weeks ahead of the campaign, and the sad reality was that they were running out of money and were way over budget. Both Fred and Anna were sitting on the couch going through the numbers.

Anna asked concerned, "Give it to me straight, Fred."

"Well, we are exactly 10,000 over budget, and if we can't come up with money, then—"

If they wanted to continue the campaign, they needed to get more funds and fast, or they would have to drop out. Ron on the other hand didn't have to worry. Coming from an upper-class family, he never had to worry about money or bills. Anna let out another sigh. Great. She was finally winning in life, and now she was going to have to quit. Her moment of victory was crushed by reality.

Ella and Edward's faces went from excited to sad. "Don't worry, Anna. We will figure something out."

Anna picked up her e-cigarette. "I am going for a walk." She said, walking out the front door.

Anna needed to clear her head. Walking down the dark, poorly lit road, she let out a puff of smoke from her e-cigarette. She had come so close to victory, and now her chance of making real change had turned into a crushing defeat. The motivation and inspiration that kept her going was gone.

Then, in the dark of night, the shining beams from a floating limousine pulled up beside her, and a mysterious figure yelled, "Get in!"

Anna was a little worried. "Who are you?"

"Who cares? Get in!"

"No, I don't know you!"

Then, she was plunged into darkness, as someone put a bag over her head, and the car door opened. Vroom! The car had taken off.

Anna screamed out, "Who are you people? Let me go!"

One of the mysterious figures yelled out, "Quiet. The big boss wants to see you."

"What big boss? What are you people talking about?"

Then the car stopped, and the car door opened. She was dragged for a couple miles until the bag was pulled off her head, and she was sitting in an office with the one and only Adrian King.

"Let's talk."

The man sitting in front of Anna was Adrian King, the CEO of Wacco INC, the second-biggest manufacturer of arms and ammunition in the city and WeapCo's biggest rival. The man behind the table was a 40-year-old man of Japanese descent and was dressed in a white business suit. The man got up from the table.

"Apologies for my thugs' aggressive approach. They can be a bit abrasive. Allow me to introduce myself I am—"

"I know who you are," Anna snapped at him in an aggressive tone.

Adrian just smiled. "Straight to business. I like that."

Anna wasn't too impressed with Adrian kidnapping her. "I know what you want. I am not going to have my campaign sponsored by a weapon manufacturer!"

Adrian was still maintaining professionalism and a calm demeanour. "Now, now, don't think of me as an enemy. Instead, think of me as an ally."

Adrian got up from the table and walked over to a bottle of old Kentucky whisky and pulled himself a glass of neat whisky. He offered Anna a glass, but she gestured to indicate that she didn't want any.

After collecting his glass, he sat back at the table and continued talking. "WeapCo. I want them out of this campaign as much as you do. That bastard John is undercutting my business and cutting my profit.”

“I would only be supplementing one gun company for another. Why in the world would I take funding from you?”

Then playing his ace, Adrian said. “Because you don’t have a choice. I know that you’re barely holding your campaign on by a thread. You’re over budget, and I know you don’t have the resources to continue your campaign. If you don’t take the money, I am sure you will lose, and WeapCo will float their weapons onto the street.”

“But so would you! I am not falling off it, Adrian. You don’t care about my campaign all you care about is lining your own pocket.”

Then, Adrian finished the glass of whisky. “Well, I guess you’re going to have to choose. Do you supplement one evil for another, or do you leave WeapCo and the army run amok and ruin your community? Your choice.”

Anna stood there contemplating whether to accept or decline.

The limo pulled up to the front door of the house. Ella rushed out to help her. “Anna! Thank goodness. You have been gone for an hour. Where were you? Where did you go? Why were you in a limousine?”

While Edward and Fred looked up in shock, they didn’t say anything.

Anna took a deep breath in and gestured towards the couch. “Guys, take a seat. We need to talk.”

Ella returned to her seat next to Edward and Fred, and they all looked up at Anna as she stood in the middle of the living room. She turned to Fred.

“Fred, check our account. I managed to fix the budget problem.”

Fred looked at his tablet. “I don’t believe it, Anna! Where did you get a million dollars?”

“Anna, you got us another sponsor? That is great news!”

Anna gave a fake smile in response. “Yer, but we have to make a few changes.”

At that moment, Ella's face went from excited to confused. "What sort of changes?"

Anna sighed. "Well, we are going to have to remove our campaign promise on restricting gun laws."

Ella's face gave another confused look. "But Anna, that is one of our major campaign promises! Guns are flooding this level and destroying our community. What happened?"

"Well, I met with Adrian King, the CEO of Wacco INC, and he agreed to fund our campaign as long as—"

"As long as you sell out and allow him to flood his product through our level?"

"But he will fund us to remove the military exercises."

Ella was not impressed. "Yes, you want to substitute one evil for another."

"Ella, come on!"

"No, you come on! You're going to let these weapons flow into our streets? I worked in a gun shop, and I am a soldier. I have seen kids as young as 10 die because of these guns. Anna, you can't take this money!"

"It's too late! I have already accepted this money, and there's no going back now."

Ella just smirked. "Guess you really have become a politician."

"Don't take that tone with me! You worked in a gun shop selling weapons, so how is what I have done any different to what you and your father did?"

"That's different, though. We were broke and had no money, but you have a chance to make a significant change. I expected you to be better than this."

"Ella! If you don't like the way this campaign is being run, then don't be a part of it."

Both Anna and Ella were shocked at that comment, and there was a moment of silence and awkwardness in the room. Then Ella broke the silence. She got up from the couch. "Fine. I am not going to help another corrupt politician exploit this community's situation for her own political gain. I am out of here!"

"Ella don't!"

Ella was too enraged to care. She walked out and slammed the front door shut.

The situation left Anna, Fred and Edward silent.

Ella walked down the street, slowly crying and feeling betrayed that a woman who called herself a friend and treated her like she was part of the family would sell her soul to a devil in exchange for power. She felt really betrayed, but deep down, she knew that she was kind of being a hypocrite because she and her dad both ran a gun shop. But as Ella stopped walking, whack, she was hit in the back of her head, and she went scrambling to the floor unconscious.

CHAPTER 19

It's been nearly 2 weeks since I watched my mum get shot on the Holonet. The court denied me bail, because why would they let a man who blew up a nuclear power plant and indirectly cause a mass flooding that nearly wiped out the entire city and killed thousands of people walk free?

So I have just been left to rot in this jail cell until my court day. I couldn't contact my mum or my family, because I used up my last phone call. I worried about my friends and family; I mean, I only figured out about my mum surviving the assassination through a Holonet projection of one of her campaign ads.

It feels like I have been completely forgotten about. My face and hair had become so messy, I had not showered, I had the beard of a metalworker, and I hadn't seen sunlight in weeks, which had made me pale as a ghost. But I guess one of the benefits of having nothing to do is that I now have time to work out. I tried to maintain a highly rigid workout program to not go mad.

As I was about to begin my third workout for the day, the guard knocked on the cell glass. "Prisoner, lights out. Tomorrow is court day. Get ready to lose, scum."

He let out a laugh, turning off all the lights, leaving me to lie on a concrete bed in the dark with nothing to look at but a grotesque poster of half-naked women that one of the other prisoners must have brought in with him. Being alone with my thoughts, all I could think about was how rapidly my life had changed, going from a factory worker to an alleged terrorist. Somehow that night, I managed to get some sleep, until of course, I heard a series of bangs on my cell.

"Court date, inmate! Time to see if you live or die." The guard let out a laugh.

I woke up to the bright light of my cell, and as I opened my eyes, the cell door flung open, and at least four other guards came in. They removed my shirt and threw a strait-jacket over me (standard procedure), and they were rough too, leaving a few bruises.

After a few minutes, they escorted me to my feet and began to walk me down a corridor, where all the other prisoners also awaiting their court date began wolf-calling me.

In the corner of my eye, as I was walking past one of the prison cells, a prisoner came lunging towards me with a shiv in his hands. It was one of those Black Sun supporters who was not happy with my mum's political party and decided to take it out on me.

The prisoner managed to scrape my jacket, but luckily, it didn't cut me.

Two other guards came rushing over, opened the guy's cell and threw him straight to the ground. The guard just turned to me and said, "Keep walking, prisoner!"

The guards eventually escorted me to a little black van, threw me in and shut the door. Darkness, more darkness. Then the car started up and began to move, throwing me into the wall of the van with every turn and curve it made until it finally stopped. The guard entered the van and threw a sack over my head. Then I could feel four arms grab each of my limbs and begin dragging me down a hallway, but this time, I couldn't see anything, as it was pitch black. Then, I heard a door open and felt a sharp pain going through my body as the guard threw me to the table, shoved me down onto the chair and removed the bag over my head.

I was before a magistrate that consisted of one middle-aged white judge on a bench, and that was it. The court system has changed dramatically over the past thousand years due to overpopulation and a significant increase in crime. It was very much rushed. While the old doctrine of innocent until proven guilty remained, the criminal court heard over a hundred people a day, so to streamline the process, I only really had 10 minutes to prove my innocence, and the judge had free reign over the court, so he pretty much decided if I lived or died. It was my lawyer's job to prove my innocence in the limited amount of time they had, as they were overworked and rushed. There were also no more jury and no more witnesses. It was basically just me, the judge and my lawyer, who arrived late, which reduced my time to 9 minutes. Plus, the judge would get a bonus if he could reduce the prison intake. No more rights, no more innocent till proven guilty rubbish. Welcome to living in a dystopian city.

The judge banged his gavel. "Court is now in session! Defendant, where is your lawyer?"

How the hell am I supposed to know? I barely even know where I am, I was thinking to myself. "I don't know, your honour."

Then, this pipsqueak kid budged through the door; dropping all his documents on the floor as he ran to the table. "I'm here, I'm here, your honour!"

I was thinking to myself, *Seriously, this kid looks like he was barely out of high school, let alone to be my lawyer.*

He then approached me. "Nice to me you, sir. I am Richard Miles, your public defender."

He then offered me a stretched arm while he shook nervously. I was thinking to myself, *What? This guy is defending my life? Well, I am stuffed.*

But I guess I had to give him the benefit of the doubt, so I just shook his hand. "Nice to meet you. How long have you been a lawyer?"

"Oh, I just passed the bar yesterday."

My face dropped in horror. But it was not uncommon among public defenders, who were poorly paid and over-worked. All the good lawyers went to people with money. But no time to argue; he was the best I had!

The judge then opened the court session. "All rise. Prisoner 56899546, you stand accused of theft, grand theft, robbery, assault, assaulting four police officers, damage to property, fraud, conspiracy to commit terrorism, grievous bodily harm, mass murder, resisting arrest, conspiracy, tres-passing, murder, damage to government property, entering an unauthorised military zone, entering the wastelands with-out a permit, procession of illegal firearms, political espio-nage, crime against the environment, terrorism and treason. How do you plead?"

The lawyer was too busy going through court documents to notice, so I just spoke for him, "Not guilty, Your Honour!"

"Not guilty he pleads, does he? Very well, let the trail commence."

The judge then clicked a button, and the projector played a projector of images, surveillance footage, statements from witnesses and documents such as my birth certificate and ser-vice history document.

"Sargent Jacob Turner, please describe the following footage."

The screen projected CCTV footage of the entire power plant blowing up. After 2 minutes of watching the plant, explode the judge turned to me. "Your defence?"

My lawyer didn't say anything. He was looking through the mountain of paperwork, so I just decided to speak for him. "Your honour, I would like to represent myself."

The lawyer looked relieved, and he just ran out of the courtroom. He was useless. But oh well. I readjusted my tie. "Your honour, may I ask that you provide footage of the con-trol room in the hours prior to the power plant explosion?"

The judge yelled, "Granted."

Then the projector played CCTV footage that showed the officer throwing me into the console. *Perfect,* I thought to myself, and I gave my defence, "Your honour, as the footage can clearly show, I am not fully responsible for the power plant explosion. There was no *mens rea* to establish that it was my intention to destroy the power plant. Therefore, the explosion is of no guilt of mine."

The judge looked at me. "What were you doing in the building in the first place?"

"Well, all you can really charge me for is trespassing. You can't charge me for murder and terrorism, and I can't be held responsible for the destruction of the power plant."

The judge, with an angry look, continued, "Very well, then can you explain this footage?"

The judge then projected multiple CCTV pieces of footage from the petrol station, which also included body cam footage from multiple police officers and medical reports from the police officers.

"Explain this?"

"Your honour, I—"

Ding! The timer went off before I could justify my actions. It says in the constitution that I had a right to due process, but it never said how long I got to defend myself. I just stood there, scared, knowing that I most certainly was going to die. The judge lifted his hammer and was about to slam the gavel down on the bench.

"I find the defendant ... guilty! Prisoner 56899546, I sentence you to—"

But just as the judge was about to bang his gavel, some guy in a suit rushed into the room, springing the doors open and rushing down towards the judge. "Your honour!"

The judge stopped in confusion. "This better be important!"

The man rushed up to the judge's bench, and he and the judge whispered back and forth; the voices were too quiet to understand. All I could hear was mumbling and then the judge said in a shocked voice, "Oh, this is the guy?"

That was followed by some back-and-forth whispering and then a massive sigh from the judge. "Oh, very well! Prisoner 56899546, I sentence you to life in prison."

With an absolute dirty look, the judge banged his gavel. "Case dismissed!" This was followed up with the judge whispering underneath his voice, "Lucky bastard."

While I wasn't happy with the fact that I was going to prison, I guess I am happy that I survived, as someone like me with no money, from the Lower Levels and with multiple charges not being sentenced to death was a blessing.

Two guards walked over and began dragging me out of the room and back into the black van with a bag shoved over my head. I couldn't see the bag, but I did hear the guard say, "You're gonna wish you got the death penalty, my friend."

The door shut, and off we went.

CHAPTER 20

13-09-3025

The van stopped. I got out of the van, still not able to see anything. All I could hear was the car stopping, and my entire body was dragged along by the guards. The driver yelled out, "Welcome to Quincentennial Prison!"

It was a massive structure that was dug underground and contained up to 100,000 prisoners. It was a prison, aged care home and an insane asylum all in one, as it housed both the insane and sane. Normally, prisons like these were reserved for the worst of the worst. People who committed lower offences and had no money were killed, but people who were from the Middle Level or were declared insane (because it is considered 'inhumane' to kill an insane person) were sent here.

I was placed into an elevator, and then I heard a loud noise coming from a siren and through the loudspeaker, "Elevator moving. Please stand clear!"

Then, suddenly, the elevator shot down at rapid speed like I was on one of those roller-coaster rides they have at an amusement park. The elevator was moving so fast that I could literally feel my entire body floating for a few seconds. Then, the elevator stopped, and I fell to the floor, with the guard escorting me to my feet. "On your feet, prisoner! Welcome to Quincentennial Prison."

The guards removed the bag from my head, and instantly, I caught the glare from the light above, as my eyes hadn't readjusted yet to the light. The guard then yelled at me to move, as one of them hit me in the back of the head to get moving. I stumbled a bit, but eventually, I began to walk down the dark, disgusting, dimly lit corridor passing all the cells. I walked into a cell, which had a stainless-steel door with a little window on it. I could just barely see the prisoners' eyes as they were glaring at me. It was hard to make out their faces. All I could see were the dark, twisted eyes.

The guard kept dragging me along until finally I reached my cell. I stood there looking at the rusted stainless-steel door with the number 110 inscribed on it. I was shaking, and I was preparing my body to fight, because to survive in this place, I had to assert dominance. The door swung open, and the guards grabbed me and flung me so fast into the cell that I stumbled over and fell, and the door swung close so fast that it was shut within a second of opening. Then I heard the metallic click from the internal locks to the door, sealing me in this room with me and my roommate.

I was scared out of my mind. Quickly, I turned away from the door to face my new roommate. I looked throughout the cell. The room was dimly lit. The only things in this room were two bunk beds and a stainless-steel toilet. That's it. Nothing more. But what was scaring me the most was the fact that I couldn't see my roommate. So slowly I began to walk into the room and stood in the centre, and then I heard a voice come from the lower bunk. "Don't be afraid."

My immediate reaction was fear. I jumped, getting my body in a fighting stance for a potential attack. The mysterious figure got out from the bunk and stood there in front of me. Immediately, I was taken aback in surprise. I was expecting some big, swole man with tattoos like in all those prison movies. But no, what stood in front of me was this skinny, pale, 16-year-old kid with glasses and a sort of mushroom haircut. The boy just stood there in front of me. "Don't be afraid. I don't want to hurt you."

My body was still on guard, in case he had a weapon, but it was relaxed enough for me to ask, "Who are you?"

The boy let out a playful chuckle. "Oh, where are my manners? My name is Norman." He then proceeded to reach out an upstretched hand. I return the exchange.

"Name's Jacob. What are you in for, my friend?"

Allowing my heart rate to slow and my body to relax, I shook the guy's hand. He let out another playful laugh before adjusting his glasses.

"I got caught on some websites. Not important. You?"

"Ah, just some terrorism charges, no big deal."

The guy laughed again. "Jeez, I am sharing a cell with a terrorist. Anyway, I get the bottom bunk."

"All good," I responded, before I crawled into my bunk. "So Norman, how long you have been down here for?"

"Ah, don't know. You sort of lose track when you are down in this cell. Maybe 5 years. Maybe. I don't really know."

Then, there was a bang on the door, and the guard yelled out, "Lights out!"

Automatically, the lights in the cell were switched off, and we were both left in nothing but darkness.

"OK, night!" Norman had rolled over and gone to bed, while I lay on the hard concrete bed, hoping to get some sleep, but I just couldn't, so I was left alone with my thoughts. Despite being alone, I heard a strange voice whispering to me.

"Jacob," that voice said.

That strange voice. What was it? It wasn't the voice of my roommate. He had a squeaky, teenage voice. I don't think the guy had even hit puberty yet. No, it was the voice of a female.

She repeated, "Jacob!"

Her voice sounded like that of a ghost. "Jacob, I love—"

The light switched on once again. "Morning, inmates. Breakfast time."

The entire room lit up and went from dark to white in a matter of minutes, while I didn't get any sleep whatsoever. I guess that explains why all the prisoners in here had bloodshot eyes. In a hurry, Norman and I jumped down from our bunks, just as the door swung open, and like cattle, we walked in a single file line down to the cafeteria behind the 100,000 other prisoners, as we all lined up with a plastic tray in our hand, waiting for our food.

Norman was chewing my ear off about how I should learn how to code and if I had ever been on 5chan and what was my K/O ratio on Honour of Duty. To be completely honest, I had no idea what the hell this guy was talking about; all I did was nod and smile, because I guess it was good to have someone to talk to in here. After waiting for the hundred or so prisoners in front of us, it was finally our turn. Norman and I stood there with our plates in our hands, and the kitchen staff gave us free food: scrambled eggs with bacon, a protein drink and a pill.

I turned to Norman. "What does the pill do?"

He shrugged his shoulders. "Don't know. But the guard will make sure you take it, so I recommend starting with it first."

After 20 minutes to eat, the guard banged on the nearest table. "Back to your cells!"

So, not thinking, we all got up from our tables, went back into our cells and lay back on our bunks.

"Hey Norman, do we do anything else in this prison besides sleeping and eating?"

Norman shot back, "This is all we do. Isn't it awesome?"

I looked concerned. Norman didn't mind, as he was autistic. He loved repetition, but for someone like me, I knew I was going to go insane fast. I just lay there in my white cell until the lights went out, and I could literally hear the wailing from the other prisoners.

For the next couple of months, I think my life was on autopilot: eat, sleep, 'Jacob', repeat, eat, sleep, 'Jacob', repeat. Day by day, I could feel my body and my mind breaking down, until finally, with bloodshot eyes and a full-grown beard, I snapped in anger and yelled out a massive scream. Then I proceeded to kick the steel door rapidly and began banging on the door, begging for them to let me out.

Norman was in the background trying to calm me down. He said, "Jacob, you need to relax, or the guards are going to come."

But I couldn't take it anymore. I didn't care what the guards would do to me. I had no choice. I pushed my luck and screamed out, "If I don't get out of here soon, I will kill myself!"

Then sirens throughout the prison rang out, and I stopped in panic. Norman went to his bed and said in panic, "Oh no, what have you done!"

I was freaked out for a bit too.

Then, a green odourless gas started leaking from the ceiling, and the room quickly filled with gas. Norman and I went running around the cell in panic as our lungs began to burn and our eyes began to tear up. Suddenly, the guards burst through the door and threw me in a straitjacket, stuck a sedative needle in my neck, and then threw me onto the bunk and left the room with the door locked. All I could do was giggle and laugh, as my head became queasy from the needle. The room began to spin, and my vision became blurry, and then I heard that voice again. Then, for some reason, I woke up in a forest.

It was strange, I knew this forest, but I had never actually been here before. I thought it may have been a dream, but it felt too real to be a dream. The first thing I did was look down at my hand, as there was an ominous blue glow surrounding them. It was weird; I mean, I had heard about astral projection, but I never thought that I would be capable of it. Or it must be the drugs I had been given, I don't know. I looked around at the massive rows upon rows of large pine trees, and in front of me stood a big mountain with a torn barrier that was on the side of a road, as if a car had driven through it and down into the forest.

But I looked further down, and I could see dirt tracks from the barrier down into the forest. I began walking down further into the forest, following the tyre tracks as they went further and further, deeper and deeper into the forest. I looked up, and there were at least hundreds, if not thousands, of stars in the dark night sky, and in the centre of the stars was the bright full moon that lit up the entire forest.

Slowly but surely, I followed the tyre tracks to the car that had collided with one of the pine trees. It looks to be a red Subaru that had its bonnet smashed into the tree. The front of the car had completely imploded on itself, and there were bits of the car and glass lying everywhere in the grass. This whole situation was one powerful trip, but what was so strange about this whole situation was that it didn't feel like a drug high; it felt like a memory, a long-forgotten memory.

I approach the car to find a girl asleep at the wheel of the car. She looked lifeless. This whole situation was confusing. *Who was this girl? Where am I? What is this place?*

Then suddenly, I heard the voice again. "Jacob? Jacob?"

My entire body was shaking, and the hair all over my body stood up with goosebumps at the very mention of my name.

Hesitant, I turned around very slowly to find the girl awake. I was so scared at that moment, as she seemed so lifeless and dead. I could literally feel my heart about to have a heart attack. The girl was staring at me with her white eyes and what appeared to be an open, bleeding cut on her head. I stared at her with my eyes wide open, her white eyes connecting with my eyes, and then she leaned into me and said in a ghastly voice, "Jacob, you have to wake up."

Then a black raven swooped at me, as the girl had disappeared and I stumbled backwards. The voice got louder. "Jacob!"

My head was hurting badly. I was remembering things that I hadn't experienced in my life before, like the picture of me having ice cream with my daughter, despite not having any children, and a picture of me walking on the beach with my wife, but I didn't have a wife.

I lay on the forest floor, breathing heavily, and then I felt him, the child, the same child from the beach. He stood there looking at me with his white eyes. I really didn't want to, but I kind of had to look. I turned my head to face him and stared at his white eyes.

"Jacob, you have to wake up now!"

I woke up with a jerk, leaping forward as fast as I could until I banged my head on the concrete ceiling. Breathing heavily and nursing a sore head, I tried to calm myself as much as possible by looking around the room. I was back in the prison cell. I woke up to find Norman sitting on the ground bouncing a tennis ball.

"Good morning, sleepyhead!"

I was so confused. "What happened?"

Norman stopped bouncing his ball and looked at me. "Well, after your little psychotic episode, the guard followed protocol and flooded the room with tear gas, and then they administered a sedative to both of us and put you in a straitjacket."

I rubbed my eyes. "How long was I out?"

Norman stared at the wall. "Only a couple of hours. Powerful trip, aye?"

"You can say that again."

I was still in my straitjacket. I jumped off the bed and landed on the ground feet first.

Norman rushed to pick me up from the floor, as I couldn't pick myself up being in a straitjacket.

"Smooth landing!"

I just gave a smirk back at him. I just sat at the corner of the floor near the toilet. Norman looked at me with a face of concern. "How are you feeling?"

"I feel like I am losing my marbles in this place. I mean, it is the same stuff over and over again. I feel like a damn robot."

Norman wasn't very sympathetic. "Yes, well, get used to it. You got another 60 years of it!"

The concept of spending my life in here made me so depressed. "Bloody hell, I am going to die in here. What have I done?"

I noticed that Norman was waiting by the door. I didn't really care, but since there was nothing else to do, I may as well ask.

"Hey Norman, where you off to? Is it feeding time?"

Norman smirked. "Na, not yet. It's work time!"

I looked at him curious. "Wait, work time? What do you mean?"

"Oh yes, didn't I mention it? Yes, you can enter into a work program where the prison assigns you a job, and you make up to a dollar a day."

"That would have been nice to know before I went clinically insane!"

"I will put your name down for you if you like. Anyway, I have to run. See ya."

The guard opened the door, and I was left in this white padded cell with nothing to do but look around. Then, as Norman had left, another guard came in and said, "All right, prisoner, you have completed your anti-suicide treatment. You can have your freedom back."

The guard took off my straitjacket and shut the door behind me. Nothing to do, I decided to rummage through Norman's bunk and found within his bunk a smuggled vape. Thank goodness for that. I was suffering from severe withdrawal.

Sad and depressed, I sat against the wall and began to vape. But what I was most concerned about was my mum, the only family I had left. Then, I felt a strange feeling, a spiritual connection. It was as if Mum was smoking at the same time as me, so I just lay on the wall and smoked while I felt my mum's presence.

CHAPTER 21

Anna was sitting on the front steps of her house in her nice suit and blazer, smoking a vape and looking out at the night sky. Anna felt guilty for what she had done, selling out her entire campaign just to keep her campaign funded. That's modern politics for you. It's about who can sell their soul and get away with it. Anna was a complete wreck. She began to burst into tears. She had lost her son, Ella didn't respect her, and worst of all, if she did come into power, she would have changed nothing. WeapCo would be gone, but only for another corporation to take over. Anna just stood there looking at her tablet and staring at the approval rating; she was still holding the lead, but she had to get ready, as tomorrow was the debate.

She knew what she was up against, and she had to get ready. Fred popped his head out the door and said, "Hey Anna, how are you doing?"

Brushing back tears from her face. "All right, let's get this over with already."

While Anna had lost everything, she really had no choice but to keep on moving forward and not let her losses get to her, because if she was going to lose everything, then at least she could try to do some good in the world. That night, Anna practised and practised her speech repeatedly until it was embedded into her memory. Practising her movements and her posture, she watched clip after clip of politicians from Hitler to Mussolini to Obama to Regan, any archival footage of speeches she could find, watched them to practice her oratorical skills. Then she went for runs around the town and decided to do a workout with Edward to get her mind sharp for the big day.

Tomorrow was a big day for her, and unfortunately, she was going to do it alone.

The next day at 6 o'clock, the stage was lit, and on the stage were two podiums on opposing sides. This one debate would determine the outcome of the election. It would determine if Anna won political office or not. The people behind the scenes were working their arses off to ensure the lighting and the sound was correct. Also, the audience and the media were all rushing for their seats. Anna was behind the scenes in the dressing room, applying her make-up, brushing her hair, brushing her suit and rereading and rehearsing all her notes over and over.

Fred busted into the room. "One hour to the debate. Get keen!"

Then he closed the door to leave Anna alone with her thoughts. Anna tried hyping herself up in the mirror. "You got this! You got this!"

Then the hour was up, and it was time for the debate. The speakers started playing intense music, and the lights shined on the podium.

"Good afternoon, ladies and gentlemen! My name is Liz Truman, host of Holonet News, and welcome to the great debate. Tonight, we will hear from both candidates; each candidate has 2 minutes to respond. Now let's meet our candidates!"

Ron was the first on the stage, with his gelled-up hair, and he held his hand up high in the air, waving to the crowd and giving thumbs up. Then it was Anna's turn, as she walked onto the stage in a black blazer and sprayed-up hair. She waved her hand high up in the air and smiled at all the people before returning to the podium. After they all returned to the podium, she and Ron greeted each other and tried being civil as much as possible, giving each other a handshake for the Holonet.

Then, they stood there.

"If everyone is ready, let's begin! The first question is for Anna. Anna, you preach about more government and more social security for the Lower Levels, but though you plan to do that, you haven't proposed how to pay for it. How do you expect to pay for it?"

"Well, Liz, we pay for it by taxing the higher levels, as it would give the Lower Levels a chance to rebuild, and once they can get businesses up and running, the Lower Level would be able to return that money back in tax revenue."

Ron cut in. "Oh please, it's obvious they won't rebuild. They will never change. They will always be stuck falling behind. I don't see why it's our responsibility to fix these businesses if they can't survive on their own means."

Anna shot him a dirty look. There was a fire burning within Anna at how snobbish this guy was. She was now angry. "What would you know about what the working people go through, you spoilt little brat!"

The entire audience and even Ron were all taken aback. They all expected Anna to be this timid person, but when she spoke up like that, everyone was surprised.

Ron tried to defend himself. "I know what it takes to run this city, something you clearly don't know anything about. You have no qualifications, and you have no political experience, so step aside and let the adults take control!"

"Boy, I managed to raise a child, served in the military, all the while barely making enough at my minimum wage to get by. So you're right, I don't have any formal education, but I have taken care of my community through thick and thin. Don't you dare tell me to step aside, because I am what this city needs. The people don't need another spoilt rich snob in political office!"

The debate went back and forth for 2 hours. Ron won the debate on topics such as finance, recessions and bailout, but Anna won on topics such as social reform, justice system and environmental reform. But now came the main event: gun control. The moderator asked the dreadful question. "What are your stances on the gun control reform!"

Ron spoke first. "Well, I think gun control is not needed. What the city is less gun control!"

"Anna, your response?"

Her entire body wanted to scream "Yes! Yes! Gun control, yes!"

But she choked and looked at the audience. She noticed that Adrian was standing in the far corner lucking in the shadows like a bogyman or a devil.

Anna choked up for a few seconds, before bowing her head in defeat. "I believe that gun control measures should be under review and be examined in more detail."

In essence, she was saying no to gun control reform. Ron looked at her in shock as she didn't say yes to gun control reform. Anna let out a small tear at the fact that she had sold out. The debate was over, and Anna had won a significant lead over Ron in the debates.

Fred and Anna were at home on the couch watching the reruns on the new Holonet projector in her living room. Fred was just being the standard kiss-arse he always was. "Oh Anna, you were amazing."

After 2 hours of reviewing footage, Fred was tired, so he got up from the couch and walked out the front door, leaving Anna alone with her thoughts. Anna just stood there looking at the floor and not saying a word. She was supposed to be feeling happy. She had won the debate, she won the lead over the competition, but she still wasn't satisfied, and she couldn't understand why. Then it hit her; her family was gone. Jacob was gone, Ella was gone, and Edward was gone. Everyone was gone, and it was just her with nothing but a slightly cold beer in her hand. She wasn't supposed to win like this. She was meant to win on moral and principle, not by selling out, which is what killed her the most about this whole situation. What was she to do?

The next day was election day. The ballots were counted, and the results were in. Anna had won the legislative position.

Anna got up on stage in front of everyone and said, "Thank you everyone for this prestigious honour. I personally want to thank everyone for this win, and I hope to serve you the people. Change is coming. I promise to be that change."

The crowd roared.

CHAPTER 22

15-10-3025

For the past month, all I did all day was look up at the concrete ceiling above, as what else was I supposed to do in this cell. But then I heard a noise. A red siren was going off, and the outside of the cell was lit up red, which piqued my interest. Out of curiosity, I peered my head out through the window to see what was happening on the other side only to find right in front of the glass was one of the guard's head. Then the guard's entire body slowly fell to the floor. I could hear shouting from the other inmates.

"Let us out! Let us out!" The voices echo down the hall. The only other sound I could hear was the series of bangs from rubber bullets being shot at the inmates. The chants were getting louder and louder, as more and more voices could be heard. As I looked out through the window, I could see the cell doors opening one by one.

Then I realised what was happening. The prisoners were trying to break out of the prison. Good luck trying to escape a prison that is made from pure concrete and is drilled underground. But I did have to give the prisoners credit. They did manage to get control of the control room and release all the doors, except of course for my cell. Our door-locking mechanism must have been jammed.

Norman got up from his bunk. "What's happening? Is there a riot?"

"Yer, some of the prisoners are rioting again."

Norman just smirked. "Those poor souls never stood a chance."

I was only new here, so didn't know what was going to happen. Then, suddenly, two vents at the corner of my eyes opened, and within seconds, the entire outside of the cell was flooded with water. The water reached the ceiling. The entire prison was flooded. Thank goodness our cell lock had jammed, or else we would have drowned in the flood.

I watched as the outside of our cell looked like an aquarium. I turned to Norman. "What the hell was that?"

Norman looked at me. "That is the emergency flooding system. It is designed to protect the prison in case it gets overrun. This prison is built to be unescapable, so it is built to flood in the case of an emergency. All the cells are water-sealed. When it floods, all the prisoners inside their cells are safe and dry."

That was incredibly cruel. "What about the prisoners outside of their cells? What happens to them?"

Norman let out a little chuckle. "Well, let's just say they are permanently sedated."

I was shocked. "They can't do that. That is extremely cruel and inhumane!"

Norman shrugged his shoulders. "Who comes in here? The media? Ha! No one cares. They're prisoners. They're just numbers in here. No one will miss them. Plus, it frees up a few more cells for more prisoners!"

That made my blood boil. "How the hell can they get away with something like that!"

"Don't ask me, I am just a prisoner."

Then he went back to sleep in his bunk. How could Norman be so cold about this whole thing? I mean, they drown prisoners. That is sick and twisted, but what concerned me the most about this whole situation was Norman's lack of empathy. I mean, how could he not care about those people? There's something about Norman that struck me as a little off. But I guess I really didn't have a lot to go off, so all I did was shrug it off and climb up to the top of my bunk and go to sleep. But before I went to sleep, the siren went off again, and the water went through the drain at the bottom of the floor and disappeared as if it wasn't even there. I lay on my bunk and looked up at the ceiling.

Hang on! I thought to myself. Then, I leaned my head over the bunk. "Norman, how is the water activated?"

"In the control room. Why?"

I smirked. "Norman, I have a plan!"

The next morning, I came up with a game plan.

"Norman, come over here!"

Norman got up from his bunk and rushed over to meet me in the middle of the cell.

"OK, Norman, here is the plan. Do you know where the control room is?"

"Yes, the control room is one floor above our cell. Why?"

"Do you reckon if we cause another riot and gain control of the control room again, we could flood the guards in the prison and walk out of here?"

"So, your plan is to drown all the prisoners and guards? That's mass murder."

"No!" I shook my head. "Nothing like that. The plan is that once we gain control of the control room, we seal it off and alert the prisoners and guards ahead of time so that they head into the cells. Once the water turns on, the cells will automatically get sealed anyway."

Naturally, Norman was sceptical. "Hang on a minute. How do you know you would gain control of the control room? The guards are well-equipped and well-armed."

"Yes, but we have more numbers. The flooding is their only defence against an overrun really, so if we take control of the control room long enough to seal ourselves in, we could use their last line of defence against them."

Norman was confused, but it somewhat still made sense. "But how do we take control? It didn't work last time. What makes you think it will work this time?"

I stuck a finger in the air and said, "Because they were unarmed or only had primitive weapons. If we arm the prisoners, we have a better chance. Yes, but the guards still have an armoury at their disposal, so they would be more equipped, but we could hold them off long enough to seal off the room. Now where is the armoury?"

"Next to the control room."

That was some poor architectural planning, but oh well, worked to our benefit.

"All right, so do you understand the plan?"

"No, but worth a shot."

We both went to bed that night concerned. We were secretly praying to God that this plan would work out all right.

The next day arrived just as any other day, with a bright, blinding light shining through the cell and burning our retina, and of course, there was a guard screaming, "Rise and shine."

Norman and I were preparing hard. Luckily for me, Norman put my name down on the worksheet, so I was sent down to the work floor. Because this prison was privately owned by a big corporation that outsourced work to prisoners as a cheap way of saving profits, suckers like me work 10-hour shifts for only one dollar a day. How awesome.

So we hit the floor and began assembling hoverbikes. One after the other, bikes came preassembled, and it was my job to screw in the bolts. Come up, screw, repeat. I did that for nearly 10 straight hours without any breaks. Boy, I tell ya, my legs were shaking that day. But as the guards were leading us in a single file line back to our cells, I pretended to collapse on the floor from dehydration. Yes, I know it was basic, sure, but it did the trick.

After the guard kicked me a few times to see if I was faking, he finally caved in and called for a medic. Two armed guards picked me up and dragged me to the medical wing and threw me onto the next available medical bed, then strapped me on the bed. I had a bit of time, though, because I was placed in the 'non-urgent' part of the hospital. The urgent part of the hospital was for people who lost something or were close to death, so it was the perfect time for me to escape this wing and get into the control room.

First, I had to break these straps. I looked around for a sharp object, but something like a surgical knife was not going to do the trick; I needed something stronger. I guess I would just have to wait here for the time being, because it was all part of the plan. Any moment now, Norman was going to come through that door … In three, two, one … Nothing happened. Three, two, one … Nothing happened. Three, two, one, Norman came rushing in, foaming from the mouth, running around throwing things around like a rabid wolf who had just escaped his cage.

Everyone came rushing over to him. The guards pinned him down, and the nurse sedated him with a needle to calm him down. Once the guy was under sedation, they threw him onto a hospital bed. All part of the plan, of course. Once Norman was strapped into the hospital bed, he brought in a bag containing meth. In his sedated form, Norman took the bag of meth, and holy hell, you should have watched him break out of those straps and run around that hospital room. In his ICE rampage, he managed to knock my hospital bed over and flipped me onto the floor. I cracked my nose a little bit, but it disconnected my heart monitor.

A team of nurses rushed over to pick up my gurney, and just as one was about to check my pulse, I managed to grab one of the keys from the guard's pocket just, as the team rushed about. I managed to free myself after Norman was put back into his cell and given some medication to deal with meth (it was the year 3000; meth overdose was easily treatable by now).

Anyway, I got out, but unfortunately, the guards spotted me and pointed here rifles at me and demanded, "Stop. Don't move, prisoner."

Unarmed, all I could really do was surrender and put my hand above my head, all part of the plan. The guards then escorted me back to my cell, but along the way was the armoury, of course. What a surprise. Just as I was passing the armoury, I broke out of line and placed my thumb on the thumb scanner, which was used to unlock the door. The guards were quick to bash me back into line, though, and off to my cell I went. The guards threw me into my cell, where I found Norman, off the ICE, but still looking pale as a ghost and throwing up into the bathroom. Great. Now the cell was going to stink of puke for the next 2 days.

Norman looked up from the toilet bowl and looked at me with vomit down his face and asked in a ghastly voice, "Did you manage to do it?"

"Yes."

"Great," he said, before going back to throwing up in the toilet. While the guy was sick, it was all part of the plan.

I had already done my part. Now it was time for Norman to do his. Norman was granted special access to the computer lab, because the guy was underage compared to the other prisoners, so by law, he must complete his GED online. Norman was an expert hacker and possessed an IQ of 160 (he kept bragging about it over and over in his cell), so while he was in the computer lab, he managed to sneak in a USB drive, which broke through the prison firewalls and granted him access into the prison system. Norman knew time was of the essence, though, so typing his little fingers away, he managed to upload my fingerprint into the main database, which would give me access to all the facilities in this place. Then, the guard came over to Norman, just as he had closed all his tabs. "School over. Back to your cell."

Then, 2 hours later, it was lunchtime. While all the prisoners were eating their meal, Norman and I went around spreading rumours about a riot, using all different types of gang names, because they wouldn't follow our word, of course. But after an hour of talking to the other prisoners, we managed to convince them to join in.

Then, lunchtime was over, and we were back to our cell. Norman and I had to go without food that day, but it was worth it, because we knew we were not going to be in our cells for long.

Later that night, it was time for the big breakout to occur. The light went out, and now was the time to strike. Both Norman and I jumped from our bunks, and we met near the door of our cell. The door was magnetically sealed, so we had to get out of there somehow.

I turned to Norman and said in a concerned tone, "Norman, any idea of how we are going to get out of this cell?"

Norman just shrugged. "I don't know, you're the one with the plan."

I sighed and thought to myself, *Is it my job to organise everything?*

All I could do was pace around the cell trying to come up with a solution to get out of here, and then it occurred to me. I turned to Norman. "Norman, start banging on the door!"

Looking puzzled, Norman got up, and together, we began banging on the door. We kicked with all our fury and started screaming like wild apes in their cell. We screamed for hours on end. Then, just as predicted, the cell began flooding with tear gas, and any minute, the guards were going to enter the cell to restrain us. Once the gas began filling the cell, we coughed our lungs out, and our eyes began to water. Then guards entered the room, and I yelled out to Norman, "Now!"

Norman caught the guard off guard. He rammed the guard, despite the fact that Norman was a skinny guy and the guard was heavily armoured. The second guard began whopping Norman with a baton, so I jumped in, grabbed the guy's arm and pushed him away while managing to disarm the guy. Prisoner guards are trained only to subdue, so I had the upper hand in this fight due to my combat experience. After being disarmed, the guard charged me, and I turned on the electrified part of the baton and zapped the guard on top of Norman, which knocked that guard out cold. Then the other guard managed to land a kick on me and push me back a little, but Norman tripped the guy over while on the floor, and I zapped him out cold. Then, sirens went off throughout the prison. I signalled to Norman to run, and we both managed to slip out of the door before the prison door shut on us, trapping the two prison guards inside.

Free of our cell, we began running down the hall until out the front of the door were two guards with shotguns armed at us. They demanded that we put our hands up in the air. We responded by putting our hands up in a false surrender and dropped our weapons. The guards then demanded we approach them slowly. Then in a hurry, we broke ranks and began to zigzag around to avoid being shot. The guns the guards had were pump action, so they could only fire one shot before having to reload. Once they both used up their shots, we opened all the cell doors, and all the prisoners came rushing out of their cells and began whooping on the guards. *Those poor guards,* I thought to myself , but they kind of had it coming. Yes, they were only doing their jobs, but they were incredibly cruel and awful to us, so it's not like they were saints in this whole situation.

While the guards had their hands full, I unlocked the door with my fingerprint, and off we went. We rushed to the other side of the prison and headed into the elevator, which shot us up to the next level in a second. But as we began to approach the control room, there was an entire row of guards, all with guns and electric batons drawn.

Oh, balls, I thought to myself. *How the hell are we going to get out of this one?*

But then, behind the guards, the door flung open, as a herd of prisoners began charging towards them. It was all-out warfare, guards versus prisoners. Rubber bullets went flying everywhere, and some of the guards and the prisoners were engaged in all-out hand-to-hand combat. Unfortunately, the guards had the upper hand, as they managed to push the prisoners back away from the control room, but it gave us an opportunity. The guards had their backs turned to us, so we quickly ran towards the control room door, and I opened the door with my fingerprint but no luck; the operators inside had sealed the door off. That's OK, because we rushed in and opened the vent above the door. It was just small enough for Norman to get through.

Norman slid in and, like a rat, began crawling through the vent, but for a small guy, he still weighed a lot, and the vent came off its fixtures and smashed through the control room. The operators then turned their back to the console and jumped out of their seats to find Norman lying on the floor. Norman got out of the vent and the operators, having no combat experience, just surrendered. Norman didn't want to hurt these guys, as they were just operators doing their jobs. He pushed them aside and unsealed the door for me to walk through. Using my electrified staff, I threatened the operators to get on the floor with their hands above their heads, to which they complied.

Then, jumping on the panel, I resealed the door. Now was the time for the Great Flood 2.0. I decided against unlocking the prisoners, as I didn't want them to drown, so to be a nice guy, I turned on the microphone. "To all prisoners and guards, please get to a free cell. It is going to get wet!"

Looking at the monitors, I watched as all the prisoners and guards rushed to the nearest cell and all huddled together. After locking and sealing all the doors, I pressed the emergency button, and the prison began to fill with water. But then, I felt an object near my neck which felt like a blade. I turned my head slowly, and it was Norman holding a shiv to my neck.

"Norman, what are you doing?"

He let out an evil smile. "Change of plans."

I got up from the console, as Norman grabbed my electrified stick and zapped me in the leg. The zap caused me to collapse on the floor in pain, and he zapped me again, which knocked me out.

After I came to, I found myself tied to a chair, and Norman was at the console looking at the monitor. My body was in immense pain from the shock. Angry and confused, I yelled at Norman. "Let me out!"

"Shut up, Jacob!" He walked over to me holding the shiv. "You don't call the shots anymore, Jacob. I am in control!"

"Why are you doing this?"

Norman let out an evil laugh. "Kicks! Here, come have a look at what I have done."

He dragged me to the monitor.

Oh no! I thought to myself, as I looked at the monitor. The bastard drowned all the guards and the prisoners. I was angry. We were never meant to kill anyone. We were only meant to escape.

"You bastard! You monster! Why would you do that?"

"Jacob, I am what you call an artist. I see the beauty in life and death."

Now it was all starting to make sense. "You didn't just come here on hacking charges, did you?"

Norman gave a grin. "Yer, let's just say I may have killed a few people. Maybe 30 at least. And boy, they did taste good."

My face was shocked that a skinny little guy like that could commit that many atrocities. Of course, he was one of the psychotic prisoners in this place.

"And now, Jacob my friend, before I escape here, I am going to have some fun."

He started cutting into my chick. Agh! That hurt! I flinched in pain. However, just as Norman was about to stab my stomach, I swung the chair, and the knife stabbed into the back of my chair, tearing the duct tape and allowing me to break free. Norman was now in massive trouble, because I had a size advantage over him, and from what I had seen, he didn't really have much fighting experience. Norman just stood there in shock, but he grabbed the shiv and went in to stab me, but I grabbed his hand and twisted it to disarm him and right-hooked the guy across the face. The force of the punch knocked the guy unconscious on the floor.

After gaining control of the control panel, I pressed the button to drain the entire prison, and since everyone was clearly deceased, all I really did was walk out of there. I should kill Norman for what he did to those people, but I had to rise above that, because if I had killed him, it would make me no better than him. Therefore, I decided to show him mercy by unlocking one of the cells, and I threw him in it and magnetically sealed the cell up so he could never hurt another human being again. Norman and I were the only survivors out of a prison of 10,000 people.

I still couldn't believe how easy it was to escape this prison. Not a single shot was fired at me. Though, I had to admit, I felt bad for those people. Now that Norman was behind bars, I just hopped on into the elevator, and it shot me straight up to the Ground Level at the speed of a bullet. There were no guards on the Ground Level either, but the doors leading to the outside were sealed and fingerprint protected. Luckily for me, my fingerprint was still on the computer system, so I unlocked the gates, and off I went as a free man. But I had to be careful, as I didn't know how long I was going to be free. It probably wasn't the smartest move letting Norman live, as he would probably blame the prison drowning on me. On second thoughts, I should have killed him. Oh well, nothing I could do now. Time to head home. I was curious to see if Mum won the election.

CHAPTER 23

17-10-3025

Time to head home. But I had no transportation, so I had to walk the remainder of the way home, which was on the other side of town. The only thing I had was my black jumpsuit and some boots I stole from the control room. I had no money or food, and I had a long way to go home, at least a 4-hour journey by foot.

I looked up above and saw all the cars flying and zooming past at rapid speeds. I knew the only way home by foot was to walk on the old, abandoned superhighway. The superhighway was a deserted concrete structure that was completely covered in vines. It was designed in the early years of this city, as everyone still used fuel-powered cars. But as fuel became more expensive, and technology advanced to create floating cars, no one really drove on it anymore, at least in the Middle and Upper Levels. The only reason it was still standing was because down in the Lower Levels, flying cars were expensive, so to get around places, we had to still use the old petrol cars. They were rusted, slow and outdated, but they were cheap. The superhighway was littered with them. It was like a graveyard for cars, as the bridges were filled with them, all broken down and left to rot. Nearly home, but I had to brace myself though; I was heading into the worst section of the city, Mercy Lane.

Mercy Lane was the lowest of the low places. This part of the town was the worst in everything: crime, unemployment and poverty. The place used to be the most bustling area, as it was the number one town for manufacturing, but as the city grew and jobs were outsourced, the place quickly turned into an absolute hellscape. It was the living embodiment of anarchy and chaos. It was so chaotic that there was literally gang warfare all the time down there. No one was brave enough to ever stay in this area for long. There were very few people who remained down here. It was considered the underbelly of the city. I wanted to avoid this place as much as possible, but it was the only way back home, so I had to suck it up and get walking.

Even before I entered the place, I could hear gunfire already. I walked down the broken, chipped sidewalk and passed by broken and deserted shops that were boarded up and had foreclosure stickers on them. It was a ghost town. All the places had graffiti on them or were covered in vines. The only thing illuminating the place was the light from some of the streetlights and a few bonfires. The entire street was littered with rusted and destroyed cars. In this part of the city, the peacekeepers were doing the best they could down but with no luck. The people down here were a different breed. They lived and breathed combat. They knew how to load a gun before they could even read or write. Sending reservist troops with little combat experience down there was pretty much a death sentence. I could tell that the troops had been down there, as the streets were littered with destroyed military vehicles, artillery guns, or barricades. Also, I could hear machine gun fire and explosions coming from different buildings.

But just as I was walking past, I could hear police cars, fire trucks and ambulances zooming past above my head. I believed that they were rushing towards the prison, but I could be wrong, as who would know what happens down here. I had to get off the streets somehow. It was dangerous to be out in the open like this with nothing but clothes. However, it was going to be tricky, as everything was boarded up or had who knows how many homeless people living in them. Even a battle-hardened veteran like me was no match for a place like this. Every alley I looked behind had all sorts of shady characters behind them. Pretty much the only businesses that stayed afloat down here were businesses that were against the law.

Luckily for me, I knew of a guy who lived down here. He was my mentor back in the marines. He lived in a deserted apartment block around here, from what I heard. So, if I was to get home, he was my best bet at surviving this place.

Suddenly, I felt it. I felt a bullet fly past my head. The metal bullet managed to just scrape my head and hit the nearest wall. I was so lucky. An inch closer, and it would have hit my brain. I quickly turned around and looked up right to find a man in a Halloween mask holding an ancient carbine rifle.

"Blast!" He managed to fire three shots at me before he stopped to reload the old rifle. Quickly, before he reloaded, I crouched in an alley to get some cover from the crazy person.

But it was a trap, because right above was one of his friends. He jumped off the fire escape, landing on the floor with a hammer in his hand, swinging it straight into my left shoulder.

"Agh!" I screamed out in pain and flinched back, holding my hand to nurse my shoulder. The crazy man went in for another swing, this time going for the head, but I ducked in time.

These guys were hunting for sport. Mental illness was rampant in this city. Mercy Lane was filled with mentally ill people, combat vets and downright psychopaths. Just as the guy missed me with the hammer, using my good side, I grabbed the hammer. I was struggling to hold it back, and as I turned around, I heard the metallic click from the loading mechanism of the gun. The other man had finished loading his rifle and was about to fire another shot.

Out of panic, I kicked the guy with the hammer in his kneecap, let go of the hammer and elbowed him in his nose. Then I pushed him back just as the other man fired the shot, hitting his own friend in the head. The guy dropped his hammer, as blood poured out from the wound, and he fell to the ground dead.

The other man was shocked at what he had done. Now he was pissed. I could tell by the look in his eye. But I had an advantage. He was a slow reloader. I grabbed the hammer on the ground, and as hard as I could, I threw it at him. While it didn't kill him, it did knock him back, causing him to drop his rifle on the ground. He cursed out profanity, but there was nothing to think much about it; I rushed to grab his rifle, and I ran away. At least I had a rifle now.

I kept running to give myself some distance from those nutjobs. I flinched in pain, and I stopped to remove my shirt to reveal purple swelling around the wound. That's going to be sore, but oh well, I would worry about that later. I inspected the rifle, but there was only one bullet remaining, and the rifle was dirty and rusted, so I wouldn't say it was reliable.

I had to hurry to my friend's apartment. Who knew what other nutjobs may be lurking around here. Slinging the rifle over my shoulder, I kept walking down the dark street. Now, from my memory, my friend said that he was held up in some old Chinese takeaway shop called 'Asian Pacific Chinese'. Thank goodness that was only a few blocks away,

But as I was walking, I heard a car come racing down the street. It sounded like a turbocharged GT ute. But I could hear the cheers of joy from people as they came rushing down the highway. It sounded like they were joyriding up and down the street. For safety, I had better hide behind this metal dumpster.

Thank God I did. The ute slowed down, and it was filled with people in war paint and masks and on the ute bolted into the truck was a machine gun. The thugs were shining a light down the alleyway, but luckily, they couldn't see me. I could only make out a glimpse of them. They must have been a part of the local gang and were just patrolling their side of the turf.

Behind the dumpster, I held my breath. However, my heart was pounding out of its chest, as one of the feral cats knocked over a bottle, and one of the thugs on the truck heard it and said, "What was that? Go and investigate!"

One of the thugs had an old AK-47 in his hand, and he jumped off the ute with a flashlight to investigate.

I had to stay silent and do my best to hold my breath in. I could hear the thug's boots slowly approaching me; closer and closer he came, and I could hear him raise his rifle up in a firing stance. The thug got closer. All I could do was grip my rifle closely to my chest. This rifle only had one shot, and if it jammed, I was stuffed. Plus, this type of rifle was better for long distance. He got so close that I could literally see the nozzle of the gun. I gripped the gun closer, getting ready to attack, but just my luck, the cat ran past behind the thug.

The thug turned around and realised it was a cat. He let out a sigh of relief. "Phew, just a cat!"

He screamed to the rest of the boys, "It's OK, guys, it's just a cat."

The other guys screamed back, "Stop wasting our time and get on!"

The thug headed back on the truck, and the truck zoomed off down the street. *That was a close one,* I thought to myself, and I let out a massive breath. I really needed to get off these streets ASAP. Slinging the rifle over my shoulder again, I made my way down the road, making sure to watch my back. I passed alleyways. Mercy Lane was something else entirely. The place was riddled with bullets and dead bodies, and then I heard a boom. I jumped down on the ground, as a few blocks down, a building blew up, and smoke came from the wreckage. As I looked further down, I saw it, the Chinese building. Hopefully, my friend was still held up in that building; he was really my only hope. But there was some bad news; the building was located on the main street, and there were no alleyways towards it. I let out a sigh of disappointment, and I unslung the rifle and readied it to shoot. Slowly, I began to walk down the street, holding my rifle ready. So far, so good. There was nobody here as far as I could see, as the street was pretty much deserted.

But I had to be sure, so I checked all the windows on the building and slowly made my way towards it. It wasn't silent at all down here, as the night sky was filled with gunfire from far away. But in this section, it was all clear. Then, not being out here for too long, I slung the gun over my shoulder and began sprinting as fast as I could to the Chinese building. I was nearly at the footstep at the door when the truck came flying again up the main street of the town, and this time, they saw me.

Oh bugger! One of the thugs on the machine gun turned it to me, and I did what any sane person would do. I ran. Using all my strength, I charged through the weak plywood that replaced the front window of the Chinese shop and ran towards the old, decrypted countertop. I ducked down, placing my hand over my head just as the bullets from the machine gun started firing. The machine gun ripped straight through the plywood and lit up the entire restaurant like fireworks, and anything in its way was decimated.

I had to crawl fast, because the bullets were piercing through the countertop at an alarming rate.

Then I screamed in pain. One of the rounds went straight through my left hand. I nursed my hand, trying my best not to cry, but man, it hurt. I just kept crawling through straight into the kitchen and hid behind a stove. Bullets went flying above me, and then it went silent. The bullets stopped.

But I knew it was never a good sign when things went quiet. I heard a thump, as all the thugs jumped off the ute to go search the Chinese restaurant. It looked like this was the end of the road. I had a busted-up shoulder, a hole through my left hand and a gun with a single bullet, and I was passing out from blood loss. Just as the thugs were making their way towards the kitchen, I fainted and blacked out. Then, I heard a buzzing as I slowly opened my eyes. Then I collapsed back into darkness.

I awoke to find an old light bulb hanging and flickering from the ceiling. All I could do was lie there, as my entire body was in pain. I looked down at my left hand to find it bandaged. My shoulder had an ice pack over its bandage. I was confused as to what had happened. Then, as I looked around the old dingy apartment, I saw a shadowy figure blowing smoke from a cigarette out the window. The old figure then turned his head towards me.

"Well, you're lucky I saved your arse!"

My mind was at ease, as I knew who it was. I let out a small smirk and in a sarcastic tone, said, "I'm guessing the thugs are dead."

The old figure replied, "They better be." He then got up from his old rocking chair and walked over to me into the light. I got to finally see his face. It was my old mentor. "Good to see you again, kid."

All I could do was smile after seeing him. "It's been a long time, Dex."

The old man smiled back at me. "It feels like a lifetime ago."

Dex Reymond was one of my commanding officers back when I was in the marines. We served multiple tours together and lost many of our brothers over many different conflicts, but Dex and I managed to get by. Despite being my commanding officer, I started to look at him like as a surrogate father figure in my life. After my discharge, we both took different paths in life. I went back to take care of my mother, and he, well, let's just say he took the path of the lonely eagle. Unfortunately for Dex, the war was never over for him. Every day was a struggle and another battle, and it took a toll on both his mental and physical health.

Dex was in his late 60s with a grey beard, receding hairline and a somewhat fit physique (though his beer gut was showing), and despite having retired from the military, he always wore his military cap as a badge of honour.

Dex slowly picked me up as I moped in pain, to which his response was "Oh, stop whining. You've been through worse!"

He then sat me down on a chair next to me and bandaged me up. Then he got up from his chair opened one of his cabinets and got a full bottle of Gentleman Jack and two glasses. After pouring a glass for each of us, we both began to chuckle as the alcohol hit our brains, but we were both men, so we could take it.

That night, we told old war stories and giggled, as Dex still had that dark humour despite his old age. But as the alcohol buzz began to wear off and as we just sat there in the dark smoking a cigarette, Dex turned to me. "So, how are you holding up since the war, kiddo?"

"I am all right. Just fighting a different battle."

"Yer, I know. I watched your court appearance on the Holonet. Quite a show you put on!"

I let out a chuckle and looked at my glass. "Yer, what can I say, Dex? We are a long way from the Ocean of Oceania."

He smiled. "You can say that again. Care to explain what happened at the power plant? And I am no expert, but I presume that whole incident at the prison was your handiwork?"

I wanted to laugh, but instead, I pondered. "Hey Dex, do you ever get tired?"

He looked at me confused. "Tired of what?"

"Tired of all the violence and the killing. I mean, when is it going to stop? All the horror, all the fighting, just to survive."

Dex sighed. "Look kid, we have been fighting our whole lives. The only difference is that my fight is nearly finished whereas yours is still going. Look, we are built different, you and I. Most people are built to live normal lives, but you and I, we will never live normal lives, as the war has scarred us, so we have to keep going."

I smirked. Dex got up and put out his smoke on the windowsill. "All right, night!"

I gestured to him, and all I could do before going to bed myself was contemplate.

I just curled up in a ball that night, no blankets, no air conditioning, just my naked self. I had to admit, I was a little tipsy the next morning, but the pain was starting to come back. I gave a yawn and woke to Dex gone and the door wide open. I look concerned. What happened to Dex? I got up, chucked on a shirt and went downstairs to the kitchen to find Dex making pancakes on the stove. Dex was whistling a tune.

I figured out what had happened to the thugs, as their dead bodies were lying all around the restaurant.

"Good morning, Jacob. How do you like your pancakes? With or without syrup?"

I looked mortified. For an old man, he definitely hadn't lost his touch.

"With!"

Dex served me pancakes, and I pulled up the one chair that wasn't shot to hell and sat next to Dex.

"So, when are you leaving this hellhole?" he asked me.

"Well, that's why I am here. I need your help getting out of here, especially in this state. I am not capable of navigating myself out of here."

Dex gave a chuckle. "Yer, you look pretty dinged up, if I do say so."

"Will you help me?"

His face just turned serious. "It's not going to be easy. To get out of Mercy Lane, you have to go deep into gang territory, and with the peacekeepers in town, it's going to be hell trying to leave this area."

The peacekeeping force for months had been coordinating efforts with the active military to take down the gangs. Unfortunately, the only issue was that the peacekeeping force was blocking all entrances in and out of the district to prevent the spread of crime. It was going to be tough, especially since I had escaped prison. That made me a prime target. Plus, I couldn't defend myself in this state.

Dex had a plan, and I was invested. "The peacekeeping force has set up roadblocks at the only exit out of Mercy

Lane. If we have any chance at all, it is there, but there is only one problem. It is highly secure, full of drones, turrets, the hole works.”

I had a look of concern over the very idea of getting through all that security.

“This place seems too secure. How do you propose we get in and out without being detected?”

Dex let out a big smile. “Remember the Battle of the Solomon Islands?”

My face dropped as he mentioned that, and all I could think of was what was going to happen next. What unfolded next was not going to be pretty at all.

The next day arrived, and we arrived at the security checkpoint in and out of Mercy Lane. Just as Dex had predicted, the place was swarming with at least 100 armed guards, 50 drones, 10 automatic turrets and snipers surrounding the nearest building. All the entrances and exits were covered, and there was no way out of this one in one piece. However, Dex and I had a plan. It was a simple plan, one that surprisingly didn’t involve any guns or killing.

Dex pulled up to the checkpoint in the truck that he took off the thugs, but he was stopped.

“Halt!”

One of the guards walked over, holding his machine gun in his hand to check the truck. Dex stood there, smoking a cigarette. “Afternoon, Officers. What can I do you for?”

“You know what! No one leaves this place, under orders from the American Division Government.”

Dex then went on to smile. “Unfortunately for you, that isn’t going to fly.”

They raised their guns in attention at that comment. The senior guard then walked up behind his colleague. “We strongly advise you to turn back around now, or else we will have to use force.”

Dex with a smirk on his face just shrugged his shoulders. “All right! Well, do you hear that?”

All the guards looked confused. Then the noise grew louder and louder, and to be cocky, I decided to honk the horn.

All the guards just ducked and fled for cover as I rammed into the back of Dex's car with an old diesel garbage truck that I managed to hotwire. The smash from behind startled Dex, which caused them to yell out a few profanities. The front hooks from the garbage truck stabbed into the back of Dex's car, as it provided an artificial battering ram to get through the checkpoint. Dex jumped onto the roof of the car and onto the passenger-side door of the garbage truck, showing us young people how to do it.

The soldiers, in a panic, began to fire at the body of the car. Armed with their laser rifle, they fired bolts towards the garbage truck; through the window, I could see at least five plasma bolts pass me. However, while a few of them managed to hit the truck, it didn't cause enough damage to stop it. We managed to get over the old, abandoned bridge which, connected Mercy Lane and our district, Commonwealth Ave. Still, it was going to be tricky, as the peacekeeping force on the other side had set up barricades.

Then, the soldiers from Mercy Lane surrounded us from either side, with drones shining their lights on us, which lit up the bridge as if it were daylight. The soldiers all had their weapons ready to fire at us if we even tried to make a single move off this bridge. One of the officers at the front of the bridge began to walk slowly towards us with a speakerphone in his hand and addressed us. "Attention, assailants. This is the American Division Army. We have your entire vehicle surrounded, and you are outnumbered. If you try to drive forward or backward, you will be shot! Surrender your vehicle now!"

There was a brief pause for a moment, as the guards watched on to see what we would do. In that pause, I turned to Dex. "What do we do?"

"Jacob, switch seats with me and let me drive."

We both got out of our seats and swapped. From my previous battles with Dex, I knew he was known to be impulsive and reckless, which the military hated, but one thing about Dex is that he got results. Dex then put his hand on the gear shift and put it in reverse.

The soldiers from both sides could see what was happening and were ready. The drones armed up, as did the rows of soldiers. You could hear the rows of clicks as all the rifles were armed. But the soldiers were waiting to fire, as they didn't know if we were going to surrender or drive back. Then, Dex, with a thrilled look on his face, put his foot as fast as he could on the pedal, and the front tyre spun so rapidly that it began to produce smoke from the tyres. The soldiers opened fire.

Dex and I ducked, then Dex pushed down the brake, and the truck went flying off, which scared the hell out of me. Because we couldn't see, as we had to duck from the bolts, Dex reactively turned the wheel, sending the truck to turn on its side. It flipped and smashed through the concrete barrier on the bridge, sending the truck rolling into the barely filled river. The truck came crashing down, with its roof now on the ground. I was scared as hell. My heart was beating at least several beats a second, and my breathing was so heavy that I felt as if I had run a marathon. The truck flipping surprisingly didn't cause us that many injuries, apart from a gash to the head and the pain further exacerbated from my shoulder and my gun wound. But besides that, I was somewhat OK. But I couldn't say the same for Dex. It looked like one of the bolts hit his shoulder. Luckily, it didn't bleed, as the bolt was hot enough to cauterise the wound.

Dex was also breathing heavily, so out of concern, I turned to him. "You all right, big fella?"

He let out a groan and laughed. "Ah! Just a shoulder wound. No biggie."

Something like that was nothing Dex couldn't handle; he may be old, but he was built like a quarterback. Thank gosh none of us had major injuries, but that probably wasn't going to last for long. The drones began descending from the bridge and down towards the truck, while the soldiers began stumbling and slowly making their way down the hill. Stuck again. What was new, really?

Then Dex looked at me and smiled. "Solomon Islands!"

At that moment, all I could do was smile. "Solomon Islands!"

We clicked a button on the dump truck, and nothing happened. We both shared a look of concern. Then Dex clicked the button again, and techno music blasted from the back of the truck. The techno music was set to a specific frequency that would cause the drones to go haywire and make them crash.

Then, once the drones were out of the picture, we reached underneath our seats, grabbed our AK-47s and leaned out from the broken window, and we just opened fire. Now, we knew that the AK-47 bullets wouldn't be able to pierce the body armour of the peacekeepers, but that was not the plan. The surprise attack was meant to catch the soldiers off guard, which it did. The surprise attack forced nearby troops to go on the defence and hide behind bushes and any cover they could find. The soldiers didn't know what type of guns we had. Though they would soon find out, the distraction would be able to buy me and Dex some time to flee.

After we opened fire for a few minutes, barely able to hold the weight of the guns with one arm, we threw them to the ground and started running. After realising that the guns were duds, the troops started advancing towards us, firing around as they slowly made their way down the hill. Dex and I kept sprinting to our heart's content, hopeful we could lose them at the Sewer Level. We rushed through the barely sanitised water as fast as we could, as the soldiers were shooting behind us. Luckily, the range on those rifles was awful, as they were for close quarters, which gave us a bit of an advantage. However, the bolts were becoming more accurate and more lethal as the troops got closer and closer.

We were almost there. We weren't that far from the sewer drain. Just a little more. Dex and I were rushing so hard that our hearts and lungs were about to give out. Closer and closer the drain became, and closer and closer the soldiers and the bolts projected were getting.

We finally made it to the drain opening when the bolt from one of the soldiers cut straight through the air and with unerring accuracy, hit Dex straight in the back.

"Agggggggh!" He let out a massive scream.

Out of fear and adrenaline, I rushed over to pick him up with my one good arm and began dragging him into the storm drain as the laser bolts got closer and closer.

I was breathing heavily. Having to carry a full-grown man with one arm wasn't all it was cracked up to be. I was running out of breath fast, and if I slowed down, I would be dead.

We finally made it into the storm drain. However, the soldiers were gaining on us. I couldn't take it anymore. I collapsed in exhaustion and dropped Dex on the floor. Lying on the concrete floor, breathing heavily, I could feel my entire body aching.

But I had to get up off the floor, or I would be dead. The bolts and the soldiers were getting closer to the point that they were getting lethal. But I couldn't get up anymore. I just couldn't.

Then, a conscious Dex yelled at me. "Get up!"

I was exhausted. "I can't! I just can't."

Dex snapped back to his old drill sergeant ways. "SOLDIER! GET UP NOW! THAT IS AN ORDER!"

"I can't! I am sorry, I just can't!"

Dex looked sad. "Jacob, please, leave me behind."

My face turned to shock. "Dex, I can't do that."

Dex took a deep breath in. "Jacob, look man, I am sorry, my fight is done. But your fight is still beginning. Please don't give up ... GET UP! JACOB, GET UP NOW!"

I breathed heavily, trying to push myself.

Then Dex snapped, and in the loudest voice, he screamed, "GET UP!"

I let out a scream of pain, trying to push my body.

"Hey Jacob!" I turned back around one last time. "It has been an honour serving beside you, Jacob. Keep up the good fight."

I responded by letting out another scream. Using whatever strength I had left, I punched the floor multiple times to give myself an adrenaline rush, and I ran as fast as I could back up onto my feet. I began bolting down into the Sewer Level, as the troops entered the sewer gate.

I took one last look at Dex saluting before he disappeared, and when he was out of sight, I heard a bang coming from a pistol. But something weird happened. After hearing that pistol, I kept thinking of my time in the Solomons. I had the flashback of a gun being fired towards Dex. It was eerily similar. But I had no time to investigate. I had to get away from the peacekeepers.

Because I had spent months at a time down in the Sewer Level, I knew it like the back of my hand, which gave me an advantage over my enemies. One of the things Dex had taught me was that if I couldn't fight at full strength, then I had to use the environment to fight. Luckily for me, the deeper into the sewer system I went, the darker it got. Also, there were multiple hanging pipes that I could climb and take them out from.

The advancement of soldiers suddenly stopped, as the darkness proved too much for the soldiers, and they needed time to recalculate and adjust their strategy. They had no night-vision gear and thus were walking into this situation blind. The commander took charge, and in the distance, I could hear him dictate the movement of the soldiers. Half of the soldiers were told to return to the checkpoint, and the other half had to come down and fight me, which was going to be tricky. They all nodded, and the remaining soldiers all walked slowly down into the level.

I could hear the footsteps in the sewer water, as the soldiers approached closer and closer. I had to be like a ninja and not make a sound whatsoever, not even leaving a footprint. I had to use the pipes to my advantage. I climbed up onto the pipe and stayed up there, waiting to pounce on any soldiers from above, using guerrilla warfare tactics. I heard two soldiers approach me from the opposite direction, but something caught my eye about these two. These soldiers were not like the other soldiers. They were equipped with night-vision goggles, which caught me by surprise. Then, one of the soldiers quickly turned around and shined the rifle in my face, catching me instantly.

"What the—"

It took them only a second to catch me. These soldiers were professionals. But what was weirder was that these soldiers were dressed in different uniforms compared to the standard military gear the soldiers wore.

Then, before I could move, the soldier who spotted me shot me with a Taser.

"Aghhhh!" The Taser hit me and sent an electrical charge through my body. The charge caused me to fall off the pipe. But luckily, my fall was stopped by the two soldiers, but just as I was about to fall to sleep, I noticed a symbol. These soldiers weren't peacekeepers. I knew that symbol, but ... My eyes shut, and I fell unconscious.

I regained consciousness again. Man, I am getting so sick and tired of being knocked out. I awoke to find myself on a medical bed, and my wounds had been patched up by nanites. I looked over to find the two soldiers who had knocked me out, who were standing over my bedside.

These soldiers weren't AD soldiers but were private mercenaries who were dressed in dark army camo gear and had laser-proof masks. I then looked at the symbol on their shoulder: the symbol consisted of a silver skull with a plasma bolt in the middle. I knew these mercenaries. It was the Wacco Group. The Wacco Group were part of a rival private military. They were opposed to WeapCo and instead belonged in the pocket of the rival, Wacco INC, the second-biggest warmonger in the city. I was confused as hell at what was happening.

I looked at the two guards and turned to them. "What the hell are you two looking at?"

The guards then shot each other a dirty look, or at least that's what I think they did; I don't know. It was hard to tell with those masks on.

Suddenly, one was about to hit me in the nose with the butt of his gun when a familiar voice screamed out, "Stop!"

I heard the clitter-clatter of high heels on the tile floors. Then, I saw Mum behind the guards dressed all official in a black suit with an American flag pin. Mum was not happy. "Don't you dare lay a finger on my son!"

One of the guards had the nerve to talk back to my mum. "We don't take orders from you!"

"No, but you do take orders from the CEO. So go away, and leave me alone with my son."

Both the guards huffed and puffed, but eventually, they complied with the orders and left the room.

"Mum, thank goodness!"

"What the hell did you do?" she interrupted, looking confused.

"Excuse me?"

"We had a plan, Jacob. You were supposed to follow it!"

"Well, you know plans change, Mum."

She wanted to stay mad, but she couldn't. She leaned in and hugged me. "I am so glad you are all right. How are you feeling?"

I shrugged it off. "Boy, I tell you, I am so sick and tired of being knocked out and ending up in a hospital bed."

She let out a small giggle. "Come on, I will buy you a cup of coffee."

That was the best piece of news I had heard all day.

After getting out of my nursing gown and throwing on some freshly washed clothes that Mum had brought for me, we walked around the hospital with coffee in our hands. I caught Mum up on everything in the prison and what had unfolded in Mercy Lane. But I had a question for her.

"Hey Mum, where are we?"

She looked confused. "What do you mean? We are in a hospital?"

"But I am not handcuffed to the bed. What's that all about? Also, why did you hire mercenaries?"

But before I could speak further, she interrupted. "Never mind about that now. Answer me this. Why the hell did you think it was a good idea to go to Mercy Lane by yourself?"

I looked confused. Mum was clearly hiding something, and I didn't like it.

"Mum, what is going on? I want to know right now."

But just as I was about to speak, the two guards from the hospital showed up again.

"Time's up. Get back to bed." Mum signalled me to get back to bed, so I did. I hopped back on the bed, where the guards slapped cuffs on me. I was confused. What is going on here?

Mum then winked. "Follow my lead."

Mum slipped me a key to the cuffs which she had taken from one of the guards' belts. She then walked up to the guards. "All right, you got your bounty, let go—Ow!"

She pretended to roll her ankle on the hospital floor, giving me enough time to unlock my cuffs.

I didn't know what Mum was planning, but I had to trust her. So I got up and out of the hospital bed and took out one of the guards, while Mum took out the other. Then she turned to me. "Quick, we don't have much time. Listen to me, I have gotten involved in some trouble in the real world."

"Real world?"

"No time for that! Now, you are in a private military hospital. I managed to disable the cameras. Just go and don't look back. That is the new plan!"

I gave Mum a final hug, and I rushed off, with Mum shooting me a look of concern as I fled out of there. In the background, the alarms started to ring, and the guards all started rushing after me.

I made my way down the hospital corridor, rushing as the guards came after me.

But then, I heard a strange voice calling out to me, "Jacob! Jacob!"

Out of confusion, I stopped. *What the hell was that?*

In a panic, I looked behind me, and the guards were all gone. It was as if they had all disappeared. Confused, I looked around and realised that the entire hospital was empty. I couldn't see a single person for miles.

Then, I heard that ghostly voice calling me once more. "Jacob!"

It kept repeating itself. All I could really do was follow that voice. I walked down the hallway, but something strange was happening; my eyes were becoming dazed and confused, and my body was feeling weak. Then, the situation got weirder. I started hearing voices in my head from multiple different people. I approached the source of the ghostly spirit, but the voice grew louder and louder, and they began to appear. I could see Anna's spirit and Ella's. I had to keep going. There was nowhere else to really go. As I got closer to the source, the background behind me began to fade into nothingness, and then I saw the ghost of Dex, who said, "Keep going, kid."

Now, that was strange, because Dex had died years ago on the beaches of the Solomon Islands.

The voices were all cheering me on to keep moving forward. Then I approached the two hospital doors, and I swung them open to find a morgue. The morgue was completely empty; no equipment, just empty metal tables, except for one, as there was one dead person who lay on the bench, lifeless. I was so scared now, but what was most strange was that I knew that dead person. It looked familiar. I approached the person, not knowing what I was in for.

Once I approached the table, I realised that it was my father's dead body lying on the table. I stepped back in shock, stumbling and landing on the floor. My heart was pounding at several beats per second. I quickly rushed to my feet to find that the body was gone. The table was completely empty. I looked around completely scared, and I turned to see the hospital doors swing completely open. Confused, I walked through the doors, not knowing what to expect.

After walking through the doors, the hospital behind me completely disappeared, as if it wasn't even there. Looking behind me, I couldn't even see the hospital doors anymore. Instead, I was standing in the middle of the darkened streets while it was pouring down rain. But I couldn't feel any of the rain. I walked past a house. I began to approach the house, and it was my house, the house I grew up in and lived in my whole life. I stood out the front, not knowing what was going to happen. Taking a deep breath, I slowly opened the door, and the door creaked a little bit. Once the door was completely open, it was my living room and my kitchen just the way I had left it before I went to prison.

Then I heard that voice again. "Jacob!"

I was still confused as to what was happening. I then noticed the figure sitting on the couch. It was Dad. I made my way to the couch. "Dad?"

The ghostly figure was there drinking an imaginary beer, and then the figure got up off the couch with his back turned to me. "Jacob," the ghostly voice said to me. "Jacob, you need to stop killing and cease all the violence! Stop killing your fellow men. Instead, be the good shepherd and lead them to a better tomorrow."

The figure turned around to reveal the face of my father, but instead of his brown eyes; they were pure white. "Jacob, remember as Martin Luther King said. *'Through violence, you may murder the hater, but you do not murder hate!'.*"

I took that quote to heart. My first thought was *Who was Martin Luther King?* But it didn't matter, as what Dad had said really resonated with me. But before I could ask him some more questions, I had a massive headache, and my ears started ringing. The only thing I could hear now was gunfire and artillery explosions and people screaming out in pain.

Then I heard a voice scream at me, "Jacob!"

I recognised the voice. It wasn't from Dad. Instead, it was from Norman, though I thought he had died.

Then the voice repeated itself, "Jacob!"

At the same time, the noises grew louder and louder. This time, I could hear the sound of a car crash and a little girl crying. Then I heard the voice for a third time, and the intensity of the voices got louder, and I was receiving flashbacks of memories I didn't even know I had. The flashback showed me memories of hanging out with the girl and the mysterious woman I had seen in previous hallucinations, and then I felt something rock me. My eyes began to slowly open, and I heard that voice again.

"Jacob!"

Then I realised that I was beginning to wake up. The first thing I saw was Norman's face looking back at me, and I was even more confused. I was back at the prison.

"Jacob! Jacob! Jacob, wake up, man."

I shot my head straight up, only to bang my head on the concrete bunk. I began huffing and puffing. I looked around, and I was back in my cell at Quintennial Prison. I was breathing heavily and looked around trying to keep my composure.

"Well, good morning, sleepyhead!"

"Norman, you're alive?"

"Of course! Why wouldn't I be?"

I looked down at my body to find I still had the straitjacket on from when I had my meltdown. I then looked up at Norman. "What happened?"

"The doctor gave you a powerful sedative."

What? Must have been a powerful sedative. "So we didn't drown the prison?"

Norman shot me a dirty look. "Drown the prison? You do know that is impossible, right? Are you all right?"

"So that whole thing with the prison break and walking through Mercy Lane, that never happened?"

Norman didn't know what the hell I was talking about, I could tell by his face. "No, nothing like that happened. I guess you must have had a hallucination."

I took a deep sigh of relief. Norman got back under his bunk, but then it dawned on me to ask him this. "Hey Norman, how did you end up here again?"

"I told you, Jacob, I got here on hacking a government website!"

"So, you didn't kill and eat people?"

Norman just laughed. "No, nothing like that. Now, you should probably just rest and let the rest of the sedative wear off."

Then the guard banged on the prison door. "Lights out, inmates!"

I just lay there on my concrete bed, pondering what just happened. I had so many questions. How was I able to meet Dex when he died years ago? How did the soldiers not manage to hit me? How did I manage to flood an entire prison?

I had so many questions and so many concerns, but most importantly, I didn't know what reality was and what wasn't. I guess all I could really do was contemplate, and here was the important question. *What was the main message my father was trying to give me? I mean, what did he mean when he said 'just be yourself'? I was so confused. I am a soldier through and through. Killing and completing my mission was who I meant to be – to keep fighting. If wasn't a soldier, then who was I?*

I tried to move around to get myself comfy enough to get back to sleep, but I couldn't. These straitjackets were itchy and annoying as hell to have on your body. I took in a deep breath and rolled over to fall asleep.

Then I heard a female voice say, "Goodnight, Jacob."

The voice caused me to shoot straight up and look around the room. Not knowing where that came from, I just shrugged it off.

"Guess it must have been the last of my sedative wearing off, or the medication I took at lunch is kicking in. Who really knows."

I just laid my head down on my pillow and went to sleep.

CHAPTER 24

18-10-3025

The next morning, I was losing it. I didn't know what was real or what was fake.

This place, this place has driven me to breaking point. What do I do? Who do I talk to?

Then, the same old thing happened. The lights turned on, turning the walls from dark black to pure white in an instant. I just lay there on the concrete bed with bloodshot eyes and hallucinations running through my mind. All I could hear were voices from the past, people I killed, people who died, people who I wronged, all screaming at me and commanding me. It was absolute madness, and I couldn't go anywhere or do anything, as the mental health support in this prison was next to nothing. So I just lay there for hours and hours at a time until the same old guard yelled out, "Lunchtime, inmates!"

Then Norman finally got up from his bunk. "Oooh, lunchtime. Time for more gruel!"

Not saying a word, I got up and began making my way like cattle to the same old cafeteria. I sat down at the metal table, eating my meal and suspiciously looking at Norman. I didn't know if he was telling the truth about being a killer or if he was just a hacker. I didn't know anymore. I turned to

Norman, and I was defeated. A physical battle was one thing, but a battle against the mind was a battle I was not ready for.

"Edward, sorry, I mean Norman, am I going to die?"

Norman's face just turned at me confused, as he held a spoonful of slop in his hand. "Where did that come from? What makes you think that? Did you piss someone off in here?"

I was barely eating my food. "No, it's just that this place is driving me insane!"

Norman just gave out a laugh. "Yer, this place does that to you. It must be something in the medication, I think. Most people don't last in here long. It's actually quite sad."

Norman seemed so calm, as if this place didn't faze him. "How do you survive in this place?"

Norman then looked down at his food. "I don't know, really. I mean, I think about having a normal life outside and what it would be like to leave this place."

Norman wasn't hungry. He pushed the plate aside. I guess I ruined his appetite, and he joined me in being sad. "Hey Jacob, what was it like?"

"What was what like?"

"To grow up, going to school and having a normal life, really." Then a tear came from Norman's face. "I mean, I spent my teenage years in prison, and I haven't seen sunlight in years. You on the other hand were lucky … So, tell me, what was it like?"

I forgot that I wasn't alone in feeling trapped here. Poor Norman never got to experience high school and having friends. He practically grew up here.

"Don't worry, Norman, you will eventually get out of here."

That comment only made Norman sadder, and he looked hopeless. "Na, man, I have been given a life sentence. I am never getting out of here alive! Hey, um, I don't feel like eating today. I am going to go back to my cell."

He then signalled to the guard, and he walked away from the table. I felt horrible at what I had asked of Norman.

After lunch, I returned to my cell thinking about these hallucinations. What did they all mean? And what was their purpose? And what did Dad mean by not using violence? That pessimistic comment didn't make any sense to me whatsoever. Dad was never a pessimistic person at all. Hell, he got into so many bar fights that when he didn't come home with a bruise, we were all very surprised. Also, how could I not fight or kill anyone? I mean, what about WeapCo? What about John? How can we let such an evil man who had destroyed the lives of so many people just live? He destroyed my community, hurt the people I love, and worst of all, he tried to kill me. I mean, what was I supposed to do? Just let him walk free to continue his evil enterprise that kills millions around the globe? Or what? Get him arrested, where he could just pay his way out of the legal system and walk the streets with a slap on his wrist? But then again, he was sitting in an air-conditioned office, whereas I was in this concrete box with some nerd who probably hasn't even touched his first boob. I felt so lost and so alone. I had no Mum, no friends – well, except Norman – and I felt isolated in this place. I mean, where could I go? I needed something spiritual to get me out of here.

"Hey, Norman?"

Norman just rolled over and spoke back, "Yer, man?"

"Does this place have a chapel?"

Norman gave a small chuckle.

Boy, I tell ya, I am getting so sick of Norman's sarcasm.

"That little hellhole? Sure, the guards will let you go every day for an extra hour if you subscribe as a religious zealot. You're not religious, are you?"

The next morning after lunch, I walked into a small, deserted room. The concrete room was full of old, dusty rows of chairs. It was also laminated with fake stained-glass windows of old, dead people, and in the centre of the room was a stage that looked like it hadn't been touched in years, and on it was a book. On the wall behind the stage was a wooden cross. I don't know what it was about this place. Yes, it looked deserted, but I felt so at peace in this place. This place was the only place in this prison where my voices were at peace. I needed to figure out why. So, lost, I walked up to the stage and looked at the old book, which had in golden ink written 'Holy Bible'. I looked confused.

"Holy Bible? Never heard of it."

Curious, I picked up the book and looked it over, flipping through the barely visible pages, but I didn't know how to navigate it.

Then, I heard an old voice scream at me. "Lost?"

I looked up from the old book to find a 70-year-old man dressed in white robes with a wooden cross hanging over his neck looking at me. I looked the guy up and down.

"Pfft, nice outfit."

"Well, it may not be the prettiest outfit in the world, but it does the job."

I looked him up and down again and looked around the room. "What's the cross for?"

"It's a symbol; a symbol of sacrifice, redemption and healing."

I just nodded in agreement. I mean, I couldn't really say anything bad about that. All I did was look around the empty church. "Where is everyone?"

The chaplain just shrugged. "I am afraid in this day and age, everyone is more concerned with chasing after money and self-satisfaction, and they fail to pay attention to the most important thing."

"What thing?"

"Why, spiritual health, of course, my boy. You see, what everyone fails to understand is that there are two bodies: the physical and the spiritual body. Unfortunately, no one pays attention to their spirits. They just focus on their physical body's needs, but what people fail to understand is that the spirit is intertwined with the mind and the body. So an unhealthy spirit means an unhealthy body and mind and thus an unhealthy life.”

I just looked at him. I wanted to think this guy was crazy, but with what I had been through, I was in no place to judge.

The chaplain signalled to me, “Please take a seat.”

I got off the stage and sat right next to him. He then looked me straight in the eyes with his blue watery eyes and said in a relaxed tone of voice, “What is bothering you, my son?”

Where do you want me to begin? I thought to myself.

I took a deep breath in and said, “Well, I feel like I have lost control of reality, and I feel like I am at constant war with my mind and my body. I just don’t know what to do.”

I had thought in my head that the priest was going to judge, but he just lowered his tone of voice. “Well, you are not the only one. Everyone has demons or secrets to hide, and eventually, those demons manifest themselves as voices in the back of your mind or as false hallucinations.” He readjusted his seating position before continuing. “They can either do one of two things. They can either push you to be a better person, or they can destroy you entirely. It’s your choice.”

I was more confused than ever. “What will it take for my demons to go away?”

The chaplain was pleased with that statement. “You have to confront them and use them to your advantage. Learn from them. Remember, history is doomed to repeat itself if you don’t learn from it.”

Amazing, I thought to myself. What he was saying made sense to me. “But Father, with the way of the world, how do I not commit violence? I mean, we have to fight for everything, and sometimes, people get hurt. How do I avoid that?”

The chaplain then leaned a bit forward, and I could hear the creaking from the old wooden chairs. “Anyone can kill someone or hurt someone, but it is very rare for someone to help another person. The world has so many people out there who are only in it for themselves. But what this world is in short supply of is healers, people who want to change the world. Now, I don't know you or any of the things you have done, but it is time to take a spiritual journey and discover who you really are and figure out what kind of a person you are and who you want to become."

The chaplain then handed me the Bible that he was holding, and he got up and went to the altar. "All right. You want communion?"

I had no idea what that was. "Sure, I guess."

I got out of my chair and walked over to the altar. Then the chaplain said some stuff and poured vials of wine and water and prepared biscuits. The chaplain then turned to me and said, "Kneel!"

I did. He then handed me a biscuit and some wine. "The blood of Christ will give you eternal life!"

I didn't know what that meant, so I dipped the biscuit in the wine and ate it. I didn't know what was happening. After the communion, the chaplain turned to me. "Your sins are forgiven. You are reborn. You are now a blank canvas. Use it well."

I looked down at the floor, and when I looked up, the chaplain was gone. I scoped out the entire church, but he was gone. I thought to myself, *What just happened?*

Then, a guard entered the room. "Time's up! Get back in your cell, inmate."

I got up from the old, decrypt chairs and followed him back to my cell. Once I reached the cell door, the guards opened it and shoved me inside. "Lights out!"

The cell went from white to black in an instant. Stumbling, I couldn't find my bunk, but then, the blue light from Norman's smuggled-in laptop lit up the room.

"Hey man, you all right?" he asked in a concerned tone.

"Yer. Went to that chapel you were telling me about."

"Oh, yer? How was it?" he asked.

"Yer, it was something. The chaplain gave me this book to read."

Norman looked confused. "What chaplain?"

Now I was confused. "What do you mean? The old guy?"

"Well, I have been to that church multiple times, and I never saw any chaplain."

I laughed. "Maybe you weren't holy enough."

"Hahaha, probably! Hey man, listen, about what happened at the cafeteria—"

"Forget about it, Norman. It's in the past."

But something still bugged me. "Hey Norman, where did you get that laptop?"

He had a big grin on his face. "Let's just say that I have a few connections and a few favours."

"Wouldn't the guard see it?" I asked.

"Na. Remember, these cells are soundproof, and if I turn the brightness down a little, it will barely shine through the window." Norman had an even bigger grin on his face. "You know what else I smuggled in?"

"What?"

Norman then got up and went to the stainless-steel toilet bowl and pulled out a small bag of weed.

"Want to get high?"

All I could do was smile.

For the next hour, we just lit up that weed and laughed our heads off while listening to some music that Norman had saved on his laptop. Both our eyes were shot red, and our throats were burnt as well, but we were in too good of a mood to care, really. We were both giggling our heads off.

"Hey Norman, man?"

He laughed. "Yer, man?"

"Do you, like, ever wonder why it is we were put on this earth for?"

"Yer, I don't know, man. I think we are just products, really. Our mum pops us out, and we just contribute to society like gear in the economic machine."

I laughed. "Wow, way to bring the mood down, man."

Curious, Norman asked, "Well, why do you think we are on this earth for?"

"Well, I think we were put on this earth to explore, to gather, to learn and, most of all, to enjoy."

Norman then looked down and blew out a puff of smoke. "Not much exploring we can do in a concrete box."

My joy then turned to sadness. "Come on, man, it's not all that it's cracked up to be out there. I mean, the real world is hard. Crappy jobs, high inflation, illnesses."

"Yer, but I would rather enjoy that than being stuck here the rest of my life."

We both just sat there in silence for a few minutes.

"So, can I ask a personal question?"

I shrugged my shoulders. "Shoot!"

"Why did you kill all those people?"

I took a deep breath in. "Well, the nuclear power plant wasn't my fault."

"I know, but why do you feel the need to kill people?"

"Well, I was a soldier for most of my life, and so was my family. It's in my blood."

"But you're not one anymore. I don't know, you just seem so troubled."

"Didn't you serve?"

"Na. I never finished school, remember?"

I looked down and blew out some smoke. "Well, yer, it's hard to explain. I mean, I have hurt so many people; some to survive, some to serve and others just for vengeance. I mean, it's not like I like killing people. I hate it. All I want is a normal life and to be normal. You know, my dream was to live a life like the people up above, with the white-picket fence, a beautiful wife, and rushing the children to school. The boring life."

"I can so imagine you in a sweater."

I laughed. "Oh, shut up, you!"

"But unfortunately, you and I are not normal people. We will never have that life, so we just got to enjoy what we have until it's gone, even if we are stuck in here."

Listening to what Norman said was quite moving in a way. I didn't expect that from Norman. Most of the time, he was a cold robot. Just as I was about to speak, we saw a light shine through the peephole. We both quickly closed the laptop and went to bed.

Then, the door opened, and the guard walked in with a flashlight. "Why are you both awake?"

Trying not to sound high, I said to him, "We were asleep until your fat arse woke us up."

We were both trying our very best to hold in our laughter.

"You watch your mouth with me, prisoner. Final warning. Get to bed now!"

The cell closed, and once again, we were back in darkness. We both let out a few laughs. Man, it felt good to laugh again. I hadn't done that in a long time, and tonight, I was actually surprised. I mean, most of the time, Norman was a cold prick, but when high, he was actually a pretty good guy to talk to.

Then the weed wore off, and I was back to my depressed self. I couldn't stop thinking about all the people on the outside that I may never see again: Ella, Anna and Edward. That made me sad. All I could really do was roll over and go back to bed. Hopefully, Anna would let me out soon. I was counting on her to get me out. She was really my only hope. But I wish I could contact her and ask her to spring out Norman as well. Guess I was going to have to wait.

The next day arrived, and it was the same old guard, cafeteria and all that. But one thing did change. Norman and I were closer than ever. He finally let his guard down, and we ended up being good friends. At the dinner table, we were both joking around and just chilling.

Then out of curiosity, I asked, "Hey Norman, do you think you could use your connections to get me something?"

"Depends on what you need to get."

"A phone."

He smirked. "Sure. Easy. One condition. I am hungry. Give me your food."

I slid the tray over to him. The food was crap, anyway. No big loss.

After Norman got back from school, he re-entered the cell and handed me an old holographic projector.

"All right, here is the deal. I have managed to hack into the Wi-Fi for the computer. I will lend you a hotspot but make it quick."

I quickly turned on the phone and texted Mum, not caring about the spelling mistakes:

"Hay, Mum its Jacob listen I am ahive in queintennal prisom, I surevived the trail and am stuck in a sell with the coolest guy, how it life for you."

"Done!"

"Sorry, man, that is all I could do for you."

I was happy that Norman did that for me. I looked down at the phone, and it sent. YES! Out of joy and impulse, I hugged Norman. "Thanks, man."

He just patted me on the back. "All good, bro."

I then gave a pat on the back and went back into my bunk. Norman then hopped back into his bunk and flipped open his laptop, but something caught his eye. Norman looked at his laptop confused. "Hey Jacob, who did you say your mum was?"

"Anna Turner, why?"

"The politician?"

I looked at him weird. "Yer, why?"

"You might want to come look at this?"

I jumped off my bunk, and Norman turned the laptop to face me. As I looked at the screen, I was in complete shock. The picture on the screen showed Mum winning the election, which I was happy about. But it also showed Mum shaking hands with Adrian King. I was furious. I mean, I went to jail for her so she could win political office to make a difference, and in one campaign, she sold me out.

I just shook my head and clenched my fist. All this suffering for nothing. No change whatsoever. How could Mum do this to me? Her only son. I just exploded. I got up from the bunk and started punching the wall repeatedly until my fists bled. I wanted my physical pain to match my emotional pain.

"Why, Mum, why?"

I just kept going until the tears rolled down my eyes and my body began to sweat. I was breathing heavily. Screw redemption. Screw trying to be the good guy. In the end, all there really is power and those who have it.

"Screw it!" I screamed out loud. "Screw it all!" I screamed louder.

Norman just looked at me like I was an absolute weirdo. "Screw what?"

"Screw waiting for someone to come save us. No one is going to save us. Only we can save ourselves."

Norman shrugged. "OK, but how are we going to do that?"

I then turned to Norman. "Hey Norman, how good of a hacker are you?"

Norman smiled. "The best!"

"Good. Then in that case, can you get us access to the dark web?"

"Sure!"

"Do it then!"

"Give me 15 minutes."

I watched as Norman typed away on his laptop, then I heard a click. "Done! Here."

Norman then gave me the laptop, and it was my turn.

"Fine, if Mum has money to blow now, then she will have no problem paying for someone to get me and Norman out of here."

I put on an ad for a $500,000 bounty to anyone who was willing to break us out of Quintennial Prison. Now, we just sit back and wait for someone to get us out of here.

Days and weeks went by, cafeteria and back to the cell, repeat until one night I heard something. Norman and I were lying asleep in our cell when we heard a knock on the door. We were shocked.

"Who's there?"

Then the door swung open, revealing a security guard, but he wasn't like the others. His face was covered in tattoos.

I looked at him. "I didn't know that security guards were allowed face tattoos."

The guard wasn't in a joking mood.

"You got the money?" he asked in a stern tone of voice.

Now a normal person would be intimidated by this thug, like little Norman, who was shaking in his boots, but I was from the Lower Levels. I said to him in a commanding tone of voice, "You will get your money when you bust us out of this hellhole."

He looked at us angrily and growled, but I wasn't scared. I didn't flinch.

"Fine, come with me!"

He left the door wide open, and Norman and I looked at him, confused as hell as to what was going on. But not wanting to spend another moment in this cell, we both decided to follow him.

It was quiet. There were no alarms, no security guards coming after us. This was a major red flag.

"Hey, what is going on here? Where are all the guards?"

"Don't worry about it. Follow me."

This was way too easy. Norman and I were more nervous than ever at what was happening, but with no other option, we just followed him through the corridors and out the stairs. Still no alarms or warning bells of any kind.

"What is going on?"

But then, it looked like there was going to be trouble, as we came close to the armoury and control room. I signalled to Norman to get ready for a fight, but the mercenary didn't flinch or anything. He just kept walking.

The guard looked up from his post. "Hey, what is going on here?"

The mercenary answered, "Prison transfer."

The guard shrugged. "Fair enough."

Now, at this moment, I was completely confused. What the hell had just happened?

I had to admit even I was getting anxious and was thinking of scenarios in my head that involved us shooting our way out of there. Then, we got to the next checkpoint, which was the front door. I was readying my body for a fight. But no, they just let us walk out the front like we were visitors. *OK, what the hell is going on here? No way it is this easy.*

After walking out the front door and outside of the prison, the mercenary pointed to us and said, "Wait there and don't move."

Now, normally, I would take that kind of attitude, but considering there was an entire prison worth of guards, it was best not to argue with the man. Norman and I just stood there in the dark with some stranger.

"Did you pay off the guards?"

He gave me a dirty look. "No, my boss did?"

"Wait, boss? Who's your boss?"

The mercenary snapped back. "I said no talking!"

I was curious who would want to break me and Norman out of prison. Then it came rushing in. A black limousine came flying in and parked right in front of the mercenary. The limousine stopped for a few seconds and winded down its windows. "Here! As promised, the packages are in one piece."

The mysterious figure then held out a holographic projector, and the mercenary completed their business transaction. After the mercenary got his money, he disappeared back into the night to do who knows what with it. It was just me, Norman and the mysterious figure in the limousine.

We couldn't see the figure's face. Then he screamed at us, "Get in."

"We are not going anywhere with you."

The car door opened, and my fear turned to gladness as my mum stood there in a professional-looking suit. "Not even for your own mother!"

Mum held out an outstretched hand, coming in for a hug, but I blocked her. I wasn't in a hugging mood. "Mum! What the actual hell is going on here? Who was that guy? And why are you in a limousine? And how did you know to get us?"

So many questions and so few answers. Mum signalled to us, "Get in! We have a lot to talk about."

Not wanting to spend another minute anywhere near this prison, we both walked into the limousine. The car then sped away from the prison at hypersonic speed.

Norman and I were enjoying being in a limousine. We were both sipping on glasses of champagne as Mum explained everything: how she made a deal with Adrian to fund her campaign, how one of her staffers came across the dark web ad after I used her credit card to fund the mercenary, and how we got to this point.

I was glad to be out of that prison, but I was furious that my sacrifice was for nothing. "How could you?"

Anna wasn't having it, and she said, "Jacob, don't give me that self-righteous rubbish. You got yourself into that mess."

I screamed back at her. "For you, Mum. To help you win the campaign, only to find out you sold me out to a warmonger."

"I didn't sell out, Jacob. I did what was necessary for our community."

"What, by flooding it with more guns from another corporation?"

"OK, yes, I had to make a deal with the devil, but so what? If we are going to fight, we need to fight fire with fire."

"We were supposed to do it the right way, Mum. Now, we are no better than WeapCo."

"Jacob, if we are to win this fight, we need resources, the same resources that got you out of prison, I may add."

"Thanks!" Norman cut in.

"Who are you, by the way?"

"Don't you worry who he is, Mum. We campaigned believing in you because we knew that you were on our side.

We fought for you. How could you do this to us?" I was so disappointed. "I mean, you were our community's only hope of actually making a difference."

"Jacob, I am not your enemy here!"

I shook my head. "Worse, you have become it."

Anna wasn't having it. "Jacob, you blew up a power plant, which contributed to flooding the city. How dare you look down your nose at me?"

I got up out of my seat and got up in her face. "Mum, you knew I didn't cause that, but so what if I did? You were supposed to learn from me. You're supposed to be the better person."

"You're making me out to be Alienize!"

I shrugged my shoulders. "Frankly, I didn't see any difference."

Out of anger, I banged on the door to signal to the driver to let me out here. The limousine stopped, floated down to Ground Level, and Norman and I both got out of the limousine as it sped off in a hurry.

With tears rolling down my eyes, I signalled to Norman and said, "Come on, Norman, let's go. I need a smoke."

I looked around and noticed that Norman was looking around.

"Norman?" I asked, curious.

He looked around happily and said, "I am free at last."

I forgot that Norman hadn't seen night-time in ages. Then, my sadness turned to happiness, and I said, "Congrats, man, you're finally free."

CHAPTER 25

I just sat there and watched in joy at the fact that Norman finally got the one thing he was hoping and dreaming for. Norman was definitely not the guy I thought he was at all. I don't know why my mind thought he was a serial killer. I walked over to him. "Hey man, do you have a place to go?"

"Um, yer, well, I don't know if my mum is alive or not, so I am going to try and track her down."

I just gave him a polite smile. "Well, my friend, it looks like we are at a crossroads. Good luck!"

I offered him an outstretched hand, and he shook it in response.

"You know, we are probably not out of the woods yet. I mean, we may have to watch over our shoulder for the rest of our lives."

"What's new? At least we would be able to get some decent food."

We both laughed.

"Nice knowing you, pal."

I smiled. "Yer, you too, my friend."

He walked away in the complete opposite direction as me. "I really hope I get to see him again."

After Norman walked away out of sight, I began making my way down through the streets, hoping to make my way home in peace. Luckily for me, the streets were dark, deserted and quiet. It was quite beautiful at night, but then something caught my eye as I looked over at the power line. A crow. It was fully black with white eyes, and all it did was squawk at me.

That is interesting, I thought to myself. I thought all the crows went extinct in the nuclear winter. I looked at it with intense curiosity, and then I heard a beer bottle be knocked, and as I looked away for a brief second, the crow was gone. That was weird. Not knowing what to do I just kept on walking, not thinking much into it. Once again, it was just me alone with my thoughts.

I was extremely angry at my mum for what she did. I mean, how could she just sell out to a warmonger so easily? She had lived and experienced what we had gone through. But deep down, I couldn't really blame her. She did what she had to keep the goal alive. Politics is a corrupt game, and sometimes, you must bend the rules to get where you need to go. I guess we all think our parents are gods among men, and we sometimes need to realise that they are human beings just like us.

After the confrontation with Anna, I finally made it home, only to find Edward sitting on the couch.

"Hey Jacob man, you got out?"

"Hey, good to see you again, Edward."

We then hugged each other after missing each other for so long, but that reunion was cut short by a loud engine sound.

"What was that? Are we under attack again?"

"All good. It's just Anna!"

Even worse, now I had to confront my mum again after storming out of the limousine. Oh man, this was going to be difficult. Personally, I wasn't a big feelings guy. I mean, it was easy for me to punch my way out of trouble, but talking and expressing my feelings, that's what I hated doing.

Then the door swung open, and Anna walked in looking exhausted and tired.

"Hey Edward, apologies, I will find us some—" She stopped mid-sentence as she saw me standing there in the middle of the kitchen.

"Hey Mum."

Mum just crossed her arms, not at all impressed that I was standing there.

"Come to yell at me and call me a sell-out again?"

Ugh! Here we go.

"Anna! Ella is missing! We do not have time to go on about your politics."

"NO! I think now is the perfect time. I mean, we are supposed to be a team, a family!"

I just crossed my arms like it was somehow my fault. "OK, then family sticks together. I gave up months of my life, my mental sanity, just so you can sell out our entire campaign!"

"No! You know what, Jacob, I am not having this discussion with you. I am tired, I have worked 9 hours, and I need some sleep. Goodnight!"

Of course, why would Mum face the truth when she could just blame it all on me. I grabbed my vape from the counter and went out to have a smoke on the front balcony to blow off some steam. I sat there looking at the night sky while blowing rings of smoke into the air.

Edward came out with me. "Care if I sit down next to you?"

"Go ahead."

Edward pulled up a seat next to me. We both sat there in silence, not saying a word.

Then, I broke the ice with a question. "Did you know about the whole situation with Anna?"

Edward sighed, pinched the vape out of my hand and blew smoke into the air with me. "No, not until after the deal was made. But come on, Jacob, don't be so hard on her. She is just doing the best she can."

"I know, Edward, but it's just so annoying. We finally had a chance to do good, and now, it's gone, thanks to Anna. All that suffering for nothing!"

"Oh, Jacob, come on, man. We have all made deals with the devil in our lifetime. We all have a dirty rap sheet. So don't act like you're a saint or anything."

I really wanted to hit back at Edward, but I couldn't. *Damn it! I hate it when he is right.*

I did accidentally blow up a power station, and Edward did betray me for WeapCo; who were we to judge?

I took the vape out of Edward's hand. "Yer, I guess you're right, Edward."

"Look Jacob, your mum felt guilty for selling out. It's not like she wanted to sell out, but she needed it, and I could hear her every night, praying for you to come home. Now, I don't know how I turned into a relationship counsellor or anything, but your mum loves you, and it's not like she failed her mission. I mean, she got you out. Maybe not in the way you wanted to, but you got out."

We both heard a slight little knock, and behind us was Anna standing there in her PJs. "Hey Edward, can you give us a few minutes?"

Edward gave me back my vape and walked back inside, with Anna coming to sit down next to me with her own vape in her hand. We both just sat there for a solid 5 minutes before she broke the silence. "Hey Jacob, listen I will resign from that position if it means keeping our family together."

I just placed a hand on her shoulder. "No, I don't want you to do that. Look, I am disappointed, but I get it. You were doing anything to stay on mission, like a good soldier would."

Mum lost all her strength and broke into tears. "I just don't want to lose you. You are more important than any little campaign."

I went in for a hug. "You can never lose me, Mum. We will both get through this as a family."

Mum cried on my shoulder and said in a teary voice, "I love you, Jacob."

"And I love you, Mum."

At the end of the day, despite all the horrible things we had done, we were family, and nothing could come between us. Mum wiped her tears and went back inside.

"Night, son. Love you."

I gestured at her and sat there alone on the front balcony finishing my vape.

The next morning was game time. I woke up and rushed downstairs to find Edward cooking us pancakes with bacon and maple syrup. He looked up from the pan in an apron.

"Good morning, sleepyhead."

"Morning yourself."

Now, one thing you should know about Edward: he had a lot of good skills and was a smart guy, but he was a terrible cook. Even these pancakes were burnt to a crisp. Then, Mum rushed down the stairs in her suit.

"Morning, Anna."

"Morning, Edward." Then she walked over to the table and kissed me on the cheek. "Morning, son."

"Good morning, Mum. Busy day?"

She sat next to me and shook her head. "Agh, you have no idea."

"Hey Mum, since I have been in prison, has this guy's cooking skills got any better?"

She just smiled. "Nah. I just rush across to the local café down the road."

I couldn't help but laugh my head off.

"I heard that, arseholes," Edward replied, which made us laugh even louder. Then, once Edward was done burning the pancake, we all sat down like a family. It felt so good to have breakfast as a family again.

After breakfast, I banged on the kitchen table a couple of times to grab the family's attention. "All right, everyone, what is the game plan here?"

Mum jumped in and took the lead. "All right, the vote to extend the military occupation bill is coming up on the floor, as the senate had rejected the bill. Now Jacob, it turns out the guard reneged on our agreement and has reported you as 'broken out', so you are going to have to go into hiding."

"OK, but you better make sure to stick to the shadows. It's not just about my campaign's image. I am concerned for your safety, as there is no telling what the authorities will do to you now that you have escaped prison. I mean, it was strenuous enough trying to get you a life sentence in prison. There will be nothing I can do once they capture you again."

So that explains why the man in the suit interrupted my trial.

"I appreciate the concern, Mum, but I have managed to survive this long. I am more than capable of taking care of myself."

She just shook her head. "All right, no point talking to you, is there?"

I smiled. "You know me too well, Mum."

Edward was not impressed, though. "Don't worry, Anna, I will take care of him."

"All right, fine, then you two go out and see if you can try to find Ella while I focus on getting the votes for the bill to pass."

I agreed. "Sounds like a plan!"

"Hey Jacob, a word?" Mum added. Edward got up from the table to clean his plate.

She continued, "Now Jacob, by the looks of things, the bill is probably not going to pass in both the house and the senate. But just because the military is gone doesn't mean that getting to WeapCo is going to be easy. WeapCo still has an empire behind them with resources and influence."

"I know, Mum. But if we are going to save this community, we are going to have to get WeapCo out of our community, and then, once they are gone, Wacco is next."

"Son, listen! You don't owe Yandan anything. Please don't let his foolish crusade be your downfall."

I shook my head. "This isn't just about Yandan or Ella. This is about justice. John has hurt this community and treated our home as a playground for his weapons. But worst of all, they tortured you and tried to kill me. So this is personal!"

Mum grabbed my hand. "Just give me your word that you're not going to get yourself killed just to get vengeance. I mean, you have to let go. Your life is more important to me than anything."

I grabbed Mum's hand in return. "Mum, look, we have come this far. I can't just move forward. Not yet. Not until all these corporations learn to stop messing with the Lower Levels. Mum, in prison, I went on a spiritual journey of some sort. As much as I want to change and become a better man, I need to defeat this demon before I can change and can heal from the damage he has caused."

I could tell from Mum's face that she was concerned for me. To comfort her, I kissed her on the cheek. "Love you, Mum."

She gave out a pity smile, though still concerned for me.

"All right, well, I have to go to work. Please take care."

She got up from the table and left, as a black limousine pulled up to take her to work.

I got up from the table. "Hey Edward, get your arse over here!"

Edward walked over to the table. "Yer?"

He was still eating his burnt pancake in his hands.

"Come and sit down!"

Edward pulled up a seat and sat down.

CHAPTER 26

28-12-3025

After that whole argument, we all settled whatever dispute we had as a family. In fact, on our way home, we shared a few giggles. I was telling Ella and Edward about what prison was like, Ella was informing us about her encounter with a killer, but that was a story for another time and Edward, well, he just talked about his time on the couch. Good times. It was great to have the gang all back together.

But then the good times stopped as we reached the front door of my house, and Ella knew that she would have to confront Anna.

"Ella, are you all right?"

She just shrugged. "Fine, why wouldn't I be? I just can't wait to give that bitch a piece of my mind."

Furious, Ella swung open the front door with such force that it nearly took the door off its hinges.

Standing in front of her was Anna with an outstretched hand. "Hi, darling."

Ella's mood went from that of an angry lion to a sad puppy. She rushed into Anna's arms. "I am sorry that I was angry at you."

Anna wrapped her arms around Ella. "I am sorry too, darling."

They both began to cry. Ella looked up to Anna, as their bond helped her establish Anna as a surrogate mother figure in her life.

"I am sorry for betraying you, Ella."

"I love you like a mum, Anna. I just don't want to see you get hurt."

Edward and I just stood there and watched those two hug it out, trying not to say anything that would bring the mood down.

After those two hugged it out for a couple of minutes, we all just sat around the dinner table and ordered some Chinese food and a few bottles of Cola and told war stories.

Once everyone got caught up, the questions began to fly.

"So, what happened to Norman?"

"How did you escape with just a booby pin?"

We shared a few laughs. Unfortunately, poor Edward copped the butt of the jokes.

"I am glad that poor Edward had such troubles sitting on the couch."

"Leave Edward alone. It's hard work walking from the couch to the fridge."

But Edward was a trooper. He just brushed it off with a simple "Screw you guys."

After dinner, now was the time to get down to business. We all gathered around to listen to Anna.

"OK, guys, here is the situation. Jacob is still wanted by the police, and our campaign is in debt to a rival gun company. Any idea of what we are to do?"

We all looked at each other, trying to figure it out, and we just sat there in silence, pondering how we would get out of this.

Ella was the first to speak. "We are in a mess at the moment, but we need to stay true to ourselves and our mission."

"And that is?"

"Simple, Edward: get the military out of the Lower Levels and take down WeapCo. Anything else in our lives is just an obstacle in our way."

"And that we will overcome together."

"Agreed, Jacob. So, what's the plan?"

"All right, everyone, here is the plan," Anna started to speak. "I will use my influence in Wacco to get this bill passed. If we are going to make a deal with the devil, then he better pay up! Edward and Ella, you two need to be out in the community, maintaining disapproval of the bill. The military can silence our voices, but they can't silence our faith. And Jacob, I need you to be a shadow in the background."

"The police are still after my head, but that doesn't mean I am out of the fight. I will try to drum up support in the underworld, particularly in Mercy Lane. If we gain support from Mercy Lane, Wacco and the entire Lower-Level community, then WeapCo will not stand a chance!"

We all agreed to the plan. "I like this plan, Jacob. You stick to the shadows and stand by while we will work our arses off to get that bill pass. This level has suffered enough pain and tragedy, but it is not going to be for nothing, I can tell you that! We take down WeapCo and then Wacco. Who is with me?"

We all put our hands in a circle and yelled, "3, 2, 1, GO TEAM!"

"All right, let's do this thing."

The next day arrived, and it was Anna's first Congressional sitting as newly elected ParliaCongresswoman. She walked into ParliaCongress in her suit and blazer ready to cause some mischief, with Ella by her side as her newly appointed aide.

But little did she know that she was a cat in a room full of dogs. She walked along the row of middle-aged men, with none of them saying hello and morning, just ignoring her. When she finally made it to her office, a fellow colleague came up to her.

"Hey, new girl, what do you think you are doing?"

Anna looked confused. "What do you mean?"

"I think you damn well know what I mean. What are you doing voting against the military bill?"

"I am doing what's right. I am getting the military out of my level, with or without your approval."

Then out of anger, the politician grabbed Anna by the neck and slammed her against the wall. "Listen to me, little girl, I don't think you know how things work around here. It is not smart to make enemies on your first day."

Ella had to step in. "I don't know, but you better let Anna go if you don't want your nuts kicked in. Now back off!"

The politician loosened his grip on Anna and walked away. "You're making a big mistake, girl."

Ella rushed over to help Anna, as she coughed up on the floor. "Are you all right, Anna?"

"I am fine," she said as she got to her feet, while all the other people just ignored what had happened.

"Come on, let's get you some water." Ella then escorted Anna into her personal office. Anna was in absolute shock; she was only in the building for 5 minutes, and she was already being threatened. How horrible.

Anna's head was jumbled trying to process what had just happened. She was in absolute shock.

Ella tried to be her voice of support. "Don't let that prick get to you, Anna. He is just trying to scare you. He won't be able to hurt you."

"You're right." Anna wasn't completely aware that politics was a blood sport. But no matter, she just tried to shake it off and focused on getting through her first sitting.

After an hour rehearsing with Ella and going over her lines back and forth and talking to herself in the mirror, she was ready, or at least she thought she was ready. She entered the big hall in amazement, looking at the rows of seats at the legislative building.

Anna was still taking it all in, trying to process how she'd gone from a retail worker to a ParliaCongresswoman.

They took their seats just as the speaker demanded silence, and he banged his gavel. "All rise! Can everyone say the pledge?"

All the members stood up in perfect unison. "We pledge allegiance to the flag and American Division City, a new America."

They took their seats. The speaker took his seat and spoke through the microphone that projected his voice through the hall. "On the floor of the house today, we move to the newly proposed military exercise bill. ParliaCongresswoman from the Lower Level, you have the call."

But just as Anna was about to speak, the politician who had threatened Anna cut in. "Mr Speaker, can I interject here?"

Anna was baffled. She didn't even have a chance to speak; no way would the speaker let him continue.

"Go ahead," the speaker said. Anna was confused as hell.

"Your honour, this bill is incredibly important for two reasons. Number one, it strengthens the capacity of the reservist military. Number two, the Lower Level is riddled with crime. By sending the military down, it helps with the policing effort to crack down on gangs and street crime."

Anna thought to herself, *That's not true at all. We are decent hard-working people who are trying to get by. What a load of rubbish.*

Anna tried her best to project her voice, but it was shut down by one male politician after the other. Anna was screaming in her head, *Let me talk! Let me talk!* But no luck. She just sat there in silence as the old men screamed from one side of the room to the other. What could Anna do but sit there as the bill got sidelined due to a filibuster.

After the speaker called the sitting adjourned, Anna just stood there with sweat dripping down her face and the glass of water on her table half-empty. She was still processing what had happened.

Anna was not happy. She walked back into her office and was so angry that she threw the door open to the point that it nearly broke the doorframe. Ella was just sitting on the couch, watching the hearing again on the Holonet projector. After Anna entered the room, Ella got off the couch and went to hug her.

"Are you all right, Anna?"

Anna was breathing heavily. "No. I don't know what happened in there. Where did I go wrong?"

Ella sat Anna down on the couch and explained to her that she wasn't assertive enough. To win in politics, you need to be ruthless and have a voice. Ella explained that this place was a boy's club and that if she wanted to get ahead, she needed to do two things: number one, form a club of supporters to back her, and number two, project confidence.

Anna didn't realise there was a lot of work involved and began to question herself. She slouched on the couch and breathed heavy. "I am not cut out for this type of work."

Ella was baffled. "Yes, you are, Anna. This was your first sitting. Look, you have your work cut out for you, but we will get through this. You have me by your side."

Then Ella gave her a playful laugh. "Come on, there's this little pizza shop down the road. I will buy you a slice."

"I will meet you there."

Ella left the room, leaving Anna by herself. In every politician's office, there was a bar, because so many politicians were alcoholics that the designer thought, *What the hell.* Anna got up off the couch and went over to the bar to pour herself a glass of brandy.

She sat there thinking of where she was and contemplating what Ella was saying. Maybe Ella was right; maybe to survive, she needed to get hard.

Walking over to her tablet, she went through old achieves and watched some of the famous orators throughout history to figure out how to project confidence. She watched Martin Luther King, Mussolini and Obama, and what she noticed about those figures was their passion. She needed passion and anger and depth in what she was saying. So over and over in the mirror, she practised. Then she realised that she had left Ella at the pizza shop and quickly rushed out the door to go meet her.

The next morning, Ella and Anna met at an old-style boxing gym called Punching Blows. They walked into the gym in their workout gear.

Anna was not thrilled about going to a gym. "Come on, Ella, I've got a lot of work to do. I don't have time to work out."

"Anna, the problem you had at the meeting was that you lacked confidence in speaking." She began strapping on her boxing gloves. "Boxing will help to build confidence and bring back the fighting instinct that you have suppressed over the years."

Anna smirked. "I have plenty of fight!"

"Yer, but you fight like a mum. We need to get the beast within you."

Anna shook her head. "This is stupid. I am too old to box."

Ella had a smile on her face. "Really?"

Whack! Ella right-hooked Anna across the head.

"Aw, what the hell?"

"What are you going to do about it?" *Whack!*

"I am warning you, little lady," said Anna, this time raising her voice.

"Oh yea?" Whack!

At that point, Anna was pissed. She jumped in the ring and strapped on her gloves. Suddenly, Ella threw some punches, with Anna dodging out of the way, and she returned with some power punches of her own.

However, Ella still had the upper hand, and she knocked Anna to the floor. Anna was sore and lying on the floor huffing and puffing.

"You good, Anna?" Ella asked to check.

Anna smiled. "Damn it!"

"From now on, every morning, we are going to get up at 4.00 am and train to unlock that beast within you." Ella then threw a towel on the ground for Anna.

After the intense training workout, they both walked into Anna's private office holding protein smoothies, with Anna still nursing a sore jaw.

"That right hook hurt!" she moaned in pain.

"Yer, well, should have kept your guard. Basic boxing 101."

After their little boxing match, they walked down the street to get smoothies and went back to their offices. Anna then walked over to the couch and sat down drinking her smoothie.

"Now, lesson number two. Stand up."

"Ella, please, if you are going to punch me again, I will knock you out."

"Hahaha, no, no punches this time. Now, we are going to learn speaking techniques."

"OK, well, I must warn you, I have been practising my oratorical skills."

"Fine, then, old lady, show me!"

"Who you are calling old lady?"

"And begin."

"Umm ... OK, well, umm, so anyway, umm, the bill I am proposing is about, umm, military reducing—"

"Stop! What are you, a bee? How many times are you going to say 'umm'? Anna, if you want to be a good public speaker, then you got to learn how to speak with confidence. I mean, what happened to the Anna who projected confidence at the rallies? In here, it is no different. Just a different playpen."

"I wasn't that bad, was it?"

"Honestly, Anna, if I catch you using the word 'umm' again, I am going to throw a book at you."

Anna was shocked at how cruel Ella was being.

"And what is up with your posture? What, do you have a hunchback?"

Anna was at a breaking point. "Ella, why are you being so mean to me today?"

Ella put down her smoothie and stood up. "Because Anna, I love you like a mother, but if you can't handle me being mean to you, what chance are you going to have out in the political arena?"

Anna thought over what Ella was saying, and she was right. In the first sitting, she got pushed around; hell. She didn't even get to speak her mind. Anna took in a sad sigh and sat down at her desk, looking in despair.

"I think you're right, Ella. I honestly don't think I am cut out for politics. It's too cutthroat. Maybe we should have elected Edward instead of me."

"No! Don't say that, Anna. Edward is a wimp. He doesn't have half the courage you do. Look, Anna, you are perfect for politics. You are smart, compassionate, caring and a fighter. You've just got to ignite that fire in you."

Anna just looked down sad. "But I just don't know how. I am a mother, not a politician."

Ella wasn't having Anna's quitting attitude. "Fine, then we will help you become a politician. Anna, we got you through the door, but you still have a long journey ahead of you. All the greatest politicians didn't start off being great politicians. They have to sacrifice and fight. Anna, you were given a gift, the gift of public speaking. You just need to master your craft."

Anna's face went from sad to determined. "All right, Ella, what do I do?"

Ella just smiled. "It's already began."

CHAPTER 27

Anna went home that day still feeling defeated from the first sitting and feeling ignored that she was strangled and shot down in her first sitting. Yet, despite her grief, she walked away with a lesson learnt from Ella that she couldn't stop thinking about. She knew that Ella was right; the old Anna was never going to get far in politics. If she wanted to survive, she needed to change her mindset. But little did she know that she was never going to be the same again.

Anna got into bed that night nursing a hurt jaw and a life lesson. But the next morning at 4 o'clock on the dot, she arrived at the gym in her workout gear ready for round two. She was tired, sleepless and sore, but she was determined to kick Ella's arse. Just as Ella arrived, Anna was all ready to go with her boxing gloves on and jumping with joy. Ella slapped on her gloves, and the bell rang.

This time, Anna learnt and ducked and swerved from Ella's punches and even managed to throw a few at herself. But with all the punches she threw, she fell straight to the floor, this time with a bleeding nose.

Ella jumped around in victory. "Is that all you got, old woman?"

Great, now Anna had to support a hurt jaw and bleeding nose. Ella rushed to pick Anna up from the floor, and she gave her some support.

"Good. That was much better, but you are still not there yet."

Ella got Anna to work. She made her work the bag for 10 minutes, then do push-ups, sit-ups, burpees and 10 minutes on the treadmill.

That was lesson one; then onto lesson two. "OK, Ella, now that you've built your physical strength, now is the time to build your public-speaking skills. First, adjust your posture. Back straight, shoulders apart, project confidence."

Anna followed Ella's feedback to the letter.

"Good. Now let's hear your proposal."

"Thank you, Mr Speaker. I am here today to tell you why you need to—"

"Booo! Stupid woman!"

Anna was surprised by her and kept going. "I am here—"

"Boo! Boo Anna, boo!"

Anna stopped speaking. "Ella, what are you doing?"

"Anna, you can't be so timid. Remember, project confidence. Clap back! If someone interrupts, you say, 'I am talking!'"

Anna looked down at the floor disappointed. After seeing how sad Anna was, Ella rushed to comfort her. "Hey, it's OK, you are doing so well!"

Anna sighed. "Na, this is stupid. I don't want to be a politician."

Ella was annoyed at that statement. "Then why did you become a politician?"

"Because I wanted to help people and to end the military occupation. I am just a retail worker and a mother."

Ella looked at her. "So what, you want to get rid of the military occupation, but you don't want to put in the hard work?"

Anna went to the bar and poured herself a scotch. "I don't know. I didn't think it would be so hard."

"Well, welcome to life, Anna. If you truly want something in your life, you are going to have to fight for it."

"But I just can't get over being strangled, talked down and treated like a piece of crap! I mean look what they call me on social media." Anna held up her phone, revealing posts of death threats and verbal abuse.

Ella shook her head in shock. "That is awful, Anna."

Ella then got off the couch, and before Anna could have a drink of the scotch, she poured the glass into the sink.

"Look Anna, yes, that stuff hurt, but you can't care about what anyone thinks about you. Look, they are trying to get to you because they are scared of who you will become. All you got to do is become something they fear: a stronger, better version of you. We all have our skills: Jacob is our soldier, Edward is the brains, I am the coordinator and you are the face of the operation. If you fail, this whole operation fails."

Anna took a deep breath in. "I just don't know how."

"Anna, Dad is gone. He is dead, and you are our only hope at saving this thing."

Ella got up and walked to the door. "Anna, keep going. You're on the right path."

Before leaving, she smiled and added, "See you tomorrow at the gym."

Ella then walked out the door, leaving Anna by herself. Anna looked out the window and started thinking about who exactly she was.

After a long day, she picked up her coat and walked out of her office. But just as she was about to leave the building, she heard chatter from across the hall. Curious, she decided to hide behind the corner and eavesdrop on the conversation. The conversation was between two men. She recognised the first voice, as it was the man who had his hand around her neck, Richard Ardwick, the politician from the Upper Level. She didn't recognise the other voice. Must be his friend. But what they were saying struck her to her core.

"How was that female politician trying to go against the bill?"

Richard just scoffed. "She's not going to last here long. She's a female. Look, I am all for female empowerment, but I just reckon this is a man's game, and she is not cut out."

"Hell, who knows, she is probably better in bed than she is in politics."

Both politicians laughed. Anna was furious at the disrespect, and she really wanted to walk up and punch both, but she wouldn't. It was beneath her.

All she did was clench her fist and storm out of that building so fast with fury in her eyes. She could not believe what they had said about her, but she had to thank them, because not only did she want to defeat them, but she wanted to destroy their whole political careers.

Ella was at home sitting on the couch watching the Holonet when Anna stormed into the house. "I will see you tomorrow at the gym!"

Ella could notice that something in Anna had changed; she could tell by the look in her eyes. Anna then stomped up the stairs and slammed the door into her room. Anna lay there in her bed, and she wanted to cry, but she was above that. Now, she just wanted to fight.

Ella was both proud and confused at what had just happened. But one thing she knew for certain was that Anna's fire had definitely been ignited.

The next morning had arrived. Anna was at the gym an hour early at 3 o'clock. She wanted to get started. Her goal was to kick Ella's arse. She began working on the bag, running on the treadmill and lifting weights until her shoulders felt as if they were about to rip off their socket.

When Ella arrived at the gym, Anna was all strapped and ready to go. Ella jumped into the ring and the bell rang. Ella was caught off guard by Anna's punches, and she managed to land a few on her. But soon, Ella got the upper hand and knocked her to the floor, for the third day in a row. Her jaw hurt again, but something had changed. Anna didn't care about the physical pain pulsing through her body, as her mind was distracted and racing with thoughts; the thoughts of all the names and all the slander she had endured.

But the one memory she couldn't erase was what the guys had said about her. "She's better in bed."

Now, that one boiled her blood. Anna banged on the ground for a few seconds and stood back up. This time, she was not going to stay lying down on the floor. Anna screamed to Ella, "Hey Ella, I didn't hear any bells."

Ella turned around in shock and was caught completely surprised, as right in front of her, Anna stood there with fire in her eyes. Ella rushed up to Anna, throwing punch after punch at her, but she was not going down. She blocked all the punches, and in her mind, all she could see were images of Richard's ugly face. The veins on her forehead nearly exploded, and she let out a scream and began bombarding Ella with punches. Ella tried her best to block them all, but they came from all directions and with such velocity that they broke down her guard within seconds. Then, all of Anna's punches began to land on Ella's face, and within minutes, Ella was knocked to the floor with bruises all over her face.

Ella didn't know what had just happened. She was on the floor breathing and coughing up blood.

Anna calmed down and offered Ella an outstretched hand. "Need a hand?"

Ella was in pain but proud of Anna. "Boy, you hit hard."

Anna just laughed.

That day, Anna powered through the workout like a lion. She hit the bag so hard that she nearly knocked it off its hinges. Ella was nursing her wounds with an ice pack on her face. Guess payback's a bitch.

After the workout, they stopped off and picked up some protein smoothies and laughed about how Anna managed to knock Ella out. As she entered the ParliaCongress building, she accidentally brushed shoulders with Richard.

Richard, the smug politician, looked her up and down. "Watch it."

Anna wanted to treat him with humility and grace, but honestly, she was in a fighting mood. She shot Richard a dirty look. "Watch yourself."

Richard just paused and was shocked at what Anna just said.

"Excuse me, who do you think you are talking to?" he growled, pointing a finger at Anna.

The old Anna would have been frightened, but she stood her ground. "I don't think you really want to know the answer to that."

Richard was now pissed. He placed an arm on her shoulder. "Hey listen—"

But before he could say another word, she socked him straight in the jaw, knocking him down. Richard just held his nose; it was bleeding. He looked up at Anna in fear.

Anna looked him right in his frightened eyes. "Don't you ever put your hands on me again, or the next time, I will break more than your nose."

Ella just stood there holding her smoothie and was absolutely lost for words.

Anna just picked up her smoothie and signalled to Ella. "Come on, Ella, we have work to do."

"Yes, ma'am."

Anna walked into her office with a step in her shoes and was a bit proud of herself. Yes, violence is never the answer, and she shouldn't have hit him, but oh well, it happened, and believe you me, that spoilt brat deserved it. She stared at the mirror with a bit of pride and did a bit of shadowboxing in the mirror of her office.

Her transformation was complete. She had finally learnt to unleash the beast within her, and now, she was a completely different person.

"So, my favourite assistant, what's on the agenda today?"

Ella then looked down at her tablet, and the two got to work plugging away at rehearsing for the second sitting.

After hours and hours of having Ella whack her on the back with a ruler to keep her posture straight and reading the speech so much that it was melted into her eyes, Anna was done. She was completely drained of energy for the day, plugging away at a 9-hour shift. By the time she was done, it was nightfall. However, it was hard to tell in this city, as there was so much light on that it looked like daytime. Anna and Ella both decided to walk back home down into the Lower Levels. They were both laughing and telling funny stories of a young Jacob and the multiple knockouts while sipping store-bought coffees. However, for some reason, Anna stopped and stared at her old high school.

Confused, Ella walked over to Anna. "Hey Anna, are you all right?"

"Yer, I am just looking at the school. I used to go here, you know."

Ella looked around for anyone watching them. Then she whispered to Ella, "Do you want to go in?"

Anna let out a bit of a giggle. "That's breaking and entering."

Ella smiled. "Only if we get caught."

Ella walked up to the locked door and used her credit card to unlock it, to Anna's shock. "Ella!"

Ella just looked over with a smile. "We are only going for a look around."

Ella rushed in. Anna hesitated for a few moments, looking around for any witness, then followed Ella in.

The two of them, looked around at the dark, empty high school, hearing the auditory ghosts of schoolchildren laughing and rushing up and down the halls and looking at the empty lockers and classroom, where 2 hours ago, this school was full of teachers and students. There was something about seeing an empty high school at night. It was creepy yet beautiful. Being back in high school was a trip down memory lane for them.

"Anna, what do you want to look at in this building? It's just an old high school."

Anna looked through the windows of the empty classroom looking for something.

"Do you remember your school days, Ella?"

"I got expelled from so many schools, I just don't bother remembering those times anymore."

Anna laughed at that statement. "Well, you may have hated it, but I loved it. They were the best years of my life."

"Let me guess, you were one of those honour roll students, weren't you?"

Anna laughed again. "Yep. School captain, honour roll, sport captain, you name it."

Then Anna stopped and looked at classroom 14A. "There it is, Ella. Do you mind being a dear and opening it?"

Ella pulled the same card trick and opened the door. Anna walked over to the teacher's desk and began admiring it.

"All the potential!" she said, while shaking her head and looking at the empty tables. She then repeated, "All the potential."

"Anna, what are you talking?"

"Oh, nothing. Just looking back at old memories. Did you know, my dream job was to be a history teacher."

"Really? You wanted to be a teacher?"

"Yer. It was my goal after my military service. I would come home, go to university and study teaching. I had my life all mapped out. I studied day and night and made sure to get nothing but a 99 per cent on all exams."

Ella was amazed.

"Wow! What happened? How come you gave it up?" she asked, taking a seat on one of the students' desks.

Anna gave a little smirk. "Well, that was the plan, but life had different plans. After my military service, I came home and met a boy."

"Oooh! A boy."

"Yep. Jacob's dad. It was only meant to be a fling, but I fell pregnant with Jacob, and the bills started piling up. Then came the excuses: Jacob's dad died, and I had a mortgage and bills to pay by myself while raising Jacob."

Anna then let out a sigh and shook her head.

"Then by that point, I had so much debt over my head that I needed to take any minimum-wage job I could to get by, and I just never had the time to study. I threw away my dreams."

She looked down in sorrow and let out a small smile. "Life really is hard, isn't it, Ella?"

Ella looked down at her feet. She was saddened to hear Anna gave up her dream, but in a way, she could relate to her on a personal level. "I know how you feel. My dream was to be an architect."

Anna looked up at Ella. "Really, you wanted to be an architect?"

"Yer. I grew up in a very poor family and never had a lot. Being poor meant I grew up in neighbourhoods that were ugly and decrepit, and I hated walking past buildings that were abandoned and served no purpose. I wanted to be an architect so I could design new, beautiful buildings. I wanted to build skyscrapers that reached the heavens."

Anna was surprised. "I didn't know how artistic you truly were."

"Yer. I mean, I loved drawing and designing. I couldn't spell for shit but could draw buildings and designed models."

Ella let out a laugh and told Anna how in one of the houses that her family was renting, she painted the house from white to pink, which got her grounded by her parents. Anna laughed. "So, what happened?"

Ella looked down at her feet. "Well, I never paid attention at school. I couldn't afford the books or resources that other kids got, so my grades slipped, and I ended up dropping out. Out of desperation, I joined the army as an air dome technician, came home and did night school, but Dad needed help with his gun shop. I got my GED, but Dad was struggling to get by, and I couldn't abandon him. So, I just put my dreams on hold and got work."

Anna now was the one who felt sorry for Ella and decided to give her advice. "Well, you are still young, Ella. Why not consider doing it?"

But Ella just looked down at her feet and began shaking her head. "Na, it's too late for me."

There was an awkward silence, and they both just looked at their feet. Hoping to not ruin the moment, Ella spoke up, "Hey Anna."

"Yer, Ella?"

Ella smiled and said, "Sorry, but I had sex with your son."

Both Ella and Anna just burst out laughing. "Doesn't surprise me. I mean, you could cut the sexual tension between you two with a knife."

Ella and Anna laughed their heads off at that comment. "Life is hard, isn't it, Anna?"

"You said it. Sometimes, you feel like you sacrifice and work your fingers to the bone, only to move backwards instead of forward."

"What was Jacob's dream? He never told me what he wanted to do."

Anna looked down. "Jacob never really had a dream. All he wanted was a normal life up in the Middle Levels."

Ella shook her head. "That guy, I tell ya, he lives his life like a robot. Sometimes, he scares me. All he focuses on is revenge."

"He didn't always use to be like that. The military changed him. He saw things."

Ella shook her head. "Didn't we all?"

"He didn't always use to be this way, you know, all brutish and moody. He used to be such a sweet kid. So happy and optimistic. Believed there was good in the world."

"What is he now?"

"A tired, scared little kid who would do anything to get out of this hellhole."

Ella was about to speak when she heard a voice. "Who's there?"

Ella and Anna both spotted the torchlight shining through the door window. They both ducked out of reflex, trying not to be spotted. They waited a few minutes for the guard to pass and then quickly bolted out the classroom and down the hall.

"Hey, stop, you kids, or I will shoot."

What was so funny was that he didn't even have a gun. Ella, and Anna both rushed down the hall and out the door so fast that they huffed and puffed as if their lungs were about to give up.

Man, they felt so young, and they both laughed. They were so close to getting caught. Anna hadn't got into that much mischief in years.

"All right, Anna, it is getting pretty late."

"Agreed. Let's just head home."

They both began walking home, but then Anna grabbed Ella by the arm. "Ella, listen to me. Your dad, well, he didn't make good choices in his life. He let hate and vengeance consume him. But you are still young and have a chance to change your life around. So take my advice. GO!"

Anna began walking off without Ella. Ella just stood there for a few minutes and then caught up with Anna.

CHAPTER *28*

02-01-3026

Ella and Anna were making their way to ParliaCongress as they prepared for a busy day of reading bill drafts and shaking hands with other politicians to get their bill passed.

It was a nice day; the weather machine was generating a clear sky and a sunny day.

Before they made their way back, they decided to stop off at a local café and get a protein smoothie, as they needed something to calm their tense muscles. Ella got a raspberry shake, and Anna got a banana shake, and they sipped down their drink while they were both running through the schedule for the day.

But a loud sound caught their attention. Ella looked concerned. "Hey Anna, did you hear that?"

Anna paused and tried her best to listen to the sound. But then, alarm bells went off in Anna's head. "It sounds like a rocket!"

Suddenly, a projectile went zooming past the shop at hypersonic speed, moving so fast that its force blew Anna's and Ella's hair back.

"What the hell was that?" Ella rushed over to the sidewalk to get a better look. "That looks like a hypersonic missile!"

"Yer, but what—"

BOOM! Anna was interrupted when the missile made an impact on its target. Anna and Ella looked at each other in concern. "Oh my gosh, that rocket just hit the private school."

Anna, Ella and everyone around them looked in shock as the rocket crumbled the strong structure into tiny little pieces, and a fireball shot up from the wreckage.

Anna and Ella threw down their smoothies and began rushing towards the crash site, sprinting down the sidewalk and brushing over concerned citizens.

Anna and Ella could see overhead emergency vehicles from the police, fire and ambulance services rushing to the crash site with their sirens on. Once Anna and Ella made it to the private school, they found it completely decimated, and all that was left was rubble. Anna and Ella just stood there behind the taped-off area watching as emergency service made their way through the rubble to try and find what remained. What was most depressing was the fact that it was 9 o'clock on a Monday, and the school was packed with students and teachers. It was awful to watch as emergency services sifted through the rubble, pulling out dead body after dead body that was covered in blood-soaked linen clothes. It was awful. Students emerged from the rubble covered in blood, and almost all were in tears. While a lucky few managed to survive the missile strike, most of them lost their lives.

A crowd of hundreds gathered around and watched, while some in the local community rolled up their sleeve to help sort through the rubble.

But Anna and Ella were still confused. *Why? Why would anyone strike a school, especially a prestigious school such as St Michael School Private School?*

This school was so prestigious that politicians and business owners sent their kids there. After at least 2 hours of watching the emergency crew sift through the rubble, Ella and Anna began to make their way back to Anna's office to watch the news. All their questions were answered. The head of the peacekeeping force read out a prepared speech detailing that a hypersonic missile flew off its target and accidentally flew up into the Middle Levels and collided with the school.

The new anchor estimated that at least 5 teachers and at least 100 students were killed in the blast. Anna was in complete shock, holding her hands above her mouth and feeling the grief of the poor parents and families who lost their children.

Ella too was in shock, with tears rolling down her face. It was horrible. How could they do that? The newscast got so unbearable, watching all the crying parents, that they had to switch off the television. Anna, Ella and all the other staffers didn't say anything. They just all stood there in silence.

Anna was the first to break the silence. "So, what does this all mean?"

Ella didn't answer. She had zoned out for a couple of minutes, but Anna snapped her fingers. "Ella!"

Ella snapped back into attention, still a bit dazed. "Oh! Well, um, this doesn't look good, I am afraid. We are going to have to give a press conference addressing what has happened."

Anna nodded in agreement. "OK, then let's get prepared for what we should address."

"Ma'am, Richard is going to speak."

Anna sighed. "Oh, this is going to be good."

Ella switched the Holonet projector back on to reveal Richard in a black suit wearing a ribbon. He clearly wasn't there to show solidarity to the victims. He was there to do PR to spin the situation. The first thing Richard said was "my thoughts and prayers are with the family and victims of this terrible tragedy." The news team went on to ask Richard about the situation, but Richard repeated what the head of the peacekeeping force said, "This was a terrible 'misfire'. There is no need for an investigation." Standard stuff.

However, it was what he said next that made Anna's skin crawl. One of the reporters asked, "So, this incident doesn't call for further investigation into the army reserve and their military exercises?"

Richard paused for a few seconds. "Look, this was just an isolated incident. Now, I feel for the schoolchildren, I do, but I am not going to stand here and let you scrutinise and demonise our military forces."

Anna was completely baffled. "What? Scrutinise? What was that twat on about? They blew up a school full of children. They deserve all the scrutiny they can get."

But what the public didn't realise was that destroying the school in the Middle Level was the tip of the iceberg compared to what the peacekeeping force had done down in the Lower Levels.

The peacekeepers, since their occupation, had levelled buildings and killed hundreds of men, women and children, but did they get any media attention or investigation? No! Because it was the Lower Levels, and no one cared about the Lower Level. When people even mention the Lower Levels, it just got swept under the rug with PR stunts and 'internal investigations'. But when one rocket strikes a school in the Middle Levels, then watch out and face the fury of the public. That is what annoyed Anna the most, the injustice that some people live are more valuable than others. However, in this circumstance, she would just have to suck it up, as the court of political opinion could be turned in Anna's favour. Now, Anna knew that what she was about to do was wrong, but she was going to twist this disaster to support her removal of the military occupation bill. It needed to be done.

Within hours of the strike, thousands upon thousands of people gathered at the step of ParliaCongress that was held back by rows upon rows of riot and capital police. The crowd was angry at the incident. They were all holding picket signs and chanting, "No more bullets, no more guns."

The rubble that remained of St Michael Private School was littered with flowers and pictures of school children who had died in the explosion. In front of the protesters was a podium, and Anna was preparing herself to speak to the crowd. She was backstage rehearsing and reciting her speech, nervous at the idea of talking to thousands of people with the whole city watching her.

Then it was showtime! Anna walked outside towards the podium, with the crowd cheering in applause at her mere presence, and the cameras were following her with every move she made.

Anna looked down, as it would be embarrassing for her campaign if she tripped on national Holonet. Then the crowd went silent as she grabbed the mic, took a deep breath in, calming her mind, and looked back at Ella for support.

"Ladies and Gentlemen of the American Division City, I feel your pain. As a single mother, I know your struggle. First, I would like to say that my heart goes out to the families who had lost loved ones to the accident."

She looked around, trying to fight back her stage fright. Then, out of nowhere, she slammed her fist on the podium. "No more! No more dying! No more death! No longer would we stand here and let the army use our city as a playground for their toys. I have a truth to tell you all, and that truth is that the army has been fighting a secret war down under, down in the Lower Level, that has killed thousands over the past couple of months. Well, I say, no longer will the Lower, Middle and Upper Levels tolerate their baboonery and tolerate their disregard for human life. Am I right?"

The crowd roared in applause. "Who says that the military is to have a free reign? I mean, what is this? Asia City? Wasn't this city built on freedom and democracy? If so, go forth and spread the word. No more military occupation!"

The crowd exploded in applause. Anna stood there proud. She had turned from a retail worker to a political icon in a matter of minutes.

The crowd began to roar: "No more occupation! No more occupation!"

At that point, Anna walked inside for her own safety, as the police held back the crowd with ease.

Anna walked inside and was met with a hug from Ella.

"Anna, that was amazing!"

"I know! Thank you!"

Anna and Ella turned on the news to find Anna on every news outlet. Some slandered her, and others praised her for her courage. But regardless, her political career was about to take shape. Also, victims from the Lower Level came forth and told their side of the story from their time under occupation. Some Anna knew, and others were complete strangers to her. It was remarkable. Anna had started a revolution. She had created friends, but she also created enemies.

Within the first 40 minutes of Anna's speech, defence stocks on the stock market crashed by 5 per cent, which was the first time in that month that had happened. Normally, defence stocks were blue chip and were having a bullish run this year. But thanks to Anna, the defence industry was having its first bearish rush in 6 months. Anna was on top of the world. She watched the Holonet as the WeapCo CEO rushed to save face by 'pledging millions of dollars to charities of gun violence', but you could tell by the look on his face that he was not impressed at all.

Anna loved it. She loved the power and influence she had because of her speech, but that was all about to change when her phone began to ring. She picked up her phone to reveal an unknown number. She answered it. "Hello?"

The voice of Adrian could be heard yelling, "We need to talk!"

"Hang on," Anna begged kindly. She then placed the phone down and yelled out, "Can everyone please get out of the room?"

Ella shot up straight away. "Anna, is everything all right?"

"Fine. I just need to talk in private."

"All right. Everyone! The lady needs the room. Come on, let's go." Ella ushered everyone out of the room, leaving Anna alone with the phone.

"Is everyone gone?" Adrian asked.

"Yes Adrian, it is just you and me."

"Great. I have a bone to pick with you!" Adrian screamed through the phone. "How dare you!"

"How dare I what?"

"Anna, Wacco put you in that position so that you could take down WeapCo, but I just found out that your silly little speech has caused my company to lose one million dollars in the past hour, and I don't like to lose."

"Well, what do you want from me? I went out there and gave a speech. The crowd loved it, and we now have support for the end of the bill."

"But it is costing me valuable money. The goal was not to cost me money. It was for you to get the military occupation bill removed off the senate floor so WeapCo loses money and Wacco takes the spot as the number one arms dealer. But I have found out that not only has WeapCo still retained its spot as the number one arms dealer in the city, but now I am losing money and am about to be taken over by my enemies."

"So, what do you want me to do?"

"In the next hour, I am going to email you a prepared speech that could save my company from losing profits. You are to read it."

"And if I refuse?"

"Anna, I am not a man to toy around with. I put you in that position, and I can be sure as hell remove you as well."

"But Adrian, reading out that speech, you compromise my morals, and it would ruin my position with the community."

"I couldn't care less about your morals. My company is losing money, and I don't like to lose. So, as I see, you have two choices. You can either read out the prepared speech and compromise your 'morals' and remain a politician, or you can refuse and 'see what happens'. The choice is yours."

Adrian hung up the phone. Anna instantly went back to her desk and opened her laptop to read an email sent straight from the desk of Adrian himself. Anna opened the email herself. In essence, it was pretty much an email outlining how

Wacco was an ethical gun company and was committed to limiting gun sales in the Middle Level.

However, the only problem was that it meant that Wacco would make up for the lost profit by flooding the Lower Level with even more guns, which meant more dead people and more weapons on top of the guns that WeapCo supplied. The speech was an absolute nightmare. That meant she would break her promise of eliminating guns off the street by flooding the levels with even more guns. Anna knew she was at a crossroads in her political career, but she wasn't surprised. When you make a deal with the devil, eventually, he comes to collect, as the old saying goes.

But the question was, does she sell her soul for power, or does she risk ending her political career in her first term? The choice was hers.

Ella burst through the room. "Hey Anna, is it safe to come in?"

Anna didn't say anything. She was deep in thought as to what to do. Ella saw the concern on her face. "Hey Anna, are you OK?"

"I was on the phone to Adrian, the CEO of Wacco."

Ella rolled her eyes. "Oh goodness me, what does he want?"

"He wants me to read out this pre-planned email in a news conference."

"Or?"

"I could potentially lose my position."

Ella was shocked. "What? Can he do that?"

"He is a very powerful man, Ella, who has almost the same amount of influence in this city as WeapCo."

"So, Anna, are you going to do it?"

Anna sighed. "I may have to?"

Ella looked shocked. "Anna, no. You're better than this."

"What choice do I have, Ella? He is right he got me into this chair."

"Anna, you can't say that stuff. It's a lie. If you do it, you will lose more than your position, you lose the respect of the Lower Level, and you will lose me."

Ella stormed out of the room, leaving Anna to look down at her desk and try to decide. She felt a little bit ashamed that she got herself into this position.

The media and supporters all gathered on the steps of ParliaCongress, as the podium stood empty. Where only a few hours ago, Anna made the biggest political speech of her career, now the crowds of people and the media team were all waiting for Anna to again take her place. The camera crew were all preparing their cameras, and the light shined bright on the podium, as it remained empty. Anna's social media team had given out an alert. Anna was going to make another speech.

Then, the cameras all roared on as Anna walked out from the ParliaCongress building and began marching towards the podium, waving to the crowd as her sight was blinded by the flashes from photographers. Then, there was an eerie silence as Anna ruffled through papers, readying herself to speak. This was a make-or-break for her. Anna let out a cough.

"Thank you everyone for being here today."

Anna paused, looking down at the pre-prepared speech, but in an act of defiance, she chucked the paper and threw it onto the floor, which caught the attention of the media. Then, Anna continued with her own speech.

"My people, just a few hours ago, I stood here and gave possibly the biggest speech of my political career. And now, I stand here now with that same defiance. The truth of the matter is that my campaign is built on a lie. Wacco had funded me to promote their agenda."

The media crew all gasped in shock at that statement, and the photographers took photos from many angles.

"But I stand here today to so say no! No to gun lobbyists, and no to independent warmongers that ravage and plague our great city with weapons of mass destruction. And I say to you, to all companies, big or small, your weapons are no longer going to touch our streets and kill our children. And I say to anyone that threatens my campaign or tries to derail me, bring it on. Thank you, and goodnight."

The crowd roared in cheers as Anna walked away. Then she looked at her phone, and a message from Adrian read, 'You just committed political suicide tonight'.

Anna walked back into her office proud as a peacock, with Ella rushing over to give her a hug.

"Anna, you did amazing, girl."

Anna had a big smile on her face from the speech she gave. "Thank you."

"Not only did you just stand by your morals, but you gave the middle finger to two of the biggest gun companies in the city."

"I know! Adrian can suck it. No one can take my morals that easily."

"I know, but Anna, what are we going to do about Adrian?"

"I don't know."

"Can he really bring down our campaign? I mean, you said it yourself, he has an immense amount of power and influence."

"I am not worried about that at this stage. What's important now is getting this military occupation bill revoked."

"OK, but still—"

"Ella, don't worry, no one is going to hurt you or my family. I won't allow that!"

Anna then made her way and sat down on the couch in her office. "Let's see what the news says about me now?"

Anna switched on the Holonet, hoping to find positive news about her. But to her disappointment, it was the complete opposite. Every news channel she went on slandered her. Anna now realised it was because she had admitted to taking money from a gun company. Anna had told the truth, and she was paying the price. Now, channels far and wide had hurtful banners. She was hated by the right and the left with names such as 'Gun Hoe Barbie' or 'Corrupt Anna'.

The media was having a field day with her. Her best day was becoming her worst nightmare, and it looked as if her political career was going to be short-lived.

Anna watched on the hologram, as her approval ratings were dropping from 55 to 45 per cent. Then, two capital police officers barged into her office.

"Anna Turner, you are under arrest for political espionage, voter suppression and embezzlement. Please turn around."

Anna and Ella were in complete shock, as the officers slapped handcuffs on Anna and began escorting her out of the office.

Anna didn't know what to say. Political espionage? Voter suppression? Where did all those charges come from? She never did any of that stuff. But nonetheless, she complied with the officers as they escorted her out of the building and down the steps of ParliaCongress.

There were swarms of crowds and flashes from all directions, blocking her view, to the point that capital police had to push them out of her way. Then, the officers shoved Anna in the back of a black floating car, and the car flew off into the distance. Anna was confused about what was happening. She was both scared and confused. It was only a moment ago that Anna was on top of the world, full of confidence and grace; now, she was at rock bottom once again. Her political career was tanking in the polls, she was being punished for telling the truth, and now by the looks of things, she was not only facing criminal charges but impeachment as well. Anna just lay in the back seat of her SUV in tears and shock at what was happening. She was going to lose everything: her family and her career.

The police escorted her out of the van and began marching her in her wrinkly black suit down the corridors, past jail cells of prisoners wolf-calling her while she just cried. Next, the police took mugshots of her, and finally, they threw her into a jail cell, where she sat feeling like an absolute disgrace.

Anna sat there for hours on end, but then Ella burst into the room. "Anna!"

After seeing Ella's face, she just rushed towards her and gave her a big hug and broke down into tears. "Oh, thank God. I missed you so much. I don't know what had happened."

Anna was so scared of everything.

"It's OK, Anna. It's OK. We will get through this. Now, we have paid for your bail. Grab your things and let's go home. Your trial is not for another week. Come on."

Ella escorted Anna out of her cell, as the capital police held the door. Both Ella and Anna got into the Black SUV as it took off making its way home.

Ella entered the house in a fit of rage. "Can't believe they put you through all that. It sucks. Agh! Screw the government, screw Wacco and screw the police! Fine, they think that they can destroy us? Well, we will show them. We will show them all, right Anna?"

Anna didn't respond, and Ella turned around to find Anna breaking down in tears at the front door with her hands buried in her face.

"Anna? What's wrong?"

Ella walked overlooking concerned.

"No, it's just my life."

"What about it, Anna?"

She broke down at the front doorstep. "I feel like I have let everyone down. I feel like an absolute failure."

"Hey, no, come on, Anna, that is simply not true at all. Look, you did the right thing. It was dirty money. Who cares if you lose your crummy job? We are all here for you, Anna."

Then, Jacob and Edward both walked down the stairs.

"It's all right, Mum. We are all here for you." Jacob walked over and gave her a hug. "Mum, remember, you are a Turner, and a Turner never gives up."

Anna burst into tears again. "I love you all!"

The group gathered around Anna and gave her a big hug. Later that night, after a big family dinner and a few laughs, Jacob was about to head to bed when he saw smoke coming from the front step of the porch. He decided to go talk to Anna who was on the porch, smoking a blunt alone in the dark.

"Mum, is everything OK?"

Anna then burst into tears. "I am sorry, Jacob. I know you don't like to see your mum cry, but I can't help it."

Jacob then took a seat next to her. "It's all right, Mum. It doesn't matter about the position. I mean, we will find a solution."

Anna just dried her tears. "It's not that. It's just, ain't you getting tired of working your fingers to the bone, giving 110 per cent, standing by your morals, only to be constantly shot down, having to pick yourself up, again just to be shot down?"

Jacob stood there in absolute silence for a minute, contemplating what his mother was saying to him. "Hey Mum, do you remember when dad died and you were struggling to figure out how you were ever going to survive?"

Anna let out a small giggle. "I ran around town with about 30 resumes hoping to find work."

"But you managed to find work, didn't you?"

"Yer, I got that retail job."

"Do you also remember that time when you thought you were going to lose the house?"

"Yer, you and I had to pull doubles just to make the mortgage payment. Jacob, where are you getting with this?"

"The point is that while we have faced storms in our lifetimes, we have always braced through them and survived to tell the story. Mum, you're right; all we do is work and work non-stop, and sometimes, it feels like our work leads us nowhere. But we still have to hold on to the faith. Even when we feel like we don't deserve it or we feel unloved or when we want to give up, you got to believe. Do you know what I got from reading all those superhero comic books?"

"What?"

"I learnt that it wasn't the powers or money or fancy suits that made them heroes. It was their morals and their values. Batman never killed, neither did Superman, and people looked up to them and called them 'heroes'. That is why, Anna, you are a hero, because despite the fact that you messed up, despite the fact you humiliated yourself on Holonet News, and despite the fact that you may be facing prison and may lose your power, you still emerge victorious. Victorious because you choose to be the person you are, and no amount of money or power could ever change that. And while we tend to lose ourselves down the road, there is nothing to say that you can't amend and try again and again and again until you are able to look at yourself in the mirror."

"But that's the thing, Jacob, I can't. I can't just wake up and let the bad guys win. I mean, that position—"

"That position was evil, Mum. 'Absolute power corrupts absolute all'. You had to lie and take dirty money just to get ahead. Now, we may never get another chance like this, so even if we lose anything, we have to take WeapCo down. Taking out one business, while it may not change things in the long run, it can change the lives of a few, including ours, and that to me is worth fighting for."

Jacob put out his cigarette and began to walk inside.

"Jacob, do you truly believe that this plan is going to work? Do you honestly expect to take down one of the most powerful and most corrupt businesses in this city?"

Jacob just smirked at Anna. "I have faith."

Anna contemplated what Jacob was saying. First, she was surprised that the guy who still liked the crust cut off his toast was being so philosophical. But also, on what he was saying, he was right. If there was any chance at all, a chance at a better life where soldiers didn't march down their streets with tanks and drones, then they had to take it, consequence be damned.

That night, while the rest slept, Anna went inside and sat on the kitchen bench. Deep in thought, she had a light bulb idea. She grabbed a beer out of the fridge and got to work using a pen and paper. She began jotting ideas down, trying to figure out what to do, and then she realised that she only had 5 days before her impeachment trial, but the seating for the military occupation bill was only in 2 days, which meant that despite her impeachment, she still had voted in the bill. That excited Anna. But then, reality hit her again, which destroyed her mood. Anna had confessed to political corruption. No one was going to follow her lead. Anna tried to think of how to get out of this. She pondered, and then, it came to her.

"Of course!"

Anna ran up to the top of the staircase and yelled out, "Everyone, get down here."

Then she ran down the stairs in excitement, waiting for the rest of her family to get up.

Suddenly, just like bears awakening from hibernation, Jacob, Ella and Edward all walked down like zombies with bags under their eyes. After all the family members made it down the stairs, they all just stood there with her.

"Mum, it is 4.30 in the morning. What going on?"

Anna was just buzzing around. "OK, everyone, here is the plan."

The team all stopped at attention.

"So, here is the situation. I am going to face an impeachment trial in the next month. However, the vote on the bill is about to enter the floor in 2 days, which means that until I am impeached, I still have a vote on the bill. But the problem is, we don't have enough support from the public to get the bill revoked, as the scandal has destroyed my reputation. That's why it comes down to you guys. I know what I am asking of you is a lot, but we only get one shot at this, and we need to make it count."

Ella, Edward and Jacob all looked at each other for a split second. But they were committed. "OK, so what's the plan then?"

"Great question. Ella, go get your tablet."

Ella looked confused, but in a hurry, she rushed up the stairs and back down in a hurry, holding the tablet in her hand.

"Start recording." Anna began to speak. "Good morning, my fellow people. I know most of you regard me as a corrupt politician or a criminal, but today, I come to you in faith and ask not for forgiveness but instead to listen to what it is I have to say. My dream was to be a teacher, a high school teacher to be exact, not because I wanted to mark papers but because I wanted to inspire and teach the next generation. Sadly, I never got that chance. However, when you elected me to office, I made a promise, not just for change, but to inspire you all to take action. Unfortunately, I have failed in that mission, but I intend to make it right. I get that many of you lack trust in me, but please do not lack trust in the work that I am doing. The work that I am doing is more important than either me or you. It is about our community. I am sure many of you still believe there is a chance for change, and I ask you today, to please vote and say 'no' to the military occupation bill. Thank you!"

Ella stopped the recording. "Anna, that was beautiful. But will that be enough, though?"

"No. So all of you, come with me and bring a lighter."

The group all ran upstairs to slap on some clothes and made their way outside.

"OK, Mum, we are you outside, and we have the lighters. Now what?"

Anna turned to Jacob and said, "Start walking and hold the lighter in the air."

Anna was the first one to start. She held up the lighter straight into the dark sky and began marching down the road. Then Jacob joined, and Ella and Edward joined too. However, they still had their doubts and thought it was stupid, but for now, they just played along.

However, they were wrong. One after the other, people began to join in, holding their lighters up high. The crowd grew by the moment. They went from one additional person to ten to a hundred, and after making our way down the streets, the crowd reached a thousand people. All of them were walking slowly down the road with their lighters. It grew to the point that the media team gathered around to see what they were doing. It was incredible. Anna didn't know if it would work, but with a miracle, she had started a movement.

However, the crowd's path was blocked by a row of peacekeepers all dressed in riot gear and standing in unison. But they were determined to get by, so Anna walked to the front of the crowd. "Let us pass."

The captain looked her dead in the eye. "No one is getting into Mercy Lane."

"Soldier, we are going to walk through every mile of this level, as it is our God-given right to travel freely, and we will not be bullied or be coerced in any way. Because nothing to us is more important than faith."

The captain looked at them confused. "What are you all hoping to achieve here? You think marching with lighters is going to solve anything?"

"Yes, because it is to show that even in the darkest of times, the light will steer the way to salvation."

The row of soldiers laughed at her. "You look like idiots, holding your silly lighters."

"You may not understand, but together, we are unified. Your forces can't stop us. So soldier, step aside, or we will walk through you."

Suddenly, the row of soldiers armed their guns and pointed at the crowd.

"Turn back around. That is your final warning."

The crowd shivered in fear, but Anna comforted the crowd. "Don't respond to fear. They will let us pass."

The crowd slowly marched forward.

The captain yelled, "Stop! I said stop."

But the crowd was unwavering in its stance. Then the captain yelled out once more, "Open fire."

The soldiers all nodded and opened fire with their rubber bullets. The bullets went flying in every direction, picking off one after the other. But the crowd did not stop. They kept approaching. While they did close their eyes out of fear, they managed to keep going. The captain grew fearful and ordered his troops to retreat. The soldiers kept moving backward while opening fire at the crowd.

The crowd kept going, as the soldiers began to move back. While the rubber bullets managed to pick off a few, more people joined in with the crowd, which quickly replenished their lost numbers. It was remarkable. It was like an invincible wave of people steamrolling the soldiers back without saying a word or firing a single shot. The crowd kept going and moving, pushing the soldiers back as they advanced through the city, with the crowd going from one thousand to ten thousand to a hundred thousand. The crowd slowly ascended into the Middle Levels, pushing the soldiers back through the street. All soldiers could do was fire and shoot, and at its peak, the crowd grew to one million, which was about 10 per cent of the city's population.

Finally, the crowd stopped. The soldiers had been pushed back to the steps of ParliaCongress. It was remarkable. The crowd had marched for nearly an hour to the centre of the city. Anna walked up the step and turned her back to the soldiers in defiance of them knowing full well they wouldn't dare open fire.

Anna faced the crowd. "The people have spoken, and the point has been made. Today, we showed the city that no matter the weapons they have or how intimidating they may be, we showed not just the military but the government and the big corporations who really are in control. You! The people are the ultimate source of power, and we did it without firing a single shot, for the people, by the people! We are the people, and it is all on camera."

The crowd roared in applause.

"Everyone, this is the face of your so-called peacekeepers. Wave! Wave to the cameras and to the millions of people who today saw your true colours. You showed the people that you don't give a rat's arse about peace. Today, you showed the city that you are brutes, bullies and tyrants who hide behind weapons and equipment.”

The crowd roared in applause as the troops stood there in embarrassment.

“Today, let it be known that when you were supposed to cower in fear, you stood, and remember that when it comes time to vote, vote for no more force! Vote for removal of these bullies, and vote for freedom and liberty.”

The crowd roared in applause, “End the occupation! No more weapons! No more weapons!”

Anna then dispersed into the crowd, merging as a faceless entity in a tidal wave of change and the crowd that would not stop. “No more violence! No more violence!”

The peacekeepers were overwhelmed and had to go on the defensive, doing the best they could, as they began clubbing the protesters and firing rubber bullets at them, but it was no good. There were too many of them for the peacekeepers to handle. The peacekeepers were getting more and more desperate. Therefore, they began getting more and more violent. They began lashing out at journalists to prevent them from broadcasting their actions for the people to see. It was all going according to plan. Showing the true nature of the peacekeeping force would change the hearts and minds of the people for sure.

Eventually, the situation escalated. The peacekeepers called in the actual military; the entire place was swarming with killer drones, helicopters and tanks. That’s when the situation truly got out of hand. After warning the crowd once, they began to use live rounds on the protesters, which really caused the protesters to panic. After at least 3 hours of protesting, the crowd began to disperse, and eventually, they all returned home. Among them, 100 were jailed, 500 were injured and, sadly, 100 people were killed.

CHAPTER 29

While Ella and Anna fought the political fight, it was up to Edward and me to rally up the support from the criminal underworld, and what better place than Mercy Lane?

Rumours had been circulating that the crime gangs had been forming resistance against the military occupation. Mercy Lane was hit hard by the peacekeeping forces. Buildings and shops were bombed and shelled, and the people of Mercy Lane were hit with night raids and attacks. It was absolute brutality in this city, and this time, it was real life, not some silly hallucination. Believe me, I checked.

Edward and I had to move like rats, scurrying around through the sewer, because up top, soldiers and military equipment littered the entire area. For some reason, I had a feeling that there would be checkpoints and aircraft there as well. Call it a hunch.

"Yuck! Jacob, why do we have to crawl through all this sewer water?"

"Oh, stop your whining, Edward. Goodness gracious me, you have been whining for the past 30 minutes."

"Well, I am sorry, but I am not exactly fond of walking through sewer water and having rats constantly bite my legs."

"I told you to wear long pants, but you didn't, so deal with it."

"Well, sorry for not wanting to wear wet trousers."

"I swear, Edward, you should have served a term in the military. It would have hardened you up a little bit."

"So, what's the plan here, Jacob?"

"Simple. We need more support; since I am a wanted criminal, I can't gather support from the community, so I need your help to rally up support from the crime gangs."

"How do you know that the gang is going to vote for you, Mom? I mean, these people aren't exactly known for following the voting process."

"They will if they want their profits to return and the military off their arse. And stop saying 'those people'. They're human beings, Edward."

Edward sometimes annoyed me with his bougie attitude. He doesn't forget to remind us that he grew up in the Upper Levels.

Edward was so lucky that he got everything handed to him. He never had to struggle for anything in his life, and you could tell by his attitude. He went to a fancy private school, grew up in a rich house with successful parents, went and trained as an officer, got a medical discharge for a bone spur and then went to pharmacy school. But Edward was a good person; except, I was still pissed that he betrayed me and tried to kill me. If he thought I was going to let that slide, he had got another thing coming. Edward was an opportunist; he may have been my friend and a good person at heart, but he would do anything to be rich, and I couldn't trust someone like that. I would never leave my back turned to Edward, and as the old saying goes, "Keep your friends close and your enemies closer."

"Almost there, Edward." We stopped at the front of the sewer gate.

"Hey Jacob, how did you know this entrance existed?"

"I saw it in my mind."

"In your mind? Jacob, are you feeling all right?"

"Yer. Why, Edward?"

"It's just that since you came out of prison, you have been acting different. You don't smoke and drink, and why did you let that serial killer go free?"

"We can't just go around killing people, Edward. The old us may have done that, but we have to grow as people."

Edward laughed. "Boy, you're really buying into that spiritual BS, aren't ya?"

"Edward, since we have lived in this city, how many people have we killed?"

"I don't know. Too many to count. Why?"

"Well, I am just getting tired of the guilt and pain on my shoulders. I just thought that since I had left the military, I wouldn't have to kill anyone. But since I have been out, I feel like all I am doing is just shooting and murdering my way out of problems. There has to be another way."

Edward smirked at that comment. "Pfft! Oh, boo hoo. Man up, Jacob. We live in the real world. Just stop thinking about that sort of stuff. It's better if you don't."

"You know what, Edward, sometimes, your cold and callous attitude gets really tiresome."

"Yea, you have said that. All right, you know my life hasn't all been so easy."

"What, you tired of the latest gold nugget to fall out of your arse?"

"Ha ha! I am just saying, you shouldn't assume stuff about people. I mean, you have no idea what I have been through in my life."

Edward just let out a sigh. "So, are we going to open this sewer gate?"

The only difference between my vision and reality was that the gate was bolted shut, but I had a plan. I walked over to the gate and asked Edward to pass the bag that was strapped across his back. Edward threw me the bag, and I caught it with one arm.

Out of the bag, I grabbed the clay and C4 and attached it to the lock.

"Stand back!"

Click, click, boom! A puff of grey smoke appeared from the gate, and the gate swung open.

"After you, good sir."

Edward and I both walked out of the sewer and looked in front of us to see the military tanks and vehicles completely blockading the bridge in and out of the city.

"When you're right, you're right, I guess." Edward shrugged, actually surprised that my spiritual delusions had come true.

I tapped Edward on the shoulder. "Come on, this place is crawling with soldiers. We need to get off the streets."

Edward looked at me shocked. "How are we supposed to sneak up on them when there are drones and soldiers posted at every corner?"

Edward was always the optimist, but he had a point. How were we going to get into the most occupied part of the city? I looked around, hoping to find a way into the city, but nothing, until Edward and I heard ute ties. Suddenly, a pickup truck bolted towards the bridge, and the gunner on the back opened fire on the soldiers. It was a local cartel trying to flood their product into the rest of the city. The cartel managed to cut down a few of the soldiers but not enough to get through the bridge. The truck stopped at the bridge, and a firefight between the soldiers and the cartel ensued.

Now was our chance. As quickly as we could, we ran towards the bridge while the drones were busy taking care of the firefight. We had to be quick, because those cartels weren't going to last long against the heavily armed soldiers. We rushed as fast as we could and somehow managed to make it under the bridge without getting spotted by the drones.

Under the bridge, we could hear the gunfire, and up above, we could see the drones opening fire from all sides towards the cartel. Speed was our greatest enemy. We were in dangerous territory here, so Edward and I took deep breaths in.

"Run!"

We both rushed up that hill with lightning speed, and we could see the fight. That one truck turned into five, and there had to be at least a small army taking on the peacekeeping force. The cartel managed to pin down the peacekeeping force, but it wasn't going to last, as they were calling in reinforcement from all over the city. Bullets and lasers blasted from all sides. There were trucks on both sides that were destroyed and in flames.

Edward and I rushed from the hill and onto the bridge, ducking and weaving through burning cars and getting low from the bullets that were flying overhead. We both hid underneath cars and began crawling past dead bodies and bullet shells that were lying on the floor. We kept crawling as soldiers from each side dropped dead in front of us.

But we were in the homestretch. We made it to our final car, and in front of us was the entrance to Mercy Lane. I tapped Edward on the shoulder. "Come on, man, we could make it."

Edward nodded in response, and we both got up and bolted towards the entrance. While some of the peacekeeping soldiers began to turn their rifles on us, they were quickly cut down by the cartel members who were close to breaking through the stronghold. We could make it, we both thought to ourselves, but standing in front of us rolling in came a tank that was ambushing the cartel from the back. The reinforcements had arrived. Edward and I stood there in shock as a tank shell went flying past us towards one of the cartel trucks. BOOM! The truck went up in flames. While we weren't close enough to the truck to get burnt, the blast did cause us to get shot forward and land directly on our faces, breaking my nose and perhaps causing a mild concussion.

My ears were ringing, and my vision was blurry. Edward ran towards me and picked me up; I could barely hear what the guy was saying.

"Edward, we have to keep going."

I got up, barely recovering from the blast, but I had to keep moving forward. We rushed to get into Mercy Lane.

The peacekeepers began opening fire on the group with tear gas, covering the entire area with smoke and attacking them from both sides.

Great, I was thinking to myself. My eyes were blurry and burning, my head was hurting and my lungs were burning. But we had to keep going. We rushed some of the soldiers who were trying to shoot at us, but they quickly became distracted by the cartels firing at them.

Finally, we made it into the city, taking shelter behind the nearest building and peering out as the reinforcements slaughtered the final members of the cartel. We heard the last round of shots, followed by silence. The cartel's mission to get past the checkpoint had failed. The forces were too well-equipped and had too much manpower. Still, they managed to do some damage, while providing us some much-needed cover to get into the city.

"I need five minutes."

"Me too."

We both collapsed from exhaustion and pain, lying on the floor huffing and puffing, trying to get the tear gas out of our lungs. After about 20 minutes of lying on the ground crying and coughing out our lungs, we both pulled each other up.

"I am sure Ella and Anna don't have to put up with this sort of BS."

I wanted to smile and laugh, but I was in too much pain to react to what Edward was saying. "Come on, let's move out."

"Where are we going to go? This place is running with criminal cartels and the peacekeeping force."

I took a deep breath in, trying to push the last of the tear gas out of our lungs. "I have a mate of mine who I met in prison. I have contact with him. Let's just say he owes me – or, in this case, Anna – a favour."

"And this friend, would you say he is reliable?"

"Well, he wouldn't shoot me," I replied, giving him a big smirk. Edward, however, wasn't impressed. "Come on, the hideout is a few miles that way."

Edward began to nod as he followed me into Norman's place.

Edward and I both began making our way to Norman's house. If there was any time to get out our guns, now would be – crap!

Edward let out a sigh. "You dropped your guns in the fight, didn't you?"

"Me? You're the one who was carrying the bag."

"Great. Now we are walking into one of the most dangerous parts of the city unarmed."

"I guess so. Oh, well, we don't need them. We have brains. I am sure we can figure something out. When there is a problem, what do we do? We solve it."

"We are so screwed."

I couldn't help but laugh at that comment. "Come on, it's not that bad. We have survived worse."

We both continued in silence, making sure to remain extra vigilant, as in this place, you never knew who may try to hurt you.

"How long until we reach your friend's house?"

"He is only a couple of blocks down the road. We can make it that far."

"I never knew you were so familiar with Mercy Lane."

"Well, it's hard to explain. I have been here, but I haven't. It is sort of a spiritual hallucination type thing."

"Jacob, what is going on with you lately? I mean, you keep going on about going on spiritual journeys, and then you didn't want to kill that serial killer. Like, who cares."

"Edward, I don't want to kill anymore. I have been a soldier my whole life, and we have killed enough."

"Listen, Saint Jacob, you may find this hard to believe, but down here, it's killed or be killed. We don't have the luxury to go to the police or take people to court, so we have to rely on vigilante justice."

"That's how we used to do things. And don't preach to me about life being cruel. You grew up with everything."

Edward just stopped and turned around at the comment. "What the hell do you mean by that!"

I stood my ground. "I am just saying my family and I have worked for scraps, whereas your family just had a bit of bad luck."

"Bad luck? Jacob, my family lost everything. My dad took his own life, and my mum and I had to fight for scraps. Yes, I may have had some luxury in my life, like a decent education, but that doesn't mean I have had an easier life than you. Life is hard for everyone."

"Look man, I—"

"Just shut up and walk to your friend's house, already."

This trip just got a lot more awkward; it was just awkward silence for the next few minutes until we finally reached Norman's hideout.

"There!" I pointed to this apartment building. "He told me that his apartment is on the second floor."

"Nice-looking place he got here."

"Just get walking."

We managed to open the door to the abandoned apartment building. Hard to believe that someone lived here. Hell, the door had a condemned sticker on the front of it. There were hardly any lights on, and the entire hallway was empty. The paint was chipped and damaged, with rats running everywhere. "Norman, where are you?"

A door on the second floor opened, revealing a blue light shining through it, and Norman appeared on the balcony. "Hey boys, get up here!" Norman said.

"This is the guy?"

"Yep!"

"The kid looks like he hasn't even hit puberty yet."

Both Edward and I walked into the apartment, revealing an empty place with a laptop and blanket on the floor, with a rifle lining on the wall next to the fire escape.

"Nice place you got here."

"Just ignore him. How you been, Norman?"

"Good. Been great to be out of prison."

I had no time for pleasantries, but I couldn't say it out loud. "So, you have intel for us?"

"Yes. OK, well, there has been a lot of dark web chatter, and apparently, the gangs are trying to form a coalition to take the peacekeeping force head-on."

"Who's involved?"

"All the crime families from the city are. Since the forces rolled in, they have lost product and profit in all industries: drugs, weapons smuggling, the works. So I was thinking that if we can get them to invest their time into something more constructive, like the vote, we could beat WeapCo."

He was right. If we could win over Mercy Lane, we would have won over the entire district of the Lower Levels, plus with a majority vote from the Middle Level, we can get the forces through the ParliaCongress.

"So where is this 'coalition' planning to meet?"

"I will take you to them in the morning."

"Take us now!"

Norman stood his ground. "I can't. The forces are at full force at night, so we are going to have to bunk during the night."

I sighed, but if we wanted to survive, we had to do what he said. "All right. We leave first thing in the morning, Goodnight."

Norman turned off his laptop, threw a blanket over his body and went to sleep, completely ignoring that we were standing right in front of him.

Edward turned to me. "What a weird guy."

"Tell me about it. That's Norman for ya."

"Well, I guess we will just set up shop somewhere."

I just shrugged. "I guess so."

Edward and I just leaned beside the apartment window, as it was the only light source from the street lamps. "Man, I can't believe we are actually in Mercy Lane."

We stood by each other awkwardly, as there was nothing else to do. We stood in silence, but I decided to break the silence. "Hey, listen, man, I just want to say—"

"No, Jacob, I get it. It was wrong to tell you how to act. I think it's good that you don't want to kill anyone anymore."

"Yer, I am just sick of having my past come back to haunt me. I am sure your demons are keeping you up just as much as they keep me up."

"Na, man, I just zone them out, really. I mean, what else am I meant to do? Life is full of regret."

"Yep, that's true. Hey Edward, I noticed you never really talk much about your dad. I am sorry about what happened."

"Well, to be honest, I never really knew the guy. He was always busy working, always on business trips or at board meetings. Look, my dad put work above everything else, even his own family, even me. So when he lost his job, it killed him inside. He was left without a purpose, and then—"

There was a pause in the room. We didn't want to think about it, but the look on Edward's face said it all. We sat in silence for a few minutes, and Edward broke the silence. "Um, Jacob, I just wanted to say that I am sorry for trying to kill you."

I never truly forgave Edward for what he did to me. I mean, we were on much friendlier terms, but deep down, I still held internal anger towards him.

"I just want to know why, Edward. Why, after everything we did for you? We took you in. I treated you like a brother, and you did that to me."

"Look, I screwed up. I panicked, all right. I mean, I saw a chance to get back on top, and I took it."

"Edward, when you are going to learn to appreciate what you have? I mean, yer, it's not much and we live in a craphole, but we stick together as a family. You have got to learn to stop trying to exploit people for personal gain. Not everything is about money and power. Sometimes, it's about a person's character. The character of a person is wealth in itself."

Edward couldn't respond to that, so he just looked down at the floor not saying a word.

I just stood there awkwardly. "Anyway, Edward, have a good night."

I closed my eyes, but before I did, I could see that Edward was deep in thought.

The room was peaceful, when suddenly, a bang was heard downstairs, which woke us up instantly. Norman shot up, awakening from his slumber: "Oh no! It's a raid!"

Edward was confused. "Why is the peacekeeping force raiding an empty building?"

Norman was constantly peering out through the door. "They go block to block, looking through every building to weed out any of the gangs. It's part of their patrols."

Norman continued to peer out through the door, looking out in fear, when suddenly, the downstairs door broke down, and soldiers who were all armoured up began making their way through the building.

"Quick! Edward and Norman, get out through the fire escape!"

We all, as fast as we could, rushed out through the window, but we were too late. The soldiers all rushed up the stairs with their guns drawn, screaming, "Freeze! Don't move!"

We all shot our hands up. How were we all going to get out of this one? But I noticed something about the fire escape. The bolts were not screwed on properly, and the escape was rusty. So, using my foot, I kicked the fire escape, and just my luck, the thing pushed out from the wall and dropped us down onto the floor before crashing down to the bottom.

Ow, I thought to myself, but no time. We had to keep running. We bolted in different directions as the soldiers scrambled downstairs to catch us.

We ran down the alleyway to try and put as much distance between the soldiers as possible, when whack, I felt the butt of a gun land directly on my face, knocking me down to the ground.

I lay there on the ground, looking over and seeing Edward having a bag thrown over his head. Then, I looked upwards and saw a guy in a Halloween mask throw a black bag over my head, and just like that, my vision was gone. I could feel two thugs picking me up from the ground by my arms and dragging me along the ground. I tried to break free, but no luck. The thugs had a strong grip on me. Then, one of the thugs handcuffed me, picked me up from my feet and threw me onto the back of a ute. I could feel another body next to me.

I screamed out, "Edward?"

A voice then screamed out, "Jacob? What the hell is going on?"

Honestly, at this point, I had no idea; I was so sick of getting drugged and thrown into trucks.

"I don't know, Edward, but we have been in this situation before. Just stay quiet and follow their instruction."

I could feel the ute rock up and down over every pothole, which sent me flying up and landing down on the tray repeatedly, thanks to gravity. Then, the ute then took a sharp turn, and I could hear a roller door being pulled. We must have arrived, as the ute stopped, and I could feel four thugs picking me up and carrying me like a dead body. Then, they placed me on the cold cement floor and removed the bag over my head to reveal a factory full of guns and modified utes with machine guns on the back of them.

This must be the cartel's hideout. I looked around the room and saw at least 500 armed men, and they were all standing around in a circle, with Edward and I in the centre.

I looked over at Edward. "Edward, are you all right?"

"Jacob, are we going to die?"

"I don't know, probably."

That comment only made Edward even more concerned.

Then we both heard footsteps slowly approaching us, and then an unknown voice called out to the thugs. "Release them!"

One of the thugs unlocked the cuffs and returned us to our feet. After we got to our feet, we both turned around to find 10 people in business suits with gang tattoos and all different ethnicities. But I did begin to recognise the thug in the middle. He was the guy in the brothel who pointed our guns at us.

"Gentleman, we have some business to take care of?"

I thought I had to speak. "Look, about what happened—"

I remember this guy; we met him when we tried to track down Ella when she was kidnapped by a murderer. But that was a long story.

The brothel owner snapped his finger, and a thug hit me in the head for me to be quiet. Then, the brothel owner signalled to one of his henchmen to bring him a cigar, and he lit it for him. The owner just stood there and let out a few puffs of smoke before taking the cigar out of his mouth.

"Gentleman, let's get down to business."

Edward tried to speak. "Sir I—"

But just as he did to me, he snapped at Edward, and he was hit in the head.

"Don't interrupt me when I am talking, please." He turned to the 10 businessmen. "Can you believe this guy? So rude."

All the men started laughing.

"I get it, guys. You were looking for your lost girl, and tensions got heated. Ain't nothing personal. But you see, gentlemen, the thing that keeping you alive is him." He pointed to me. "The politician's son."

Now I knew what this was all about. I interrupted. "Yes, I am, and my mother has the power to make your lives easy or hard."

The owner just smiled. "Now we are talking business. You see, boys, these peacekeepers have been a complete pain in the arse for the past month. Profits are being squeezed out from decent, honest, hard-working Joes like me and my fine gentlemen here. We are so desperate that we actually had to combine our forces together in order to save our businesses. But even then, we are losing men and resources to those pigs out there. Every day, they raid our businesses and rob our profits, and we are ready to fight back. So when I heard that a politician's son was back in Mercy Lane, then we just had to get this man again. So, boys, what is it going to be? Are we going to work together?”

Working with these thugs was the last thing I wanted to do, but if we were to win against WeapCo, then we had to get everyone on board. Mom needed the money and all the resources she needed. So all I could do was bite my teeth and agree.

“Looks like we all have an understanding of the situation, then.”

But the brothel owner snapped his finger, and two thugs brought a masked figure in front of him. “It’s not that simple, I am afraid. You see, you came into my brothel, which I get is business. But I can’t have people walking into my place of business and pointing guns at me. That is just bad business.”

Then the owner snapped his finger, and the henchman removed the bag off the masked figure’s head to reveal Norman lying there in handcuffs.

One of the thugs came over and handed the brothel owner a golden Glock, which he picked up and pointed at Norman’s head.

“Now, you have two choices of how this is going to go down. I either shoot him, or I shoot your friend next to you. Your choice.”

Edward freaked out, and the owner snapped his finger again, and two henchmen threw Edward to the ground and pinned him down.

“Your choice, Mister Politician’s Son. The one near me, or the one beside you?”

I stood there in shock, as two people’s lives were in my hands, but who do I choose? Edward let out a sigh of relief.

“That is a no-brainer, he is obviously going to choose me. Tell him, Jacob.”

My head was thinking over and over, and then, suddenly, I blurted, “I choose Norman.”

Edward looked at me. “Wait, what?”

I looked at him with puppy-dog eyes. “I am sorry, Edward. He is just a young kid.”

Edward looked at me with fear in his eyes.

The brothel owner slowly walked over to Edward with the golden gun in his hand, and Edward began to panic and pleaded for his life.

"I don't want to die! I don't want to die!" Tears began to roll down Edward's face. Then, the thug pointed the gun at Edward's head, and he screamed out, "NOOO!"

The owner pulled the trigger, and Edward closed his eyes waiting to die. But when clicked, nothing happened. The gun was empty. The brothel owner leaned near Edward's ear and whispered, "Now we are even."

Everyone in the room burst out in laughter at what had happened. The thugs picked up Edward, and he stood up with piss going down his pants and his eyes filled with tears.

I wanted to speak and justify my answer, but I couldn't; I had never felt so ashamed in my life. I had literally sentenced my friend to death. Edward looked directly at me. He didn't say a single word. He just looked at me with killer eyes as if he wanted to rip my throat out. But to be fair, I really couldn't blame him.

"Now we have an understanding, gentlemen," the brothel owner said to the three of us, and he signalled to the thugs to let Norman go. Norman ran towards us to rejoin us.

Suddenly, we heard a sound coming from outside that caught us off guard. We all just stood there in shock. Then we heard another one. Now we were concerned. What was happening? But we heard a third one, and all the thugs rushed to the front entrance and began to point their guns at the hanger door. The 10 bosses just stood there shocked, and the brothel owner asked the thugs, "What is going on?"

The front door opened, with all the thugs pointing their rifles, ready for anything that could be coming through that door. Then, a silver canister came flying into the room. Everyone in the room knew was it was, and one of the thugs yelled out, "Get down!"

Everyone jumped out of the way. Bang! The canister emitted sparks and smoke; it was a flash grenade. Once the smoke dispensed, hundreds upon hundreds of police and peacekeeping officers bragged into the hangar, running in and opening fire in all directions.

"It's a raid!" one of the thugs screamed.

The forces went on to mow down at least half of the men on the site. The henchmen were caught off guard, but then they snapped back into action. Hiding behind whatever cover they could find, they began opening fire at the soldiers. But the soldiers were all well armoured, and there was a consent supply of them, as there was another hundred outside surrounding the building. We were all trapped inside. It was a nightmare. Bullets went flying across the room, and we were losing men by the minute.

But Norman, Edward and I were not waiting to die. I picked up one of the AK-47s lying beside the dead henchman and opened fire. Unfortunately for us, the soldiers were wearing high-tech body armour, which made bullet fire from the AK ineffective unless shot at the head.

The whole thing was a massacre. Everyone joined in, and even the crime bosses were being slaughtered.

I screamed at Edward, "Edward, we have to get out of here!"

Edward wasn't in the mood to talk to me, but he wanted to survive too. "How? We are in the middle of a firefight, dummy. There is no way out!"

I quickly scoped the room out, and it looked like there was only one way out of there: to run into the middle of the firefight and hijack the modified ute. Quickly, I turned to Edward, "Cover me!"

Edward just gave me a dirty look. "Cover yourself. I have my own problem."

I screamed at him and gestured towards the truck. Edward looked at me confused for a few seconds, then he realised what I was pointing at.

Edward sighed. "Throw me your gun."

I chucked him the AK-47, and Edward stood up from behind cover and began shooting at the peacekeeping officers while I quickly rushed to the armoured truck. It was a close call, but after nearly getting shot like five times, I managed to make it up the tray of the ute. I took a deep breath in and jumped onto the machine and unloaded at least 50 rounds a second towards the soldiers.

The soldiers were caught off guard, ducking and jumping out of the way of the gun. The gunfire was a perfect distraction, so I yelled out, "Go! Go! Go!"

Norman, Edward and the brothel owner hopped onto the back of the tray.

"Edward, take over!" Edward and I changed position, and I hopped into the driver's seat of the ute. "Hold on, everyone."

Everyone in the tray of the ute ducked down, and I switched the ute on. The engine roared to life.

Quickly, I switched the gear shift from N to R, and the ute went charging backward and smashed straight through the hanger wall and straight into the sewer canal, collapsing the tray inward. However, luckily Norman, Edward and the brothel owner jumped out just before impact.

I quickly jumped out of the ute as it flipped forward, landing on its front wheels. Everyone began to rush towards the sewer gate as fast as we could. Some of the soldiers from outside the hangar had signalled to the others, and they all opened fire in our direction. While I didn't have time to analyse the situation, as I was busy running from the plasma bolts, it did feel like the hallucination I had, with Yandan and I running towards the sewer gate. What a coincidence. But I had no time; Edward, Norman, the brothel owner, and I all began to run towards the sewer gate as fast as we could, but the laser fire was getting closer and closer to us, as the soldiers were moving within range of us. As we finally made it to the sewer gate, the brothel owner got hit in the back with the plasma bolt. He let out a groan and fell to the ground dead. There was no point mourning the guy, though, as he had tried to kill Edward, and he was a crime lord, so honestly, good riddance.

Yes, we made it just in time to the sewer gate. I quickly stopped and rushed down towards the sewer gate to close it, and just in time, two blaster bolts went flying past my head, narrowly missing us. After the gate was down, we all ran as fast as we could deeper into the Sewer Levels.

After running for about 5 minutes, we all ran out of steam and stopped to catch our breath. There was a silence, as we were all breathing heavily. Norman finally broke the silence. "Pfft, thank God that's over with."

But was it? Edward stopped breathing and looked at me with those killer eyes again. He got up and walked towards me, and he threw a right hook directly into my jaw. I couldn't say it wasn't deserved, as I nearly killed the guy.

"You bastard, you could have killed me!"

"Oh, well, you shot me, remember?"

"Oh, that is it. Screw you and your mum's damn campaign. I am going back to my pharmacy."

"Fine, go back to your pharmacy, you spoilt little brat. It's nice to know you have that luxury."

Edward exploded. "Jacob! Your campaign is a dud. Your mum is a corrupt sell-out, your friends are all dying, and now your only chance at victory is lying dead near the sewer gate. This whole taking on the big dog bullshit has gotten us nowhere. It's gotten so bad that you have lost your damn mind."

"Well, we all know whose side you are on: the one with the most amount of money."

Edward threw up his hands. "Fine. You're all going to end up floating in this sewer when you two are done."

"Edward!" I screamed out, but he just ignored me and walked away.

"Some friend you got there, man, Jacob."

"Oh, he will calm down. He just needs some time to breathe."

But really, I was in the wrong. It was wrong to put him in danger like that. Oh, well, got to keep moving forward. I turned to Norman. "All right, this whole thing was a complete bust. Let's just head home."

"Aye, Jacob?"

"Yes, Norman, I am aware. You can crash at my joint, but only if you are ready for the fight ahead."

Norman just smirked. "Oh, well, I am already in too deep, so you may as well catch me up on the game plan."

I smiled at that comment. "That's the spirit. Come on, I will take you back home."

After walking through the dark and disgusting water of the Sewer Level, we finally made it back to Ground Level, though our pants still smelt of sewer water. I still couldn't stop thinking about what I had put Edward through. I almost killed him, and here I was giving him a hard time about shooting me. But I didn't know how to find him or what to really say to him, so all I could really do was change my pants and try to think of a plan B. Mercy Lane was a complete waste of time. Not only did I lose my friend, but we didn't get the support we needed, as the criminals had most likely gone underground.

Norman and I made our way up the front stairs to our house when the front door swung open to reveal Edward standing there with his fist clenched and his eyes bloodshot red. I stood back in shock.

"Edward?"

Suddenly, Edward charged at me like a raging bull and tackled me straight onto the ground, pinning me down. Edward was furious. He started throwing punches at me while I was lying on the ground.

"You bastard, how could you try to kill me!" he screamed, with tears coming down his face.

Norman just stood there, mortified at what was happening, and all I did was try to block the oncoming punches, as one after the other, they landed directly on my face. But after the third punch, I rolled him over and head-locked him.

Edward looked over and grabbed a garden ornament and smashed it across my head.

Jeez, that hurt, I thought to myself as blood came rushing from my head. Then, not paying attention, Edward kicked me in the face, which caused me to lie on the ground for a few seconds. Using the last of my strength I retaliated by slapping his nuts with an open palm.

Edward screamed out in pain, and it caused him to lie next to me in pain. The both of us just lay there groaning in pain before I turned around to Edward. "Look, man, I am sorry. I wasn't thinking."

"But why choose him over me? Am I not your best friend?"

"You are, but I chose Norman because he was only a kid, and I knew you could handle yourself. Plus, don't forget, you shot me."

Edward paused for a moment, breathing heavily. He then rolled over to me. "Look, I am sorry for nearly killing you. You are right, I made a mistake, but you nearly got me killed, so we are even."

I let out an upstretched hand and patted him on his shoulder. "There, there."

The both of us just lay there out of breath, while Norman stood there awkwardly not knowing what to do.

After a few minutes, I turned to Edward. "We cool?"

Edward just smiled. "Yer, we're cool."

We made our way to our feet. "Come on, I have some beers in the fridge."

"Count me in." We made our way into the house to have a few beers, smoked a few cones and watched some old TV show with Norman.

Later that night., it was peaceful and quiet, except for all the rushing cars and the occasional sound of the railways rushing past. I needed some time to think. I grabbed a packet of Winnie Blue cigarettes and decided to try something new. I climbed out the window and onto the roof of the house. I lay there and looked at the skyscrapers that were as tall as heaven. I looked up at the sky and let out the occasional smoke from my cigarette. I just needed time to think, to think about life. But most of all, I needed time to think about who I was fundamentally as a person.

Am I a killer? Am I a failure? Am I a hero? Am I a good person? Or a bad person? Am I— "Edward?" My train of thought was interrupted as I saw Edward looking at me.

"What are you doing on the roof?"

I turned to him. "Just smoking and thinking."

"Mind if I join you?"

"Be my guest."

Edward hopped onto the roof and lay next to me, so I offered him a cigarette and lit it for him, as we both looked up at the night sky. We both lay there, as the puffs of smoke emerged from a cigarette, and there was an awkward pause, when I decided to break the silence. "Hey Edward, do you think this is all real?"

Edward gave me a dirty look and blew out a puff of smoke. "What do you mean by that?"

"Well, I know you are going to find this hard to believe, but sometimes, I think that the moment we are in is not actually happening. It's all just a construct of our imagination."

Edward just laughed at that question. "Jacob, did you take LSD or any other psychedelic?"

"I am serious, Edward. Do you ever just stop to think that maybe the world we live in and the people we lost and the things we have done have all been for nothing?"

Edward was a very close-minded person and was logical in nature, so he was not used to conceptual ideas of reality, "Jacob, where is all this talk coming from? Of course, you are, and of course reality is real. This is all real, Jacob. What is going on with you?"

"Edward, I have to be honest, I don't think what is happening now and what we are doing at this very point in time is real. I think my mind has just created this reality to hide my internal pain and trauma."

"Jeez, Jacob, I didn't realise how stoic you are." Edward then turned to me and punched me in the shoulder.

"Ow, that hurt, Edward."

"Did that hurt?"

"Yes. Why did you do that?"

"To show you that the pain you felt was real. See. I don't believe in that philosophical BS, because life is just about getting up and moving forward. That's it. You don't need some inspirational quote to hang on your wall. You exist. Simple as that."

All I could do was smoke and think about what Edward had just said.

There was a pause, and then Edward turned to me. "Look, I know you are on some spiritual journey of redemption or self-discovery or what not, but stop trying to decipher your own life, Jacob. You just got to live, breathe, forget, forgive and stop trying to question or justify your own experience. Just accept it. That's life."

I smiled. "Thank you, Edward. Good to know you can keep me grounded."

Edward just turned to look up at the sky. "Jacob, listen, I want to say this as a friend; you need to stop with this high moral BS, because if you want to take down WeapCo and free the Lower Level, I need the old Jacob back. I need the Jacob who is not afraid to kill any person that comes in his way. I know you are sick of killing, but what's one more?"

I sat there contemplating what he had said, and I looked up at the sky for a few minutes. "OK, Edward, you are right, I am probably losing my mind."

"Probably?"

I paused, trying not to smile. "But if we are to complete the mission and free our community, then I will put aside these religious obligations and morality to get the job done, like a good soldier."

That comment brought a simile to Edward's face. He tapped me on the shoulder. "That's the spirit. Hey Jacob, what time is it?"

I looked at him confused and looked down at my watch. "9 o'clock, why?"

"Cool, let's go." Edward got up before jumping back into my bedroom window.

I threw my cigarette butt off the roof. "Where are you going, Edward?"

"Follow me. It will be fun!"

Curious, I re-entered my room and began to follow him down the stairs and out the door, leaving Norman asleep on the couch.

Edward screamed out, "Hurry up, slowpoke."

After walking 5 minutes, Edward led me down to a deserted alley. I was concerned for my own safety. "Edward, why are we here?"

Edward and I then walked up to an old, rusty door and banged on it. Suddenly, the door swung open, and the inside was blurring with light. It was completely out of character for a dark place like this. Edward began to walk down, and I peered my head through and saw a staircase that was illuminated with LED lights. I could hear music coming from downstairs.

I followed Edward inside, and it was hidden, underground club. The entire place was illuminated with strobe lights and coloured LEDs. There were people everywhere rocking out and dancing to music. I was amazed and surprised at this place. I couldn't believe it. How did I not know of this place?

Edward handed me a blue cocktail filled with rainbow strips and so much sugar that my heart nearly gave out. We downed so many shots and drank so many beers that our eyes began going blurry, and my head began to swirl around. After drinking more and more beers, the night began to become less and less memorable, but that really wasn't such a bad thing, because at that moment, my only focus was on dancing, not the worry and fear of what to do next, only dancing and laughing.

I ran up to Edward in my drunken state of mind and began to hug him. "Thanks, man. I love you!"

Edward returned the hug. "I love you too, man."

After that point, the rest of the night was a blur. I woke up the next day to find the club completely abandoned, and I was just lying on the floor with a pounding headache and bloodshot eyes. I was hungover as hell, and I got up and ran to one of the fake plants to throw up in.

Then, Edward patted me on the back. "There, there. Come on, let's get you home."

The two of us walked out of the nightclub with the same clothes we had on – only now they were covered in vomit and were all wrinkled up. After exiting the nightclub, the light burnt our eyes. The walk home was terrible. We were both disorientated to the point that we couldn't even walk in a straight line. It was terrible.

We finally made it to the front door of the house, and I turned to Edward. "Hey, Edward!"

Edward stopped. "Yer?"

I smiled. "Thank you for a good night."

"No sweat, Jacob. Anytime, buddy. We will figure something out, Jacob. Do not worry. One way or another, we will take down WeapCo. For Yandan."

We both entered the living room and collapsed on the floor.

CHAPTER *30*

While the protesting may have ceased, the impact was far from over. After the military had placed a mandatory curfew on the city, given to them under the emergency powers act, Anna, Ella, Edward and I were at home with no other options.

When we switched on the Holonet, we were met with a perfect surprise. Every news broadcast portrayed the protests. But what was most interesting was how negative it was towards the peacekeepers.

The plan had worked, and every news broadcast had negative things to say about the so-called peacekeepers. While some of the far right–wing broadcasters took the position of the peacekeepers, many of the left and neutral ones took the position of the protesters.

Across nearly 20 channels, there were banners that read: 'Military Reservists Kill Protesters' or 'Military Coup'. Even some of the centre-right news outlets were not pleased with the use of military use of force and the curfews; they said that it was an invasion of their rights. The move tonight had changed the political battlefield. While WeapCo defended the military actions, Wacco and other smaller defence companies began to shift their allegiances to the protesters, pledging money and support to help the victims and condemning the use of force.

The only thing Anna could think to herself was, *Thank goodness the news isn't focusing on her, for a change.*

Anna, Edward, Ella and I were watching in glee. Anna's approval rating had jumped from 36 per cent to a whopping 76 per cent overnight. It was a remarkable turnaround. That didn't fix the issue of the impeachment, but Anna was happy knowing that the court of public opinion was on her side, and she was going to need it, as the vote was in a week.

Anna got up from the couch. "I am going to get a beer."

"OK!"

Anna then got up from the couch and walked over to the fridge, whistling a tone with every step she made, as she was buzzing with joy. But then her phone rang. She looked at it, and it read 'unknown caller'.

"Who could that be?" Anna said out loud, but not loud enough for the rest to hear them.

"Hello," Anna said, confused.

"Perhaps I was a little bit too hasty."

"Adrian!"

Ella, Edward and I all turned around in shock at that name.

"What do you want?"

"No need for hostility, Anna. I am on your side. The peacekeepers have got to go. The people need freedom, and Wacco can provide your level with the money and the weapons needed to fight WeapCo and the peacekeepers. Anna, I am giving you an opportunity to turn your career around. Call it a second chance."

"And if I refuse?"

Adrian sighed. "Then I will have to take away—"

"Take away what, Adrian? You have already ruined my career. What else can you take away from me?"

"Enjoying the beer."

Anna looked down at her beer and was concerned. "How did you—"

"Know? Simple. I have your place surrounded with my private military group. Look outside your window."

Anna moved to the window and looked over at the neighbours' roof to find a sniper pointed directly at her. Anna quickly yelled out, "Everyone, get out of here!"

"Why?" I asked.

Then, within a second, the door came down, as 10 soldiers busted through the door and threw Edward, Ella and me to the ground and handcuffed us. Anna watched in horror, not able to do anything, as she placed the phone back to her ear.

"Now, if I have your attention, it's time to renegotiate the terms of our agreement."

"What do you want?" she asked, with her eyes fixed on the guns pointed at her family's head.

Adrian let out a small laugh. "Thought you would never ask; shall we all continue this discussion somewhere else?"

Anna took a deep breath in and asked, "Where?"

She looked up, and two of the soldiers threw a bag over Anna's head, and I watched in horror as they dragged my mum in a car, then Ella, then Edward and finally me. I was getting so sick of having bags thrown over my head and being transported to different locations. But my focus now was on my family and their well-being.

I was so tired of my family constantly being put into harm's way because of this silly little crusade. I mean, all we tried to do was make the world a better place, and now look where it had gotten us. We were constantly thrown into vans and escorted to different locations. I could fight my way out of this or try to figure out where it was that we were all heading, but no point. Frankly, I just wanted this all to be over with. But it wasn't me, though. I could feel it from Anna, Edward and Ella. The truth is that whenever we get a victory in our lives, it is quickly taken from us. Sometimes, it felt like all we do is move backwards. I mean, this must be at least the third time since we started this crusade that I had been thrown into the back of a van, but this time, my family was involved.

I screamed out through the bag, "Anna! Ella! Edward! Are you guys all right?"

"Calm down, Jacob, we are all fine."

Then a thug screamed at us, "Stop talking!"

We all went silent. Then the car stopped, and we were carried out of the van and escorted up what seemed like a flight of staircases, I heard the squeaky boots stepping up every flight of stairs, and then I was thrown onto the ground. The bag was removed, and Ella, Anna, Edward and I were all lined up in a row in an office of some sort and were placed right in front of Adrian, the CEO of Wacco.

I looked over to Edward. "Nice of you to join us."

Then, Adrian walked over to his desk and grabbed a glass of brandy and took a sip of it.

"So it appears that we have reached an impasse on the road."

Suddenly, Adrian snapped his fingers, and the thugs behind us pushed Ella, Edward and I to the ground and pointed a Glock at the back of our heads. I could feel the cold metal press up against my head. Adrian then snapped his finger again and pointed at Anna. "Let her go."

Two thugs came over and cut the zip ties around Anna's hands and escorted her to her feet.

Adrian then signalled to Anna. "Take a seat, my dear," he said, pointing to the seating facing directly at him.

Anna, with no other opinion, sat in front of his desk, with Adrian also taking a seat. Adrian then finished off his glass of brandy. Anna was concerned. "Why didn't you do this at my house?"

Adrian just looked at her. "Because I wanted to make the choice in person."

Adrian leaned in his chair, coming to eye level with Anna.

"Now, here is the deal." He slid a piece of paper in front of her to read. "You are going to take this new bill to ParliaCongress."

Anna picked up the document and looked it over, and the document read 'Peacekeeping Deactivation Bill'. Anna was confused. "What is this?"

"Like I said, an opportunity for both of us. A win-win, if you will." Adrian got out of his desk and walked past Anna, brushing her shoulders. "The bill permanently decommissions the army reserve and removes them from your level."

"OK, and how do you benefit from this?"

Adrian smirked. "Simple, in the bill, the army reserve is replaced with a new military force. My military force, the Eagle Eye Group. You see, with my group as the main protection force for home defence, I will become the main supplier of weapons. Also, I can jack up the prices on my forces, meaning more of the city's military budget goes directly into my companies' pockets."

Anna smirked. "Of course, and you have a say in the deployment of the military force."

"Exactly." Adrian smiled. "Also, being members of a private military, my men are not bound by the Geneva Convention. Think of the havoc I could unleash."

I overheard everything. It was ingenious. Adrian could basically control the city's entire military overnight.

"Furthermore, I also put in a bailout for my company as well, saving the profits you cost me and making my organisation, the biggest defence company in the city. And you win, of course, because it takes WeapCo out of the picture."

"And if I refuse?"

"Then your family dies in front of you, so sign it, damn you."

Anna looked down at the document and then looked over at her family lying on the floor. She paused for a moment and picked up the pen, ready to sign the document.

But, instead of signing the document, she paused and got out of her seat. The guards pointed their guns at her, but Adrian dismissed them, as he knew that she wouldn't do anything.

"Anna, you have no other option. Either you sign your life away, or your family dies."

Suddenly, Anna grabbed the glass that was lying on the table and threw it straight at Adrian, which he dodged, and the glass went straight through the window, shattering the window on impact. Adrian looked over at the exposed window. "Hah! You missed"

"Did I?"

Suddenly, Anna threw the pen at me, got up onto the table and kicked Adrian straight out of the 50-storey window. The guards stood there in shock, and that was enough of a distraction for me to grab the pen and stab it into the guard's leg. The soldier screamed back in pain, grabbing his leg, which gave me the opportunity to knock him off balance. Ella followed suit, swirling her body around on the floor, knocking the guard to the floor, which in a domino effect knocked Edward's guard to the floor. Anna quickly rushed to cut me loose, and she grabbed Ella's guard, who was about to get to his feet, and kneed him in the face, knocking him out.

Anna rushed to grab Ella and Edward to their feet, and she cut the zip ties off their hands, and all four of them got to their feet and knocked out the remaining soldiers. However, it was far from over, as the alarm rang out through the building and outside. We heard at least a hundred soldiers rushing up the stairs and barricading the entire building, trapping us within Adrian's office. The head of the guard yelled, "Listen up. We have the building surrounded, and in a minute, we are going to barrage in and kill you all."

Blast, I thought to myself, *how were we going to get out of?* Then I looked over at the drapes hanging on the wall of the office. This was absolute suicide, and there was no way this would work, but I was going to die either way, so may as well give it a try. I quickly rushed and grabbed the drapes, tied them to the window ledge and threw them out of the exposed window like a makeshift rope. But I had to hurry, as the fabric was cutting on the exposed glass. Without thinking, I grabbed the drape and walked down, and I pushed my body outwards to give it some momentum and smash through the glass window on the next floor, but as I did, the drape tore and fell.

However, I was lucky, as I managed to hold on to the exposed window, but I couldn't hold for long, as the exposed glass was digging into my hand and I was losing my strength as my hand bled, I really should have thought this through.

However, just as I was hanging on, Edward peered his head out of the office window. "Jacob, grab my hand."

He reached out an exposed hand. I had no other option. Using the full strength of my upper body, I pushed myself up, letting go of the windowsill and grabbing onto his hand. But my full strength pulled Edward out of the window. He grabbed onto the windowsill with one arm.

"Edward, on the count of three, let go! One! Two! And THREE!"

I pushed myself away from the window and Edward let go. While I did manage to dislocate my shoulder, it was a success, as I made it into the window. *Quick, better grab Edward before he falls to his death.*

Meanwhile, upstairs, Ella and Anna were trying to figure their own way out, as they both rummaged through Adrian's desk in the hopes of finding something. Luckily, they found a white and gold Glock. Yes.

"Jacob, lean out your hand."

I was confused about what they were up to, but nonetheless, I leaned out of the window, with Edward holding my back. Then, Anna dropped the gun.

"Thanks, Anna!" Boy, that would come in handy. I checked the gun. Full clip. I turned the safety off and rushed towards the staircase, seeing the troops all line up in rows.

Bang! Bang! Bang! I opened fire at the soldiers, which caught them completely off guard, and they all rushed to return fire. There were plasma bolts flying everywhere, cutting through everything in the office, as both Edward and I ducked under the desks.

Upstairs, Ella found a button underneath the table. She clicked the button, and a blaster-proof shield shot down in a split second, which blocked the entrance into Adrian's office. That would buy them some time. Quickly, Ella and Anna had to rush to knock the guards out and collect their rifles and handguns.

But on one of the soldiers was a grenade.

Anna yelled out, "Take cover!"

Anna grabbed the chair and moved it to the middle of the room. She pulled the pin, and both Ella and Anna ducked out of the way.

BOOM! The grenade blew a hole in the floor, with Anna signalling to Ella, and the two of them pushed Adrian's desk into the middle of the room and climbed up in the hole and onto the next level.

Meanwhile, Edward and I were pinned down, as we were both unable to move. There were hundreds of soldiers surrounding us from all sides. If we did hurry up, we would be encircled, and all we could really do was lay on the ground with our arms on top of our heads. With no other option, we surrendered, and two soldiers rushed over and placed us in handcuffs. The soldiers picked Edward and me up back onto our feet, and they began escorting both of us in handcuffs.

Upstairs, Ella and Anna had managed to climb to the next level, and using the elevator, they took it up to the rooftop. There, they found Adrian's personal flying car. They rushed into the car and flew it away from the building. Suddenly, just as Edward and I were being escorted downstairs, Ella and Anna crashed the car into the lobby of the building.

The crash caught the soldiers off guard in the distraction. Not wanting to waste this opportunity, Edward and I flipped our bodies over the railing of the stairs, falling two storeys and landing on the roof of the car.

Luckily, in this modern age, the car was built out of plastic, so the roof collapsed in on itself, but not enough to hurt Ella and Anna in any way. After falling onto the roof of the car, Edward and I rolled over, landing face first on the ground, and we both managed to pick ourselves up, went to the body of the soldier, unlocked our handcuffs and got into the car.

Quickly, Anna reversed out of the building, only for the car engine to stop working.

"For gosh sake, what do we do now?" Anna asked, as the soldiers opened fire on our car.

"RUN!" I screamed, we all bolted from the car and rushed towards the elevator, while I kicked the door off its hinges and used it as a shield from the laser bolts. But thank goodness, we made it to the elevator.

"Quick, we need to get downstairs and take out the power."

Everyone nodded in agreement, and Anna pushed the button for downstairs. The elevator took us down into the generator room that powered the entire building. After reaching the generator, I took the rifle that was slung over my shoulder and shot at the generator. After at least five shots, the generator blew up, and the power throughout the entire building went out. Everything went down: the cameras, the security doors, everything. Also, while we were down here, we went to the IT room and destroyed the archived camera footage, leaving no trace that we were ever there.

Now the real question was *How do we get out of here?*

Upstairs, there were hundreds of soldiers ready to kill us on sight. We all looked around. It looked like we were trapped. We all thought hard, but it looked like there was no way out but up. Guess we would have to head up. So, we all hopped into the elevator, waiting to face the hundreds of soldiers.

One question came to mind, though. *How would this elevator be running without power?* I didn't notice the elevator door open, and the room was immediately swarming with emergency service personnel and police officers. It was obvious that the emergency service personnel must have turned on the backup power. They were responding to the alarms in the building. The soldiers quickly disarmed. They wouldn't dare kill a politician in front of the police and the media.

We all were treated by paramedics, and the situation became an active investigation, as the investigators asked what had happened. All we could do was explain our side of the story: The soldiers from Wacco INC had kidnapped me and my family. Adrian, out of guilt, committed suicide by jumping out a window, and his soldiers tried to kill us, so we acted in self-defence. Also, we crashed the car out of duress for our lives.

After sitting around for an hour, the police investigated the soldiers on duty. The investigator could find no evidence of Adrian being pushed out of the window. Also, drone footage from the local peacekeeping force captured us being kidnapped and thrown into a van. Furthermore, eyewitness reports stated that they could hear 'plasma rifle blasts ringing out from the building'.

After the investigation into Adrian was labelled a 'suicide', a spokesperson from Wacco offered us his deepest apologies for kidnapping us against our will. They also claimed that they were unaware of Adrian's actions and that we were free to go. The people at Wacco asked if we were going to sue, but there was no real point pressing charges, as we were free to go. Because all of us just wanted to go home, this whole adventure was just a waste of time.

After an exhausting and pointless adventure, we went back home and sat on the couch, drinking a couple of beers and trying to process what had happened. But, for the life of us, none of us knew what had happened. It escalated so quickly. But, oh well, we all just shrugged it off (we were used to this sort of stuff by now) and watched the news. The headlines read 'Wacco CEO Commits Suicide' and 'RIP Adrian', and on the screen appeared John, who offered his condolences to Adrian's family.

CHAPTER 31

After the incident at Wacco INC and having to deal with the impact that Adrian's political meddling had caused, it was finally time for the vote on the military occupation bill. This moment was extremely important for Anna and the Lower Levels, as this vote meant the difference between freedom and legal tyranny. The vote consisted of two parts: first was the vote on the floor, and second, the people's referendum. It was going to be tough, so Anna had to pull out all the stumps.

It was in the living room that Ella and Anna were going over their speech at least the 20th time in order to prepare for the big day.

"OK Anna, now concentrate. Don't be timid. We need all the fight you go. Unleash the beast."

Anna took a deep breath in. "OK, unleash the beast ... Ladies and gentlemen, right now is an opportunity to—"

"NO, Anna, you've got to get angry. You're speaking too softly. Find your voice and stand up for yourself."

"OK, Ladies and—"

"NO, Anna—"

"Ella, I didn't say anything yet."

"I know, but you're still too timid. Speak with passion. None of this 'ladies and gentlemen' garbage. Now is not the time to be civil."

I didn't bother to step in because they were both under a lot of pressure, and I didn't want them to rip my eyes out.

"OK, guys, practise at the office. You're going to be late."

"You're right. Thanks, son. Don't wait up."

Anna proceeded to kiss me on the cheek, and both she and Ella headed out the door on their way to ParliaCongress.

Showtime! Ella and Anna both walked into ParliaCongress, both dressed up in their fancy blazers ready to kick some metaphorical arse. Anna's political stunt with the riot had gained her a reputation. She was so feared in ParliaCongress that interns and some politicians didn't even dare look in her direction. Finally, the day had arrived. The moment they had all been preparing for. The final seating of the bill. All the politicians were walking in to take their seats, as the voting was contested and extremely important. The entire stadium was full of legislators.

There was chattering back and forth among all the politicians until the speaker of the house got out of his seat and demanded silence in the house. "Quiet!"

The room went so quiet that not even the crickets dared to chirp.

"Attention, please. The legislative house is open on the military occupation bill. The senators from the Upper Level, you have the floor."

The Upper Level politicians were all venture capitalists, so of course, they voted in favour of the bill being passed, as they had much to benefit from the bill. But now, here is where it gets interesting. The Middle Level politicians were divided on how to vote; some were in favour of the bill, because they were in the pocket of WeapCo, but others were not so much. After the school rocket incident and the riots, some were indecisive.

Guess it was time for Ella to shine. Politics is a dirty game, so we had sent Ella in as a 'negotiator' of sorts. Ella went to some of the politicians who were indecisive and strongly urged them to vote in our favour, or certain pictures would be released to the public. After, convincing a few politicians to change their vote, she would give me a wink.

That's my girl, Anna thought to herself. Sometimes, you got to twist a few arms to get what you want.

The first hour was brutal. There was screaming back and forth, and some passionate politicians had to be removed from the chambers because they got into fistfights. Ella had played her part well. The vote was 45 per cent in favour, 45 against, 5 per cent undecided, and the bottom 5 per cent (the Lower-Level politicians) were yet to cast their vote. Suddenly, the speaker of the house turned to Anna. "The lady politician from the Lower Level, you have the floor!"

Anna's heart sunk in her chest. She had to speak in front of a thousand politicians who were eager to rip her throat out. Anna got up to the podium and took a deep breath in.

But before, she could say a word, Richard tried to demean her by interrupting. "Mr Speaker, the Lower Level—"

"Excuse me, Richard, but I am talking," Anna snapped straight back at Richard with anger in her voice, silencing him dead in his tracks. He was speechless.

Anna took another breath in and tried to calm herself down. "Mr Speaker, I would like to proceed with my speech."

"Go ahead."

Anna ruffled through her paper and composed herself and finally mustered the strength to speak.

"Mr Speaker and the people of the House, tonight, we are standing at the edge of a precipice in our city's history. Today will determine not only the actions we take but also who we are as a people, as human beings and as Americans. We stand here let troops march in our streets and enter our homes in what is to be a free and democratic city. But, if you don't care about the people down under (that comment was met by boos, and the speaker of the house demanded 'order'), then I say to you to think of the money that is being wasted on this silly little exercise. Think of the cost of repairing the destruction and the loss of revenue from the business that the military has crushed. So, ladies and gentlemen, I say to you, it's time to remove this bill and stop the military occupation bill dead in its tracks."

Anna's face had turned bright red. It had to be, as she basically screamed her speech to the entire legislative body. But her speech was met with a mixed response; half of the room booed her, and the other half cheered in applause. Ella silently slunk over to Anna and patted her on the back. "Well done. You have done well."

This session was a battleground, as politicians were screaming back and forth, with Anna screaming back at the politicians who called her 'a left-wing witch' and a 'hypocrite'. However, the room went silent as the final votes were tallied up, and all the politicians watched on the hologram projector as the numbers flicked back and forth. The current scores were 45 per cent 'yes', 50 per cent 'no' and 5 per cent 'undecided'. The fate of the race relied solely on a handful of politicians. Anna looked down over the railing in the Lower Levels of the ParliaCongress, as the politicians talked back and forth. The vote soon closed, and the results were 45 per cent 'yes' and 55 per cent 'no'. It had happened. Anna had won. The military occupation bill had been removed.

Anna was over the moon at the results. She jumped up and down in joy, high-fiving and hugging Ella. What a victory! After everything that she went through, she finally got a victory. Something finally went right in her life, and she walked out of that room victorious.

"Congratulations, Anna."

"Hey, it was a team effort. Everyone played their part."

"OK, the bill has been rejected."

"Yay! Another high five, Ella. Come on, don't keep a girl hanging."

But Ella, having to be the buzzkill, reminded her, "There is still your impeachment trial."

Anna stopped Ella from running her mouth by placing a hand on her shoulders. "There is time for all of that. Right now, let's celebrate! I am buying!"

Anna and Ella walked out of the building to find me and Edward at the bottom of the stairs. I just looked at Anna and smiled. "We did it."

Anna returned a smile, and she rushed into my arms and gave me a big hug. "We did it!"

That night was a massive celebration. Now, normally, we wouldn't eat out, as we could never afford to eat at one of those 'posh' restaurants. But now that Anna was a politician, we ordered bottle service and ate some fancy-looking steaks. There were laughs and giggles shared all around, and for good reason. Because all the sacrifices, all the time spent in prison, and all the time spent in Mercy Lane had all led up to this victory. Naturally, we all partied hard that night and got drunk but also poured a drink in the memory of all our friends and family whom we have lost over the years. After a few drinks at the club, we all took the party back home, and everyone but I crashed from all the bottles of wine.

After last night's party, we all recovered with massive hangovers. But today was not a day to take lightly, as today was Anna's impeachment trial. What a letdown. We finally got a massive win from the vote at ParliaCongress, and now everything Anna had worked for was crashing down around her. Anna's mood was not great, you could tell by her face. After having some breakfast and some coffee, Anna herself began walking into the den of the vultures that were going to rip through her political career, and she couldn't do anything about it.

After Anna entered the building, she took a deep breath in and walked into the tribunal, only to be met with camera flashing from the reporters, and in front of her was a panel of nine judges who had to be all past their prime and in their late 70s.

But Anna had to keep her cool. She couldn't show fear or guilt, so any anxiety had to keep it hidden. Anna sat down at her desk and took a sip of water to calm her nerves.

The old judge in the middle of the proceeding began, "I would like to begin the impeachment process of the Honourable Anna Turner. Please confirm for record."

Anna just coughed and said in a slightly timid voice, "Present."

"Very well. Shall we begin?" the nine judges all nodded their heads, and the impeachment trial commenced.

"Anna Turner, you stand accused of political espionage, voter suppression and embezzlement. How do you plead?"

Anna stood up and leaned into the microphone. "Not guilty, your honour!"

"Very well," said the senior judge in the middle. "Then let the trial commence."

A holoprojector then projected an image of Anna and Adrian shaking hands.

"Hon Anna Turner, do you confirm that this is you in this hologram shaking hands and accepting a payment of $500,000 towards your campaign?"

Anna leaned into the mic. "I plead the fifth (the right to remain silent)."

"OK, so you admit that you accepted campaign finance in exchange for political favours?"

"I pled the—"

"I can testify to that."

Anna was shocked at the sound of the familiar voice. She turned around and thought, *Wait, that is not impossible. Adrian!*

Adrian stood at the back of the courtroom, alive and well. Anna, Ella, Edward and I all stood there in shock. How did he survive a 100-storey fall?

Adrian walked to the front of the courtroom. "I can testify that Anna accepted funds from my company."

"Very well. Take the stand then."

But before Adrian took the stand, he leaned over to Anna and threw a syringe on the table and whispered to Anna, "You should have checked what was in my blood system."

And he took the stand. Anna turned over the syringe and on it in big letters read: Xenogren. I had taken Xenogren before. It was an incredibly potent drug, made from the essence of radiated tree bark. The effects of the drug mutated human genes for 24 hours, giving the user incredible inhuman abilities.

Adrian opened his briefcase and handed the courts some documents. "Your honour, I would like to present to you a contract signed and dated by Anna Turner confirming that she indeed took finance from my company."

All the judges looked at the paper and began scribing notes. "Anna, do you confirm that is your signature?"

"Well, yer, but—"

The judges scribbled away.

"Thank you, Adrian. You may step down!"

Adrian got up, winked at Anna and walked out of the courtroom. Anna just stood her ground. If she said anything, it would indict her. So for every question, she replied, "I plead the fifth."

"Very well, shall we proceed?" The judge on the edge spoke: "Anna, were you aware of this device?"

The judge projected an image of what looked like a microphone.

Anna was confused. She didn't even know what that thing was. "I am not aware of that device."

The judges looked sceptical and wouldn't buy that. "Really. That's not what this eyewitness said. Please send him in!"

Richard got up to the stand.

Anna was furious and shook her head. He was lying and had planted that device to get back at Anna for punching him and humiliating him in front of ParliaCongress.

Richard smiled. "I can confirm that the device was found by one of my staff members in my office and was planted by Anna and her team." Richard handed the judges a police report. "As detailed by this police report, it shows that the forensic team found fingerprints at the scene of the crime."

Anna was even more confused. How could her fingerprints be there? She didn't even know what that device was. Anna couldn't stay quiet any longer. She got up out of her chair and exploded, "I don't know what that device is, and I have no recollection of ever touching that device."

But the judges weren't buying it. "That's not what this report says, Ms Turner."

Anna slunk back into her chair. The court was unfair and biased, and the worst thing was that she had no way or evidence to prove that she wasn't guilty. This wasn't a trial; this was an execution.

Finally, the judges asked, "Anna, do you confirm the charges of voter suppression?"

"I am 100 per cent certain that I never engaged in any voter suppression whatsoever."

The judges shook their heads. "Can you confirm that Ms Ella was part of your team?"

Ella sank in her chair, and I could note her look of guilt.

Anna was even more confused. "Yes, but what does that have to do with anything?"

"Is Ella here with you?"

Ella shot up immediately. "Present!"

"Can you take the stand?"

Ella walked up guilty and nervous as hell. Anna felt guilty too. She had told her to blackmail the other politicians, and she whispered to Ella, "I am so sorry—"

"Ms Ella, can you confirm that you were a staffer for Anna Turner?"

"Yes," Ella said timidly.

"Very well. Can you confirm that you engaged in voter suppression on Anna's behalf?"

Ella shook her head. "No, no, I didn't."

"Really? Then can you explain this CCTV footage?"

Ella was in shock. *They recorded that?* The hologram projected Ella talking to some gang member behind Anna's back. In the footage, Ella was whispering, "I will do anything to help Anna win. We can make that happen! Let's just say we can take care of some district in the Lower Level for a fee."

The judges paused the video. Anna went on the defence. "Your Honour, I—"

Ella melted down and burst into tears. "Guilty, guilty, I am Guilty. I borrowed a bit of campaign money to hire some thugs to suppress certain districts that may have posed a threat. I am so sorry, Anna."

Ella threw away the mic, leapt out of the stand and ran out of the courtroom.

Anna was in complete shock. *What has she done?* This campaign and this political career have destroyed not only her morals but the morals of the woman she loved. Anna slunk back in her chair. She couldn't take this anymore. She stood up. "Your honour."

"The chair recognises the Hon. Anna Turner."

"Your honour, I would like to call for a plea bargain."

All the judges nodded in agreement. "Very well. The court calls for a recess."

Anna, the nine judges, and Adrian, Richard, Edward and I as witnesses were all placed into a different room outside of the courtroom to negotiate.

The senior judge was the first to speak.

"We are going to level with you. It is not looking good. However, thanks to the generosity of Adrian and Richard, they have agreed to look past this transgression, and if you agree to plead guilty to your charges and resign from your government position, you will walk free."

Anna looked around the room. It looked like she didn't have a chance. Anna sighed. "OK, where do I sign?"

One of the judges handed her an agreement that dismissed her criminal charges on the condition that she pled guilty to the charges, and below was a prepared letter of resignation for Anna. Anna just sighed and signed both, and just like that, her political career was over.

"Pleasure doing business with you, Ms Turner."

Anna got up out of her seat and walked out of the room with us following along. I just turned and gave her a hug. "It's all right, Mum. We know you did nothing wrong."

Anna looked defeated, but then she checked her pocket. "Excuse me, guys, I forgot my phone."

Anna slowly pushed the door and stumbled onto the nine judges, Adrian and Richard, all laughing and pouring each other drinks. Anna now realised that the whole thing was rigged from the start. Anna just shook her head. She lost, and the house won. Anna just gave up and followed me and Edward out.

Anna, Edward and I all walked down the stairs of the courthouse. Ella was bawling her eyes out. Then she looked up and ran to hug Anna. "I am so sorry, Anna."

Anna could have ripped her throat out for what she had done, but there was no point. We all did things in this campaign that were all not proud of, so instead, all Anna did was hug Ella. "There, there! It's all right. I should have never taken that dirty money. This thing was a mistake from the beginning."

"Don't say that, Mum. While you may have lost your career, we won! We got the bill removed, and to me, this is better than any victory!"

Anna just smiled at that comment. "Come on, everyone, let's go home. I feel like some Chinese takeaway."

Everyone just smiled at that comment, and we all walked away happy.

"Yer, screw the government. Let's just get shitfaced!" We all couldn't help but laugh at that.

While Anna lost her position, the legacy she left was more than what she could ever hope for. Finally, after months of fighting and campaigning, they were gone. The peacekeepers were finally gone, and the Lower Levels were free.

The next day, we all stood on the balcony drinking a beer as we watched the tanks, drones, military vehicles and all the soldiers began marching out of the city and back into the warehouses and the reservist military base, where they belonged, never to come back unless it was an emergency. It was a beautiful sight to see. It was like watching a military parade unfold in front of our eyes. And within an hour, for the first time since the forces had arrived, there was silence and nothing more. Silence fell on the city, and we were free. At long last, we were finally free.

CHAPTER 32

04-02-3026

Boy, how the time flies. Three months had passed since the peacekeepers left the Lower Levels, and the community had never been more vibrant. Businesses and shops were opening up again, people were moving back into their houses and we were free to roam the streets without the fear of being shot. People were free to sleep at night with missiles or artillery fire screaming through their bedrooms. Yep, the Lower Level had never been better, well, some parts at least. Ella had reopened her shop but decided to reopen it as a florist shop instead of a gun shop, and Edward managed to rebuild and reopen his pharmacy. Meanwhile, Mum decided to become a part-time social science teacher at the local high school. And what was I doing? Well, I was unemployed, but I had been helping at the local church. The times had been quiet. As a group, we all decided to abandon our plans of taking down WeapCo and get back to our normal lives. I was trying to reform my old ways. Over my entire lifetime, I had killed and hurt many people in the name of duty, and frankly, I was done with it all, and I was loving it.

It was another casual Saturday night, and the church that I was attending was hosting a dinner for all the people who had lost their homes during the occupation, or just for anyone going through hard times. Together, we had all managed to serve at least 20 people, and it was my job to wash the dirty dishes. Honestly, it felt nice to finally work again. But to be honest, I had kind of let myself go a little. I now had a long beard, and my muscles were getting a little frail.

After finishing the last of the dishes, I waited for everyone to leave so I could speak to Father Bruce. Father Bruce had been the practising minister at the local church for the past 30 years. He was an old man in his late 80s, and he had white hair and the signature priest attire: a black shirt with a white collar.

I waited around the hall, and then he approached me. "Jacob, fantastic work with the people, today. You were a massive hit with people."

I smirked. "Well, what can I say, Father, I have a flair for dealing with people, both difficult and not-so-difficult."

Father Bruce had been mentoring me, helping me to deal with my PTSD and trying to help me repent for all the people I had hurt and killed over the years. He gave me a cup of coffee, and we walked around the old Victorian-style church.

"So, how have you been holding up, Jacob?"

I sighed. "All right. My sleep is starting to improve. I have been able to get to sleep with having alcohol, but I can't stop the screaming and the flashbacks."

Father Bruce sat in an empty chair. "Well, I have met a lot of veterans who have been where you are. So trust me, it gets better. You just have to confront your demons head-on."

I shook my head and looked down at the floor. "I know, Father, but it is just so hard. You have lived in this city for so long. You know what it is like. How do I stop hurting people, and how do I let go of all the people I have hurt?"

Father Bruce looked at me. "Well, sometimes, all you can really do is offer a hand of kindness and generosity to people. You see, if you want to improve your life, you need to start by taking little steps. Here is how I see it, Jacob. From the killings and the hurting, you have created for yourself a world of pain and negativity that you try to drown out with alcohol.”

“But Father, I am confused. How do I make a little step to change?”

Father Bruce then placed a hand on my shoulder. “Simple. Keep helping people. Keep volunteering and being kind. Eventually, all the past hurt and demons will heal with time. All the good deeds and all the help you give accumulate, and what you put out into the world eventually comes back to help you, so be a good person, Jacob. Be the person you want to be. Pray with me, Jacob.”

I placed my hands together, and we prayed.

“Dear Lord, please help guide and steer Jacob down the right path in life and help lift him out of his world of desperation and forgive him of his trespasses. Amen.”

“Amen,” I repeated and walked out of the church, contemplating what Father Bruce had told me.

Walking down the steps of the church, I came down to find Mum standing there holding a bag of burgers and two Colas in her hand. Mum had just finished an 8-hour shift at the high school and decided to walk home and catch up, as both of us lived so busy and productive lives that we never really got to see each other anymore.

Anna was a lot different after leaving her political position. She was a lot calmer and more at peace about what happened to her. We walked home in the dark, drinking our Cola’s.

“How was church?”

“All right. I mean, as much as I can be with the way the world is.”

Anna couldn’t really argue with that logic. “So Jacob, I want to check in with you and figure out what it is we are going to do about WeapCo.”

“What do you mean, Mum? We already went through this. We need to start living normal lives.”

“No, you established it. Ella and I want to take down WeapCo, I mean, we have come this far!”

"Mum, Yandan is dead, and we removed the peacekeepers. We won. Move on."

"Come on, Jacob."

"Mum, it is not our responsibility to change the world or to seek vengeance for what has happened. Bitterness will only cause more death and more destruction."

"So, what, we just get old and fat?"

"No, we live out the rest of our lives in peace and go back to the way things were before this whole crusade started."

"Jacob, I get that you are doing this whole rebirth stuff, but—"

"But nothing, Mum. You got to stop thinking about the bigger picture and focus on what we have left."

"Fine, Jacob. If you want to sit around and play monk, that is fine by me, but don't expect us all to—"

"To what? OK, what's the plan? You run in there all guns blazing? Worked well before. No, wait, you expect to use your political position. Oh, wait—"

"OK, you proved your point. You don't need to be a smart-arse about it."

"My point is, we are all alive. We have employment, but most importantly, we are alive. Let's just keep it that way, shall we?"

Anna just sighed at that comment. "OK, no violence sounds like a plan."

I pulled Mum aside and held her by the shoulders. "Look, I get it, but we are not soldiers anymore. We don't need to resort to violence anymore. You're a teacher now, and I, well, I am out of work, but we have finally got what we wanted. Peace! So let's live with that."

"Good luck convincing Ella of that plan."

"How's her shop coming along?"

"Fine, but she finds it lonesome. She said there's always work if you ever want it."

I smiled at that comment. "I am guessing I will have to take her up on that offer. How's Norman settling into the place?"

"Yer, fine. What did you say he does for work again?"

I just looked at Mum confused. "I didn't know Norman works."

"So can you explain to me how long he is going to live with us?"

"As long as he needs. The kid's got nowhere to go, and he needs us."

"Oh Jacob, always caring for strays ... Even when you were a little kid, you would always leave out a bowl of dog food for the stray dogs."

"Hahaha, yer, Dad would get pissed because the yard was full of stray dogs in the winter. Hahaha, good times ... Hey Mum, do you think it may be time to move out of the Lower Levels?"

"Jacob, we can't afford to move. We barely make a decent wage."

"But if we sell the house and cash out some of your super, we could buy a cheap apartment in the Middle Levels. We may not have the same amount of space, but it would be a safer neighbourhood."

"What about Ella? Edward? And Norman?"

"Ella got her shop back, Edward got his pharmacy back, and if I vouch for Norman, I am sure either one of them would happily give him a job."

"What are you talking about, Jacob? That is the home that you grew up in. Our family lives there."

"Mum, I know that, but I am just tired of living in a place full of crime. I want to get out and create a better life for us. Think about it, Mum. You can go to university and become a qualified teacher for a reasonable salary, and I would go back to trade school or maybe even get into engineering school."

"I don't know. That's a big move."

I rushed up the stairs and let Mum in through the front door. "Think about it."

"OK, I will try," she said, defeated.

We walked into the living room to find Ella, Edward and Norman all sitting on the couch drinking beers and laughing.

It was amazing how quickly all our moods improved when we were not under pressure from gunfire.

Ella was the first to greet us. "Hey, hey, how did it go?"

Mum smiled. "It went great. I had to teach kids the fundamentals of sociology."

Ella nodded and continued, "How have you been, holy man? Prayed for all of us?"

I just smirked. "Real funny, Ella."

Anna dropped the bag of burgers on the coffee table, and the three of them swarmed in like a bunch of vultures ripping through a dead carcass. Everyone dug into their burgers, including myself and Mum.

Ella adjusted herself to an upright position and dropped a bombshell question, "So, when are we taking down WeapCo?"

My face just froze.

"Ugh, not this again! We all right went through this, Ella. We have agreed to abandon that plan."

"No, you agreed to that."

"That's what I said," Anna cut in.

I threw down my burger on the coffee table, ready for a fight. "But the peacekeepers are gone. We don't need to fight. Look what happened to Adrian? Nothing, right?"

Ella was now angry. "The fight is not over until he pays for what he did to my dad."

"Your dad is dead. Move on."

I had crossed the line with that comment, as everyone in the room went silent and were all staring at me. Normally, I would backtrack, but I wasn't backing down. "Ella, we have already lost so much and gained so little. How much more do we have to lose as a result of your dad's silly campaign?"

"Whatever it takes, Jacob! Why have you turned into such a little bi—"

Edward shot up, hoping for her not to finish that statement. "OK, guys, let's all calm down."

"STAY OUT OF THIS!" we both screamed.

"Jacob, we did not come all this way to back down now because you went on some spiritual journey."

"Ella, I am just trying to do what's best for all of us."

"You don't speak for all of us, Jacob."

"Well, don't expect me and Mum to follow you to your grave."

Ella shot up out of her seat. "You're such an arsehole, Jacob."

She stormed out of the door, leaving all of us in silence.

"Nice going, Jacob!" Anna retorted.

I was in a fired-up mood and not really in the mood to take any crap. "Care to contribute, Anna?"

"Jacob, don't talk to me like that."

"Then why are you encouraging her to chase after this silly vendetta against WeapCo?"

"Because I want to keep fighting, Jacob. Edward wants to keep fighting. You're the only one who doesn't seem to be following the plan."

"Mum, it's futile. WeapCo is a billion-dollar company with more resources than a third-world nation."

"Jacob, we can't just let John and WeapCo get away with what they have done to Ella, this community and us. It's not fair."

My face was as red as a tomato. "Well, news flash, life isn't fair."

"Only if we do nothing, Jacob."

"No, I will no longer be a part of this, and I am not losing any more people. Excuse me."

I needed to cool down, so I took up my jumper and went for a walk. The night air would help to calm my red and bloodshot face.

But then, I heard a noise, a scream coming from a nearby alleyway. "Help! Help!"

I looked down the alleyway and saw a man and his wife being held at knifepoint.

"Come on, move it!"

"OK, man, just don't hurt us!" The man handed the robber his wallet.

I wanted to run in there and beat the robber up, and I was really struggling to contain my anger. I clenched my fist as hard as I could. No more violence. I meant it.

Suddenly, the robber stabbed the man in the stomach and ran away with his wallet. The wife collapsed on the ground crying and holding her husband's hand as he died in her arms. "Harold, no!"

I just watched in disappointment as the robber ran down the alley. But when I went there to help, she went off at me. "Why didn't you help him? Get out of here, you coward!"

She wasn't wrong. My days of helping people through violence were over. Instead, I just wanted to focus on helping people through charitable causes. But still, I was incredibly angry with myself. I really wanted to hurt that guy, but most of all, I was angry that the people who were supposed to support me were trying to pull me back into a lifestyle I was trying to escape.

It was so annoying because I felt as if the entire world was against me. Despite all the suffering and all the pain I had to go through, I still felt as if there was a never-ending supply of it. But no matter how much I tried to redeem myself, I couldn't fight the sorrow and guilt towards the people I had killed. I could see them. I could hear their screams in my mind every night, even when I was alone. But what was strange was I could hear the voices of people I had never met before who told me stuff and gave me guidance, which made no sense whatsoever.

During these moments of reflection, I decided to look at the Bible Father Bruce had given me. It was a red worn-out book with the words 'Holy Bible' scribbled on it in gold. Riddled with guilt, I decided to open it up, only to find out that I must have been dyslexic or something, as the book had no words in it. There were only unreadable scribbles in the book. I had no idea what I was supposed to get out of this book. I kept flipping and flipping the book through, as it was all the same unreadable scribbles. Then I stopped halfway through, finally finding some distinguishable words. In the bold letter, it read: 'But those who wait on the Lord shall renew their strength; they shall mount up with wings like eagles, they shall run and not be weary, they shall walk and not faint' (Isaiah 40:31).

Something about that quote really resonated with me. I felt at ease, and I felt my anger and sadness all but disappear in this brief moment.

However, after hearing that quote ring in my head, I started to get flashbacks of moments I never lived; I had flashbacks of me holding a Bible like this in my mind. I could remember sitting beside my daughter reading it to her.

My moment of peace was suddenly broken when I heard a shrill scream pierce my eardrums, which caused me to collapse to the ground in pain. The wail started to fade, but my vision was blurry. I just want it to stop. All I could really do was scream out, "Make what stop!"

"Make what stop?"

I turned my head and saw Anna staring at my doorway with a concerned look on her face.

"Nothing, Mum, nothing at all."

I got up off the floor, wiped my tears and pretended as if nothing had happened.

"Anything I can help you with, Mum?"

"I just came here to say sorry for ganging up on you back there."

I got up off my feet and shrugged it off. "It's OK, Mum. I still love you." After what I had experienced, I wasn't concerned about that whole argument anymore. I wanted to go home.

"OK. Love you, son." Before she walked away, she turned to me. "Are you sure you're all right?"

"Fine, Mum."

She wasn't convinced, but she walked away anyway. All I could really do was breathe a heavy sigh of relief and try to figure out what was going on in my life and what the screams meant. But deep down, I knew what was happening. My internal rage was manifesting false memories of people I had never met. That, or the trauma I had taken over the years was finally accumulating, and I was losing my marbles. Either way, I was going to have to come to terms with it and move on. I placed my head on my pillow and went to sleep.

I was lying there in a light sleep when I heard a loud scream ring out from outside my door. At first, I thought it was the scream in my head. But then I realised that it was my mum's voice screaming from outside the door. I shot straight out of my bed in shock at what was going on, looking around frantically.

When I got outside, I saw Mum in a complete freeze, with her hand covering her mouth and pointing at something. I looked at what she was pointing at. It was Edward lying on the couch with his throat slit, bleeding out on the couch in the living room, but what I saw next shocked me to my core. My goodness! I saw Norman standing over Edward's dead body holding a kitchen knife in his hand, and he was looking concerned.

I was confused, but I had my suspicions. "Norman, what's going on?"

"Oh Jacob, thank goodness you are here. Edward was trying to attack me, so I had to disarm him."

I was confused. "Why would he try to attack you?"

"I don't know. He just went berserk and tried to kill me."

This wasn't making any sense. Why would he try to kill him? But then, I noticed something on Norman's face. Then it all started to occur to me. Right next to the couch, I picked up the Glock that was hidden next to the couch. I picked up the gun and pointed it directly at Norman.

"Jacob, what are you doing?"

"I can tell a fake facial expression from a mile away. You're lying! You killed Edward!"

I didn't know; I was bluffing, but I had a gut feeling that he killed Edward because of the vision.

Norman paused for a moment, and then he began to give me an evil smile like a cartoon supervillain. Then he let out a sinister laugh. "Guilty!"

I was in absolute shock. I thought he was a nice guy, and I thought that illusion of him stabbing me was just that: an illusion. But it turned out that my vision was right. Norman took me for a sucker, and I paid the price.

"Why did you do this, Norman?"

He just shrugged his shoulders. "Well, WeapCo paid me a bit of money to take out your mum over the loss of profits. But I saw Edward lying there valuable, and I thought, why not? Why not have a bit of fun?"

I shook my head. "So the reason you were in prison?"

"Mass murder! Apparently, people don't like it when you kill your classmates one by one. But hey, thanks for getting me out."

I saw the look on his face. It was devoid of all empathy and compassion. I thought he was just a nerdy, autistic introvert, but it turns out, he was just a cold-hearted killer.

I could not believe it. I was played. "I should have never trusted you."

He just laughed. "The joke's on you."

I pulled the head of the Glock and pointed it directly at him. "Don't think I am going to let you get away with this."

He just smiled and didn't flinch, as if he didn't have any fear, even swirling the knife in his fingers. "You won't shoot me, Jacob, because that would go against your little changed man bullshit. Poor Jacob, hearing screams in his head. Gonna cry." I could see the emptiness in his eyes. "Do it, kill me!"

I don't know what came over me. I began to hesitate, and my hand started to shake. I was a seasoned veteran, but something inside of me was preventing me from pulling the trigger. Was it my subconscious? But, out of nowhere, Norman rushed towards me in a sort of 'kamikaze charge', holding the knife by his side. I walked backward, putting my back to the wall and closing my eyes just as he was about to stab me, then BANG!

I held my eyes closed, knowing that when I opened them, I was going to feel a rush of adrenaline from the stab wound. So, not wanting to wait, I opened my eyes, but I couldn't feel anything different. I did see the shocked expression on Norman's face. Then I realised why. There was a bullet hole straight through his chest, and blood was pouring out onto his white shirt. I turned to the side and saw that he missed me by at least an inch, stabbing the wall behind me. Shocked, I looked upstairs, and, in my mum's hand was a Glock that was kept upstairs (we stationed guns all around the house due to multiple break-ins we have encountered).

Then, Norman's face went as white as a ghost, and he fell to the floor, coughing up blood.

"At last, I am free." With those final words, he collapsed dead with a smile on his face.

I couldn't process what had happened, but there was no time, as Mum rushed down the stairs in a panic. "Edward, NO!"

I too had just realised that my best friend had died.

Mum rushed over to Edward's deceased body on the couch and held his hand. But no response. The poor guy had passed away minutes ago. Mum grabbed his hand and started crying. I walked over, and even I began to tear up a little at his passing. I mean, he and I shared some history together. But Mum took it hard, so I gave her a hug while she cried on my shoulders. After Mum had calmed down, with two fingers, I closed his eyes, as his soul had far on moved from here.

Ella knocked on the door just in time. "Hey Jacob, I just wanted to say—"

She froze after seeing Edward's dead body on the couch, and her eyes began to water up as she burst into tears. I rushed over to give her a shoulder to cry on.

Ella, Anna and I began digging up a grave in the backyard, as this place didn't have a cemetery of any sort. We draped Edward's body in an American flag, and we buried him.

Out of respect, we placed a little makeshift white cross in the yard. I filled up the hole and gave a little ceremony his honour, followed by a moment of silence. Then, we laid him to rest. Norman wasn't so lucky. That bastard didn't deserve peace, so we did the most disrespectful thing possible. Mum and I went out back to the trash and threw his body in the closest dumpster we could find with no ceremony or words.

I felt so guilty. I should have never shown that guy any remorse or sympathy. I should have let him rot in that jail cell. But what sucked the most was the fact that I didn't suffer, but poor Edward died because of my failure. Poor Edward. I mean, despite our history, we were best friends, and I would miss him dearly and was never going to forgive myself.

After the funeral for Edward, we all just sat on the floor, as we couldn't even look at that bloodstained couch any longer. We all sat there in silence, all of us holding a beer. We were in shock at the sudden passing of Edward. I mean, it had been just a normal night, and in an hour, we lost our friend.

While I just lay near the wall, looking over at the stab mark that nearly killed me, Ella walked over to me. "Hey, are you all right?"

I just shook my head. "No, not really."

Ella just gave me a sympathetic smile. "Care to share?"

I just shook my head. "Because we showed him nothing but sympathy, he did that."

"Some people are just not good people, Jacob. It happens."

"But, why? What's wrong with this world? Why are people so cruel and evil?"

Ella just sighed. "I don't know, Jacob. This world just takes and takes. That bastard is lucky he didn't confront me. I would have destroyed that guy."

I just gave her a sympathetic smile in return, and something caught my eye.

"Ella, what happened to your face?"

Ella was confused. "What do you mean?"

"Your face is covered in bruises, and is that a black eye?"

Ella looked a bit nervous. "I just had a run-in with a guy. No big deal."

It sounded a bit sketchy, but I wasn't in the mood to argue. In a depressed state of mind, I just walked up to bed. "I am going to bed. Goodnight, everyone."

Ella and Anna just put up a hand. I don't know what happened after that, as I just collapsed back to sleep, still trying to process what had just happened. I knew that I was never going to forgive myself for letting Norman into this house.

CHAPTER 33

05-02-3026

WeapCo Industrial Factory – the main factory for WeapCo. All the weapons, aircraft, tanks and military equipment were built here and distributed to all different megacities across the world.

The factory was running in overdrive. Thanks to the effort created by Anna's political stunt, profits for defence companies were at an all-time low. WeapCo had lost over a billion dollars on the stock market and was boosting production to distribute across the globe in the hope of making back their losses through international sales.

"Unacceptable, Keith. We need those weapons distributed yesterday."

The production manager was this timid, young, 42-year-old guy with glass and a receding hairline. "Sir, the crew is already running overtime with little pay. They're on the verge of striking."

His manager didn't look so impressed at that statement. "Who gives a rat's arse about the employee? We have measures in place with the police to prevent unionising, so keep cutting pay and get it done. The CEO is breathing down my neck because that stupid girl opened her mouth on Holonet, and now the entire company is facing an economic crisis of epic proportions unless we can make back out money."

"Yes, sir."

"So, get it done then," the head manager said before storming out of the office and back into the car. The production manager was angry at being screamed at, but instead of doing the healthy thing, he decided to take it out on all the employees. He clapped his hands. "All right, let's get these weapons moving."

Behind him was an assembly line of a mixture of robots and humans building all sorts of guns at rapid rates.

Outside, the entire facility was covered with state-of-the-art security systems, including drones, metal barriers, anti-craft guns and laser turrets and was constantly being guarded by security with more weapons and manpower than the entire USD military combined. For anyone to get into this facility, it would require someone who was brave and incredibly suicidal. But there was one person who was all that and then some: Ella.

Ella would never forget, and she will never forgive WeapCo for taking her father from her, and she didn't care what Jacob was going through. She was resolute and determined to take down WeapCo. Ella was a complete contrast to Jacob; she had a fire in her soul that could not be contained. So while she wasn't running her shop, she was training and working out intensely, preparing for this moment.

On a skyscraper about four blocks away from the factory, Ella was in a prone position on a rooftop, trying to scope out the area through the scope of a state-in-the-art plasma-bolt sniper rifle, which was ironically produced and manufactured by WeapCo. But nevertheless, she had a job to do, and it was the perfect gun for it, as it was both silent and lethal.

Ella was dressed in the makeshift City Watcher outfit that Jacob hid in his little lair, looking at the state-of-the-art security to scope out the building. She noticed two guards who were heavily armoured, guarding the main gate, and like a cobra, she was ready to strike. She switched to thermal, and bang! Bang! The two guards went down to the ground from the velocity of the plasma bolts.

She had to hurry because soon, more guards would be on their way. Using her grapple gun, she fired the hook to the ground and used the gun to slide down to Ground Level.

Suddenly, the auto-turret sprang to life to take her down. Luckily, she came prepared, as on her utility belt were two makeshift shuriken, and with samurai-like precision, she managed to strike the turret scope directly, which disorientated it and caused it to shut down.

Quickly, she had to move, as the alarm blared throughout the building, and the lockdown procedures kicked in, which involved blaster and calibre-proof shutters blocking up the entire place.

Ella wasn't stuffing around, though. She bolted using her peak human speed to get to the shutter, and she managed to barely slide under the door just before it was magnetically sealed. But she had bigger problems. What was standing in front of Ella was a militia of over a hundred-foot soldiers, all heavy-armed, and above her were swarms of killer drones.

Then it occurred to her. She was going to have to do two things: first, use the shadow to her advantage, and second, use her environment. The place was littered with military equipment. Ella had been scoping this place out for months, so she knew where the generator was. She hid in an armoured Humvee, and from her back pocket, she pulled out a miniature suicide drone, which people would confuse with a fly, and with a special remote control, the drone buzzed to life. Ella began to pilot the drone towards the power generator, and once she was close, she pressed the self-destruct button, and BOOM! While the explosion wasn't powerful enough to damage the building, it shut down the generators, causing the backup generators to shoot on.

But she had another plan for that. In a rush, she sprinted out of the car and threw one of the shuriken she had retrieved from the turrets directly at the backup generator, which caused the entire place to go black and caused the production line to stop.

But that didn't stop the soldiers, as they were equipped with night-vision and thermal goggles, so the darkness didn't faze them at all. But it did give Ella – however limited – some stealth. Ella quickly bolted out of the generator room, as two soldiers came to inspect.

Ella was hiding behind the door, holding a combat knife in the belt. She attacked the first soldier and used his plasma rifle to blast through the armour of the soldier, killing him, and then took out the first soldier, killing him instantly.

She then took the impulse generated from the dead soldiers' bodies and moved quickly before the rest of the soldiers could show up. In a hurry, she bolted out of the room and rushed over to the assembly line of grenades. Then she pulled the pin, quickly bolted to the nearest Humvee, and BOOM! The grenades, like a chain of dominos, let loose fireballs that went everywhere. Luckily, the Humvee shielded her from the blast. But the fireball engulfed the room and killed half the men in the room. Now, it is for one versus fifty.

Ella quickly jumped out of the Humvee and began rushing towards the assembly line of weapons, but at that point, the soldiers took notice of her and opened fire at her. However, she was ready for a showdown, as on the conveyor belt behind her was a line with machine guns. She grabbed a mounted machine gun, loaded it up and began firing, as conveniently, the assembly line made for good cover as they were littered with planes and military equipment that she could duck and weave through.

Ella needed to use her environment if she was trying to get out of there. So she just shot at the objects around her: explosives, hanging objects, fully built planes. Anything shootable, she shot at it.

They still had a large number of highly trained soldiers, and she was completely outnumbered. But no matter, she was close to completing her objective, anyway. Trying to avoid calibre and laser fire, she quickly ran up to the manager's office and plugged her USB into the computer. Using her machine gun, she staged an uphill offence with the office window as a firing point.

Staggering the force, they all fled behind cover to return fire. But she only needed to hold on for another minute, then she heard the click as the USB memory glowed from red to green, and her mission was complete.

Quickly, she rushed to grab the USB stick, and using the override button in the manager's office, she removed the shield surrounding the building. But Ella was still stuck. How was she going to get out of there? Ella never thought that far ahead. She stopped for a minute, slowing down and ignoring the fire that was blasting past her head, then light bulb! She was just going to have to climb onto the roof.

She kicked out the manager's window and pressed the blaster-proof shutter, and a warning went out through the building. But before the shutters came down, she quickly jumped out of the window, and the shutters quickly came down, as the building became once again encased in the blaster-proof shutters. At that point, she jumped out the window and fell onto the ground. While the armour blocked some of the falls, she did feel some of the pain. Ella had to lie down for a couple of seconds before getting back up to leave the premises.

She needed some air, so she took off her helmet to take a deep breath, but she made a fatal mistake. She let her guard down. A soldier, who was outside the factory, grabbed her, threw her to the ground and began wailing at her.

Ella wasn't afraid to take a few punches, because she quickly shot the guard up and began punching the soldier in the chest, which did nothing, and the soldier began to choke her. At that point, Ella's fight-or-flight response kicked in, as a rush of adrenaline surged through her body, which made her smarter and stronger, and she quickly pushed the soldier back an inch, reached for his knife and stabbed him straight in the neck killing him instantly.

Now, with that rush of adrenaline, she began to bolt out of the factory as quickly as she could.

Ella just kept on running down the street, trying to get as much distance between her and that place as she could.

Finally, she stopped at a café, went over to the nearest person and snatched the laptop out of her hand, to which the lady responded with a "Hey!"

"I need this for a second!" Ella then plugged in the USB and logged into the dark web and leaked all of WeapCo's trade secrets online. She leaked the designs of their most simple weapons designs and specification documents, and she also sent them straight to Wacco INC. Ella gave the laptop back, sat down and took a sigh of relief. In one night, Ella not only caused structural damage to WeapCo's primary factory but also damaged WeapCo's production, causing millions in damages. But the pièce de résistance was that she leaked weapon and vehicle designs to WeapCo's competitors to replicate. Even if WeapCo was quick to take down the Infolink, it was now out in cyberspace, which meant that WeapCo's equipment was no longer superior, closing the tech gap from which WeapCo could not financially recover.

Ella was over the moon. There was no way John could ignore her now. So, in that café, she finally stopped and took a deep rest. But then, her mood was about to change from happy to shock. She left the café and quickly rushed down through the subway and into the Sewer Level to hide and place her equipment back for safekeeping. After getting undressed from the City Watcher suit, she got dressed back into her civilian clothing and made haste to Jacob's house. Ella stopped at the front door, and nothing seemed out of the ordinary, as the house was silent. But what lied inside was truly devastating.

Ella opened the door to reveal Anna and Jacob looking over the bloodstained couch where Edward's body remained, and against a far wall laid Norman's body on the floor with a bullet hole in his chest. Ella didn't know what to say. She was in shock, and then she burst into tears at the thought of

Edward being gone forever. All she could do was go over to Jacob and cry on his shoulder.

Ella was completely silent throughout the entire funeral. She barely said a word, except a lovely speech wishing Edward well. After Edward's body was buried, she struck up a conversation with Jacob, which resulted in him asking the question, "Ella, what happened to your face?"

Ella was confused and tried to think on her feet. "What do you mean?"

"Your face is covered in bruises, and is that a black eye?"

Ella looked a bit nervous but came up with a quick lie. "I just had a run-in with a guy. No big deal."

She was not going into any details.

CHAPTER 34

06-02-3026

The next day, I still couldn't fathom what had happened to Edward. I couldn't believe that Edward had been slaughtered right on our couch, and what was worse was that I wasn't able to save him. In fact, I let his killer sleep in our spare bedroom in the basement. How the hell did I let this happen? What was worse was that in my guilt, I knew he was a killer deep down; in fact, I literally saw a vision of Norman killing thousands of prisoners, and it completely slipped past my mind.

Today was definitely not a good morning, as I walked down the stairs and greeted poor Mum, who was trying to act as if everything was normal, eating cereal and drinking coffee, but I could see on her face that she was barely holding it together, as she was constantly look over at the empty space where our living room couch once stood. The breakfast was so awkward, neither of us could barely talk to each other, so I just scoffed down my breakfast, kissed Mum on the cheek and rushed to church.

I sat there looking at the cross on the altar, thinking to myself, *Who? Who am I trying to be?*

I tried so hard to live a quiet and stable life, but something deep inside of me still lingered: that burning rage to seek revenge. Because everything – and I mean everything in my life – I had to work hard for. I wasn't born into a rich family like the now-deceased Edward, and I certainly was not born a math prodigy like Ella. No, I just had to use my God-given hands and grit to get through all the tough times. But every time, every time something went right in my life, it was taken away from me: my family, my friends, all taken by people who have plenty but always want more.

While I was deep in thought, I felt a hand being placed on my shoulder, as my soldier's instinct automatically shot my entire body out of the chair, only to find Father Bruce stepping back a bit to calm me down. "Woah! Woah! Jacob, it's only just me."

After realising it was Father Bruce, I quickly calmed down. "Sorry, Father."

"Everything all right, Jacob?"

"Not really, Father. My best friend was murdered last night. Died right on my couch."

Father Bruce just looked at me shocked. "Oh my, I am sorry for your loss."

"Thank you, Father."

"How are you holding up?"

I sighed at that question. "Tell me something, Father. The Bible says, 'thou shall not kill', but I am a natural-born killer. I feel it in my bones. That's how I was programmed to respond ever since I went into the military, so how do I fight what I am programmed to do?"

Father Bruce was taken aback by that statement. "Well, I, look—"

I noticed Father Bruce was reaching for a phone of some sort.

"It's OK, Father, I am not planning to kill or hurt anyone. But I need to understand something. God created humans in his image, yet all we do is steal, lie and kill. Why?"

Father Bruce just let out a cough. "Well, Jacob, you're right. God created us in his image, and he created the heavens and the earth, but the problem is that this world has gotten sicker and sicker. Humans have only grown greedier and more bitter to the point that they not only poisoned their souls but the souls of others. Jacob, you have to seek help. You can't fight that urge by yourself."

"Father, look at where we live. Look at the state of the city. There is no help. They don't give a rat about us. They feed us with their products and expect us to just—"

"Just what, Jacob?"

I didn't finish that sentence, as it was pointless. "Father, how are we supposed to have morals in an immoral world? Forgive me, Father. I have wasted your time. I should—"

I tried to get out of my seat, but Father Bruce stopped me before I left. "Jacob, wait! Jacob, listen to me. It's easy to just lash out and hurt people, but it takes real strength to let go and move on. Jacob, if you want to find peace in this lifetime, you need to overcome that devil inside you and settle down."

Father Bruce then let me go.

"You're right, Father. Forgive me. I just need some time alone. Goodbye, Father."

Bruce gave me a sympathetic smile. "Best of luck, my boy."

I turned my back and walked out of that church deep in thought.

After stepping out of the church, I still couldn't shake the internal struggle that was gripping my soul. What was I to do? I mean, maybe Ella was right. Maybe it is not my job to be a monk. Maybe I should collude with Ella and Anna to just take down John. I mean, they were responsible for Edward's death and so many others.

But Father Bruce was also right. Killing John and seeking vengeance wouldn't solve anything, if I went down that path, I would end up destroying more than myself. There were so many paths to go down, and I felt more confused than ever. I just needed a walk to clear my head. I went for a light jog down the street. At least on a positive note, it was a bright and sunny day. But boy, it was great to see everyone, out and about since the peacekeepers were gone. Since they had been gone, businesses were bursting back to life, and people were free to roam around again and go about as they pleased.

I stopped in at the local convenience shop to grab a protein shake and a chocolate bar, but something caught my attention as I was in line about to pay for my shake. On the Holonet projector, a large banner read: "WeapCo Factory attacked!"

I was concerned. What did they mean by attack? I turned to the shop clerk. "Hey, do you mind turning it up?"

The shop clerk nodded, and I could now hear the voice of the news anchor.

"That's right, Phill. It was reported last night that a terrorist attack was launched on the factory late into the night, causing millions in damage and killing hundreds of people. The terrorist's motives were unclear, and the only image that was recovered was this person in a suit. To figure out—"

At that moment, my focus was on the image. I wasn't even listening to what the anchor was saying. I kept my concentration on the image. I had seen that before.

It occurred to me who it was. "Ella!"

I was furious. I threw the change at the clerk and stormed out of the shop. I couldn't believe Ella had been so stupid as to ignore my advice and not only kill more people but also anger one of the most powerful corporations in American Division City.

After leaving the shop, I went straight down to the Sewer Level and went into my secret hideout, where I kept that old suit. It was what I had expected. The place was loaded with weapons. The whiteboard that had all the intel on WeapCo was set up once again, and in the corner was the container with the suit. I walked over to the metal container and opened it to find the suit stacked in there neatly, but the paint on it had been chipped. It had been worn. Someone has used it. Then I began to hear splashes, as footsteps made their way into the lair. I shot up quickly and scrambled to find a place to hide.

Ella walked into the lair, rocking out to jams through her headphones, not a care in the world. But she quickly turned around to find me standing in the middle of the room with her face like a deer in headlights. She froze, and out of shock, she dropped her protein smoothie all over the floor.

"Ugh, Jacob, a—"

"What are you doing down here, Ella?"

"Oh, you know, just here to do some cleaning. This place was a bit dirty."

What a load of rubbish, but I played along. "Oh, were you? Then why is all this stuff out?"

"Oh, haha, you know me. Just like to be thorough."

"Give it up, Ella. I know you were behind that attack on the factory!"

"So what if I was? Just because you want out doesn't mean the rest of us are going to give up!"

"Does Anna know about this?"

"NO, Jacob, it was just me and me alone."

"What the actual hell are you thinking, bringing that kind of heat on us?"

"Jacob I am not just going to stand by while we have a chance to take down WeapCo. If I didn't do anything, they would recover. I saw an opportunity, and I took it."

"Ella, have you actually stopped to consider the consequences of your actions? Now they are going seek retaliation and hurt more people, more of my family. It's fine if you want to destroy yourself, but don't drag me and Anna down with your problem."

"Jacob, I never asked you to get involved. You may want to live an apple pie life, but I am not just going to stand by and let that company rise back up, not after they killed my father!"

"Ella, your father is dead and buried, and he is going to stay that way. Don't go down that road, or you will be sharing a grave next to him."

Ella was breathing heavily, and her face was as red as a tomato. "Wow, Jacob! Just, wow. You prick," she said, pointing her finger at me. "Look, I don't know what happened to you, if you have just lost your mind or whatever, but I am not going let you stand here and control my behaviour and my actions. My mission in life is to get revenge for my father, for what John has taken from me. Don't dare judge me. How many people have you killed? You encouraged us to stand and fight, and now that the going is getting tough, you just want to walk away and act holier than thou. Well, screw you, Jacob. For me, finding peace involves John's head on a platter! I don't have to take this crap!"

Ella turned around and began walking out of the lair.

"Ella, if you go down that path, you will end up no better than him."

Ella just scoffed. "No better. Fine, but at least I will die standing for my belief and being who I am. The question is, who are you, Jacob Exactly, nothing but a liar and a hypocrite, and you will die as nothing."

I was left in complete silence. Ella stormed out of the lair to who knows where, and frankly, who cares. I tried to calm down, but I couldn't. I was boiling up inside to the point, and I redirected my anger by kicking the whiteboard. How could Ella be so selfish? I kept thinking over and over in my head, "How could she?"

Then, as I calmed my mind down, it became clearer and clearer. She was just doing what she thought was right. I took in a deep breath and sighed. *She is right. I didn't know who I was, and I kept pretending to be a good guy. But the truth is, I am not. I am just a man, a flawed, broken man, and I am just kidding myself with this whole born-again stuff. The truth is that I was wearing a metaphorical mask. I am pretending to be something I am not. I am so confused.*

I just paced up and down the lair, troubled and conflicted.

CHAPTER 35

Iwas so confused. I mean, why couldn't Ella see that vigilante justice wouldn't bring her father back and that sometimes, doing the right thing is just letting go and moving on? But no, Ella was on a suicide mission, and what was worse was that she was dragging my family down with her, and that made me so mad.

After finally making it home, I walked into the house, trying to quell my anger and pretend like everything was normal for Anna. I walked in the door to find Anna sitting on the floor in the middle of the day watching the Holonet.

"Hey Ma, how are you enjoying your day off?"

She didn't respond at all. She was just staring at the Holonet as if something had caught her eye, and telling by the look of concern on her face, it wasn't good. I walked over out of concern. "Mum, is everything OK?"

Then I realised what Anna was concerned about. The Holonet was playing a news broadcast of the Warehouse Terrorist Attack on the screen.

Anna's face went from concerned to angry, and she shot me a dirty look. "Jacob, do you care to explain this?"

"I don't know, Mum."

"Don't you lie to me. I know that suit anywhere. It's modelled after the comic books you used to read as a kid."

"Mum, I don't know what you are talking about."

Anna was now angry. "Jacob, I raised you, and I can tell when you are lying to me. Do you care to explain this?"

I just sighed. "All right, fine. I designed a suit so that when we were going to take down WeapCo, it would give me protection. I hid it in Yandan's old hideout."

Anna just shook her head. "You hypocrite, Jacob! You forced me and Ella to give up violence, and here you are running around like some comic book hero."

"IT WASN'T ME, Mum! Ella found the suit and is now on some revenge mission to take down WeapCo on her own."

Anna's face looked even more concerned. "Ella? Why would she—"

I interrupted her mid-sentence. "Because she is still angry about her dad and wants to finish his mission."

"Jacob, that factory is the main production line of WeapCo, and she attacked it! John is not going to let that slide. We have to help her."

"No! Absolutely not!"

"Jacob, she is our friend and our family."

"Anna, we have gotten out! We have to focus on moving up and forward with our lives."

"No, you decided that, Jacob. When did you start to dictate our behaviour and actions?"

"Anna, all I want is peace in our life—"

"But that doesn't mean the rest of us want that. WeapCo has screwed us!"

"Anna, everything and everyone screw us. That's life. We can't just go around killing everyone who's wronged us. We just have to accept it and move on."

"Look, Jacob, I get you're scared—"

"Scared? Anna, all I am trying to do is keep us safe and alive. How many times do I have to keep explaining it?"

"But Jacob, we can't just keep hiding. WeapCo is coming after us now—"

"No, they are after Ella. We were never involved in this mess. That's Ella's doing."

"No, Jacob, she is our family. We are not going to abandon her to fight WeapCo by herself."

"Well, I am sorry, Anna, but she made her choice. Now I have to make my choice."

"Well, Jacob, you don't decide for me. That's your decision. I want to keep fighting!"

"So you want to share a grave with Ella and Yandan, do you?"

Anna just shook her head. "Oh, Jacob! When did you become so selfish?"

"When I decided that there is more than taking down corporations and killing people. I mean, we have a chance to live in peace and become better, and I am not throwing it away playing superhero."

"Let me be clear, Jacob. I am helping Ella, and you can't stop me! If you are out, that's fine, but I am going to stick with her."

"Then don't expect me to bail you out!"

Anna got up and walked out the front door. But before she left, she turned to me. "I don't know about you, but I don't turn my back on my family. Enjoy the peace, but you will have to share it by yourself. I want to keep fighting!"

"DON'T YOU DARE—"

But before I could speak, Anna slammed the door behind her, not telling me where she was going. I was so angry to the point that I punched the wall behind me, leaving a giant dent in the wall. My life and my family were crumbling because the two of them couldn't let go of their need for vengeance. So I am just supposed to let everything in my life slip away? I knew I was in the right, and no one could convince me otherwise.

But what annoyed me the most was that I had to stand alone. What was wrong with the two of them? Well, fine. I was tired of being the responsible one in the family. If they wanted to get themselves killed, it was on them. My internal rage began to boil up. I should have never made that stupid suit or even joined Yandan's stupid cause. Fed up, I grabbed a lighter from the kitchen drawer and began making my way back down to the Sewer Level. I was going to end this now once and for all.

I began heading down to the sewer lair, not thinking and not paying attention to anything around me. My plan was to find that suit, steal it, destroy it, and burn any documents down in that stupid lair. This whole thing had been a mistake from the start.

I finally arrived in the lair and opened the container, but it was gone! Ella must have been out and about, but where, I thought.

I looked around the lair for any clues and found plans of the old munitions warehouse on the whiteboard. It appeared that Ella got a source of information off the internet that appeared to indicate that WeapCo was planning to smuggle weapons down to the Lower Level.

While it was none of my business, I was concerned for my mum and Ella's safety, so I went in to investigate. But it wasn't making any sense. Where did it come from? Who was the source? And how did they know?

The information seemed to have come from an anonymous source, which was already concerning. The source had blueprints. However, the information didn't disclose the security measures or why WeapCo is using that building. This information wasn't making any sense, but suddenly, it dawned on me. *Oh no!* I thought.

This information was false. I had to find Ella and Mum quickly. Luckily for me, I knew where to find her.

Meanwhile, Ella didn't care what Jacob was saying. If he wanted to be a placid sheep, then let him. Honestly, she couldn't care less. She had a mission to complete, and she was going to fulfil it.

Ella was once again on a skyscraper, scoping out her target: the old munition factory.

Ella got a tip through the dark web that WeapCo was secretly using their surplus of weapons that they manufactured and were supplying it to gangsters and warlords down in Mercy Lane, and Ella intended to put a stop to it.

Ella looked through her sniper rifle, but there was no security in there, and when she used her thermal scope, she detected no heat signatures whatsoever. Ella didn't know what to think of it. It was indeed strange, but it was a chance to land another crippling blow to WeapCo. Of course, she would take it.

After a final scope of the building, there was still nothing. But she could see vans and cars outside.

Ella, not thinking, had to jump at the opportunity. She shot her grapple hook to one of the uncharged power cables and slid down to the road. Quickly, she rushed behind one of the cars, and still, there was nothing: no guards outside patrolling the grounds, no drones, there was nothing. Now, Ella was concerned. Was this a trap? Her inner voice was saying, *No! That's ridiculous. Maybe I've already caused more damage to WeapCo than I realised.*

Ella dropped her guard and walked to the old, rusted front door and opened it to find John himself sitting on a metal chair, on his phone, pretending there was nothing there. Ella walked in and pointed a Glock directly at his head. "Freeze, dirtbag!"

In a cocky gesture, John pointed up a finger as he was finishing a text. Ella looked confused. Didn't this guy know that she was pointing a gun directly at his head?

John then placed his phone in his pocket and looked up at Ella. "Ah, Ella, come on in," he said, smiling.

"Don't you see the gun in your face, dumbass?"

John then snapped his finger.

Crap! Ella thought. *It was a trap.*

The hologram of John disappeared, and suddenly out of nowhere, at least 50 soldiers swarmed the room with their guns drawn, all pointed at Ella. They were wearing thermal-masking ghillie suits, which explains why Ella wasn't able to pick them up on her scope.

Suddenly, Ella's phone began to buzz through her pocket. She reached into her pocket and picked it up to find that it was an 'unknown number'.

"Hello?"

"Did you think I would be that stupid?"

"John!"

"Did you really think that you and your gang of losers could not outmatch me? You destroyed my assets, ruined my company's reputation, and you think you can get away with it? No matter. Once I take care of you, I will wipe the floor with Anna and Jacob."

"THE HELL YOU WILL!" Ella threw the phone at the ground, smashing it, and then out of the back of her utility belt, she grabbed a smoke pallet and threw it to the ground, releasing a cloud of smoke that covered the warehouse.

Then, with a Glock in her hand, she began unleashing fire, but it was futile, as the guards could see through the smoke, and bang! Ella stopped in shock as she felt pain surging through her body. While she was wearing body armour, the rifle the soldiers were using used higher-calibre bullets. Thank goodness they weren't using plasma, or that would have shot straight through her and she would have died.

But there was a problem. The soldier shot her straight in the back, snapping her vertebra, and Ella's entire body went numb. She collapsed to the floor, lying in her blood. What was worse was that she couldn't feel her legs.

The soldiers encircled her, and she was powerless to do anything to get out of it. She guessed this was where she would die. She watched as the soldier in front of her pulled out a combat knife, and Ella felt so afraid to the point that she was seeing her life flash before her eyes.

The soldier gripped his knife and snickered. "Hahaha, I am going to enjoy this."

The soldier went in to stab Ella, and she quickly closed her eyes, knowing she was about to die, but she heard a whooshing sound, and she opened her eyes to find the soldier with a hole in his chest.

The soldier collapsed to the floor dead. The soldiers around him all began to panic after seeing the body of their dead mate. Their leader screamed, "Spread out!"

The remaining soldiers all ran around, trying to figure out where the shot had come from. Suddenly, another shot rang through the warehouse, as a blue plasma bolt landed straight into one of the soldiers who was standing near the door. Now Ella was curious as to who the shooter was. Then Ella saw her phone buzzing, but couldn't feel it, which was a concerning sign. Nonetheless, Ella reached into her pocket and saw on the bloodied phone screen a text from Jacob that read: 'Stay there I am coming for you'.

Ella was confused. Jacob? How did he know that I was here?

After discovering the information in the lair, I quickly made my way to the warehouse, and I managed to find Ella's sniper rifle on the rooftop that she left just outside the warehouse.

Finding it, I decided to scope out the area for any clues regarding Ella. I used its thermal scope to reveal that, just as I had expected, she had walked into an ambush. The thermal scope revealed a body signature lying on the ground, and the warehouse was surrounded by multiple different heat signatures.

I began to panic. Ella was in trouble, and I had to help her, or she was going to die!

I got into a prone position and got the rifle ready, firing the rifle into the soldier closest to Ella.

I guess I had to say goodbye to being a 'saint', but I didn't care. My friend was in trouble, and I had to help her. While I may not always agree with Ella, Mum was right. She is family, and I care for her well-being, and if it meant carrying a few more voices in my head, then so be it.

Meanwhile, inside the factory, the soldiers were panicking and scrambling around trying to figure out where the shots were coming from. Poor Ella just lay on the floor not feeling anything in her lower body. She slowly lost consciousness from the blood loss.

The soldiers finally picked up that the shots were coming from the skyscraper in front of the factory, but it still gave me an advantage. However, I had to be fast, as Ella needed medical attention.

The soldiers were quickly making their way up to me. Then I saw the grapple line that Ella had shot previously, and using the sniper rifle, I slid down the line and landed on my arse in front of the warehouse. But what I saw in front of me completely shocked me. I found Ella lying on the floor in a pool of blood.

"Ella!" I screamed out in complete shock. "What have they done to you?"

I had to get her to a hospital.

As I approached Ella's body, she looked up at me and began to cry. "Jacob, I am so—"

I just placed a finger in front of her mouth. "Don't worry about that now. Let's get you out of here."

I picked up Ella's body and slung her over my shoulders. I had to move, as the soldiers had realised that I had zip-lined down to the warehouse and were making their way back down.

The soldiers began chasing me, and I couldn't fight them back as I had Ella over my shoulders. All I could really do was run for it. Guess I only had one option. I had to suck up my pride and call Anna. Quickly using my phone, I gave Anna a call, but she didn't pick up. I sent her a text, but I didn't have time to wait for a response, as more soldiers had begun to make their way to the warehouse.

"Blast!" With no weapons or options, I just had to leg it down the street and hope for the best.

I tried the best I could, running as fast as my legs would let me, taking back alleys and turning every corner I could. It wasn't easy carrying a body over my shoulder, but I had to make do until I tripped, which caused me to fall and drop Ella's body. I tried to get back up, but a soldier had pinned me to the ground. I tried to fight back up, but there were too many of them, and all the soldiers had their guns pointed directly at me.

Then, screaming down the road came a floating car, and who was behind the wheel of the hijacked car? None other than Mum.

Mum jumped out of the car and rolled on the ground, while the car slammed into the soldiers, knocking them down temporarily. After getting to her feet, Anna rushed towards me and picked me and Ella up. "Come on, let's go."

I grabbed one of the flash grenades on Ella's utility belt and threw it at the soldier. "Bang!" It worked too, because the soldiers were more susceptible due to the goggles, they were all wearing.

Anna helped me carry Ella, and we just started running down the street. We ran as fast as we could, but no luck, as we turned a corner, it was a dead end. But we weren't really worried about our own lives, as Ella was mainly on our minds, and she was bleeding out quick. If we didn't get her medical treatment, she would die.

"Crap! What do we do now, Jacob?"

I scoped out the area. "The fire escape!"

"Jacob, stop!"

"Mum, what are you doing?"

Anna signalled to me, "Just turn around!"

I didn't argue with her, and I just showed her my back.

She tied Ella to my back with her belt and tied her utility belt around my waist, thus allowing me to climb up the fire escape.

"Jacob, get out of here! The soldiers are going to be coming down here any moment. You need to go!"

"But Mum!"

"No buts, son. I will be a distraction." She then pulled out the small pistol Ella had as a backup "NOW GO!"

"But Mum!"

"What, Jacob?"

I gave her a big hug. "I love you, Mum."

She hugged me in return. "I love you too, son. Now go!"

Not refusing her order, I climbed up the fire escape, as the soldiers came down the corner. Anna began shooting at the soldiers to get their attention, and it worked. Anna unloaded a few shots, but they were nothing against the heavily armoured soldiers, as the bullets just bounced off their armour. The soldiers laughed and rushed towards her, knocking her to the ground and pinning her down. But it worked, as their attention was off me, which allowed me to climb up the fire escape onto the roof.

I paused temporarily, as the soldier pinned her to the ground. "Where are the others?"

Instead, she told them where to stick it, which got her a punch to the head, and the soldiers picked her up and began dragging her away. I watched in horror as the soldiers carried away my mum, but I couldn't help, as Ella needed urgent medical attention.

I began parkouring across the buildings, trying to get some distance between me and the soldiers. By the time the soldiers had realised we had taken the fire escape, we were long gone.

But I had to hurry, as I could feel Ella grow weaker, and I knew she couldn't hear me. Still, I whispered to her, "Don't worry, Ella. I will get you there!"

I hopped across rooftop after rooftop, as the sky grew darker and darker. I knew where to go, but it was a matter of finding them, but my mum was still on my mind. How could I just abandon her like that? It should have been me to sacrifice myself for her. But nevertheless, I was here, and I needed to get Ella home.

Almost there, I kept thinking to myself, and finally, I made it! I walked down the fire escape and approached the basement door, and I knocked on the door once. No answer.

I knocked again, and finally, I got an answer, as Dr Kim and Courtney opened the door and found me tired and near tears, with a passed-out Ella strapped to my back. They were in complete shock to see me again and were in more shock to see Ella in that state.

"Help us, please!"

CHAPTER 36

I guess history really is doomed to repeat itself. If only Ella and Anna had listened to me.

The anxiety from Ella's injury and Mum being kidnapped was the only thing that was plaguing my mind.

What do I do? How am I supposed to fix this? I just don't how.

I felt so lost and confused at that moment, but the only thing I could really do was be patient and wait for the doctor to tell me about Ella. But still, it should have been me down there instead of Anna.

After reading the Bible for an hour, I saw Courtney rush in with the same hospital gown she wore to treat Ella's father. "How is she, Courtney?"

Courtney just sighed. "Well, we managed to keep her alive, but she has damaged her spinal cord along the A3 vertebra, so she is paralysed from the waist down. She is never going to walk again."

The two of us just stood there in silence. That poor girl.

"Can I see her?" I asked.

"No, she needs her rest, Jacob."

"Thank you for all you have done, Courtney!"

Courtney then grabbed my arm. "Hey, Jacob, are you all right?"

I shook my head. "No, not really. Ella's in the hospital, Edward is dead, my mum is either dead or being tortured, and I feel as if my life is falling apart."

Courtney then took off her gown and gave me a hug, as the tears ran down my face. "There, there, my dear boy. You have been through a lot, haven't you?"

After the hug, I brushed off the tears. "Come on, Kim's making dinner."

Both Courtney and I walked up the basement stairs into the girl's living room, and they set up a plate for me.

Kim was in an apron, and she was cooking the most delicious steak, potato bake, and veggies I had ever tasted. Over dinner, I told Kim and Courtney everything that had happened with the factory ambush, Ella getting shot, and Mum being kidnapped.

"So, Jacob, what are you going to do now?"

I just shook my head in confusion. "To tell you the truth, I don't know anymore. It's just that I have lost so much, and I don't know how to get it back."

"Are you going to get them back?"

"I don't know. I just don't know where to start or where to go."

"Well, you got to do something, Jacob."

I sighed. "But I am just one man, Courtney, and John has an entire company behind him. I can barely have my sanity. How can I get Anna back?"

Courtney and Kim didn't know how to respond to that, so we just went back to eating dinner in silence. But my appetite was gone, and I just wanted to go home, so I stood up and placed my plate in the sink. "Sorry, girls, I don't feel like eating. In fact, I need to go for a walk if you don't mind."

"OK. We will contact you when Ella is awake and able to see visitors."

I just got up, but as I was about to walk out the door, Courtney grabbed my attention. "Jacob wait! Jacob, Yandan has died, Ella is paralysed and your mum is gone. Please don't follow them by seeking revenge. Call the police or something? Just don't go after them by yourself, or you will end up losing more than—"

"Then what? My soul? That is long gone. I may have lost everything, but I can't lose my family. They are all I have left."

I walked out and slammed the door.

I didn't know what to do, honestly. I thought I could live a life of peace, but I now realised that if I wanted peace for my family, I had to prepare for war. So, trying to think about my next step, I made my way home in the dark. Something lit up the night sky. What was that? It looked like—

No! I said to myself. *No! No! No!*

I began running down the street as the glow grew brighter and brighter, and I finally arrived to find my house, my family home, lit ablaze.

The people from WeapCo must have done it. The entire house was up in flames, and I just collapsed to my knees in absolute shock, as the two-storey house crumbled down into the ground. My home! The house that we had to rebuild, the home and land we fought to keep, were all gone.

After the flames dimmed down, all that was left was ashes and nothing more. The fire had burnt all our possessions away. There was nothing left. I salvaged through anything I could find, but it was a waste. I didn't know what to say except for one question: why?

I didn't hurt anyone. I only just wanted to find peace, and this happened. I just couldn't take it anymore. I collapsed into tears. We didn't have building insurance down here, so I had no money and no home to go to.

In a last-ditch effort, I continued to search through the rubble in hopes of finding anything. There was something in the rubble. I managed to find one thing, one thing that remained intact, and it was … a samurai sword? My dad had brought it home from his time in the Pacific. He found it in the ruins of an old, Japanese Shogun Temple. It was a bit rusted, given its time, but it was still a remarkable piece of Japanese history. I looked at the sword and admired its beauty.

I pulled the sword out of its scabbard and looked at the rusty blade. But something inside me began to burn. It was the fire I thought had been extinguished years ago. I could feel my eyes burn with rage.

Screw peace, and screw being the good guy. WeapCo had hurt and killed my friends, had taken and hurt my family multiple times, and now they have taken my house. I am going to destroy that corporation if it is the last thing I do.

I threw the sword back into the rubble and walked away. I took one final look at the rubble that was my house, and I began to walk away. No point looking back, because I knew I was not coming back.

Then, I received a text from Courtney. "Ella is awake."

I rushed down to find Ella lying on the hospital bed weak and broken and full of pipes and wires. She was barely conscious, so I just stood at the end of the hospital bed waiting for her to face me. Ella saw me, and she just had a little smile on her face.

"Fancy seeing you here." She let out a series of coughs. Even when she was at her weakest, she still had her humour.

I smirked and walked over to Ella. "How are you doing, Ella?"

Her smile disappeared, and she lay back in her hospital bed. "I feel like crap. I can't feel my legs."

"Ella I—"

Before I could continue to speak, she interrupted me. "I know, Jacob. I am paralysed. I am never going to walk again."

"I am sorry, Ella."

Ella let out a tear. "That means I will never be able to run again, walk again, box again. I am confined to a wheelchair for my whole life!"

"I am sorry, Ella."

Her tears began flooding out. "What have I done?"

I rushed in to hug Ella. "There, there. Ella, you are going to be all right. You are alive! That's all that matters."

After a few tears, Ella just lay there and looked at her feet, and both of us stood there in silence, trying to take it all in. Ella looked over at the empty hospital bed next to her. "Funny, right over there—"

I was confused and looked over at the hospital bed. "Over there?" I asked.

Ella reaffirmed what I had said. "Over there is where my father died."

"Ella, I—"

"Don't, Jacob, just don't. You were right."

"About what, Ella?"

"About everything. About seeking revenge, about letting anger consume me and about paying the price. I just—" She lay back down and didn't say anything, trying to hold back her tears. "I just thought that if I managed to take down WeapCo, then my dad would finally have peace, that his death wasn't for nothing, but instead, I nearly went the same way as him."

"Ella, that's not on you. You fought all you could."

"And yet, Jacob, I have nothing. I have lost my ability to walk, and I just feel emptier than ever."

Ella lay down in her bed, tired and sad. "Can I see Anna?"

I couldn't tell her, so I just walked over to her and laid a hand on her shoulder. "She is fine back at home. You just rest."

I lied to her because she wasn't ready to know what had happened to the house and to Anna.

Ella just lay there and slowly began to close her eyes. I couldn't help but look at the blood-covered hospital bed next to her. How ironic that she lay right next to where her father had died. It was truly sad. We have come so far in our journey since then. While Ella was an independent person, it sometimes felt as if Yandan lived on the inside of Ella, as if Yandan possessed her and carried his anger and hatred inside.

I just watched her sleep like an angel, but my sorrow and sympathy for Ella quickly dispersed. Instead, I was consumed by contempt and anger towards John and WeapCo for taking everything I had in my life. I couldn't look at her anymore. The grief and sorrow had overtaken me, and I had to get out of there. I went outside to catch my breath.

I had survived so much – wars, prisons, conflicts, betrayals – but it was at this moment that I felt more alone than ever.

This must have been one of the first times in my life that I had to go into it alone. What got me through all those problems in my life were the friends and family beside me. But with Anna gone, Ella incapacitated and Edward resting in peace, I had no one to help me out of this situation. Normally, I knew all the answers to the questions ahead, thanks to my years of military experience, street smarts and age. But now I realised that maybe I didn't really know everything. But I had lost everything, all because I dropped my guard and got soft.

I couldn't stop thinking about Ella in the hospital bed and Anna being who knows where, or Edward lying on that couch with his throat slit. The memories kept replaying repeatedly in my mind. I may not be a psychologist, but even I knew what it meant. I felt as if I had failed them and let them down. Since Dad died, I had to be the protector of the family and the head of the household, being the one who had to take care of Mum, and in a way, I guess that was what I was trying to do. I was hoping that by getting Ella and Anna to live a normal life, they could get their mind off of vengeance and instead enjoy the rest of their lives. But I guess I was wrong. I should have been there for Ella, I shouldn't have let Anna sacrifice herself, and I sure as hell shouldn't have let Norman anywhere near my family. I was so lost in life, I didn't know where to go from there, and I guess there was only one person out there who I thought knew all the answers, a man who had years of experience, wisdom and knowledge over me.

So, with no other option, I decided to head to church, hoping to find some answers from Father Bruce.

I headed into an old, historic church. But it seemed like Father Bruce wasn't here, as there was not a light in sight. But even with no one in there, I could feel the building calling at me as if I was supposed to be in. I pushed open the wooden doors and looked out over the church seats that should have been filled with people, but they were completely empty, and in front of the chairs lay the altar where the white linen lay over the tables with candles that weren't lit. The only thing illuminating the church was the lights radiating through the stained-glass windows of famous figures throughout the Bible.

Honestly, it was kind of creepy looking at the church at night, and I didn't even know why I was in there, but something was calling me to the altar. I don't know if it was desperation, but I approached the altar and looked at the wooden cross, marvelling at its glory. I looked around, hoping to find Father Bruce, as he always had a way of finding me in this building.

But for the life of me, I couldn't feel him. I couldn't feel his presence in this place. Therefore, I opened the book and began reading it, but none of it was making any sense to me. How was this verse supposed to help me in life? Then, out of nowhere, a gust of wind blew through the church and blew the pages of the Bible all over the place. Luckily, I managed to stop the book on a certain page. I couldn't see the whole page, as it was too dark for me to see, but I could read a verse: "Do not be overcome by evil but overcome evil with good" (Romans 12:19).

I read the verse but didn't understand what it meant. I tried to read it out loud, but it wasn't making sense. What did it mean?

Then I heard his voice. "It means to overcome evil inside of you or the evil around you by doing good deeds."

I looked up from the Bible, and I saw him in the chairs. *Every time I need him, he is there, like a spirit or something supernatural, with his old beads and his black shirt with the white collar.*

I looked up at him. "Why are you always here whenever I need you?"

Bruce just smiled. "I get that a lot."

He then got out of the stands. With a snap of his fingers, the entire church lit up, which amazed me.

I just looked at him confused. "How did you do that?"

He smiled. "You never heard of a clapper? It's very ancient technology. Long, long before your time, my boy. But then again, the past never seems to amaze us. As we keep moving forward, we sometimes forget that the past has a lot to offer us, as we have much to learn from it."

Bruce then made his way to the altar and gave me a hug. "It's good to see you again, Jacob."

I still wasn't used to his hugs, so I just tapped him on his shoulders awkwardly.

"Come, my dear boy, take a seat."

I did, not quite knowing why.

"I sense that you are not here to talk about relics from the past. What's on your mind?"

I told Bruce everything. Finally, I ended my narration by asking, "What do I do?"

Father Bruce rubbed his beard, and he just looked at me blankly. "I don't know."

I looked at him shocked. "Father, what do you mean you don't know?"

He just shrugged. "I don't know."

"What, you don't know how to fix this, or you just don't know?"

"I don't know, Jacob. I am sorry, but I don't know how to fix the mistakes of other people. They are not your concern." Father Bruce then stood up. "Jacob, God gave people free will and the ability to make their own choice. You can't be held responsible for the decisions of other people. You see, my friend, every choice you make has consequences, whether you like it or not, consequences that are determined by the actions you take. Take your friends, for example. Your friend Ella chose to let her anger dictate her choice, and for that, she suffers in pain. Your mum, on the other hand, made the choice of love, and while she may have to suffer for it, she will rest safely knowing that her son is safe from harm. And as for your friend, yes, he only chooses to sleep on the couch, but it was the decision of another that cost him his life. Does that make any sense, Jacob?"

"Honestly, Father, that is absolutely terrible advice. I mean, I know that actions have consequences, but what does that have to do with trying to fix things."

"The advice I am trying to give you Jacob is that it's not your job to fix these things. You can help everybody some-times, but bad things happen in life because of the actions of others or themselves. But if you think you can fight evil with more evil, then you will end up causing more suffering for more people."

"But Father, what's the alternative? I just wait around and let evil people get away with what they have done to me?"

"Jacob, you can't keep using violence to solve your prob-lems. Violence is evil. You have to forgive. Forgive John. Forgive Norman. But most importantly, you must forgive yourself." Bruce then walked over to me. "Jacob, you and your family have suffered more than most, because you keep using violence to solve your problems, and I hate to tell you, but what you are fighting for will only lead to more suffering. Jacob, let go. You won't help anyone by going into WeapCo guns blazing. If you want to stop fighting, find peace and let go. Stop trying to control your circumstances by fighting. Let go!"

"Bruce, I can't just let my mum die if there is even a chance that she is still alive, and I certainly can't let John get away with hurting my family. I am sorry, Father, but I can't. I can't just let John get away with what he has done to me and to my family. I am sorry, Bruce, but you are wrong."

Then I don't know what happened next, but my vision started to go blurry, and the church began to swirl in my head. I looked at Father Bruce, and his eyes began to glow red, and his voice took an insidious turn: "THEN YOU WILL CONTINUE TO SUFFER FOREVERMORE, UNTIL YOUR RAGE BURNS AWAY WHOEVER GETS CLOSE TO YOU."

I was starting to get dizzier and dizzier, and then I collapsed onto the floor of the church.

My head felt dizzy, and I woke up to broad daylight. It appears that I had slept through the night, as there was bright yellow light shining through the stained-glass windows.

Once again, the church was empty, and there was no one in sight, but what had I seen, it must have been my mind playing tricks on me again.

Then Father Bruce walked into the church. "Hey Jacob, are you all right?"

I got up and looked around confused. "What am I doing here? Father, don't you remember what had happened last night?"

"Jacob, I don't know what you are talking about. I was at home resting. I was never here last night."

What the—, I thought to myself. What had just happened?

"Never mind, Father. I best be going on my way. Take care."

Father Bruce smiled at me. "Take care, my boy."

But as I was walking out of the church, I heard Father Bruce's voice in my head, "Remember, Jacob, unless you learn to let go, you will never find peace."

I looked over at Father Bruce, who clearly didn't say anything, and I just thought that I must be going crazy. I just walked out of the church not saying a word and began heading back to the hospital to go visit Ella. I was still weirded out by the encounter with Father Bruce, but after what I had been through the past month, I was kind of used to it. During the walk to the hospital, I kept going over in my mind what he was saying. "How could I let go when every time I try to let go, I just dragged into another war."

But anyway, I had to let that go for now. I was on a mission, so I knocked on the basement door and was greeted by Courtney. "Jacob, where have you been?"

Courtney's face looked concerned, but I decided to brush it off. "I just needed to get out of this place for a while."

"Oh, OK, well, since you are here, I am happy to report that a certain friend of yours is up and about."

Now I was excited, "Really? Ella is awake?"

"Not just awake. Come on and see her."

I rushed down the stairs and found Ella, Courtney, and Kim greet me with a "surprise!" Ella was out of bed and full of energy again.

"Ella? You're back to your old self again?"

Ella smiled. "No, Jacob, I am better than my old self again. Check it out."

Ella was in a wheelchair, which she beautifully designed herself.

While it was a massive difference seeing Ella in a wheelchair, it was great to see her almost back to her old self again. I smiled. "Ella, it's beautiful."

Ella just looked down at her legs. "It's going to be a bit of a difference, but I will adjust."

I placed my hand on her shoulder. "Well, regardless, it's a beautiful chair."

She smiled back at me. Ella turned around to Courtney and Kim. "Do you mind if Jacob takes me for a walk around town? I need some sunlight."

Courtney and Kim both looked at each other with a smile. "I don't see why not. You don't mind do you, Jacob?"

I walked behind Ella's wheelchair. "It would be my pleasure, Ella."

Courtney, Kim and I pushed Ella up the stairs, and Courtney and Kim went back inside to allow me and Ella to be alone.

Ella was still getting used to her wheelchair, so she needed me to push it. But honestly, I didn't mind. I enjoyed the company.

"How you been doing, Ella?"

"All right, Jacob. I'm still adjusting to my new life as a cripple, but I am slowly getting the hang of it. I need to build up my upper body strength a bit more. But besides that, I am doing all right. How about you, Jacob? How are you holding up?"

I just sighed. I was tired as hell, but for the sake of Ella's well-being, I had to maintain a positive attitude. "I am holding up all right, Ella, especially now that you are all right."

Ella's positive attitude quickly shifted. "Jacob, how long are you going to keep lying to me? I have been around you for a long time, and I know when you are lying to me."

I sighed. Again, of course, Ella was a smart person, and she knew me well. I bit my tongue. "The truth is, Ella, I am struggling just like you are."

Ella and I just stopped. "Jacob, you were right. The move I had made was selfish, and it got me hurt and Anna captured, and I am sorry."

"No Ella, I was wrong. I thought we could live in peace once we got rid of the peacekeepers, but I was wrong. We will never be at peace as long as WeapCo and John still exist."

Ella licked her lips. "Jacob, why didn't you tell me about Anna and our home?"

"The truth is, Ella, I wasn't ready to tell you, because you were unwell and—"

"You wanted to spare my feelings." There was a silence for a moment, and then Ella broke the silence. "Jacob, do you know what I saw when I was lying in that pool of blood?"

I didn't say a word, as it was a rhetorical question. "I saw my father, Jacob. I saw the fire go out in his eyes as he lay there on his hospital bed."

"Ella, I am going to get Anna back, and then I am going to take down WeapCo. It may not make a difference, it may just be replaced with another weapons company, but it needs to be done, for the sake of your family and ours."

Ella just took a deep breath in and shed a tear. "Even if it kills you?"

I paused after Ella had said that. "Ella, the truth is, I am not going to come back from this. You know it, and I know it, so I think this is where I have to say goodbye."

Ella let out a tear. "Don't say that, Jacob. You always say that, and you always come back or get lucky."

"But Ella, this time, it's different. I can't fail this time. Failure is not an option, and I can't get you to fight anymore, as you are in no condition. So, Ella, this is where I have to leave, you know." I pushed Ella back to the front entrance of the basement door. "Ella, listen to me. You need to remain strong. Anna will come back to you, so please, take good care of her, and please don't follow me. I have to walk alone on this one."

"Jacob, can you come a little closer?" I did, and she kissed me in the mouth, and we both couldn't help but smile afterwards. We both considered that a goodbye kiss, and I slowly began walking away, knowing I might not see Ella again.

Before I left, Ella called out to me. "Jacob?"

I turned around. "Yer?"

"Please don't go down this road."

"I am sorry, Ella. It has to be done for my family."

Then, I turned my back to Ella, and that was the last I saw of Ella. I could have just stayed with Ella, but she has been through enough. She needed to live the rest of her life in peace. It was now my mission to find Mum and take down WeapCo, no matter the cost.

My mission was now clear. I made my way back to the hospital basement, which caught Courtney off guard. "Jacob, what are you doing back here?"

"I think you know why I am here. Courtney, I need the suit."

"Jacob, don't do this. You will only lose more."

"Give me the suit, Courtney."

Courtney just shook her head. "Don't do this, Jacob!"

"Give me the suit, Courtney!"

"No, I will not!"

"COURTNEY, GIVE ME THE SUIT!"

That worked, and Courtney fearfully rushed over to Ella's medical bay and handed me the blood-covered suit that still had the hole in the back of it. "What are you going to do with that, Jacob?"

"Simple, Kim. I am going to modify it and make it stronger, and then I am going to wear it as I watch the light go out of John's eyes and as WeapCo burns to the ground."

I carried the bloodstained suit out of the hospital and headed to my old place of work, the old weapons factory where I used to work. The tools may be scattered throughout the rubble, but my skills were as sharp as ever. For the next 2 hours, I repaired the suit and upgraded it, making it even stronger and more durable. Now that Ella was in the safe hands of Courtney and Kim, I needed to find information on where WeapCo was hiding my mother.

Knowing whether my mum may not even be alive was what concerned me the most. But if there was any hope at all that she was still alive, then I had to try.

Based on previous experience, my best guess was that Anna was being held at a black site, an area outside the law and jurisdictions of American Division City, a place where law enforcement and journalists couldn't find her. But where would it be, and where could I start looking for one of these sites? There were so many places that Anna could be, and WeapCo mercenaries were known for their discretion. But after searching through the dark web, thanks to Norman's laptop, I found her.

I guess WeapCo was running out of ideas, because she was in the same spot as last time. I began loading up my weapons and gadgets and prepared myself, putting on my newly repaired and modified suit, ready to take down WeapCo. Because, you see, the old Jacob Turner was gone. In order to save my family, I needed to become who I knew I was born to be, designed and destined to be. I needed to be the soldier. I needed to become my fictional childhood superhero, City Watcher.

CHAPTER 37

Iapproached the fence of the warehouse where they were holding my mum. There were very few guards and minimal security. Guess WeapCo is running out of manpower, which is good news for me. I stood outside the fence smoking a vape to calm my mind and my nerves. I took in a quick puff and threw the capsule aside. It was game time!

I kicked down the fence, went through the bag to pull out an old M4 rifle and kicked open the door of the warehouse. I had just 10 clips left, so better make them count.

There were at least 10 guys, and in the middle, my poor mum was tied to a chair. I threw the M4 aside and pulled out a combat knife that was holstered to the side of my leg, and I thought to myself, *Let's dance.*

The thugs were lightly armoured and armed with nothing but handguns, which, against this armour, they may as well have thrown stones.

The thugs opened fire, which only fuelled my rage even more. I could feel my eyes going red. I rushed full speed. Slash! I cut the first thug's neck. Then the other thug tried to take me down with gunfire, but I flung my knife into the thug's head, killing him instantly. I pulled the knife out and stabbed it straight through the other soldier's jaw, then pulled it straight out as the blood splattered all over my armour.

The other seven thugs fled in terror, and so they should have. If I ever saw them again, I would kill every single one of them. How dare they kidnap my mother.

I walked over to my barely conscious mum, who looked as if she had been beaten and was covered in blood and lacerations across her body. It appeared she had been waterboarded. My anger quickly turned to fear at my mother's state. I rushed over to her chair and instantly cut the zip-tie bounding her to her chair.

I shook her body. "Mum, speak to me, please! Mum?"

My mum luckily responded, coughing up blood and a few teeth. "Jacob? Is that you?"

I grabbed her blood-covered hand. "Yes, it is, Mum. It's me. You're safe."

She then broke down and cried on my suit. "Oh, thank God. I thought you would never find me."

I took off my helmet revealing my face and gave my mum a big hug. "I will always find you, Mum."

Then Mum collapsed into unconsciousness, and I picked up her body and carried it out of the warehouse. It was always hard seeing my mother in such a state: weak and frail. But at least I was there for her, again.

I was saddened. If only I could have been there sooner … but all I could really do was carry her out of that hellhole like her guardian angel here to rescue her.

I walked down the cold, dark, wet streets with my mother in my arms barely conscious.

After walking for a few blocks, I finally made it to safety. I arrived at the front of the basement door, where Dr Kim and Courtney could take care of her. But as for me, I could not go in, because I knew that if I headed back down there, I would put Kim, Courtney, Ella and Mum in danger, and I couldn't allow myself to put more people in harm's way.

So I laid Mum gently at the front door and slammed my fist forcefully on the door, then ran across the street and hid behind the corner. I watched as the dark night lit up from the basement door opening, revealing an orange light and a figure coming out of the door. It was Courtney. She looked down and was shocked to see my mum in such a state. Then she called out to Kim, and the two of them picked her up and escorted her down to the basement, closing the door and leaving me in pitch-black darkness. I stopped for a few seconds to take in the fact that after this mission, I may never see any of them again, and I let out a little tear at the thought of losing my family, but I quickly brushed it away, as now was not the time to be soft.

Instead, I had to become a vengeful, heartless, cold brute, something that even as a soldier, I could never be, but I had to try for my family.

In fact, the only person I had sympathy for now was John, as I personally was going to make sure that his empire crumbled and would make sure he was deep in the ground at the depths of hell.

I walked into my lair and collapsed on the floor as my legs and my whole body were scorched in pain. All the fighting and moving around really took a toll on my body.

But I was too full of hate and anger to really care. I just threw the armour off my body, grabbed a vape and walked over to the whiteboard to plan my next attack on WeapCo. Thanks to Ella, WeapCo was at the weakest they have ever been, but there was still plenty of work that needed to be done. My first target was to take their subsidiary company, Herculean Aircraft. Then, it would be time for the one-on-one between me and John in his 500-storey skyscraper. There was a lot of work to do, and I had to get started right away.

I just stood there in the lair looking at the plans that Ella had prepared. I had to get to work. I quickly rushed over the blueprints. As I stood there in silence, I heard a ghostly voice whisper in my ear, "Let's go!"

I quickly flinched and grabbed the firearm closest to me and pointed it at the door. I scoped the room trying to find where the voice came from, but there was no one there. It was me and only me in a deep, dark lair. Probably just an echo. So, now concentrating, I got back to work. I walked over to my bag of weapons and began loading up my firearms when I heard that voice again, "Let's go!"

At that point, I jumped out of my chair and grabbed my gun, as I thought the voices were coming from outside. Opening the steel door, I walked outside of the lair, and surprise, there was nobody there. All I could hear was the rushing of running water and the dark, empty sewer that was barely visible to the naked eye.

I was definitely losing my mind now. It had been a long day, and I was incredibly stressed out, so maybe my mind was playing tricks on me. After staring out into the darkness for a couple of minutes hoping that I wasn't losing my mind, I just walked back inside. I re-entered the lair and went into the bathroom to try and cool my face off from all the fighting.

After entering the bathroom, I pulled the string that was connected to an old watt light bulb and began washing my face with the water. I looked up from the sink at the yellow eyes, and I quickly stumbled backward and tripped over my bag of weapons, landing headfirst on the concrete below, and my head went dizzy.

My mind became disorientated, as the room swirled around me. After I looked down at my forearms, my clothes began to flash. My forearms changed. The armour that covered my hand disappeared, and instead, my forearm was covered by a hospital gown and a hospital tag that read 'Jacob Turner'. Shocked, I blinked my eyes back again, and my forearm returned to armour, and my vision returned to normal. Everything was as it was. I brushed off my concussion and walked over to the whiteboards to continue my planning.

CHAPTER 38

I stood in front of the whiteboard when my phone began to ring, only to display an unknown number.

"Hello?"

"Did you really think you were going to win?"

My face turned to anger. "John Spear!"

"In the flesh."

"What the hell do you want?

"I just called to say congratulations on destroying my supplies. I am personally going to make sure that your cripple girlfriend and your deadbeat mother burn for what you did."

"That makes two of us. I am going to burn your company down to the ground for what you did to my family!"

But John just laughed. "I don't doubt that. By the way, that's a nice-looking whiteboard you got there!"

I looked over shocked at the whiteboard. "How did you—"

"Know? Well, since that little stunt your Ella pulled at my weapon factory, I have been watching you and your little family. I know your house, your friends. I know everything about you."

I looked around the lair, and then I noticed it. There in the old sewer drain was a microdrone recording my every move. "Say hi to the camera! You think you can one-up me, don't you, little punk? Well, don't worry, I will rebuild. Because if you think I am scared of some—"

"You should be scared, you rich prick! Because I am going to climb that 500-storey and kick the living hell out of you. You hear me? I will not sleep. I will not rest until you are buried deep in the concrete!" But there was an eerie silence in the room. "SAY SOMETHING, JOHN!"

John then whispered into the mic. "You can't do that if you're dead. NOW, BOYS!"

And he hung up the phone.

There was silence. Not a single sound except the sewer water rushing through. But then I heard it, the whistling sound. *What was that?* I thought to myself, and then I realised what it was. Quickly pulling out my gun, I shot the camera in the sewer pipe so that John didn't know my next move.

Then BOOM! A missile directly hit my lair, blowing it to pieces and sending my body flying and landing on the ground. I lay on the floor as the disgusting sewer water washed into my face. I got up and turned around. It looked like my lair was now rubble with the sewer water flooding it, the exposed hole in the roof of the road flooding into the sewer. I couldn't see anything but smoke and rubble, but I could hear in the background sirens, and then I collapsed into unconsciousness.

The next thing I knew, I woke up in a hospital bed covered in a hospital gown with my phone lying on the table next to me. I looked confused yet not surprised, considering I was hit with a missile. I hoped the doctors knew that I didn't have private health insurance, but I guess they would figure that part out sooner or later.

A nurse rushed over to check up on me. "Thank the Lord you are all right," she said, with a southern accent: "You are one of the luckiest men on earth. You escaped that situation with only a few lacerations and a few bruises. It's honestly a miracle."

"Ugh, thanks!"

"I will have the doctor examine you soon." The nurse walked away to go treat more urgent people.

I pulled back the curtain, and I saw them. The hospital was at full capacity, and this hospital could fit 5,000 people. I closed the curtain, as I couldn't bear to look out at the people. But I could still hear the people crying out in pain. I was surprised I wasn't buried under rubble.

But I better get out of here. First, I don't have healthcare, and second, I still had to go take down John.

As I was lying on the hospital bed, my phone began to ring. I had a gut instinct about who it was. *Speak of the devil,* I thought to myself.

"Hello!"

Surprise, surprise, it was John, but he seemed different compared to last time. He wasn't confident and calm; instead, he was angry and sad. "You bastard!" He was obviously drunk. "You destroyed my company. I have nothing left. It is all gone. Everything. My company is now worthless." Then he paused, and I could hear crying on the other end. "I built this company from the ground up!"

He actually inherited it from his dad.

Then he paused, as his crying turned to anger. "Well, fine then. If I can't win, then nobody will. Time to go scorched earth on this place!"

"Wait, John, what do you mean by scorched earth?"

But he hung up the phone before he answered my question. Now, I was now a bit concerned.

BOOM! The hospital front exploded, and WeapCo mercenaries came rushing in and opened fire on the hospital.

"Oh my—"

There was no time to finish that statement, as I flipped over the hospital bed and began crawling down on the ground.

Come on! Attacking a hospital, that is just low, I thought to myself, but all I could do was crawl while around me the hospital descended to chaos. There were people of all ages screaming, and there were lasers and gunfire going everywhere. I had to crawl under the hospital bed to get to the nearest exit. I watched around me as bodies fell to the floor.

Man, I thought I had seen it all, but seeing those innocent faces would scar me for the rest of my life.

John is so dead.

After enduring all the screams and gunfire, I managed to find an emergency exit, and I rushed as fast as I could and bolted through the exit and out of the building. But I wish I hadn't, as the outside was much worse.

I walked out of the hospital, and the entire city had been plunged into chaos. It was an absolute massacre; all levels of the city were under attack, and all buildings were smoking and burning. John had unleashed his entire private army of one million people with advanced state-of-the-art aircraft, tanks and military equipment on the city, and it was absolute anarchy. There was urban warfare on every street, and the people ran for their lives or returned fire at the troops.

The people on the Lower Levels were used to fighting and were able to hold their own, but the people on the Middle and Upper Levels were not used to fighting, so they were slaughtered by the troops. The city had descended into lawlessness, and martial law was introduced, but hardly anyone was able to enforce it. The president went into hiding, and ParliaCongress went up in flames.

The defence force tried their best to mobilise, but because a majority of the army was working through for WeapCo, it was going to take 24 hours to come back. In my entire life, I had never experienced anything like this before, particularly a full-scale invasion of the city. I could not fathom this. I mean, I knew John was breaking, but this was a whole new level of insanity. I couldn't believe I was saying this, but I was praying for the peacekeepers to come back and sort these guys out.

I could hear the missiles and artillery overhead roaring through the night sky and hitting building after building. I got such a fright when I witnessed an entire skyscraper come crashing down, covering the place in smoke.

I was honestly baffled as to what to do. I was used to war zones down in the Lower Level and at Mercy Lane, but I had never seen a citywide one before. It was crazy. All I could really think to do was go back home to the Lower Level. I made my way down through the damaged subway line that had derailed and crashed into the road in the Lower Level and dodged through the war zone, passing through soldiers. My best bet was to hide in Ella's shop.

Nothing was out of reach for the soldiers. They were attacking anything and everything near them: churches, shops and even hospitals, both normal and children's. It was horrible, as these soldiers were so cold that they would attack anything!

But no time to worry about that now. I had to make my way to Ella's old shop and find shelter there.

It wasn't going to be easy, as everywhere I looked, there was chaos after chaos. The Lower Levels were putting up heavy resistance. By the looks of things, it seemed that John's private army was losing ground, as troops and tanks lined the street, and broken artillery lay everywhere. Compared to the peacekeepers, John's private army was nothing but untrained children.

It was such a shame, though. We finally got peace down here, and now our community was thrown into yet another war. But what was important was my own survival, so I began to make my way down the street when I heard a scream coming from one of the back alleyways, and I looked over and saw a young girl being grabbed by two soldiers. I witnessed her screaming out, and I saw the soldier grab the child by her arm and legs and begin spinning her around. I couldn't just ignore this, so I rushed over and whack! I knocked the soldier out, which caused him to drop the child on the ground. Then the other soldier pulled out his knife and rushed towards me, but I was used to dealing with knife wielders. I made quick work of the soldier, and they both lay on the ground dead near the little girl. Now that they were taken care of, I had to check up on the little girl.

"Are you all right, sweetheart?"

The little girl brushed away her tears and rushed to give me a hug.

"Thank you!" she said in a sweet voice.

Then, out of the corner of my eye, I watched as a frantic woman came rushing down the alleyway to hug her daughter, as the girl called out, "Mummy!"

The two hugged, and the mother pulled her daughter away from the scene of the crime. Watching the relief on the mother's face reminded me of my mother. Maybe I needed to help shift my priority off myself and instead focus on my community. I rushed down the street, and in the middle of downtown, the soldiers were standing firm and safely guarding downtown, with over 50,000 troops barricading themselves with cars and tanks, as this was the main staging ground. As I looked out in the distance, I could see him, the head of this little operation, General Lathosiv, the head of WeapCo's private military. But it was no good. He was too far away. I needed to get a better look.

Luckily for me, I knew these streets like the back of my hand, so using the fire escapes, I climbed up the closest building and jumped over a few rooftops, and finally made it close enough to see the general in his military tank. Looking at him, I could tell he was talking to John via hologram.

John was not looking good. His suit and hair were all messed up, and he looked like he was breaking down. I could see the general pacing around anxiously through the hologram, and I was close enough to hear what he was saying. The general was screaming, "John! What is the point of this operation? We are losing troops by the hour, and once the army reserves kick in—"

"Trust me, General, this will all work out eventually. It's all part of the plan."

The general looked concerned. "And what is this plan? This seems like a suicide mission."

John screamed at the general: "Do not question my orders. You have a job to do, and I pay your salary, so get it done!"

The general wanted to talk back, but his soldier's instinct stopped him, and timidly, he bowed his head in defeat. "Yes, sir!"

The general walked out of the tank and down to his men. "All right, men! Abandon this position and begin your advance on the city. Push the insurgents back."

The troops looked concerned, and one brave soldier spoke up. "Sir! Why are we attacking our own people?"

The general screamed at him, "Don't question my order. Now move!"

The 50,000 soldiers rushed into the city, and the tanks began rolling into the city, while the rockets struck everything in sight. I watched in horror; this was just a suicide mission, and they didn't even realise it. John just wanted to watch the city burn, and he didn't care how many people he killed.

I sure as hell wasn't going to let him get away with it, and I had a plan to defeat them.

This was a city of over 20 million people, and John only had half a million soldiers. If we all banded together, we could take them out easily. Instead of heading to Ella's shop, I climbed down the building and retraced my steps to Central Park in the Middle Levels.

Once there, I stood on top of the statue of the original founding father of the old United States of America. I stood on the top of it just like Yandan did when he called for an insurrection on WeapCo and using my mobile phone, I began to stream it to the city.

"People of American Division City, my name is Jacob Turner, son of the late Anna Turner. A few months ago, my mum defeated the odds and called out the defence companies for their action. Now I am calling on all of you to stand up and fight. Remember, evil triumphs when good people do nothing. Stand and fight. There are only millions of them and a billion of us. We have never been defeated or invaded because we are Americans. We fought for this land, and we are damn well going to keep it. Who is with me?"

For a moment, I thought nothing happened. Then I witnessed something incredible, as skyscraper after skyscraper full of people exited the buildings holding any weapons they could find, as there had to be at least a million people descending on the soldiers, and there was an all-out brawl.

There was gunfire everywhere. Millions of people were brawling out with the soldiers in hand-to-hand combat and firefights.

Unfortunately, the soldiers were too well-armed and equipped, and they began to push citizens back. But a miracle happened. As the soldiers were about to kill the crowd of people, a helicopter flew in. At first, we all thought we were doomed, but it was one of ours.

The helicopters fired missiles towards WeapCo's private army, taking out all tanks, and in the far distance, the reserve army came down the street, helping us out. I stood at the front, and with the army and the crowd of people, I screamed out, "Charge!"

Now it was our turn to distribute the pain.

After an hour, we began pushing the troops into the middle of the street. The private army was defeated, as there were only 10,000 of them left, and they all stuck up their hands in surrender. Meanwhile, I began making my way to the tank to confront the general, only to find that the general had killed himself because of the loss, as he did want to be captured alive. At last, the city was safe once more. The army and the people began to help clean up the streets, and martial law was lifted. Now, the city could breathe a sigh of relief, as peace fell upon it. John's private army was destroyed, and WeapCo had nothing left but its skyscraper, which I was going to storm now!

CHAPTER 39

Imade my way back down into the rubble that remained of my lair, and while he may have destroyed it, my equipment and my bag of weapons – which held my suit in – survived.

After grabbing my bags, I made sure to grab my secret weapon: Xenogren.

After grabbing out the drug, I injected it straight into my arm, as I watched my veins go from blue to green. Then, I put on my suit, and it was time to end this once and for all! After months of waiting and preparing, the time had finally come, because I was going after the big prize. Now was the time to storm WeapCo!

I just stood there and looked in awe at the size of the 500-storey skyscraper with the name WeapCo in red neon lights stretching across the middle of the building. It was hard to believe that a month ago, I had survived a fall from that building, and 3 months ago, Ella's father and his squad were all massacred like dogs.

I needed time for the Xenogren to course through my body, so I stood there, smoking a cigarette, as the Xenogren pumped through my veins. The Xenogren gave me powers and strength beyond comprehension, but there was a catch as the Xenogren increased my anger to the point that all I could feel was intense bloodlust. But it was OK, because I directed at one man, John Spear.

The drugs kicked in soon. Showtime! After the cigarette burnt out, I threw on my helmet and got to work.

Using my newfound abilities, I used my X-ray vision to scan through the entire building. There had to be at least 1,000 soldiers in that building, but with current powers, they wouldn't stand a chance in hell. Using my strength, I kicked the front door off its hinges and sent it flying to the other side of the room, which scared the hell out of 10 guards on the top balcony of the reception. They all looked at me with shocked expressions on their face, but what freaked them out the most were my mutated green eyes.

"What the— Quick, fire!"

The soldiers offloaded their rapid-fire plasma rifles, shooting 400 bolts a minute directly at me.

Normally, that would be enough to rip a normal person to shed, but the Xenogren turned my skin to diamonds, and coupled with my high-tech body armour, the bolts just glanced off me without any damage. It was amazing. No wonder this drug was so expensive.

Now the first thing I thought to do was grab a gun, but I didn't need to. My eyes had begun to burn with a surge of energy that pulsed through them. I tried holding it back, but I couldn't, and the green beams projected from my eyes and cut down the 10 guards and anything else in my way. What was worse was that the beam increased my anger, as the pain surged through my body. But I had no time to wait around. I must keep moving to the top to face John.

WeapCo was in a sorry state. There were documents scattered over the floor, and besides the guards and John, the building was basically deserted. It was weird seeing an office with no employees in it, especially considering it was midday in the city. WeapCo was dead. All of its assets around the world were either destroyed or seized by the government, thanks to our little stunt, so WeapCo was virtually worthless. The office was in such a bad shape that across walls, there was graffiti painted in red captions that read 'WeapCo is dead' and 'WeapCo stocks at $0'. But it worked out for me, as it meant there were no innocent people in here who could get hurt. Anyone remaining in this building deserved what was coming to them.

After taking out the soldiers, I began making my way up the stairs, and I had to climb the 500 storeys. The soldiers tried to stop me as I made my way up the staircase, but it was of no use. They didn't have the tech or equipment to stop. They kept firing at me, but it was to no avail, as the bolts weren't even slowing me down. One after the other, they rushed at me, but I just threw them over the railing with my enhanced strength and let gravity do to rest.

Also, the drug gave me incredible psychic abilities like telekinesis. All this power made me feel great. I felt unstoppable, and the guards just felt like toys to me. With every floor I climbed, the more my patience began to fade. At first, I was doing my best to not kill the soldiers, but as the anger surged through me, the more brutal my killings got. I began to telekinetically push hordes of soldiers and crush some of them. I continued to overwhelm them with increasingly brilliant and creative ways until eventually, I made it to the '500th floor'. I stopped myself and took a breath of relief as behind the door was John, the cause of my problems, and now, I was finally ready to confront this man, so I just could not wait. With a swift kick, I shredded the door down and made my way to John's office.

I was preparing my drug-fuelled mind for anything that was about to come through that door. Knowing John, he probably had an army or advanced state-of-the-art drones ready to blast my head off as soon as I entered the room.

But after kicking the door down, there was nothing. I must have entered the wrong floor or something, because it was empty and dark. There was nothing there. No people, no soldiers and no drones, just rows upon rows of empty desks. He must not have paid the electricity bill, because the room was covered in complete darkness.

I was silently anticipating an attack, but nothing. Nothing came to attack me. I continued to walk slowly past the meeting room. But I stopped to have a look inside, and what I saw horrified me; the boardroom was full of dead businessmen and women. John must have really lost his mind, because he had killed his stakeholders. The bodies lay stiff and motionless on the floor, and the walls were covered in blood and flies.

Found him! I saw the only light source in the room, John's office, but could only see his back, and in his hand was a glass of brandy. I just stood there outside his office.

John took a sip of his brandy, then he paused and gave a defeated laugh. "I wondered how long it would have taken you to reach me."

I just stood there clenching my fists. "Well, I am here. Surprised?"

He turned around. John was a complete pathetic wreck. His business suit was all wrinkled up, and his hair was a complete mess, and he was obviously a little drunk and a little insane, telling by his demeanour.

John got up from his desk and looked at me. "That Xenogren is one hell of a thing, isn't it? Burns through your brain and rots it from the inside over time."

He then took a drink, and the alcohol turned him bitter.

"I still can't understand how such a small family like yours could have taken down such a big company like mine."

I looked and raised an eyebrow. "David and Goliath, I guess."

John just laughed. "That anger must be consuming you. You remind me of myself – ambitious, hungry. And where does it lead us to? Our graves?"

I laughed. "Our graves? You must be mistaken. You're the one on death row."

"Oh no, no, no, no. You destroyed my company, and now, my poor little bastard, you are going to die."

At that point, I lost my cool and snapped. I jumped over the table, not thinking, and relying on my raw strength to overwhelm him. But I had forgotten who I was dealing with, as John caught my fist in mid-air, which caught me by surprise. He baited me, as John knew I would confront him. Suddenly, a nanite suit surrounded his entire body.

In a robotic voice, he stared me down and said, "Did you really think I would come unprepared for a fight!"

He pushed me back and punched me in the chest, sending me flying back to the stairwell with his newly enhanced strength. Then he kicked his deck out of the way and stood in the middle of the room.

"Congratulations, Jacob. I am standing right here, but I'm going to make this building your damn tomb!"

I got up and stood at the end of the doorway. Then, unleashing my anger, I charged at him like a raging bull. Unfortunately, the drug hindered my intelligence, and I just relied on my brute strength and power. I grabbed John around the neck, but his suit made him stronger than me, and he had his intelligence as well. He slammed me to the ground with a full-forced kick and stomped into my chest, which caused me to crush through the ceiling and onto the 499th floor, which winded me a bit. John jumped down, as he was ready to face me.

Quickly, I jumped back to my feet and began punching at the suit, and John returned the punches in kind. But because of my drugs and his suit, we both had similar durability, and both of us were standing our ground. I soon managed to get the upper hand, as I grabbed him and threw him out the window, but his suit had built-in wings and jetpacks, which allowed him to hover outside the window. Then, with his built-in rocket launcher, he fired 10 small rockets at me, which exploded in my face. Luckily, they only did minimal damage due to my thick skin. Then I jumped straight at him, which sent John spiralling around in circles and losing control. I looked down, and I freaked out a little at how high up we were and kept telling myself to not look down. Then I dragged my foot back to the building, and I grabbed John and spun him around with my enhanced speed and slammed him to the 499th floor and began punching his back, trying to disable his jetpack. But John got to his feet and super-punched me through the wall.

As I jumped to my feet, John pulled out a telescopic sword and charged at me. I shot a bolt of lightning at him with my fingertips, but he used the sword to redirect the bolt back at me. It managed to cut through my skin, which shocked me. I looked down at the nasty cut and back up at John.

"You really thought I wouldn't have prepared for you to attack me? I know Xenogren, and believe me, this suit is going to bury you."

John then charged at me again with his sword in hand, and I tried my best to dodge every swing. Now I had the upper hand, as John was just a businessman, whereas I was a veteran and knew how to disarm an opponent with a sword. I grabbed his arm and struck it with my elbow, which caused him to drop the sword to the ground. Disoriented, he stepped back, and I rushed at him, throwing strike after strike at his face. Then I worked his body with my enhanced speed and strength, then WHACK! I delivered a punch so strong that it knocked the helmet straight off John's head and broke his nose.

But John returned the blows in kind, as he punched at my rubs out of anger. He used his jetpack and charged at me, turning his body to a 180 degrees and with the full force of his jetpack, he slammed me down through multiple storeys.

Even with my enhanced durability, I still felt that. I may have cracked a rib or two. But my blows to John had taken a toll on him too, as he was grabbing his side.

We both ran out of energy and took a moment to pause and breathe. Then John just laughed. I looked over at him.

"You want to know what the funny thing is, Jacob? You blame me for the death of your family, but—" John pulled out a remote to the Holonet projector in the main lobby, and it projected drone footage of Ella, Anna, Kim and Courtney squatting in the Sewer Level.

I looked up in shock. *They are alive!* I thought to myself. I got up off the floor and looked up in absolute shock.

John laughed. "How does it feel? You started this whole campaign because I took your family, and it turns out, they are alive. You're nothing more than a murderer and a hypocrite!"

My shock turned to anger, as I rushed towards him, grabbing at him, but John grabbed me back, and he turned on his jetpack, flew me back up to the 500th floor and threw me to the other side of the building.

Out of breath, he walked over to his desk and took a sip from the bottle of brandy that lay on the floor. I too was out of breath. Getting slammed back and forth through different floors really takes the wind out of you. But something caught John's eye. He looked over at the Holonet projector, and there was CCTV footage from inside the building as a swarm of police officers and army soldiers began to swarm the building, making their way upstairs and coming to take John to jail. John stood there in shock.

Now it was my turn to laugh. "How does it feel, John? Trust me, a rich boy someone like you wouldn't last long in prison. Oh, how the mighty have fallen."

John's face turned red with anger.

As I was catching my breath and coughed up blood, I looked into his smug face. "It's over. You're done!'"

That comment pissed John off, and he rushed at me, throwing punch after punch, and I returned the same, and once the jetpack was powered up, he shot me and him straight up through the roof onto the helipad that contained John's private helicopter.

Unfortunately, the brushes and smashing through floors had wrecked his suit, so he ripped it off completely.

"Fine! You want a fair fight?" John reached for his pocket and grabbed out a syringe of Xenogren and injected it straight into his arm, and his eyes began to glow green. "Then let's have a fair fight to the death!"

He then charged at me, and I charged at him. We both threw punches so powerful that each punch left shockwaves. But what John didn't realise was that I had a lot more combat experience, so I grabbed his upper body and sent him flying to the ground, and my anger exploded, as I threw punch after punch at him.

"Ugh!" I screamed out. "This is for Yandan." Punch! "This is for Ella!" Punch! "And John, this is for my community." Punch!

John lay there, bruised and bloodied. In a last-ditch effort, he tried to reach for another syringe of Xenogren to double his power, but I grabbed his hand and took it.

"Thanks for the power up," I said, as I injected the needle into my vein, and it healed all of my wounds and doubled my strength, turning my eyes red. Then I began whooping on him, as his face became barely unrecognisable. But suddenly, I stopped, as the drug caused me to hallucinate. Just as I was about to deliver the killing blow; I began to see my father. I released John from his grip and paused, as I was confused. "Dad?"

But John took advantage of my weakness, and with all his strength, he pushed me away from him, which sent me flying a few feet. Then he got up and rushed towards his private helicopter, turning on the autopilot with its preset location. I jumped back to my feet, but at that point, the helicopter was away from the building. Quickly, I rushed towards the helicopter, but John drew in his energy into a ball of pure energy and launched it straight at the bottom of the building. BOOM! I looked around confused, but then I felt it – the shake of the building. John had blown the bottom half of the skyscraper, and the 500-storey skyscraper began to implode in on itself. Finally, I had achieved my mission. WeapCo was destroyed. But I couldn't let John get away, so I bolted as fast as I could on the roof just as the building was coming down, and using my strength, I leapt off the building just as the entire thing came crumbling down to the ground, covering the entire city with smoke and possibly killing the soldiers and police inside. I was still too far away from the helicopter, so I telekinetically pushed myself towards it and caught it with my hands. I used my legs and kicked in the door, but my weight caused the helicopter to sink an inch.

John got out of his seat, and we were once again throwing punches at each other, damaging the helicopter with every hit. Then I managed to get the upper head, but I looked back and realised that I had damaged the autopilot, and the helicopter began to spiral out of control. But what was worse was the helicopter was approaching the border wall, and I could hear over the comms: "This is the USD Army move. Away from the wall, or you will be shot. I repeat, move away now!"

After hearing that, I rushed towards the helicopter controls to try to steer it, but I didn't know how to fly a helicopter. Then, without realising it, John grabbed me by the throat and had me in a headlock. I looked over and saw a hypersonic missile head directly towards our helicopter.

John let out a maniacal laugh. "We are going to die! Hahahah!"

I broke his hold, and having enough of John, I turned around and elbowed him in the Adam's apple, causing him to fall to the floor, coughing up blood. Now I tried to jump out, but it was too high. I would probably die. Best not to risk it. Then, the hypersonic missile malfunctioned and got stuck in the back of the helicopter, and it began to flick.

This is where I die!

I just looked down at the floor, and my final words were "Mission complete!"

The hypersonic missile kicked in and blasted the helicopter out of the sky and through the dome window, only leaving behind a trail of smoke and rubble as remains of a once multi-billion-dollar empire.

CHAPTER 40

Two months had passed since WeapCo fell. Jacob had been declared dead, and the world had moved on, but not for everyone.

Anna was sitting in the rubble of her old house, watching the Holonet News and watching Adrian's statement on the anniversary of the destruction of WeapCo. He was dressed nicely, as his company was now the number one weapons company in the city. Then Anna turned off the news and began smoking a cigarette. But something had caught her attention … or someone. Ella rocked up to the rubble site, dressed in a nice suit.

"Hey! Mind if I join you?"

Anna shot up and approached Ella, "Hey Ella, it's great to see you again."

The two of them hugged each other. "Anna, you are looking nice."

"Thank you!"

"What have you been up to, Ella?"

"I did it!"

"Did what?"

"I got accepted."

"You did?"

"Yep. I got a scholarship to study architecture."

Anna hugged Ella. "That is fantastic. I am so proud of you."

"Thank you, Anna. And what are you up to?"

"Well, I've gotten myself an apartment in the Middle Level, and I am now working full-time as a teacher and studying for my Bachelor of Education."

"Anna, that is so great!"

But then their joy turned to sadness as they looked over at the rubble.

"How are you holding up, Anna?"

Anna looked down at the rubble sad.

"I miss him. I miss my son. It's just so hard."

Ella grabbed her arm and leaned her head to Anna's side. "I miss him too!"

"I will never forget the memories of my baby boy. His first step. His first birthday." Tears rolled down Anna's face. Then Ella hugged her tight, and she began to cry as well.

"I am sure he is finally at peace."

They stood in silence, and Ella began to roll away, but Anna stopped her.

"Hey Ella, take care, will you?"

She gave a smile and rolled away.

Anna was now left alone, looking at the rubble, enjoying the memories that once were. Then she grabbed her cigarette and threw it into the rubble.

"Goodbye, Jacob. Your mum will always love you. Remember that. Please rest in peace, my beautiful boy."

She brushed away her tears and walked away from the rubble of her old life, never to return.

EPILOGUE

The voice stirred up in Jacob's mind, and he heard his mother scream. 'Jacob!'

Then Jacob woke up in the rubble of the crashed helicopter and looked around, as sand and green skies surrounded him. Jacob began to panic, as he realised, he was in the wasteland a light year away from his home, lying upside down in a crashed helicopter. Jacob reached into his pocket and lit a cigarette, waiting for the radiation to kill him.

ABOUT THE AUTHOR

Ronin Matthews was born in Nowra, New South Wales, Australia, and began writing when he was 6 years old.

While he has never written a book before, he felt that he needed to share his story with the world, as it has always been his dream since primary school. Therefore, *The Concrete Jungle* is his first novel. Having worked as a public servant and studied psychology in his free time, he has tried to combine his interest in politics with his passion for fiction and superheroes into one action-filled and political novel.